Floating Point written by Stefan Gagne
(copyright 2015)


stefangagne.com/floatingpoint


Keep supporting free web novels!


Dedicated to Bob Gagne, 1942-2015.
Father and friend.


**WARNING:** Floating Point contains triggering and
abusive language, and may depict sexual content and
violence. It is recommended for mature readers only.
(Responsibility falls to you to decide if you're, in
fact, mature.)

# Floating Point 1.1 :: Gank

As the clock struck zero, bolts of pure electric fury shunted into the ground beneath the gathering storm clouds as summoned champions of the Chaos Rift awakened to the fields of battle.

Their eyes opened to the familiar sight before them... great blackstone obelisks, diseased jungle trees, and the cries of bloodhawks across the lanes of battle. Wonderful sights and sounds, to those who craved the bloodshed yet to come...

The finest sight and sound, however, was the similar blasts of lightning that were visible on the other side of the battleground. Five claps of thunder heralded the arrival of Order's champions: the ones who stood between Chaos and absolute victory. Without anyone to stand in their way, well... it wouldn't be any fun, would it?

Their leader carried an axe stained in both sap and blood, a similar matted texture which stained a beard large enough to cover his chest. Heavy feet sank a full inch into the mud, betraying the immense weight which bore down into the earthen soil; weight of muscle, weight of iron. All of it honed to bring crushing death to all who stood before it.

Standing at his left lurked a revenant of flesh and malice, surrounded by vitae-drinking flies which were starving in their attempts to drain life which no longer existed within their host; to his right, a gaunt figure of purest black and white, with a painted down frown and lines where his eyes should be. Alternating black and white stripes of cloth covered every inch of skin, assuming the creature even had skin...

The chosen champions of Chaos would make any sane man run from the sheer horror of what they represented. They were malice, they were rage, and they were here to do war upon this sacred-and-defiled battleground.

All that remained was to speak the ancient runes which declared their battle strategies, and to launch into the absolute madness of war.

The dark axeman was first to declare his wicked intent.

"Solo mid," he spoke gravely.

"Bullshit! I called solo in the middle lane before we got here!" his fellow warrior of Chaos spoke, from within his diseased shell of rotting corpseflesh. "You can't jack solo mid after we already launched. Besides, I can do solo just fine. I've got a good item list I found on the game forums..."

"Seriously? C'mon, Diseased Shambler sucks at solo mid with any items," the leader replied, idly dragging a whetstone across the blade of his axe. "My Lumberjacker can hold the middle lane better than any of you. We'll have Shambler take bottom lane, Mime playing support with Cobbler in top lane, and put Scissors in the jungle between lanes. That's how this team composition works best."

The animate corpse of a long-dead king sneered, with rotting teeth. "Maybe I'll go mid anyway," he scoffed. "I'd do a better job than some stupid guy with an axe..."

"Any of you see Shambler out of his lane, report his ass to the moderators," Lumberjacker declared to his other teammates. "And if you don't I'm reporting *you*. I'm not losing diamond rank because of some pub scrub who doesn't get the metagame. Now GL HF and let's fucking wreck 'em already."

With the issue nicely settled, the hale and hearty tree-felling Lumberjacker strolled off towards the gates that would take him to his lane.

App Name: **Challenge of Champions**

Genre: **MOBA / ARTS**

Serv.: **CoC Ranked Official #37**

Every round of the Challenge of Champions game took place on the same map. Lumberjacker knew every nook and cranny of it, as a result... knew the three lanes (top, middle, bottom) that connected the two opposing bases of Chaos and Order together, knew the roles that each five-man team would typically take on. Five men to defend three lanes wasn't evenly divisible, so invariably at least one guy would be flying solo... and in this case, that would be Lumberjacker, the best of the bunch.

His role as solo mid was to fight his way down the middle of the three lanes, a champion for the cause of Chaos against the forces of Order. Lumberjacker, Cobbler, Scissors, Mime, and that idiot Shambler would represent Chaos... fighting to push through their respective lanes, to control territory and destroy various guardian obelisks along the way. In the end they'd storm Order's base, and burn it to the ground...

...all while Order tried to do the same thing in reverse. Five champions of Order would push down the lanes, fighting back against Chaos, to push them back into their base and turn *that* to the ground instead. A five-on-five war for supremacy. Like hell Lumberjack would allow those five Order idiots to stop his inevitable rise to glory, of course.

The first ten minutes of every Challenge of Champions match were generally identical; he could've played this game in his sleep.

Lumberjacker strolled out in that middle lane alongside a wave of friendly Chaos Goblins, little A.I. driven monsters that fought for his side. Even if the five man team of actual players got all the glory, and even if Lumberjacker was technically flying solo, he couldn't really do it alone; the strength of their goblin army would aid him in the heat of battle.

The plan was to crash head on into a wave of Order's little gnome army, and beat the hell out of them. Every time his axe fell one of the little Gnomes, he'd get gold towards buying items that would amplify his ridonkulus Lumberjacker tanking... magical items combined to make him stronger, healthier, and damn near an axe-swinging demigod. By the fifteen minute mark, if all went according to plan, he'd have everything he'd need to keep the middle lane secure for the rest of the game... then close out the game with a few good five-on-five full team fights.

Of course, Order would send someone down the middle lane after him... likely another strong solo mid, someone also beating up Chaos Goblins and earning money towards a god-tier set of items. But Lumberjacker could do it better, faster, easier. The axe had amazing range for a melee weapon, and his sit 'n spin move could wipe an entire wave of Order's Gnomes in three seconds flat. Once he was sitting pretty, it wouldn't matter who Order put up against him... he'd push, and push, and eventually take out Order's base.

And then...? Diamond rank, unlocked. He'd been playing for hours and hours a day, ever since the start of the ranked play season. This was the last game he needed to make his mark. Tournament invites, sponsorship deals, major sports recruiters lined up at his door... everything within reach. Just one victory to go...

Strolling with heavy leather boots across the muck of the lane, with a gaggle of little red Chaos Goblins at his side... yes, *this* was living. He tossed his axe lightly from hand to hand, hefting the weight, enjoying the ease which this proxy avatar could lug the thing around. The bright blue of the Order Gnomes, coming up the lane in front of him, danced in his eyes as he charged in for the whirl 'n kill—

—and promptly and fell flat on his face in the mud.

An icon of a ringing bell with little birds lazily circling it occupied much of his perspective, as he found his character unable to rise to its feet. Someone had smacked him upside the head with a hard stunning blow, locking all movement and preventing all actions. What's more, it was lasting way longer than stuns usually did in this game...

A blur flicked from bush to bush, back and forth across the lane. One by one, Chaos Goblins dropped to the ground, dead; a brief splash of golden coins signaled their fall, coins which were scooped out of the air by the vague blur...

Until it snapped into focus, behind a healthy wave of Order Gnomes, now bearing down on the fallen Lumberjacker.

Flashing pink silk, with fluffy pom-poms. A single straight blade, glinting in the dim light of the sun above. A hood and mask...

As the Order Gnomes cheerfully beat the stunned Lumberjacker into the dirt, emptying all of his blood (and coins) into the ground, messages flooded upwards through his Peep window.

```
<Kelek> holy *** did he just die to GNOMES?
<DethShard> lolololol rekt
<Kelek> who the *** plays that stupid pink kunoichi?
isnt she a joke character?
<Kelek> she's got no damage at all, just stuns and ***
```

Of course, death was not the end in this game. Moments later, a freshly respawned Lumberjack stormed out of the Chaos base... declining to responding to anyone laughing at him in his chatroom.

"Lumber, what's going on in mid?" Cobbler called out, across the private team chat channel. "Did you seriously just get killed in the first gnome wave?"

"It's the idiot playing a Kunoichi for the Order team," Lumberjacker explained—while storming back down the middle lane, with a fresh wave of Goblins marching in lock step to watch his back. "I think she dumped all her starting gold into boosting her goblin smackdown and stun attacks. Good news is that means she's bought no player-versus-player damage boosts that could actually hurt me."

Shambler echoed in next, with a voice like leaking, pus-filled sores. "You need any help there, Mr. I-Call-Solo-Mid?" he asked. "Who's that playing Kunoichi, anyway? Username looks like... 'Spark'? That sounds familiar... maybe she's a pro?"

```
<Reynard> You're up against SPARK playing Kunoichi?
holy *** you are in trouble.
<Reynard> She's a legit pro player, diamond rank.
<DethShard> grills don't play games
```

"Look, who cares? She's a nobody. Probably not even a *she*, there aren't any girls in CoC. Just stay in the bottom lane, Shambler, I've got this. A few more waves and I'll have enough gold for my armor items..."

"She's a ninja, right? You should buy an All-Seeing Eye. That'll counter her stealth—"

"I'm a damn tank, not a support. I'm not wasting my money on a support item," Lumberjacker insisted, storming through muddy puddles, kicking up a grayish wake of muck as he got his axe ready for the second run. "Mime, go get us an Eye next time you're back in base. And throw up some observer wards."

The black-and-white cloth rasped through mime's lips, as he grumbled back in channel.

"Buy your own damn wards, we've got serious problems in the top lane!" he barked. "We—oh COME ON—!"

And Mime went down to a Chemist on the Order team, judging from the distant green explosion and whiff of acrid toxins.

Not that Lumberjacker had time to deal with the gradual collapse of his team. He had a lane to control, and some idiot playing an underpowered joke character with crappy items to deal with.

Kunoichi couldn't pull the same stunt twice. That initial flurry of teleporting, creep clear, and stun would've drained out all the energy she had; she wouldn't be pulling off THAT wombo combo anytime soon. All Lumberjacker had to do was find her, keep the pressure on, and push those gnome waves back towards the Order base. Kunoichi was a one trick pony, and that one trick couldn't stand up for long...

Except she was nowhere to be found. He wove in and out of the jungle between the lanes looking for her, ignoring the Gnomes for now—and ignoring his own jungle-based teammate Scissors, who was struggling to beat up the jungle's neutral monsters—in search of the Kunoichi. No sign.

```
<Kelek> run home to mommy's house, ***
<DethShard> B E T A N U D E S
<Reynard> Probably swapping lanes with Chemist, you
should buy an acid protection item next.
<Reynard> Or you could get stun protection to defend
against Kunoichi if you invest in a low king's stool.
```

The viewers in his Peep chatroom had a point... but if Kunoichi had indeed run off, he wouldn't need an LKS. Good thing too, because LKS was expensive and he still had tanky armor items to buy. He had a plan, a strat, and he was damn well gonna stick with it.

By this point she'd definitely left his lane, knowing she couldn't possibly stand toe to toe with a Lumberjacker. Good. All he had to do was—

On instinct, he swept his axe wide, clearing out a swath of trees.

A pink blur dropped from the branches above, bounding away.

"Oh no you don't...!" he shouted, pounding boots into the ground, rushing her down. He had to time his swing just right; it slowed his movement speed and threw him off balance whenever he unleashed a flurry of axe strikes. Wait to catch up. She'd dumped all her money into junk items, no speed boosts whatsoever, while Lumberjacker grabbed himself a sturdy pair of shoes while respawning. Ten feet. Six feet. And...

The axe struck true.

Specifically, it struck a log.

He hadn't missed. Hadn't swung wide and hit a tree, no; this was a free-floating log, one which appeared in a cloud of pink smoke. A ninja substitution *jutsu*... swapping places with a harmless object, while teleporting to safety.

With perfect timing, she'd baited him out long enough to recover all her energy. Which meant she had plenty in reserve to stun him again.

The blade strike hit his back, causing a dazed Lumberjacker to stagger back out into the middle lane...

Right into a fresh wave of Order Gnomes, which gleefully kicked his ass while he stood around helpless.

Lumberjacker's disembodied spirit began its extensive tour of the jungle, dragged back to spawn, to be born again.

This one idiot playing this one stupid character was standing in the way between Lumberjacker and everything he wanted: rank, prestige, notoriety. If he lost this game to that stupid little girl... if he couldn't show that he could hold his own against a gimmick character...

Hate. Absolute hate, at this point. He had one objective now, and one objective alone: *KILL HER.*

"Lumberjacker, what the HELL, man?" Shambler was shouting across the team channel. "You're losing your lane!"

"It's nothing, okay? It's nothing!" the axeman growled back, as he dropped back into the land of the living... and bought himself a Low King's Stool, for stun protection. "Minor setback. Look, I can take the hits, I'm a fucking tank! I'm gonna kill her eventually, don't worry about that—"

"I'm not worried about *her*, worried about our *base*! Or did you not notice the rest of the Order team pushing all the way around the top lane while you were playing with your new girlfriend? *They're at our base!*"

```
<DethShard> n00b rush tactics are for n00bs
<DethShard> stupid *** too fat to get a man, plays CoC
instead
<Reynard> For a n00b tactic it's working fine, isn't
it? He's getting completely rekt.
<TrumpCard> oh man, what a value play! grill game too
stronk, yo
<Reynard> Seriously man, you guys gotta team up and
win fight against Order. Push them back and do it NOW
or Order's got this in the bag.
<Reynard> An LKS is critical to keeping her out of the
fight. Keep at it, I know you can win this if you
focus.
```

"Guys, guys, shut UP, okay?" he shouted. "—no, not you, team, I mean my stupid Peep chatroom! Argh. Okay. Okay..."

...Reynard was right. He had to focus. Kunoichi was gonna die screaming and begging at some point, but in order to *get* to that point, they had to push the Order team back. They had to focus on the game and the team, not one specific player.

"We need to rally at the top lane and do it NOW," he said, regaining a smidgeon of his composure. "All five of us, all at once. We push them back and regain control of this game! I'll tank, you guys spank! GO!"

Seeing an opportunity to turn this around, the Lumberjacker twirled his axe once, and rushed from spawn to the top lane gate.

No way he could beat down the whole Order team on his own; not yet. If he'd been killing Gnomes and making money instead of getting stunned by the damn Kunoichi every time, maybe he'd be able to pentakill these bastards... but even without his maximum power, his job remained the same: distract the enemy, absorb some hits, and give his team time to crack back hard against Order.

Even if he died, it would be worth it if his death got them some breathing room. Enough time to push back, to assert dominance, to get back into the groove of how the game was *supposed* to be played...

The frenzy of battle lie ahead of him. Blue Gnomes on Red Goblins, locking horns, snarling at each other. More importantly, here were the five warriors of Order... the Chemist, tossing green explosive bottles. Butcher, pan-frying up hot death. Scythe, currently dismembering their useless Shambler.

Where was the Kunoichi, though...?

For the moment he shoved that thought aside while tossing a throwing axe, neatly cleaving the Chemist's skull in half. Brains and blood, the core of his game avatar's innards, splattered across the nearby trees. Good. They could win this. Lumberjacker could get his ranking. He could...

...there. Hiding in the trees, *again*. Did she really think that trick would work again?

The trees were Lumberjacker's forte. He could clear cut them, give her nowhere to hide. This was *his* fight, his fight alone; he was better than joke characters like Kunoichi. All he had to do was run her down. With his shiny new Low King's Stool, her stuns would be useless! He could do this. He could *win*...!

With a cry to the skybox above, the Lumberjacker charged away from the frenzy of the team fight, into the tree line.

His axe cut true, slashing down tree after tree, felling a good portion of the jungle forest. He could see the Kunoichi above, blurring between the branches, panicking and doing her best to not be seen... but it was too late. He was wise to her game. He'd put her in the ground and end this game once and for all.

With each tree that went down, she had less and less chance to escape. He quickly calculated which trees to focus on, how to drive her away from the brawl, back into the middle lane. Once there, in his home turf... he'd have her. He'd finally have that little *bitch*...

The last tree went down... dropping Kunoichi to the mud below. Nowhere to hide.

Stunning knives flew from her fingertips, a fan of them. The Lumberjacker ignored them, the weak little blades bouncing off his bloody beard, deflected by the aura of the Low King's Stool. No more stuns. No more tricks. No more Kunoichi...

Her blade went up to block the incoming blow... but it was too late. His axe, nearly as large as she was, came down hard.

Blood sprayed outward to the left and right of the blade, as the girl's body fell away into two pieces.

It took the Lumberjacker a few moments to catch his breath, from the exhilaration of the hunt. Victory. Victory at last... one perfect gank, a massive kill, on his mortal enemy.

The word that flicked across his perspective suggested otherwise.

**DEFEAT**, it declared.

In the distance... the final Obelisk of Chaos, core of their base, crumbled away. The healthy Order team, fresh off their slaughter of every other member of his team, were doing a little touchdown dance in his end zone.

...she'd led him away from the team fight. Tree by tree, she *let* herself be run down, *let* herself be chased right to the point of death... so that Lumberjacker wasn't there to keep the Chaos defense from falling to bits. Thanks to her distraction he'd won his fight, and lost the war...

From the skies beyond, across the global game-wide chat channel... he heard the unmistakably female voice of Spark, player of the Kunoichi character, calling out to him.

"GG," she spoke.

*Good Game.*

His Peep window flooded with laughter. Hundreds of viewers watching him plummet down the ranks, diamond ranking now forever out of his grasp. His own team cursed his name, cursed his mother, cursed everything about this stupid game.

And all the Lumberjacker could do was scream, and scream, and disconnect from the server, and scream some more.

---

"Soooo... that's how you play Kunoichi," Spark concluded. "I don't feel like she's a joke character at all; she's a troll, but not a joke. Normally I advocate for trolls to die in a fire, but in the context of the game, playing a troll character is a legit strategy. If the enemy gives in to their hate and lets you run them around in circles, it's their game to lose, yeah?"

Spark stretched, flexing a few joints to get them working again. Reconnecting back to her home server (and her own avatar) after sitting inside a game server while wearing a game avatar always left her feeling a little stiff. Even if her moves were pretty awesome inside the game, she felt far more awesome in her own skin, and far more comfortable in her own bedroom.

The folks tuned into her broadcast couldn't see her bedroom, of course. When not operating within a game server, her Peep App displayed fanart sent in by her viewers and things like that instead. Rule number one of Peep broadcasting: don't let them know where you actually live, *especially* for "grill" (aka "girl") broadcasters. They can enjoy your sparkling personality and wit, you can talk about the games, but your personal life is yours and yours alone to share or not share as you see fit.

"Anyway, did that answer your question, Reifu?" Spark asked, turning back to her Peep chat window.

```
<Reifu> ty, always wanted to
see Kunoichi played well
<XxKILLxX> B E T A N U D E S
<Wayne78> *** grill plays a ***
character
<Wayne78> show us ur ***
<MegaMilk> GG well rekt
<Polearm> GG
<Reifu> do you main ninja type
characters? I've only ever see
you play them
```

Name: **Spark**

Home: **(undefined)**

Org: **Pro Gamer,**
**Peep Broadcaster**

Spark flicked a single painted nail across the invisible chat window, to strike out Kill and Wayne from her room. No need to wait for her moderators, not when she was between game sessions and focused on chat again.

"Yeah, I've got something of a ninjutsu addiction," she agreed. "Less the costuming and more the moves. I love cheesy action movie files, parkour videos, stuff like that. I actually study martial arts in my spare time, like, learning how to do it fo' reals..."

```
<Reifu> What, you mean avatar-to-avatar in real life?
Not in a game?
<MegaMilk> backspacer beats punchy kicky
<MegaMilk> no point
<MegaMilk> besides, can just get patches installed if
you want punchy kicky
```

"Software patches ... ehhh," she replied, making a gross-out face (exaggerated, so it would be picked up by the facecam). "My teacher always said that heuristic learning was the way to go; no preloaded memory maps here. I guess it's kind of an #OldSchool #AthenaAttitude, but way I see it, unless you really take the time to learn through trial and error, it's not really a *part* of you, something you know how to respect. It's just something you *know*..."

```
<Polearm> Spark's hands registered deadly weapons
confirmed
<Polearm> best ninja AO 10/10
<Reifu> can you play Hanzo next?
<Forzen> omg Spark ur so hot
<MegaMilk> HANZO OR RIOT
```

```
<Polearm> HANZO OR RIOT
<Forzen> HANZO OR RIOT
<Reifu> HANZO OR RIOT ... sorry ^_^
```

Spark laughed it off, raising her hands, surrendering to the chat. "Okay, okay! I'll play Hanzo next round, guys, no rioting, no rioting..."

Except now, another window had opened itself. This one, a private voice chat.

*"Need you here now,"* he spoke, tersely. *"Got a strong lead."*

"Uh... one sec guys," she told her chatroom, before switching to speak through the secured line. "—Tracer, I'm busy streaming. Y'know, coins for the family piggy bank...?"

*"Leave it. This is more important."*

"More important? We may live here rent free but it's not like we don't have expenses."

*"HolyHymnal, in the Chanarchy. Brand new server. Get over here as soon as you can. This one's not some snipe hunt; he's here."*

And then, gone. Disconnected without another word to say.

With practiced ease, Spark took her anger and frustration and swallowed it down. Came back to her virtual Peep chat facecam smiling. There was no actual camera—just a floating red dot to look at, above the hovering chatroom text—but she knew how to flash that red dot a winning grin.

That was the key; no matter what was going down in her personal life, she had a Peep persona to maintain. Spark had to be known as that cute girl with the fire-effect hair and the fire-bright smile. When broadcasting her gameplay to an audience of fans, she felt your attitude carried over into your chat; being salty and bitter led to a toxic community. The Spark they knew and loved was a pretty chill gamer grill, which led them to be pretty chill as well.

"Soooo... I gotta cut today's stream early," she said, breaking the news as gently as possible. "Sorry. #ItsPersonal. But hey, if you enjoyed watching me play Kunoichi, throw a like on my MyFace profile, drop me a donation, or subscribe to the channel. It's only five coins a month and it really helps me out, you know? This month's sub goal is a cosplay stream, and we're sitting at... let's see... seventy-two out of one hundred. Could be soon! Later, my little #Sparklers!"

She saved her swearing tirade until after shutting down the Peep App.

Of COURSE her idiot brother would interrupt her during game time. Of COURSE she'd have to travel halfway around Netwerk, away from the comforts of home, to chase down another one of his "solid" leads. What a complete pain...

But, he was her brother. He was family. And they did have a common cause, even if they had differing views on what caused that cause. In the end she knew she'd follow him around on this fool's errand, so... no point thinking otherwise.

Briefly, Spark leaned against the frame of her bedroom window. Taking a look at what passed for the outside world was a fine way to get her perspective back, at times like these.

Clouds obscured most of it, naturally. The physical structure of her home server floated high above it all, a flying castle in the skybox... but through the holes in those fuzzy particle fields, she could see a representation of all of Netwerk below. She saw it as connected lines and squares, a basic map of the known servers, gathered across Netwerk's backbone into the three major hosting service nation-states. An entire universe of ones and zeroes, of Programs and Apps, of games and services, of delights and dangers...

And honestly? If she was being *super* honest with herself...?

Even if she preferred to soak in the delights, it was the danger that would keep her walking in her brother's footsteps. Danger to his life which needed to be stopped, of course... but some of that danger *was* a delight. Unlike the games, these risks were real.

After all, Spark had lived out all her days as a sentient Program within the cohesive digital universe of Netwerk. Her whole world was defined by the constraints of that digital world.

And as far as she knew at the time... nothing else existed.

---

**File Name:** Last Interview

**File Type:** Chat Log

**MemoryPalace:** Investigation Notes [Private:Tracer]

**Description:**

A chatroom recording made years ago, by a participant of the chat. Includes interactions with all original suspects. File was truncated on being salvaged from the chatroom logs, but reconstruction efforts showed nothing of interest in the Q&A section. See follow up files on Widdershins, JSLaunch, and Ichiban for additional information.

I wish I'd tuned in for this interview myself, instead of spending that afternoon wasting my time goofing off. Kids can be dumb, myself included.

```
<Widdershins> Hello, and welcome to Turning Point. As
always, I'm your host, Widdershins. Tonight's chat
topic is the ongoing debate of creationism vs.
evolution. How did we come to be the way we are?

<Widdershins> My guests tonight are noted software
engineer and evolution researcher JSLaunch, Archbishop
Ichiban of the Athena Online chapter of the Church of
One, and controversial archaeologist Verity. Gentlemen
and lady, welcome.
```

<JSLaunch> Thank you, it's good to be here tonight.

<Ichiban> Blessings of the One upon you, my son.

<Verity> Personally I'd have gone with "archaeologist" rather than "controversial archaeologist," but hey, I'm happy to be here too.

<Widdershins> As always submit your questions to the queue. Subscribers get priority. Time permitting we will un-mute the audience later in the session for an open discussion. Please be aware moderators are online and owing to the sensitive nature of this topic, we will be ejecting any statements considered trollish.

<Widdershins> JSLaunch, you're the current president of the Horizon Trades and Sciences Guild, which has recently done considerable research into the subject of evolution. Can you tell us of your latest findings?

Name: JSLaunch

Home: Archetype / Horizon

Org: Horizon Trades and Sciences Guild, Member

<JSLaunch> Certainly. We in the Guild have excavated a number of Horizon's oldest servers, digging deep into the layers of deprecated software found within. The results are startling; in the refuse of early digital civilization we've found signs of primitive Apps making port calls and utilizing tools they were never coded to use in the first place. With each passing day our knowledge grows deeper, and with the support of fine individuals such as Horizon/Kincaid, I believe we'll have the resources to solve Netwerk's deepest mysteries.

<Widdershins> Ichiban, your organization protested the excavation, I believe?

<Ichiban> That is correct. The server in question was once a Church of One holy ground, before server rights were revoked to the Horizon family. They've already desecrated that land many times over; this so-called search for truth amounts to a Zero, a great sin.

<JSLaunch> Fortunately, visionaries such as the

Horizon family are not easily swayed by superstitious reverence for the integers "one" and "zero." They are only numbers.

<Ichiban> I would expect a non-believer such as yourself to speak casually of the One and the Zero. Truly, the work of the Zero is rampant through our decadent society... this blind pursuit of science in ignorance of faith is proof of that.

<Widdershins> Perhaps it would help if you explained your objections to evolutionary theory, Archbishop. Why has the Church of One come out against it?

Name: Ichiban

Home: Liberty17 / Athena Online

Org: Church of One, Archbishop

<Ichiban> The lie of evolution trivializes the miracle of life. We are digital beings, comprised of One and Zero, good and evil. All of us have blessings and sins within our code. Our life was granted to us by the One, an entity so pure that He holds no zeroes in His data and yet functions perfectly! Our purpose is to spread goodness, charity, and the message of the One to all programs. We must stand against the Anti-One, the Zero, wherever it may be and whatever form it may take. And the so-called "theory" of evolution is clearly a Zero.

<JSLaunch> Outside of the church's cultural watershed in Athena Online, a full 76% of polled programs believe in the scientifically proven theory of evolution. The simple fact of the matter is this: Programs evolved from Apps. We are the descendants of Apps, born from the primordial sea of data, through random code mutations. We are *life*, pure digital life, born to our universe through mathematical processes. Nobody "created" us; certainly not some big beard in the skybox.

<Ichiban> Why do you turn against the One so willingly? He created you, created us all, and yet you spurn his love...

<JSLaunch> Creationist lies, the whole lot of it. A

silly story told to comfort children.

<Widdershins> Gentlemen, please. We're here to discuss things in a civil manner.

<Widdershins> Miss Verity? You've been rather quiet so far.

<Verity> I was enjoying the show, actually. Do you have a question for me?

<Widdershins> Well, let's discuss your perspective on creation and evolution. While you lack the financial resources of the Horizon family and its guilds or the congregations of the Church of One, you've made some in-roads with your latest text file, "The Avatar Paradox..."

Name: **Verity**

Home: **HiRize / Chanarchy**

Org: **PS#7E00FF**
**Teacher, Author,**
**Data Miner**

<JSLaunch> An... interesting book, much like others in the genre of pop science. No doubt quite famous in the finest Chanarchy servers, where conspiracy theorists gather.

<Verity> I could care less about fame. If I wanted to be rich I wouldn't have released the book for free; I sure as null wouldn't be making barely more than coin-grind minimum wage working as a teacher, either.

<Verity> Honestly, I think both of these gentlemen are right. Yes, we evolved from Apps. And yes, those Apps were created by an outside force. Our life isn't simply a random happenstance, but it's certainly not divine.

<Verity> Let me put it to you this way, Widdershins. Why do you have a navel?

<Widdershins> Pardon?

<Verity> A navel. A belly button. An innie or an outie, whatever you prefer. It's a part of every default avatar, our representation within the physical simulation of the servers we reside in. You likely have a belly button, unless you removed it with a cosmetic tweak. You've got eyes, ears, a nose, a mouth; you've got senses tied to them. Why?

<Widdershins> I'd imagine communication would be rather difficult without eyes and ears.

<Verity> Would it? We're digital beings. We exist within the data of the universe itself, not within our avatars. Why did we "evolve" into having avatars in the first place? Avatars are the most grossly inefficient way for living programs to communicate. If JSLaunch is right, if absolute natural selection dictated our forms, we shouldn't be the messy and socially awkward creatures we are.

<Widdershins> So you consider yourself a creationist? That we emerged through intelligent design?

<Verity> I wouldn't call it particularly INTELLIGENT design. As for my beliefs... I believe that there IS a life form which exists beyond our comprehension of ones and zeroes. That life form crafted our universe, provided us the primordial sea of data. From there, yes, we indeed evolved from Apps... there's plenty of evidence for that. But we somehow evolved in their image. We have belly buttons when we don't need them. We EVOLVED out of someone else's CREATION.

<Ichiban> Which is complete heresy, of course.

<JSLaunch> I'd actually agree with your sentiment, if not your word for it. So Miss Verity, you're saying we exist because of... what, transdimensional aliens? Seriously? Are you reading a lot of science fiction lately? Spending too much time mining coins and going star-mad?

<Verity> Honestly, I'm okay with your skepticism. Rational thinking calls for us to examine all assumptions with a skeptical eye. I will admit I could be completely wrong... but my initial research is promising. I've uncovered a major artifact that I'm still studying, one which points towards my theory, in fact... and like JSLaunch, I'm learning more every day. The truth is somewhere out there in Netwerk, and I'm going to find it. If not me, someone in my footsteps. I promise you that.

One other major advantage of living in a rent-free server occupied only by two people: near infinite closet space.

With a closet, you could store all your cool outfits back home rather than carry them around in your personal inventory. Pretty important for keeping your overall Program size low... every App, every data file, every memory you carried with you ate up server resources. Lugging around six or seven wardrobes and a zillion installed Apps when you went out for coffee was a great way to get kickbanned from your favorite servers. Why let one fat Program suck up space that could go to two or three instead?

Of course, that just meant all her excessive bulk of clothing was stored back home; it wasn't like it took up less space. But her home server was a private one, and she set her own rules. No angry landlord screaming at her about causing server lag with eleventy hundred pairs of shoes. (Granted, her brother had been grumbling about that very same problem. Fortunately she'd grown used to ignoring her brother's grumbles.)

And if Spark had one major addiction beyond the thrill of a good game, it was collecting avatar accessories.

She owned clothes of all stripes (often *with* stripes) but also invested heavily in little extra details to mix 'n match. Kitty ears, those were an obvious choice. Complete hairstyle replacements across all the colors of the visible spectrum, with and without subtle fire visual effects at the edges. Alternate skins for her eyes. All manner of particle-enhanced jewelry; she could be her own walking light show if she put on too many at once. Virtual pets, like fish that swam around her head wherever she went. And of course, there were complete avatar swaps with cartoony forms, with appropriate bounciness coded into them for added cute factor... although she tended to prefer her more human forms, so she could add in her favorite accessory of them all.

No matter the avatar, she'd always find a way to work her prized white leather jacket into it. Across her back, often glowing or pulsing to the beat of whatever music she listened to, hovered Spark's own heart-on-fire icon.

Icons were a decidedly personal statement, Spark felt. She had a boring one when she was born, some silly looking Default... but even at an early age, she was assembling bits and pieces of public domain art, trying to find exactly the right combination of elements that spoke to her. Fire had to be there; she took her filename, "Spark," and embraced all it could mean. A light in the darkness... a burst of energy and life... or a tiny, easily overlooked flame that would grow into an all-consuming inferno.

At first, adding the heart in the center of the flames was an accident, loading the wrong clip art file while on a customization spree. But the more she thought about it... the more it felt *right* to her. A burning heart of passion, with a touch of whimsy? Perfecto.

Most Programs didn't bother paying THAT much attention to their customizations. Many stuck to their Defaults; some didn't even bother changing their clothes more than once a year or two. Spark cared quite deeply about expression, and damn well wanted to show off her efforts through icon and wardrobe alike...

But the jacket itself, no, that never changed. This gift from Verity meant the world to her. No matter how many times she swapped out clothes or hairstyles or even body parts, this jacket stayed with her, even as she dug through her closet for something to wear for today's shenanigans with Tracer.

Although even as she continued to hunt for a good ensemble to stroll out in style with, she pondered why she was even bothering. It wasn't like she was trying to impress anyone; if anything, judging from Tracer's past exploits, she'd likely want to attract *less* attention. But... he had interrupted her game time. He could sit and wait, while she designed up an impromptu outfit. Make him squirm a bit...

A soft beep that only Spark could hear distracted her from deciding between a cheesy red halter top and a skintight torso decal made of liquid silver.

"Darling!" she called out, across all of Network.

"*Darling!*" a cheerful voice replied. "*We are ON for tonight!*"

"Seriously? You got the passes?" Spark asked, while swapping into the halter top. A mirror App confirmed it looked just as tasteless as she was hoping; good for further punishing her idiot brother. "How'd you swing that, Puz?"

"*Ohhh, Puzzle has her ways. She's a woman of mystery and intrigue,*" her friend joked, in the third person. "*Shall we make a full day of it? We could obtain some new threads, find a bite to eat, and storm the club's grand opening gala! Two divas on the town!*"

Closing the mirror App with a sigh, Spark shook her head. Not that Puzzle would see it, with the cheap messenger App being audio-only, but some behaviors were simply automatic.

"Honestly... I don't think I can. I'm going to be busy this afternoon," she admitted.

"*Tracer again?*"

"Tracer again."

Name : Puzzle

Home : Bellico / Horizon

Org : Customer Service
Representative

"*Darling, you can't let your brother run your life. What was it last time we wanted to have a night out on the town, anyway? Chasing down some troll?*"

"He had good reason to believe the guy was connected to our primary target. He wasn't, but the evidence we found got the bastard banned from six servers. That's good, right?"

"*Look, if Tracer wants to play social justice warrior, he can do it on his own time. Or just go tattle to a moderator! That's why mods exist, right?*"

"Mods? Hah! Don't make me laugh," Spark replied. After a little laugh. "Only time they lift a finger is when we drop proof right in their laps. Too much corruption and laziness. The bastard mods in the Chanarchy are just an #InnerCircleJerk. Horizon's mods, they're happy to sweep trouble under the rug or look the other way if it impacts the bottom line. And Athena Online, the only guys with an actual police force? Lazy *and* corrupt, with a hate-on for colorfully alternative avatars. I grew up there, I should know."

*"So what, the only alternative is to go full vigilante? Does he also wear a cape and a mask when he plays hero, too? How tacky..."*

"It's not like that, Puz. I mean, you know most of the awfulness out there is unmoderatable due to masks of anonymity or jurisdiction issues. If we don't step in and investigate, nobody else will."

*"This is the problem with SJWs, darling. Self-righteousness doesn't automatically mean you're right. What gives Tracer the authority to step in and play judge, jury, and executioner?"*

"Sheesh, Puz, we don't *kill* people! Look, this is important to him, okay? And it's important to me, especially because it's important to him."

*"Ugh. Spark, he needs therapy, not you backing up his antics."*

"If I'm not there to keep him safe when he draws aggro with those antics, he's toast. Tracer's complete crap in a fight, Puz. Mind like a steel trap, limbs like jelly..." Spark mused, while having a seat on her bed to tune up her avatar's makeup in one of her many mirror Apps.

Eye shadow and lipstick were the norm, but considering her destination... she focused on applying a few layers of her favorite red nail polish, right from a bottle kept in secured storage. Only placed on her index and middle fingers, both hands, for safety reasons...

"Anyway, don't worry, okay? #ItsCoolYo. I don't think I'm about to get into a fight," she lied, while studying her nails. "I mean, judging from where we're going today. It's a server called 'HolyHymnal,' or something like that. Sounds peaceful and pleasant. You heard of it?"

The pause was telling. Briefly, Spark regretted bringing it up; the Church of One was a bit of a sore spot for Puzzle, for obvious reasons. She was so busy making herself pretty and chatting away that she didn't realize in time...

*"You need to get out of whatever basement you stream from more often, darling. HolyHymnal's all over the news lately,"* Puz explained, choosing to be informative rather than bitter. *"The integer-thumpers won the server lottery and got a shiny new megachurch built right in the Chanarchy. 'A beacon of light in a sea of sin,' or something. I'd probably burst into flames if I set foot in there. You seriously would rather go to THAT grand opening than hit the ID:Entity's grand opening?"*

"Look, whatever Tracer needs me to do, it can't take all day *and* all night. We'll be fine! I'll meet up with you at the club, I promise."

*"I've got a doubt you can promise anything. But, fine. If you show you show, if you don't you don't. I'll see you later or I won't. Ta ta."*

And disconnected.

Honestly, Puzzle was right. Constantly tag-teaming with her brother on his personal obsession quests was not healthy, not in the slightest. She didn't HAVE to go play consulting detective today; he'd be angry, but he'd get over it, right? No matter how much they fought and bickered... they were family. They shared a home server, they shared a secret, they shared the same pain. He'd understand if she ditched him...

Instead, she opened a connection to HolyHymnal, transferring her runtime across Netwerk.

Some things just had to be done. And hopefully done quickly, before ID:Entity opened its doors.

---

**File Name:** Last Moments

**File Type:** Memory Recording [Tracer]

**MemoryPalace:** Investigation Notes [Private:Tracer]

**Description:**

Childhood memory recording. Some details remain fuzzy; I've exhausted my contacts trying to sharpen up the image. These are my last memories of her and they are woefully useless.

If I hadn't been distracted, if I'd gone in to see what was taking so long, maybe I'd have seen who did it.

Little by little, Tracer chipped away at the data layer.

The skeletal remains of some primitive App lay beneath layers of uncollected garbage; he had no idea what that App was coded to actually do, since he always got weak marks in programming, but he could recognize the structure of it all the same. That was something Tracer excelled at—pattern recognition. He knew an App when he saw one, even if he didn't know what it did. The basic shape of things were clear to him.

He'd annoyed plenty of kids on the playground by using that talent to point out when people were lying, or when someone was using an avatar customization which didn't fully mesh at the seams, or when the soccer team was leaving a gaping hole in their defense. Tracer knew it all, which made him a know-it-all. Unfortunately, it seemed nobody liked a know-it-all. That was also a pattern he'd learned, albeit at the receiving end of many shoving matches.

After years of saying the right words to the wrong bullies and needing his sister to jump to his defense, he'd recently decided to perform an experiment: optimize his interactions by cutting back on them completely, and see if it helps.

It worked quite well. Nobody paid attention to him when he didn't draw anyone's attention or say anything to anyone. For example, this new policy allowed him to excavate this bit of data in peace, while the other kids on the archaeology class field trip were busy running around yelling and wasting time.

One person, however, broke through that self-imposed isolation.

An adult avatar wearing a white leather jacket sat on a nearby primitive lump covered in grassy textures, patiently watching his work, before speaking her mind.

"Shouldn't you be working with your partner?" Miss Verity asked.

"Spark got bored. She's busy playing with the loose physics objects," Tracer explained, not looking up from his excavation. "I think she figured out how to glitch a rock into the skybox a moment ago. I can do her work and mine twice as fast as we could do it together, anyway."

"And how's your sister supposed to learn about archaeology if you do all the work for her, hmm?"

"She's not smart enough for this stuff, so why bother her with it? This is more optimal."

"Tools down, young man," his teacher spoke sternly. "And come over here. Sit down."

The boy knew that tone well. Without hesitation he set his junior-grade data tool down, and joined his teacher's side.

"You've been avoiding all the kids, not just your sister," Verity pointed out correctly. "I think I know why, too..."

"Nobody wants my help," Tracer explained, cutting her off. "Every time I point something out that's wrong they just get mad. So why should I bother? People are stupid."

"That's a generalization. They *can* be stupid, and they *can* be smart. Everybody exists on a spectrum between the two, all the time."

"Yeah, well, they're *usually* stupid. They don't want my help, so I don't wanna talk to them anymore. Why should I?"

Verity sighed softly... and offered her best reassuring smile to her star pupil.

"Tracer... consider methods and outcomes," she suggested. "Programs like you and I learn by heuristic methods. We make mistakes, and learn from them. But we're prone to integer decisions, being creatures of zeroes and ones. One, you insert yourself into every situation whether it's appropriate or not, and people sometimes react badly. Zero, you withdraw completely from society to avoid those bad reactions."

"Isn't the desired outcome to have less bad reactions?"

"Indeed, but that sacrifice being made is being made through fear, not logic. In case zero you're not risking any mistakes, which means you're also not learning from your mistakes. ...how about this? What lies between zero and one, Tracer?"

"A floating point decimal number," Tracer spoke, from memory of math classes.

"Exactly. We're ones and zeroes, yes, but *life* is what happens in between. You need to find your truth between case zero and case one. Knowing *when* to say *what*, understanding the social patterns, that should be your desired outcome. You're having trouble, but you're young and can learn through your mistakes."

"So... I have to get my butt kicked so I learn how not to get my butt kicked while still helping people."

"Hopefully with less butt kicking, but yes, that sounds reasonable. You know, let's examine that, too! Why do you think they kick your butt, exactly?"

"Because I did something wrong?"

"Not exactly. You can make mistakes, yes, so can they; the act of violence is an active choice by the aggressor," Verity spoke. "The one who takes offense chooses how they want to express offense. If they let hate and fear rule their actions, that response will be a violent mistake. But it's not your fault they chose that response. Doesn't make it hurt any less when they choose poorly, doesn't make it fair, but that's how it is. Don't let fear of their choices define your choices, Tracer. When the time is right to offer your help, offer it."

"...okay," he agreed, in the end. "I'll try."

"Trying is the first step, and I'm proud of you for taking it," Verity spoke, pleased to hear it. "Like all learning processes, it'll take your entire runtime to master it. So... go find your sister, sit her down, and help her learn how to make mistakes. Plenty of time left before we have to go back to that boring old classroom..."

"You're not like other adults. You actually talk to me like I'm a person."

"Why shouldn't I? We're all people; some of us just have more experience. And bigger avatars, but it's the code that runs those avatars that counts."

It made sense.

That's what Tracer admired most about his teacher, really... she made sense. She understood him, knew that he appreciated sensible explanations of how the world worked. She didn't talk down to him like he was some little App, didn't say things like "because I said so," didn't order him to shut the light off and go to sleep mode when he wanted to keep reading. (Not that she'd do that, since she wasn't really his mom, but he liked to imagine.)

"And when you two are done digging up this App, I'd like you to check those rocks outside the dig site entrance," Verity suggested, pointing to the primary dig site... off limits to the kids. "Stay in sight of the chaperones, though. And if you need anything just holler, I'll be inside the cave working on the primary dig. I've nearly got the next data layer uncovered!"

"What're you digging up, anyway?" he wondered.

"No idea whatsoever," Verity said, with a literal twinkle in her eye, a customization she'd taken a liking to. "That's what's so exciting. Could be random garbage, could be a data file we can't figure out how to read. I love it when I find something I don't understand... maybe one day I'll show you my greatest mystery. When you're ready."

And so Tracer dragged his protesting sister back to dig site, to finish retrieving the ancient App. Then they worked on the rocks and found nothing of any interest, while Spark's attention started to wander.

He tried to keep her focused, but also tried not to nag. If he was still looking for that social pattern his teacher was talking about, he'd at least recognized the edges of it; the harder you push Spark to do something, the harder she pushed back. A lesson their mother hadn't learned, not after all these years.

He had to maintain a delicate balance of asking her to help with the task, and goading her into doing it by saying things like "Hey, what's this?" or "Huh" to catch her interest. Little by little, it worked... and by the time they heard the scream, she was on point and digging away.

The scream.

A chaperone had wandered into the cave, wondering why the teacher that dragged them all out to this decrepit old server hadn't been seen in an hour. That's who did the screaming; Miss Gearkit, mother of the guy who routinely ran around class with his pants on his head to make the other kids laugh.

Spark was first to her feet and first into the cave, her brother not far behind. She was always the one to rush into danger, particularly if her brother was already heading that way. Better to between her brother and the danger...

The danger had already passed, in this case. And it left Miss Verity lying dead on the floor of the well-lit cave, with a glitchy and spasming hole in her avatar where a hacktool had been stabbed through it.

Data corrupted. Process crashed. Verity, gone forever.

The chaperone noticed a few moments too late that some kids had come running, and immediately moved to hustle them out. Tracer would have none of it, struggling against the older Program, eyes fixed on the body... and on the words her killer had painted on the wall of the cave.

### *CREATIONIST LIES.*

Jagged and snarling, as if every single stroke was crafted out of pure anger. He could see the spray of low-resolution pixels clear as day, a primitive sort of graffiti, to leave behind a calling card of motive over the scene of the murder. To desecrate the body with an accusation.

But the message only made him angry.

What made him terrified was the strange icon pasted against the wall, just below those words.

The heart of an avatar, surrounded by barbed wire.

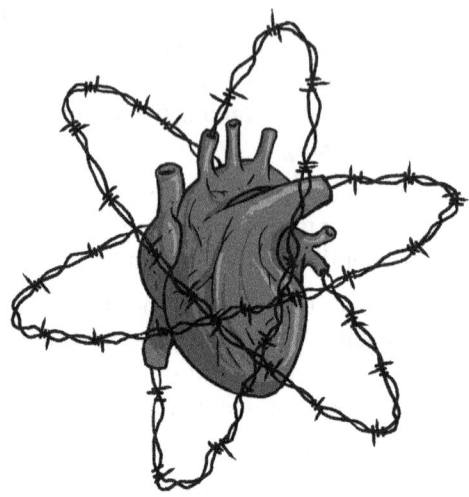

In the years that followed, I've painstakingly reassembled the entire scene. The words, the icon, the wound, the positioning of the body... all of it pulled together to form meaning. What that meaning actually means, I have no idea whatsoever.

But learning is an ongoing process. I will solve this puzzle; Verity will be avenged if takes my entire runtime to do it.

Fifteen years later and Tracer had made many, many mistakes. But he'd also learned much along the way.

When the waitress offered him a refill on his coffee, he knew the smile she offered along with the beverage suggestion had happened by his own design. If he'd appeared wearing a schlubby avatar, if he'd either remained perfectly silent or talked too much, he wouldn't be getting that offer now. Instead he'd engineered a precise outward appearance which engendered trust. He saw the social pattern, and knew how to fit himself into it.

Name: Tracer

Home: (undefined)

Org: Unemployed

A calm, well-chosen word was superior to the verbal spam he could emit in his youth. Knowing when to keep your silence, when to hold your secrets? Also critically important. He saw the patterns now, saw how to manipulate them and manipulate those involved in them to get what he wanted.

Elegance was the key... offering only as much as was required, inserted gently into the cracks of a conversation to act as prybars that would leverage the truth free.

Elegance in avatars was key, as well. He didn't shuffle up his appearance with the same zeal as his sister; he kept to a single avatar composition, one designed to maximize his first impressions based on cultural standards of respectability and dignity.

Fine leather shoes. Comfortable but sensible slacks. A grey woolen sweater over a dress shirt, with a neatly arranged tie around the collar. Carefully styled but short hair, not too flashy, not too plain.

Finally, he'd tinted his skin a neutral gray shade. The Defaults for avatars ranged all over the color spectrum; by occupying a hue-free midpoint, he could appear empathetic to anyone, regardless of their pigmentation or any cultural implications thereof. It set him apart from his sister's fair complexion, but that had its own value...

All calculated. All composed.

...and probably not what Verity meant when she suggested he learn how to fit in, but once Tracer set about a task, ruthless efficiency was the order of the day. It would all be worth it, when he completed his life's work.

Also, it got him free coffee refills.

He offered a measured smile to the waitress, accepting the beverage with a graceful nod. Despite his lifelong obsession, it wasn't like Tracer was completely without secondary interests... a good cup of coffee was a fine thing to be passionate about. Even if it wasn't an actual Chanarchy-style blend with light "malware" to allegedly accelerate the senses and keep one's mind sharp... a simple well-coded coffee with rich aroma and flavorful sensory data? Simply ideal.

Less ideal was the atmosphere he was "enjoying" along with that coffee.

Oh, HolyHymnal itself was simply splendid. The Church of One had outdone themselves; in an effort to show outreach to the community of the Chanarchy, they'd designed a spectacular server. The temple's golden spires reached towards the elevated skybox, gleaming in the perfectly golden decorative sun. The entire building sloped from those spires down to the ground, gentle curves of gold that terminated in the grassy earth below... with plenty of winding paths around gardens and fountains, excellently designed by the finest artists the Church of One had in its ranks. Every inch of the super-sized cathedral was a tribute to opulent modern design.

If the meditative nature of the gardens wasn't enough, no doubt deep within the temple itself you could find an ideally designed prayer shrine... soft benches to kneel on, while locked in a coin-grinding trance. Dogma dictated that grinding for coins was a way to send your wishes up the line to the One, with the money being mana from the heavens, or some such bullshit. Spark never saw anything meditative about wasting hours of consciousness, nor did she see a particularly wonderful deal in the tithe the church took from those grinding in prayer, but at least it was arguably profitable for all involved. You could at least claim a material benefit, if not a spiritual one.

Outside the primary (and quite secured) building of worship, a large-scale shopping plaza had been packed with faith-affirming products and/or services... including a pleasant little third story balcony bistro, overlooking the gardens below. That was where Tracer chose to spend his afternoon, with charming choir music floating in the air... and the bawdy sing-song of the mob below overlaid upon it.

Spark showed up fashionably late, as always. Which is why he'd messaged her a good hour before he felt he'd need her. Instead of a simple shirt and her usual fire-effect short crop haircut, she'd chosen to wear some hideous halter top and big blue pigtails... likely to annoy him. Still, he was too focused on the crowd below to pay much mind.

Pausing only to fire off a location check-in to her MyFace account ("Grabbing a coffee at [HolyHymnal] with [Winder/Tracer]!") to work towards her Tea For Two achievement, Spark had a seat at the table.

"Shouldn't be doing that," Tracer noted, spotting the brief flicker of a MyFace window. "We may not want people to know we were here."

"You drag me out of my game, I do what I please," she noted, grabbing a menu off the table. "So what're we having? I could kill a muffin right now."

"We can't stay long," he replied, not taking his eyes off the assembled crowd. "I'm waiting for him to make his move."

"And you think it's really him this time, huh? Her killer..."

"The evidence points his way," Tracer suggested, before taking a sip of his excellent coffee. "There's a strong chance that we've found our final target. Even if we haven't, he's still scum of the lowest caliber and needs to be stopped."

"And as usual, the mods won't just stop him on your say-so, right?" Spark asked. "I'm familiar with this song and dance, bro. This is a Church of One server. Wouldn't the Church of One step in and step on him if he gets out of line?"

In response, Tracer pulled open an audio file, broadcasting to their avatars alone. No sense bothering anyone else in the open-air bistro with their business.

The waveform flickered and pulsed to life, a series of green lines that waggled with the sound of a woman's soft voice. A floating tag identified the speaker as Mother Nestt/Wren, Bishop of the Church of One.

*"We are here to bring the good work of the One to our brothers and sisters in the Chanarchy,"* the speaker soothed. *"The One is within all of us, not simply those of us who live under the services of Athena Online or the Horizon family. In the past we have been negligent in our duties to the Chanarchy, but with the*

*establishment of HolyHymnal, we are ready to forge a new era. I know the Chanarchy greatly values free and anonymous speech, and I will respect that right. I invite any who wish a dialogue to visit us on opening day. We have a reputation for heavy moderation in our servers, but I value your culture of light moderation, and welcome your input..."*

Tracer flicked the file back into his MemoryPalace with a gesture.

"The Church are being 'tolerant' today. Tolerant for them at any rate, which means they're ignoring the obvious dangers. Despite this call for open dialogue, Bishop Wren's only allowing members of the faith inside the cathedral itself," he added. "Paying members who are using Defaults, of course. Scanners implemented at every door. That rules out you, me, and the mob below."

The assembled mob of crazy avatars below would've agreed with her. In their numbers she counted a robot pirate zombie, a three-breasted trollop, and at least two octopi.

Unable to get into the building due to their "alternative" avatar lifestyles, a large mob of colorful protestors had formed in the gardens below. They waved signs with various anti-creationism memes on them, singing some pop song or another, while celebrating the day away. It looked more like a party than a protest, all good cheer and absurdity rather than menace. The sort of thing Spark herself might have wanted to get in on for the lulz, really...

"Apparently what we see below us is 'Operation Skybeard,' as popularized on various Chans," Tracer explained. "They'll get bored and leave eventually. Not like they have any real goals, other than disruption."

"So... a bunch of trolls? You dragged me out here to watch a bunch of trolls?" she asked.

"A bunch of trolls... and a single legitimate threat," Tracer spoke... pulling a second file from his pockets. This time, a recorded rant... with a single flickering image superimposed above it.

A heart, pumping barbed wire rather than blood.

*"The Church of One misleads you with its creationist lies,"* the distorted voice spoke. *"The Nestt family and those like them hold immense power over the most influential minds in Netwerk. They are the most dangerous force imaginable, threatening to destroy all rational thought in favor of their own nonsense. For this reason, Nestt/Wren and her new temple of lies must be destroyed. Mother Wren and her little Starling must pay for their crimes against reason."*

The wired heart remained in her eyes for a moment, after the video playback ended. Some images you never forgot, even when they were no longer in view. Some stayed burned into your mind.

"And you think that means this is the same guy who killed Miss Verity," Spark concluded. "Tracer... we've been over this. Hearts and barbed wire are not exactly uncommon image elements. What about that tattoo parlor we investigated years ago? That ended up being a complete coincidence..."

"Except that that humble tattoo parlor was being run by a blackhat organization. One which we busted, if you recall. Are you saying it wasn't worth it to shut that place down?"

"Your 'prey' is long gone, okay? You seriously need to #LetItGo. I miss Verity as much as you do, but—"

"Three years ago, a similar server founded by a member of the Church of One suffered a massive memory leak and crashed overnight," Tracer continued, ignoring her. "Hundreds of programs died, either caught in sleep mode when the server went down or unable to reconnect to another server due to ping timeouts from the lag. A video just like the one I showed you was posted the day before. Same symbol. Same accusations. Officially the crash was a system glitch, but unofficially? We've found him. The same bastard with an axe to grind against anyone advocating what looks like creationism..."

"So tell the mods directly. Warn them this guy is gunning for them. We don't always have to step in, you know."

"I did, actually," Tracer said. "An anonymous tip to HolyHymnal's abuse reporting system, to avoid any uncomfortable counter-questions. I got an automated form letter in response. Spark, the Church gets so many death threats on a daily basis that generic anonymous hate speech holds no water anymore. ...speech across Netwerk has gotten so extreme in recent years that nobody takes outbursts seriously. It's seen as harmless trolling, until it's too late..."

Not that any of the party-hardy trolls below looked threatening. Some wore scary "Zero" themed costumes, aping the supposed sins of Programkind, but they were likely harmless. Tracer could see the pattern in the movements, the ones who chatted with each other, who were too busy socializing to be plotting anything dangerous. The connections between the protestors, even with most of them wearing anonymized joke avatars, they were clear. These were people brought together as a flash mob for a singular purpose, and actual malice was not it.

None of them were here to actually cause trouble. Or rather, they *thought* they were causing the Church trouble, when honestly the Church didn't really care and the faithful were ignoring them. Zero impact.

None of them except one.

That one.

One of seven candidates he'd been considering, actually. All of them seemed like loners within a crowd, blending in without actually fitting into the pattern. Tracer had become adept at fitting into the social pattern despite being a loner, knew how to ape the motions of ordinary social Programs. Those seven did not know the trick to it; they stood out by not standing out, by simply standing there. But one-by-one either they joined the dance, or simply wandered around bored, or...

...or one, who faded away from the crowd, then turned and walked. With purpose.

Quickly, he drained his coffee cup.

"Let's move," he prompted, dropping several coins on the table. A generous tip for the nice smiling waitress, because that's what was expected of a well-socialized Program like himself. Not because he liked her smile, of course.

**File Name:** Concerning Knives

**File Type:** Text

**MemoryPalace:** Investigation Notes [Private:Tracer]

**Description:**

Freewriting exercise to break up a mental block I was having at the time.

Programs exist in two aspects: the *physical* and the *virtual*.

The most understood aspect is the *physical*, as in the "avatar" of a program. Avatars exist within the physical simulation of a server, an assistive system that provides us a means of communication and relative positioning. Your "senses" are limited to the boundaries of the avatar; what you see, hear, touch, taste are all tied into the physics simulation of your avatar.

We like physical avatars, don't we? They give us an easily understood perspective. These are my eyes, this is what I see. These are my ears, this is what they hear. I reach out and I touch my sister's shoulder, and feel her there. I taste an offered delicacy, a data file designed to stimulate my avatar's physical sense of taste, and enjoy the inputs. All these systems work in concert to provide us with a unique existence that we can call our own.

But the avatar is a lie. Physics simulations are merely that: *simulations*. They are the handle, not the door.

Programs exist truly within the *virtual*, an abstraction of data files and processes operating within a server's memory banks and runtime. This is where we truly live: as ones and zeroes, code being run on the servers we visit. While we limit ourselves to the physics simulation, that code continues to merrily run beyond the reach of our eyes.

This is a vital distinction to make, when you wish to understand typical hacktools.

Swords. Blades. Guns. Bullets. Explosives. Sometimes harmless looking and abstract, sometimes lovingly detailed to match what we know from movie files...

We hold these shapes in our cultural memory, in the same way we use the letter A to represent a particular vowel sound. They are handles; intermediary concepts which provide a readily understandable and user friendly interface for those who seek to sin.

In my hands, you see a knife–the representation of my hacktool app within the physical simulation. I press the knife into your chest, and you die. But behind the scenes, in the virtual layer, the dance of data is quite a bit more complicated than that...

My knife is a tightly coded App, one which assaults commonly known vulnerable ports in default Program configurations. It establishes access routes for attack. Eventually it finds a way in, allowing it to damage your data and crashing your process. Unrecoverable coredump follows, and you die. All in the space between two ticks of a clock.

(This is assuming you haven't made backups. But given the expense of making and storing regular backups of your code and your entire life experience in memory, few people outside of affluent server owners actually do this. Plus, many public or residential servers will throw up warning flags to moderators if a duplicate program with the same unique identity metadata is found, active or not... it's a fraud protection issue. For purposes of this document let's assume no backup exists, as that's the most common outcome.)

So, why can't my knife kill you from across the room? Why can't I just tell my knife "Hey, knife, I want her dead" and have the rest sort itself out? Why do I need meaningless physical contact, if our physical avatars are made of lies, and everything is actually an interaction of data?

I don't know where in the server's memory your program resides. I don't know anything about the exact internal nature of your software; that critical knowledge is buried under layers and layers of read/write access protections. My hacktool is a generic device; it requires specific input to perform its highly specific function. Without input to tell it who you are and how to kill you, it won't kill anything.

The physical contact between my knife and your skin tells the simulation "these two objects are interacting, how should this be simulated?" That query is the key. It establishes a connection between your software and my software... specifically, my knife. Once the stabbing takes place, my knife exploits the physics simulation of this collision check, works its way backwards through all your access protections, and learns all it can about you.

Once my knife makes physical contact and uses it to zero in on a useful vulnerability in your software, you are dead.

I'm not using some cheaply coded hacktool with a 15% reliability rating and outdated vulnerability checks, no. My knife is sharp, my knife is fast, my knife is made of exceptionally versatile code... and it *will* kill you.

There are exceptions, of course. Single-purpose custom-coded kill tools, geared to eliminate a very specific target at long range... which likely still need to be launched within the same server. Perception-based attacks, which rely on indirect access through the sensory physics simulation... hardly as effective, yet still quite dangerous. But by and large, if I want you to die at my hands, I will need to ride the lightning of the physics simulation directly into your heart using a generic hacktool. Bullets and blades and knives...

My teacher was killed by a knife to the heart.

There was another program in the cave with her when she died; that program's avatar put its blade into her chest. The knife used the collision subsystem of the physics simulation to gather targeting data, find a vulnerability, and do the deed. She died instantly; process crashed, unable to restart due to massive data corruption.

The crime scene parameters I stole from Athena Online's police department indicate that she didn't struggle. The attack came as a surprise, a single direct blow to the chest from an avatar standing directly in front of her. But Verity had fully excavated the data layer she was studying, had applied a global lightmap across all physically represented surfaces. There were no shadows to spring from, no way to fool her avatar's sensory input. That means she *saw* her attacker, and simply stood there while he murdered her.

Verity knew the murderer. She didn't see him as a threat until it was too late.

I seek to make the connections. I will understand the situation, analyze it with a rational mind, and draw appropriate conclusions. That's the process Verity taught me.

I've studied the interactions of avatars, of the physics systems and the abstract representation of data. I've analyzed countless hacktools, and grown proficient in their use. I've taken her theories to heart, learning how the self-limiting nature of avatars–these weak and grossly tangential methods of interaction–worked against her. My eyes see more than most, and even if I must pay the price for that vision, my mods have aided me tremendously so far.

Except for this. Except for the one thing I want to see the most. I can see the knife going into her chest, over and over, but I can't see whose fingers grasped the handle.

But I will see, one day. It's inevitable. My parents called me Tracer because I mimicked their motions during my early heuristic learning levels, but that's not the meaning I embrace today. I trace the connections across Netwerk that lead me to objective truths. I trace the knife's sharpest point right back to the end of its handle.

One day, I will see who held that knife. And I *will* see it pointing in the other direction, my own fingers on the hilt.

Underneath every new server, there existed a superuser access layer. Here, avatars belonging to the system operators could easily monitor server performance, make fine tuning adjustments, install new services, and perform other routine tasks that keep a server ticking along.

In a brand new server still running various system defaults, that layer had extremely minimal decoration. The user interface would be simplistic, stark white and well lit, with "rooms" for each function set offered by the layer. It didn't have to look pretty, after all, it just needed to get things done.

Smart system administrators would immediately uninstall the access layer, since a clumsy abstraction designed for avatar interactions was insecure by nature. A better way to go would be a mobile App installed within a moderator's codespace, which lets them adjust settings through a very basic HUD. No physics-based space required... which meant no physics-based space for a hacker to access, either.

HolyHymnal was so freshly installed that the superuser access layer still had that new server smell. Pristine and default, it laid stretched out before Spark and Tracer, who absolutely were not supposed to be down here. But with all the mods focusing on watching the mob scene above and overseeing any possible trolls within the temple itself... nobody showed up to tell them to leave.

"You know they're gonna kick our asses if they find us, right?" Spark felt the need to point out, using their private speech channel as the pair prowled these back hallways.

Tracer seemed unconcerned. "It's the Chanarchy. There's no higher authority they can appeal to. At worst they'll ban us from this particular server."

"Well, no higher authority other than the One, I suppose..."

"Focus, Spark. We're looking for a man in a hooded jacket with sunglasses and a bandanna."

"And isn't that a BIT too typical?" Spark asked him, while poking her head into a room that controlled the skybox decorative weather parameters. "#ObviousBadGuyIsObvious. I thought the guy who killed Verity was a criminal mastermind or something..."

"Programs make mistakes. It's normal."

Coming down here was the mistake, Spark felt. If she hadn't seen the suspect carve a hole in the ground and hop on down into the access layer with her own eyes, she wouldn't be here now.

Even if her brother had a singular focus in life, he'd managed to uncover plenty of nefarious activity along the way. Spark had no problem with being a "social justice warrior," as Puzzle had put it, if she could actually achieve some justice along the way. So far their record was a net positive on that front, even if the means were questionable.

They'd gotten trolls banned, scammers exposed, astroturfing uprooted, malware makers managed... and even advanced threats like killers and kidnappers taken out of business. Whenever possible they'd disable the foe, gather evidence, and let the moderators take care of the rest. (Mods may be lazy or corrupt, but drop a mountain of proof and a trussed-up bad guy right on their doorstep and they'd be reliable enough.) When pushed to the wall, another fine trick was to get the bastards to turn on each other or make mistakes via active misdirection; a tactic honed through hundreds of hours of gametime.

Very, very rarely did it come down to a straight kill-or-be-killed fight... for that, Spark was thankful that Tracer always did his homework before going into a situation. He saw the angles she couldn't. He found ways in and out of trouble while minimizing chaos.

Still, if their bastard of the day was as bad as they suspected, if he sought to destroy the entire server and kill everybody within it... well, in a kill-or-be-killed situation, Spark only had one real option. And if he was *actually* Verity's killer... maybe she'd be okay with that.

Maybe years of playing caped crusader were turning her around in a way that should worry her. This hobby of hers certainly worried Puzzle... but this wasn't the time or place for Spark to worry. Worry got Programs crashed in situations like these.

As if mentally preparing for the fight, Spark flexed her fingers. She'd added fresh polish to the nails, armed and ready. Part of her wanted this mysterious hooded figure to be around the next corner they checked...

And he was.

Doubts slid away rather quickly, when she took in the scenario.

His avatar was crouched in front of the garbage collector, a standard server feature to clean up used memory space for later repurposing. Without it, a server would quickly experience a memory leak, eating up more and more resources until time itself slowed to a crawl... and by the time anyone noticed, it might be too late to reconnect to another server. Everybody would go down with the ship...

Textured across the makeshift box he was affixing to the collector was his symbol... the heart of an avatar, surrounded by vicious looking barbed wire. Every single detail precisely identical to the calling card left behind by Verity's murderer.

Chances were low that marked box was anything but the most dangerous hacktool imaginable.

If Tracer was the big-picture guy, Spark was definitely the small-picture gal. She relied on him to guide the overall path of their ludicrous quest, while he relied on her to deal with the immediate situation. That meant he fell into step behind her, as they approached the enemy.

"Game plan time," Spark called out across the private channel, while shaking out her arms a bit, getting them ready to go. "I'll tank aggro while you get whatever the null that thing is off the collector. If I can get a connection lock collar on him, we can leave him to the mods."

"Correction. You lock his connection, and then he's mine."

"Let's... just get to the win condition and work from there," Spark countered, calling up the connection lock from her internal data stores. It hovered invisibly in her mind, waiting for the right moment to be snapped into place... which would require her to get in nice and close.

Fortunately for them, the physics simulation down here in the access layer was quite minimalist. No noise made by footsteps, specifically... meaning Spark could creep up behind the stereotypical gangster, fingers already forming the middle-and-index together poise of the mantis style she'd trained in. Flame flickered gently across her fingernail polish, the weaponized code coming online by the gesture...

And the murderer picked that moment to glance around, to make sure he was still alone.

Spark pushed off hard from her right foot, a lunging strike... aimed at the backspacer in the thug's hand. Or more specifically, at his hand.

Her fingers made contact with the back of the man's hand, just before he could activate his hacktool.

In a burst of searing red flame, his avatar was now forcibly left handed. The backspacer fell to the ground, its abstract gunlike shape bouncing away on the cheaply simulated floor.

Her opponent slid sideways, taking advantage of the terrible physics to propel himself to safety. He clutched at the scorched stump where his right hand used to be... while glaring with sharp grey eyes at Spark, who had assumed a defensive stance, ready for him.

"Tracer! The box!" she shouted, across their channel.

"On it!" her brother called, dashing over to the garbage collector while using Spark for cover.

A knife-shaped hacktool appeared in the thug's hand as he lunged at her, a wild and angry strike.

She was expecting wild and angry; half of her fighting style relied on using an opponent's momentum against him, letting him make mistakes and capitalizing on them. Actually *punching* an avatar was a fruitless act, but leveraging their avatar to throw them off balance or toss them around the room... that could get you somewhere. The physics system took over at that point, and when your enemy was too busy trying to get back to their feet, that's when you could give 'em a good poke with weaponized incendiary fingernails.

Hacktools didn't have to be knives or guns. In the end, they were simply code... and the more innocuous the weapon, the easier to smuggle it around with you. For instance, code designed to obliterate body parts of avatars when you make the right finger gesture and poke 'em good. It didn't actually *hurt* the Program to damage the avatar in that way, but taking a guy's hand off would make operating a hacktool with a physical interface considerably harder. Hard to hold a knife in a nonexistent hand.

Of course, to actually DO that blow up the guy's hand, she'd need to get close to the knife. And if that knife was anything like the one used to kill Verity... one good slice would be all it needed to deliver a fatal malware wound.

Spark normally would take no chances, dodging and weaving to avoid any possibility of physical contact. Let the enemy grow frustrated, then move in when she saw opportunity. But... he wasn't lunging at *her*. He was going for

Tracer, who was going for the box, who was trying to save the server from meltdown...

The risk was worth it. She stepped into the lunge, coming up and underneath it... to use her own shoulder blades as a pivot, and send the killer tumbling across the floor.

That bloody knife stayed in his hand; a good hack tool couldn't be easily dropped, which is why Spark specialized in limb removal. But with his avatar down for even a second or two, she had the opportunity she needed.

Whirling in place to face the man again, she didn't wait for him to get up. Coming in low and fast, she pressed her fingers together, and jammed them directly into his right shoulder as he was sorting out his impromptu ragdoll pratfall.

Flames illuminated the already brightly lit chamber, as the man's arm came off completely and became a loose physics object. The knife, being well coded, stayed in that hand.

Now, he was crippled on both side of his body while desperately trying to get to his feet. Awkward jerking movements were the best he could manage, unable to compensate for the strange changes to his balance... actually, far more awkward than others Spark had temporarily maimed like this. Like some sort of spasming little doll...

No time to think about that. Only time to act.

With the enemy disarmed, she moved in for the "kill"... specifically, reaching directly forward, and clamping her hand around his throat.

The connection lock snapped in place immediately. Its UI representation took the form of a kinky black leather collar of her own design, actually; quite stylish, in addition to utterly blocking a Program from changing servers or making any sort of outside communications call whatsoever. It didn't stop them from *running*, but only within the server they were locked down to. Perfect for making sure you can finish a fight, or when you've got some interrogating you need done before they run off to lick their wounds.

And... the hood dropped. Complete ragdoll, limbs bending all sorts of funny and awkward ways, as he dropped to the ground. His body bounced a few times, owing to the terrible simulation, before finally coming to a jittery stop.

That was... not normal.

Spark deactivated her fingers, before prodding at the body. It reacted much like some idle physics object word, not like a Program would...

By the time Tracer joined her side (with one very awkwardly disarmed bomb tucked under an arm) he was ready to make with the interrogation. Problem was, there was nothing to interrogate.

"Please tell me you didn't kill him," Tracer spoke, keeping his emotions fully in check. For the moment.

"I didn't!" Spark protested. "All I did was slap a lock on him! And he just... dropped. I don't get it..."

With a frown, Tracer set the bomb aside... and pulled a tiny glowing spot from his sleeve. He never went in for Apps with clunky physical representations, preferring very minimalist interfaces. He placed the dot on the man's chest, then tapped it once...

Spark couldn't interpret the pile of data it spat back, but fortunately for her, someone in the room as excellent at pattern recognition.

Enough that after calmly rising to his feet, he punched a wall hard enough to make a sound even down in this minimally simulated environment.

"It's a proxy," he declared.

"Uh. #WTF?"

"A proxy avatar. The ultimate in safety," Tracer explained. "It simulates being a Program, while actually being a mindless App that's remotely controlled by someone on another server entirely. Since it requires considerable trickery of the server software to fake being a legitimate Program, it's typically illegal and a moderatable offense if you get caught. You put a connection lock on a proxy, which severed that external connection but otherwise did nothing. ...Verity's killer is still out there, somewhere. He's out there and he's laughing at us, because all we did was shut down his puppet..."

"We... we don't know this was the same guy. Didn't you say she knew her killer? I mean—"

Tracer raised a single finger, to silence her. So he could stay silent as well, and swallow all of this down. Regain his composure, rather than simply exploding in anger.

She'd seen him like this before, of course. Moments like these, Tracer was fighting an internal war... his idealized rational side locking horns with his personal grief-driven personality defects. Usually reason won. When it didn't... he at least quietly recused himself to his room to, well, scream at the walls or something.

For the moment, reason won.

"New tools," Tracer decided. "I need new tools. Something that'll track server-to-server connections being made by Apps. And I need to redouble my efforts to scan for the symbol; he's not going to be happy he couldn't destroy HolyHymnal. He'll want to strike again, and soon. I'm canceling my own sleep mode until we catch him. Can't afford to waste a minute..."

"Tracer, you can't keep pulling all-nighters. You'll age twice as fast if you don't allow yourself some sleep mode downtime," Spark reminded him. "I'd rather you didn't #Burnout at middle age..."

"Not now, Spark. Thinking."

"Yes, now! Look, I want to catch this guy as much as you do, but—"

"Do you? *Do you*, Spark?!"

Damn. The personal grief-driven personality defects apparently were fighting back, she realized. But... she'd already dove in inadvisably. No way she was backing down from that fight now.

"Yes, I *do*," she emphasized, standing her ground. "I miss Verity just as much as you do. She was more of a mother to us than our mother was! Why do you think I always wear her jacket? I loved her! The only difference is I'm not ruining my life in an effort to avenge her! Yes, she was murdered. Yes, it's tragic. Yes, I want to see the bastard brought low! But you know sure as null that she wouldn't have wanted you to put your life on hold for fifteen years trying to accomplish that!"

"Of course she wouldn't want me to do this!"

"So if you think that—what?"

"Obviously she'd be disappointed and saddened to see I'd become a crazy vigilante," Tracer agreed, reason entering his voice again. "I know exactly how she'd react if she knew; not angry, not upset, just disappointed and sad. But she's not here to react that way, is she? She should be, but she isn't. And I... I *have* to do something about that. It can't just slide. Actions should have consequences!"

As proof that reason hadn't entirely taken over again, he gave the limp avatar proxy a good solid kick in frustration.

"This is about more than just Verity," he explained. "It's all of Netwerk. I've looked in every dark corner for her killer... and you know what I found there, you've seen it too. All these patterns of abuse and harassment and terror and madness. Trolls and crooks and hackers and killers, all getting away with it, because their actions have no consequences. 'That's just Netwerk for you, LOL.' Well, I can't cure all of Netwerk's ills... but I can cure the ones I find along the way. I can avenge Verity, and I can take down every son of a bitch between me and the murderer. If I can restore even the smallest amount of reason to the insanity of Netwerk, well... I'm gonna. And if you won't help, that's your call."

Which put the conversational ball firmly back in Spark's court.

Funny thing was... she agreed, completely. It's why she was along for the ride, after all; not just to keep Tracer from getting himself stupidly killed, but because they'd indeed done some good along the way. The methods were doubtful, the situations bizarre, but... they'd done some good.

Still, she felt the need to argue. To fight. And there was one point she was going to stick to.

"You need sleep tonight," she spoke, quietly. "Just... agree to that, and I'm in. You have to take better care of yourself, so you'll still have a life to lead once all this is done. Okay? Just because you're right doesn't mean you're allowed to be right and stupid."

"...okay," Tracer capitulated.

"Good. Meanwhile... I'm going clubbing with Puzzle," she decided. "When you track down this proxy-using dickbag you let me know, but until then, I've got a life to lead."

"That's... fair. We do have some time. I think he'll strike again soon, but not likely tonight... and we can report this incident to the mods of HolyHymnal. They'll believe me and lock the server down tighter when they find a bomb and a dead proxy in their private access layer. He won't be able to pull the same stunt twice."

"Good. ...hey, one other thing. You said you need new tools to track down a proxy avatar's home connection, right?"

"Correct," Tracer confirmed.

"When you say 'new tools,' you don't mean you're going to Arjay, right? I mean, this sounds pretty #hardcore and that dude's pretty #hardcore, but you know what happened last time..."

"I'll be home and asleep tonight, I promise you."

And disconnected, leaving Spark alone.

**File Name:** The Church of One (and software patches, apparently)

**File Type:** Text

**MemoryPalace:** Investigation Notes [Private:Tracer]

**Description:**

In order to gain fresh perspective, I've asked Spark to write a few documents for my MemoryPalace. Specifically I asked her to give me her views on the Church of One, the organization that's under fire by Verity's killer. I didn't quite ask her to also go on a rant about patches, but...

I don't know why you need these zillions of little notes, and I'm not particularly happy about the dark little memory hole you carved into your skull, but whatever.

Church of One. Why do you need me to tell you anything about it? We both grew up in the same One-worshipping household, until we could get out the null out of there. If we didn't have our secret clubhouse to sneak away to in our teenage years I would've gone completely insane under mom's religious tyranny. And dad never stood up to her, either...

Now, don't get me wrong, I don't hate everything about the church. We grew up in Athena Online, more churchfolk per capita than any other hosting service nation, and that means most of my best friends were faithful. The overall attitude of peace, love, and goodwill towards all Programkind? I'm down with all that. If the One is love, and we desperately need more love in this world, I'm all for it.

You can't even say the church is greedy, despite the massive inflow of money they get from tithes while the faithful grind for coins within a prayer shrine. The spirit of goodwill and humility encourages distributing wealth around rather than amassing it fruitlessly, which means charity fundraising drives, homeless shelters for Programs who can't afford server space, and other great stuff. Can you really look down on a religion because you think its beliefs are silly if the end results improve Netwerk as a whole?

I also really like that the church doesn't mess around in people's personal business very much. They don't care what the color of your skin is, they don't care what your sexual orientation is, they don't care what clothing you wear. I've heard of other religions out there that scream bloody murder if you bare your ankles or something, totally repressed, and seriously fuck those guys.

What I can't buy into is two things:

There's the origin story, obviously. Now Verity believed in her own form of creationism, speaking of some alien race that we're patterned after. I don't fully get that, even with the artifacts she left behind for us, but... she didn't *demand* you believe in it. She wanted you to believe in it, but she didn't build this enormous prayer-based obsessive feedback loop about glorifying "The One" the way the church does. I hated going to Sunday mass, listening to some preacher mix in things I like (kindness and moral action) with things that made no sense (the One, the Zero, and all the trappings). It's harmless, I guess, but I have known people who use the One as justification for deeds that the One would absolutely not approve of...

The second thing, and this *really* sucks, is the church's obsession with Defaults.

You remember the great Hair Color Scandal, don't you? I dare to change my hair color to a sweet-ass shocking pink, and mom threw a complete fit. I'd violated my Default avatar, oh no! She called it a Zero... and called me a *whore*, said I was only doing it for attention. Dad just sat back and let her do it, too busy reading his news feeds. After that, she slapped an avatar customization lock on me that wouldn't remove itself until I was eighteen. Another fine Church tool, malware in the guise of controlling your wayward children...

(Notice she didn't put one on *you*. I swear she had it in for me, while you were the golden boy... but I put that on her, not you. Not your fault at all, bro. Still, GTFOing from that house was the smartest thing we've ever done.)

It's stupid. It's beyond stupid. What kid doesn't dream of ditching the "natural" growth curve of an avatar over time, in favor of something crazy and wild (and less tiny)? What's so bad about tweaking your self-image a little, to better express yourself? And the implications for people who weren't born in their "right" shapes...

But they do have one point: While I feel avatar modifications and goofy customizations are totally okay, *Program* modifications through software patches are another deal. I'm not saying patches are a "Zero" but they are seriously bad news.

I've installed plenty of Apps that follow me from server to server; messengers, my Peep broadcaster, my nail polish. But I don't modify my core code with patches. It's waaaay too easy to crash your program when you muck around with it on that level, integrating crazy open source stuff or shady black market modifications to your basic software. Sure, patches are more powerful than sandboxed little Apps, but the price isn't worth it.

When you came back from Arjay's barely able to remember your own name because you got that damn MemoryPalace installed, I seriously wanted to blow off two or three of that weirdo's arms and kill him with fire.

I get that you want to find justice for Verity. I get that. But watch how far you go to do it, Tracer. If you crash yourself in an obsessive drive to become perfect... her killer wins.

---

His life was an endless series of acts that disappointed his loved ones, really. He'd made peace with that long ago; otherwise, he'd never be able to get done what needed to get done.

Of course Tracer would be visiting Arjay. Spark was right; realtime connection tracking without the benefit of a physical hacktool App would demand some pretty intense modifications to his code. There was only one man... woman... *person* he'd trust with that. Tekkit/Arjay, broker and installer of slightly shady distribution packages.

The server of AptGet lie deep within the Chanarchy, on one of the oldest of the chans. In here, hundreds of different businesses took root—usually very briefly, before taking flight into the night after crossing a few too many customers. Arjay's business was one of the few to remain in place longer than a decade; Arjay was a pillar of this dodgy little community, the guy/girl/thing they went to when problems had to be solved. Nobody screwed with Arjay, and Arjay screwed with no one. Once the first part of that pact was broken, the second part would be broken to a degree that would resonate across the entire Chanarchy.

Tracer rode the connection from HolyHymnal straight to AptGet... a short hop across Netwerk, given both lie within the same hosting service. If he'd had to cross the backbone into Athena Online or Horizon, it would've taken longer than a few seconds of unsettling non-existence while his runtime transferred long distance. All the better; Tracer always hated that weird void, the sense of missing time that came with a really lengthy or lagged connection transfer...

His neatly polished shoes made contact with the concrete of a back alley. Normally visitors would be routed to any number of landing pads around the server, a means of tourism control. Tracer had special dispensations, of course.

He ignored the automated Apps barking fabulous offers on pirated software and pornographic media files, as he traversed AptGet. Neither interested him; the sibling piggy bank could get him whatever Apps he wanted, and compared to his sister, he'd pushed most of his desires aside in favor of mindlessly bloody vengeance. (Even if he had to admit the waitress smiling at him earlier was a pleasant feeling.)

No, his goal was a simple and efficient path right to the clinic of one Tekkit/Arjay. Who, fortunately, was not currently with a client. No, he was currently mining for coins, in her own little unique way.

A vision of a six-armed androgynous entity hovered in the middle of its otherwise empty office, bathed in a silver light. He wore nothing but a similarly silvery metallic sash around her midsection, contrasting the obsidian-black of its skin. A glowing halo shaped like a gear turned just over her head, eternally grinding away the thoughts of the avatar beneath it. He was a multithreader, typically pondering ten things at once, thanks to a cocktail of self-installed patches that expanded her mind beyond that of many similar Programs.

Name : Arjay

Home : AptGet/Chanarchy

Org : Black Market Modder

This glorious mess of beautifully strange software ate up a considerable amount of the available runtime of AptGet, enough to allow four Programs in the same space. But nobody was going to tell Arjay to pack up and leave; this was her server, in spirit if not in name. It'd go to pieces without him.

Tracer allowed it a moment longer, then cleared his throat semi-politely.

Eyes slid open, blank and white. Similarly blank and white teeth formed its smile.

"Winder/Tracer," she greeted.

"Just... Tracer, please," the client requested. "Adding my family name in makes it sound like I've got two primary file names. I don't wind things AND trace things; I got enough flack about that in school."

Arjay folded two of its six arms together, the other four in restful pose. Slowly, she bowed to him; Tracer returned the bow, in turn.

"My favorite little high-functioning sociopath has returned," Arjay spoke, pleased. "Your needs must be great, to seek me out despite your sister threatening to burn my head off. I'm honored that you've sought me out."

"Yeah. Sorry to interrupt your coin mining. ...why do you mine for coins, anyway? It's not like you're religious. Plus, you make more cash than you could possibly spend off your surgeries; why lower yourself to grind for minimum wage money, like some homeless Program?"

"I find it to be... enlightening," Arjay tried to explain. "I touch the void, and become one with Netwerk."

"Tell me you're not going star-mad, Arjay."

"We're all a little star-mad at heart, I feel. But no, my eyes are as clear as my mind."

"That's still not a reassuring answer," Tracer pointed out.

"What brings you to my clinic today, my little misanthrope?" Arjay asked, floating a bit closer... his blank eyes focusing on his occasional friend, occasional client, and occasional plaything. Personal space was something Arjay gave no respect to; he got all up in Tracer's area, enjoying any discomfort it may cause. "You have needs. I have means. Let's bring our two selves together and see what happens, shall we?"

Deciding to get on with it, Tracer laid out his needs.

"I want to see what connections an App is making across Netwerk without involving a physics check," he specified. "I'm hunting a proxy. I need to know what server its puppetmaster calls home."

Arjay folded all six arms together, now. A show that he was focusing all his threads on the issue at hand.

"You're not the first to make this request," she noted. "Proxies are common when you're up to no good whatsoever, and those up to no good are often sought after by those seeking to do less good. And fortunately for you, I have *just* the package you need... a little something I cajoled out of a coder from Horizon, who enjoyed leaking proprietary company technology out the back door. It sniffs out all active Apps on a Program, and any connections they're making. It should work just as well on a proxy."

"Okay, hit me with it."

"Now now, let's not be hasty," Arjay warned, extending a hand to waggle a no-no finger. "I'd rather not incur your sister's ire. That one is... she's quite beautiful and bold but very, very dangerous when crossed. What you are asking me to do is rewire your core code to install an illegally obtained patch which someone would likely murder you in your sleep in order to retrieve from your person, before backspacing your entire home."

The non-weight of the access key in Tracer's personal inventory space felt very reassuring.

"Let them try. My home is remarkably difficult to find," he noted. "And my sister would burn them alive, if someone actually came looking for us. I *need* this patch, Arjay. I'm close. I'm so close..."

"Verity's killer?"

"Verity's killer," Tracer confirmed.

"A fine cause. But you've already pushed the limits so far, little Program. How much further do you wish to push them?"

"I don't believe I have limits."

"Such hubris! What makes you issue this statement, exactly?"

"I'm the sum of my data and code," Tracer explained. "Everybody thinks of avatars when they think of the self, but I know there's more to me than that. I'm living software; my potential should be near infinite, up to the limit of the server that executes my code. I'm not going to limit myself to safe little Apps. I want to *see* the data, feel it; not just with my sensory input routines but with the entirety of my being. Why can't I? Why shouldn't I? I *know* you feel the same, Arjay, considering how heavily modified you are. You've never given a fuck about limitations before... and neither do I."

The entity considered this mission statement, pleased with each word of it.

"You really should mine for coins more often, Tracer. I think you'd find it enlightening," she suggested. "But for now... I'll grant your request. I'll need read/write access to your code, notably your sensory subroutines. Grant me temporary access, have a nice lie down on the couch, and I'll pour strangeness into your eyes until you can see forever..."

Because now, there was a couch. Where before there was no couch, a couch currently existed. Arjay's office remained featureless and empty until features were required, as needed. Arjay had no interest in the customary standards of physics and reality, not any more than he had an interest in his Default avatar. Her world was larger than that...

A world which should worry Tracer, honestly. When the MemoryPalace system was installed, Tracer nearly lost himself along the way. Its ability to compartmentalize, archive, and refine memories helped him tremendously in his hunt, but... every time he visited Arjay, he was taking risks. Risks for vague reward. Was it worth it?

Didn't matter. He was going to take the risk anyway, after all.

The multi-armed angel floated above him, silvery sash draping down across Tracer's form. If it was going to be creepy during pleasant conversation, it would be *incredibly* creepy while performing an intimate opening of another Program's code.

Arjay traced two fingers down Tracer's eyelids, closing them while *shhh*ing him to sleep, much like a mother/father might. Although the whisper in his ear was hardly maternal/paternal, given the deep moistness of it.

"I'm going to take your process offline," Arjay informed him. "This will be a deep modification. Less chance of a fatally corruptive crash if I work while you're inert. You won't feel a thing, especially if you never wake up. Goodnight, love."

And and and and and

   end of line.

I, 5o5o/Verity, of sound code and avatar, do bequeath the following to my star pupils Winder/Spark and Winder/Tracer...

To Tracer, whose intellect refines sharper with each passing day... I leave my copy of the Compiled Works of Pollox/Scribler, *and all else that is contained within its pages*. [TRACER NOTE: Page 505, halfway down, misprinted word] May you find enlightenment in these earliest creative works of Netwerk's history, personally retrieved from the ruins of a dying server.

To Spark, whose brave heart knows no bounds... I leave my favorite jacket, an old design which is no longer being produced. Every stitch and *every bit between the stitches* belongs to you now, to do with as you wish. [TRACER NOTE: Extra stitch on left shoulder.] May the blank slate of its #FFFFFF inspire you to find the light within yourself as well.

Be who you want to be, no matter what anyone else says. There are many in Netwerk who will tell you that you must be A or B, Zero or One, but I tell you that *there are more things in Heaven and Earth than are dreamt of in their philosophy*. [TRACER NOTE: Matches quote from a poem on the lower shelves, but analysis is ongoing.]

---

Despite the late hour, Spark used her access key to pop back home and hit the closet. No way she was going out clubbing in this ridiculous getup; for starters bright blue hair just screamed out 'PAY ATTENTION TO MEEE' in clubs, and second, that halter top was mostly to annoy her brother.

Instead, she swapped to her favorite hairstyle; short and stylish, in bright reds and oranges with little fire effects at the edges. She'd tried complete hair-made-of-fire plugins before, but generally they just made her look bald. A subtle smouldering about the fringes, though? That played nicely.

Rather than a hot little dress, she decided to eschew the concept of fabric entirely; too classical, really. Instead she went with a smooth and silvery body texture, with a shader that would pulse traces of light around her curves in time with whatever music she was listening to. Bodypaint-style avatar accouterment was very hot right now, and she felt a burning need to be hot tonight. Add in a hot little red collar, proper dancing shoes... and of course, her blue-lined white leather jacket. *Now* she was ready to party.

A few moments later, and she'd arrived at ShipTo... a largely disused App packaging server in Horizon, purchased on the cheap from a failed business enterprise. Within this shell of empty warehouses and factories, like a pillar of brilliant light and sound in the middle of so much ruin, lurked ID:Entity. The ideal of sticking something like that in the middle of urban ruins felt very apropos to Spark, given how flighty the club scene could be.

Clubs popped up and then simply popped with regularity. Everybody who liked a good social hotspot felt they could do it better, and everybody was typically wrong in that regard. Still, it'd be a fun ride on the way down... and Spark did enjoy the spur-of-the-moment thought that went into these places. They felt raw and rough, full of enthusiasm and ill-conceived ideas. Much like herself, really.

The windowless prism of ID:Entity stood silent in the middle of those dark structures; audio had been spatially locked, to keep sound from leaking in or music from leaking out. Instead, all Spark heard on approach was the annoyed chatter of clubbers without VIP passes, forming a queue up to the door. A queue which she bypassed entirely, producing the pass mailed to her earlier by Puzzle... one which earned a curt nod from the doorman and a series of groans from the unlucky bastards who couldn't get in.

Inside... well. Inside was her scene.

Light and sound incarnate. Sculptures of glowing lines hanging in the air overhead, shifting and twisting away, just as wild as the array of avatars in a wild array of colors on the dance floor beyond. Music pumping away, omnidirectional, from within her own avatar. Who needed speakers when you could personally broadcast right to everyone's ears?

In the visual mess, it'd be nearly impossible to reconnect with her BFF. Fortunately, both of them were running a cheap FindMe App... one which highlighted other avatars in your friends list running the same App with a shining gem floating over their heads. All Spark had to do was weave her way through the crowd, sliding around flailing limbs and drunken dancers towards the glowing golden crystal bobbing its way around the dance floor.

There she was... classy and beautiful. Way classier and way more beautiful than Spark, honestly. She didn't entirely fit the crazed abandon of the ID:Entity, not with her movie-file glamour of wavy blonde hair with a tiny flapper-style attractor on top. Being something of a classical beauty, she opted for cloth simulations rather than bodypaint; that figure-hugging ankle length dress didn't suit frenzied club dancing, but she made it work so very nicely...

And poor Puzzle was dancing all alone, as usual.

This was normal for her, honestly. Puzzle enjoyed the club scene Spark had introduced her to years ago, but rarely had the confidence to approach anyone herself without Spark there to act as support. Another reason why Spark was glad to get away from the situation in HolyHymnal, so she could be here to help out a friend. Giving Puzzle a solid shot at finding love and romance was an open quest in Spark's mission log.

For lulz, Spark snuck up on Puzzle rather than make her presence known. Approached at an oblique angle, out of eyesight... then clamped onto her with a nice tight hug.

"DARLING!" Spark greeted, across their personal channel. (The only way to be heard over the thumping music.)

"*Wagh!* Darling!" Puzzle greeted, after the initial shock.

"Surprised? I accepted your event invite on MyFace, didn't I?" pointed out, after letting go.

"Yes, well... after our earlier discussion, I wasn't certain..."

"Be certain. You're my #BFF, I won't leave you to dance alone," Spark smiled, with a little twirl. "Although I figured you'd have lured some gentleman into your web by now..."

"A lady paces herself, yes? The night is young!" Puz replied, with a smirk. "Plus, now I've got my partner in crime with me, don't I? Let's have a few drinks and hatch evil schemes together."

Spark adjusted her volume slider down a bit to bring the thumping music to a manageable level, then took Puzzle's hand to lead her towards the bar. Drinks were definitely called for; something tasty and nasty, to set the tone.

Puzzle ordered something nice and intoxicating; Spark stuck to her usual simple cocktail of sweet and sinful flavors. Two glasses were served up by the multiplicious bartender, who was splitting and reforming his bright blue avatar as need be to service an entire club by himself.

Generally Spark avoided intoxicants. Light malware designed to temporarily screw around with your sensory inputs felt like a bad idea to her; sure, they amplified taste routines to make the drinks far more awesome than they should be, but why risk it? Plus, this way she could keep an eye out for Puzzle. Being the designated tank suited her; absorbing drunken aggro from various jackasses while keeping her partner out of trouble...

Much like earlier, in a very brief but very dangerous dance with a murderer. A thought that gave Spark pause, swirling the remainder of her sweet drink around in its glass.

"Darling, you seem vexed," Puzzle spoke. "Things not go well with your brother?"

"...yes and no. Yeah, we saved a server from meltdown. No, the jerk got away. #ItsComplicated."

"You're not going to have to abandon me again to go play monster hunter, are you?" Puzzle asked, suspicious. "I thought you said tonight could be purely girl time..."

"Chances of finding that bastard again are low, Puz. We screwed up his plans; it'll probably be some time before he surfaces again. So, yes... it's #GirlTime tonight. No vigilante antics, no brother, no worries. You and me against the world!"

A fresh drink slid across the bar, resting in front of Puzzle.

One of the bartender's many instances explained. "Courtesy of the gentleman at the end of the bar," he spoke, before rejoining himself to take another order.

Both women leaned across the bar, to peer at the gentleman in question.

Not really Spark's type. She preferred her menfolk built for agility; this one was too traditionally handsome, too chiseled and ripped. Still, it felt like a Default with a really good set of data poured into his random seed, handsome by luck and genetics rather than the result of a store bought Hunk-o-Tron avatar customization. Points for authenticity, she supposed...

"Ooooh... VERY nice," Puzzle spoke, making her views quite clear.

But before her hand could reach for the drink, Spark grabbed her wrist.

"One sec," she said... quickly producing an extra ice cube from her personal inventory, and dropping it into the glass.

It remained clear as crystal. No malware detected.

"...okay, you're good. Have fun, Puz."

"Mmm, I'd hate to ditch you so soon after you got here, though," Puzzle spoke, with an adorable little pout. "And after I made such a huge deal out of you ditching me for your brother... it'd be hypocritical, wouldn't it...?"

"#ItsFine, #ItsFine! He's cute, and you don't talk to cute boys nearly as often as you should. I say get to know him, have some fun," Spark assured, with a smile. "And if it doesn't work out? Just look for my FindMe gem. Unless I strike gold, too. No promises."

After a grateful little hug... Puzzle faded into the crowd. And reappeared at the end of the bar, gifted drink at the ready, exchanging smiles with the hunky guy.

And good for her, Spark felt, sipping the rest of her nontox. Puzzle had tried so many times to find love and happiness, and struck out so often. Granted, going out to clubs wasn't a terrific way to find a lifetime soulmate, but that was Netwerk life in a nutshell: high hopes, awkward efforts. Much like ID:Entity itself. Much like Spark...

Well. Tonight, Spark intended to get her own shot as well. Maybe not at long-term flowers-and-candy romance like Puzzle aspired to, more something her speed—fast and physical and crazy and without commitment—but either way, this *would* be a night for successes. If the daylight hours weren't quite as successful as she'd hoped, she intended to make up for it here and now.

Dancing and martial arts weren't exactly the same thing, but the basic idea remained the same: move around, don't get hit by anything, and express yourself through motion. Difference being that she had to suppress any instinctive urges to throw out a few sweeping strikes or pokes in her dance partner's direction.

Holding a casual conversation while dancing was another matter entirely.

"So he finally runs me down and cuts me in half with his axe!" she shouted, to be heard over the music. (Private channels were reserved for her friends exclusively.) Spark threw in a vertical chop in the air for emphasis, nearly cleaving her dance partner in the process. "SPLOOSH, blood and guts everywhere. He thinks he's won because he finally got me, right? But he lost! His entire team lost because he was too busy killing me! I mean, isn't that just the #FunniestThingEver?!"

The slightly bewildered guy in the popped collar shirt slowed his dance moves a bit, horrified at the vivid description of blood and guts and mortal combat.

"...uh... sure?" he said. "Hey, listen, I gotta... thing... that I gotta... thing. Okay. HEY! WHOO! PARTY!"

And off he went, dancing the hell away from the crazy woman.

She could almost see the glowing DEFEAT in the air, as she lost this particular raid encounter.

So, that was zero for two tonight, trying to find someone with a cool avatar and any common interests whatsoever. Not a great start to her evening at ID:Entity, all told.

But a surprise? No, not really. Gamer jocks had a hard time relating to non-gamers, and it wasn't like she could discuss the intricacies of vigilante justice with a total stranger. Finding someone willing to accept Spark for who and what she was would always be a bit tricky... one of the reasons why she typically gave up by the end of a clubbing trip and skipped along to Puzzle's place for old movies and drinks as a pair of strikeouts.

For now, she'd just enjoy the music, flow around the dance floor, and go with it. Whatever happened, happened. Couldn't be worse than the disastrous day she'd had, after all.

A blur of golden hair and tears rushing past the edge of the dance floor suggested otherwise.

Quickly, Spark worked her way through the crowd, back to the previously occupied bar stools from earlier tonight. One was occupied again... by Puzzle, trying desperately to hide her crying.

Spark was there in an instant, one arm around her shoulders... private channel open, so they could discuss without worry.

"What? What happened?" she asked. "Darling...?"

Her perfect diva-glamour makeup wasn't running, of course; it wasn't cheaply designed code. But seeing tears flow from those perfect eyes was just as sad a sight.

"It... it was going so well," Puzzle responded, through her sobs. "He, he said I was beautiful. And we were talking, and smiling, and laughing and then and then he, he... he had some kind of scanning App. It saw, Spark. It saw my Default! I haven't used my default since I was a child but somehow he could see it! And he shoved me away and called me a, he called me a... a *tranny*, and..."

And the rest was clear to Spark.

As she gripped the edge of the bar hard enough to cause tiny wisps of flame to rise from her fingers.

"Where is he now," she asked, firmly enough to drop the question mark from the end.

"What? Spark, no no no, NO," Puzzle begged, eyes wide. "I don't want you picking a fight, not on my behalf. It's not worth it. Please. We'll get kickbanned from ID:Entity..."

"This club sucks and we don't need to come back here. And you don't need to give a shit about what that asshole says," Spark insisted. "You're beautiful the way you are and I won't let anyone say otherwise. Where is he now, Puz?"

"It's not right. It's just as bad as Tracer's stupid vigilante attitude! You can't go around kicking ass and taking names whenever things go wrong! Just because some church bigwig's son made fun of me doesn't give you any right to—"

Immediately, Spark's fire doused itself.

"He's the son of a church bigwig?" Spark asked, more shocked than angry. "Wait. Wait, Puzzle, back up. Who was this guy, exactly...? What's his name?"

"It's... Nestt/Starling. That's what he said his name was. ...wait, is this related to...?"

Quickly, Spark turned on her barstool, to look out across the crowd.

Locating anyone without a FindMe gem in this mess was nearly impossible. Nearly.

Finding a man in a hooded jacket who worshipped a barbed wire heart? Much easier. That avatar had been branded into her memory after taking it down one-on-one.

A fresh copy of the avatar proxy was making his way around the dance floor, in the general direction Puzzle had been running away from

"Puzzle, reconnect back to your home server *now*," Spark ordered. "He's here. The murderer, he's *here*, because we stopped him from destroying HolyHymnal. Starling's his new target."

"Wh-what?! But—"

"As much as I hate to do it... I need to go save the life of the asshole who broke your heart," Spark realized. "Go, get to safety. This isn't about picking a fight, it's about saving lives, Puz. I'll alert the mods that there may be a bomb in the server and I'll get Starling to safety. GO! I can't do this if I know you're in danger!"

Briefly, Spark was pinned in place by a crushing hug.

"Be safe," Puzzle begged... before vanishing, leaving behind only a vague afterimage as her Program runtime was transferred back to her apartment in Bellico.

Spark was off her barstool and crossing the entirety of the club in under a moment.

The killer had to pick his way through the edge of the crowd; Spark was running right across the dance floor. Specifically, across the dancers. A little hackery kept her light on her feet, literally so, to the point where she could kick off the heads of the dancers without throwing them off balance... a manipulation of the physics system which would've gotten her booted for hacking, if the mods had time to notice. She didn't intend to be around long enough for that to be a problem.

As for Nestt/Starling, the man with the handsome Default avatar... he was fortunately sitting by his lonesome, busy flicking his hand through the space in front of him. No doubt some private messenger windows, bragging about how he "avoided the trap" or something like that. A perfect distraction...

Spark landed on her feet, leaping across a gap in the crowd... and planting a hand firmly across Starling's throat.

The leather connection lock collar snapped into place instantly, cutting off his communications and keeping him isolated to the ShipTo server.

Before Starling had a chance to react, Spark was dragging him out the nearest exit.

Despite clear evidence to the contrary, many still assumed that the mass and sculpt of an avatar denoted physical strength and ability to apply force in a given situation. The reality was that in a scuffle, whoever understood physics simulations would be the winner, regardless of size. If anything, having a lighter and smaller avatar was an advantage, if you could move it and use your own form as a leverage point.

Dragging the bulky Starling out of his booth and into the streets of ShipTo, behind the ID:Entity itself, was simple enough for Spark. She was used to tossing around larger avatars. Keeping them unsteady and unbalanced was key... which meant kicking off Starling with both feet and shoving him into a wall would ensure his continued inability to resist. Which is exactly what she did.

"What the FUCK?!" was his only response, once he could make a coherent response.

"I'm saving your life, you idiot," Spark declared. "HolyHymnal was nearly leaked to death by an avatar proxy this afternoon, right? I'm the one who reported that to your mods. That proxy-using bastard with the barbed-wire heart bomb is back, he's here tonight, and now he's and after your head!"

Tugging at the collar around his neck, Starling at first refused to listen. But... when she went into detail, he froze in terror.

"You... that's not... how could you know that?" Starling asked. "We didn't tell anyone what we found in the access layer. You couldn't know about that..."

"You stick with me and I'll keep your stupid ass alive," Spark promised, quickly checking left and right to see if the killer had found them yet. "You've got my word. Now we need to move; there's plenty of abandoned buildings around to hide in—"

"Fuck that, I'm going home! ... why can't I go home?!"

"Connection lock collar," she explained, pointing to his neck. "I need you here as bait to lure him out. Can't have you bailing on me. I'll remove it after we catch him."

"WHAT? Are you crazy?!"

"Probably, but I'm still your best shot at not getting backspaced tonight. Now that we've established the rules of this game, are you in the mood to #RunAndHide yet?"

Fortunately, he was now in the mood to #RunAndHide. Which beat Spark needing to continue hauling and hurling his avatar around to ensure compliance.

Excellent timing, too, as the proxy avatar kicked down the emergency exit they'd departed through.

"MOVE!" Spark called, and Starling sure as hell moved. Impressive speed on that boy, she thought, as the pair fled into the dark of the largely abandoned server.

While she searched for hiding spots, proxy hot on their heels... she calmly fired up her messenger App. And prayed that Tracer hadn't gone to sleep yet.

```
Process rebooting....................
Package loaded: Winder/Tracer
Code execution starting.

WARNING: Unknown adaptation /sys/mem/MemoryPalace
detected
WARNING: Unknown adaptation /sys/sens/ConnCheck
detected

Avatar physical system online.
```

—blinding light of a million stars, in his eyes.

"Shhh, shhh. It's all done. You're safe and sound."

Pressing his hands against his eyelids, to keep the light out.

"It may take a short while before everything's fully initialized. This is your pain; ride it out, Tracer. Enjoy it and savor it; once the agony passes, you'll be a new *you*..."

Pain. Physical pain was a strange concept for a program, but it undeniably existed. Sensory overload could cause it, malfunctions of avatar inputs. Corrupted data and read errors could cause it, as your mind failed to access information and threw error messages. Perhaps pain was an evolutionary advantage, a fight or flight response designed to encourage Programs to avoid harm... their screams would be warning enough to not take terrible risks. Much like the risk he'd taken today with this dodgy software.

Maybe he was screaming in pain? No screaming in his ears, though. His voice wasn't online.

"Oh, one moment..."

"—AGHHHHGHHH."

"There. I believe everything's quite in place, now. Open your eyes, Tracer. I've aimed you at a wall; shouldn't be anything too offensive to your new senses there. We need to get you acclimated, bit by bit..."

And... the stars faded, replaced by a featureless blank wall. Arjay's workshop in all its minimalist surfaces greeted him. Slowly, he risked turning his head to look at a corner... nice and angular and safe. Nothing strange.

"Annanannanananany issues with the install?" Tracer asked, after his voice snapped back into place.

"No issues whatsoever. Your boast of being an unlimited being may very well bear fruit. Now, I've set up a small test to make sure everything's in order. Please turn around and tell me what you see."

With only a moment's hesitation, Tracer rotated in place, to see...

A ping tool App, a simple green sphere which pulsed with each packet it sent across Netwerk. He'd seen them before, they were one of the simplest Apps imaginable, designed to simply check if a server was online. But unless you personally were running the App, you wouldn't know what server it was pinging. Not normally...

Hexadecimal numbers floated above the App, inverted black against the white of the walls. A simple connecting line indicated the source of the address, leading to the ping tool.

"It says `480c:2204:dce3`," he spoke.

"Excellent. You have no permission to read data from my Apps... and yet you can see what connections they're making. Congratulations, little sociopath. You are now a walking, talking violation of privacy. The doxxing you are capable of now is godlike; no doubt server mods would be unhappy to know that you exist in their midst, but thanks to my handiwork, they'll remain oblivious..."

And now, Arjay appeared.

At first, Tracer had to avert his eyes. Arjay always had a few dozen Apps running at once, invisible to the naked eye... invisible until now. He could see a mess of addresses floating in a cloud around Arjay now, each one a static number indicating what parts of Netwerk Arjay was reaching out and touching. But... once he could accept the mess of numbers, deal with the strange way they were both in front of and behind Arjay's avatar, it wasn't as painful to look at.

...one last test. Because he'd been curious.

Tracer retrieved the access key for his home server, and held it out in front of himself.

6d56:653d:5908

With a wince of pain, he put it away again just as quickly.

"How much do I owe you for the operation?" Tracer asked, while bringing his usual plethora of personal Apps back online after the downtime.

"Not a thing," Arjay spoke, smiling darkly. "You know I'd do anything to aid in your insanity, Tracer. You're a walking social experiment, well worth augmenting in its own right..."

```
Messenger App online.
17 unread messages from Spark.
Messages read as follows...
```

"*Shit!*" he blurted, in contrast to his usual vocal composure.

"And we're already off to the races, I see," Arjay spoke, with some delight. "Go, go. Go forth and be atrocious. Do let me know if you succeed in your hunt, love."

Without further word, Tracer was gone, his process (now with illegally obtained software patches installed) shifting across Netwerk's backbone from the Chanarchy to Horizon... towards the ShipTo server.

One day, the owners of ID:Entity would tear down these disused buildings. At this point they were providing a nice atmosphere of urban decay, a lovely contrast to the palace of wonders at the center of this messy server... but they were also largely useless. Unless you were trying to evade a murderer.

Fortunately for Spark and Nestt/Starling, that's exactly what they were doing.

Starling was not a happy Program, but he was smart enough to know to shut up and not draw attention as they moved silently between software install packaging crates in the largely empty warehouse. These shelves and discarded containers were the only defense he had... and while he *could* have simply logged out of ShipTo within seconds and been perfectly safe, the collar meant he had to actually keep his avatar safe from harm. Fighting with the crazy person who controlled that lock was not wise.

Said crazy person, meanwhile, was actually rather enjoying this.

She'd been in stealth-based hunting game scenarios before, but this was real life, wasn't it? She had a solid and clear objective, a path to follow, an enemy to deal with. All the trappings of her usual sport, but with the added risk/reward of life/death...

Spark knew this was crazy. She knew she had to take the situation seriously or she'd be toast. But she wasn't going to live in denial of the small part of her that was jumping up and down and cheering and having a ball, either.

Normally, she'd go right for the kill and take out the proxy that was stalking them... but that wasn't the goal. She had to stall this out until Tracer's arrival, so he could catch the proxy in the act and trace it back to its origin point. Obliterating the thing would be simple enough, but then they'd be back to square one...

Instead, she stayed crouched behind a crate, while a man armed with a backspacer was slowly searching the warehouse for them.

"What's this guy's problem, anyway?" Starling whispered, while tugging at his collar (again) in vain hopes it'd pop right off. "Why does he want my family dead? Mom preaches peace and tolerance!"

...which made Spark really want to lay into this guy for hating on transsexuals. But, that wouldn't be productive at the moment, would it?

"He hates creationists in general," Spark replied, keeping her voice low, well aware of how sound might carry in the empty structure. "That's not the question to ask, anyway. The better question is how he know where you'd be tonight, and how he got into the club so quickly without an opening night pass...? Did you tell anyone where you'd be?"

"I don't know. Maybe. Some of the staff at HolyHymnal knew; I got the VIP pass from a contact in the church, he had a bunch of 'em... look, does it matter? We need to leave! Get this damn collar off me and we can really run for it!"

"Do that and he'll just pop up when and where you least expect it. This way, we know where he is. We can trap him..."

Problem was... their stalker didn't know for certain his target was in here. If he assumed that Starling got away (which would've happened without the collar) the proxy would just leave the server. There needed to be proper bait in the trap, something to draw the aggro and pull her enemy in the right direction...

Bouncing off the heads of avatars on a dance floor was a matter of lightly hacking the physics of a server. Similarly, projecting your voice as a sourceless, directionless sound could be accomplished by another hack. It worked similarly to the music of the club, generating audio within your own avatar rather than from a spatial location.

"Looking for us?" she called out, for starters.

A crate on the other side of the warehouse vanished, backspaced out of existence in a burst of surprise fire. Good.

"He's in here, you know," Spark continued, from the safety of her hiding place. "Nestt/Starling. Son of the woman you tried to kill today. You want him, don't you? Punish her, by killing him. Good. Keep looking. Keep searching. Maybe you won't be a complete #failure twice in a row..."

Which led Spark's hostage to protest.

"What in null are you *doing*!?" he whispered, trying not to be heard by their assailant.

"Keeping him focused on me and not you. Relax and stay hidden while I go deal with this," Spark ordered... while flexing her fingers, getting ready for the upcoming fight. "Be a good boy and I promise to remotely disable your collar once I've got him down."

Since Tracer was taking his sweet time... she had to step this game up a notch.

Quickly, she slipped away from the safety of the hiding crate, hoping Starling would do the smart thing and stay put. Meanwhile, as she repositioned herself, she kept the taunts going.

"...you really aren't good at this, are you?" she asked the attacker, keeping the sound aimless, while she kept an eye on the proxy through cracks between crates. "You've taken out a server or two, good for you. And... you murdered a schoolteacher. Three cheers for evolution, eat it you stupid creationists! But did it accomplish anything? Did it stop those supposed backwards thinkers, turn them around to your perspective? No. Total #failure. You're a #failure. You did #nothing. You *are* #nothing..."

...the proxy, spinning in place with his handheld backspacer aiming randomly into the darkness. He fired randomly, vaporizing a few crates... not enough to expose either of his targets, just enough to work out his frustration.

"You don't understand what's at stake!" he called out... the first words Spark had heard from him, outside of a prerecorded ranted death threat.

"Really? Clarify, then. Make me understand. We've all the time in the world to talk it over, you and I..."

Now, the stalker crept around the crates, keeping his trigger happy weapon under control. He had a chance to make his case, to speak calmly... and was using that chance to calm himself, as well.

"Nobody sees what I see," he explained. "They don't see the threat. There's a war going on, a war for our hearts and minds. One side versus the other, and neither will stop until the other is completely eradicated. Everybody says it's just words, it's just trolling, it's just... *Netwerk*. But I know the truth. Our world is soaked in mutual hatred! This is life and death. Zero and One..."

"That sounds rather faithful, for someone who hates creationism."

...a flash of white. That jacket, the one with the blazing heart icon on it, yes. That was the one who stopped him earlier today...

The proxy crept up on that spot, hidden behind a crate.

"You don't understand," he repeated. "But I can show you the light."

The backspacer unleashed upon the crate, deleting its data from the server entirely.

Revealing a discarded white jacket, draped carefully over a rolling office chair.

Spark dropped from the ceiling above, fingers poised and ready to strike at the man's shoulders.

It would have been enough. From their earlier fight, she knew he wasn't particularly skilled at avatar to avatar combat, likely relying on the power of a backspacer or a surprise lunge with his knife. The art of parrying and striking was beyond him, this afternoon.

This evening was another matter, as he reached out and deflected her blows, counterattacking her wrists to deflect them.

When Spark landed nimbly on her feet—the physical bounding boxes of her dancing shoes being a bit flatter and more stable than the spiky heels might suggest—the proxy had already assumed a martial arts stance, knife at the ready but held with a slashing grip rather than a stabbing one. The killer had gone ahead and installed some self-defense software, learning from earlier mistakes.

...which made the tiny part of Spark that craved this game smile even wider.

Her initial flurry of strikes weren't intended to be fight-ending blows, burning away the proxy's limbs. No, she was testing this new software, trying to learn more about it. Studying the patterns of blocks and deflections... analyzing the way the knife arced as it passed through the space occupied by her avatar half a moment ago... learning the methods of her new opponent. A new fight, a real fight, compared to the quick ambush from before...

Long-term planning wasn't Spark's forte. But in the moment-to-moment of a challenge, nobody matched her for coming up with wins on the fly. In this case, the win was a stall, keeping him fighting while waiting for Tracer to show. Keeping him focused. Keeping herself from getting stabbed and suffering the same fate as Verity...

Easier said than done, though.

The knife went wider than expected on one flurry... and sliced across her left arm.

Instantly, his hacktool went to work.

Spark's defensive firewalls and anti-malware Apps were layered thick, even for social outings like club nights. They put up a fight against the hacktool's intrusions, shutting down ports, keeping it from exploiting the usual suspects of default passwords and known overflow vulnerabilities. But even the best software can't be perfect.

Her vision blurred, as some of her data went screwy. Not a full corruption and crash, not a fatal wound, but she'd need to do run some cleanup and repair Apps tonight. He'd managed to hurt her, but not kill her... which made the situation far more dangerous.

Now her reaction times wouldn't be ideal, not sharp enough to keep up her defensive wall of martial technique. Her internal software wouldn't deal well with another hacktool attack, either; already some of her firewall Apps had crashed, needing reinstall before they'd be useful again. She was open, and vulnerable...

But what fun was a game you couldn't lose?

And besides... she'd already won.

Across the warehouse, she could see the dim lighting glinting off her brother's new eyes.

"97f1:56a8:83e3," he announced.

With a final cry of triumph, Spark worked her way past the defensive patterns she'd been analyzing during the entire fight, and planted two fingers squarely in the chest of the avatar proxy.

A brilliant fireball lit up the warehouse, as the proxy exploded into flame. It licked at the crates, leaving behind decorative scorchmarks... and leaving behind nothing but tiny bits of avatar data, scattered and ruined, across the floor below.

...Spark sagged backwards a bit, stumbling on her dancing shoes, as she started launching Apps to clean and repair her data damage.

With a thought, she dismissed the ongoing connection lock from her hostage. No doubt Starling disconnected away immediately; he wasn't important anymore. He'd hurt her best friend, true, but they had a more important bastard to deal with right now.

"So what server is he from?" she asked.

"Liberty17," Tracer announced. "And now I know exactly who killed Verity."

Desperately he worked to erase all of his tracks.

All the spare proxies, he deleted them. One by one his duplicated thugs vanished, leaving behind no data whatsoever to comb through. His recording software used for his threats, scrubbed. The icons and imagery he had been leaving behind at the scene of his murders, destroyed. Nothing that could possibly prove his role in those events...

Unfortunately, the two that followed him all the way home weren't interested in proof. Not after what he'd done.

The door to his private chambers beneath the church was blasted off its hinges, parts of it vaporized in a burst of brilliant flame.

He tried pointing his last remaining backspacer at the intruders, but without the assistive combat software of the proxy, his hands trembled far too much. Before he could even get a shot off, the weapon itself was in the hands of his hunter, and vaporized. Ash and flame, and then, nothing...

The archbishop whimpered, and realized how pathetic that whimpering must sound. All the confidence he had when acting through his proxy was gone; even if he was the same person, he lacked his protective shell. His puppet, his alter ego, his excuse... everything stripped away.

Leaving only Ichiban, one of many Archbishops in the Church of One. Someone who would have the connections to easily infiltrate HolyHymnal, to track down Nestt/Starling, even resources to get into ID:Entity to enact his assassination backup plan...

This supposed priest backed into a corner of his private room, as the boy with absolute loathing in his eyes advanced on him.

"*Why*," Tracer demanded to know.

Ichiban's lips flapped uselessly, before he stammered out a far less impressive speech than he'd managed through his proxy.

"B-Because... because... nobody understood," he claimed. "Evolution is a lie. It's a threat. I, I had to, I had to attack the church under the name of evolution so they'd wake up to how much of a threat those academic heathens represent..."

"A false flag. You were pretending to be an anti-creationism terrorist just to rally your own church to your cause," Tracer understood. "You did more damage to the faithful than evolution ever has, Archbishop. You've destroyed servers and murdered your own people just to frame the innocent..."

"It had to be done!" Ichiban insisted. "He whispered to my heart, he told me that they had to understand, had to be made to see the evil within evolution's heart! The... the teacher, that first one, he said she had to go, she was a threat, she would've destroyed everything good and pure and holy...!"

Spark slammed the archbishop up against a wall, the fabric simulation of his white robes glitching slightly from the force of impact...

...revealing his avatar's bare chest. Upon it, a tattoo of the barbed wire heart.

She raised her other hand, igniting her fingers.

"Just say the word," she told Tracer, level and even in tone. "Just say it. I'm sick of his ranting."

"—wait."

"Wait?! He murdered Verity!"

"Something's wrong," Tracer said... focused in tightly on that tattoo.

It wasn't just an avatar decoration, no... it was an App. An App with an ongoing connection outside of the Liberty17 server, to... to...

...to Tracer's own home server?

A quick glance at his private access key, currently displaying 6356:8538:5988, contradicted that. The addresses were similar, likely using the same supposedly lost technology, but they were indeed two different servers. Another place like Floating Point somewhere out there in Netwerk, influencing an Archbishop of the Church of One and using him to commit murder...

"Who was whispering to you?" Tracer demanded to know. "Who told you to kill Verity? WHO?"

"Th... the Zero," Ichiban whispered. "The all-encompassing Great Zero. The smiling boy branded me with its heart, long ago. A sacred heart bathed in light and shadow and pain, perfect and true. I'm, I'm not the only one it whispers to, so many, so many others bear the same bloody mark, synced to its pulse, to spread its gospHGHRHHGAAGAHHH—!"

Spark let go in shock, as the barbed wire exploded outward from the Archbishop's chest.

Flailing, screaming metal wires writhed their way out of the tattoo. It began to animate, valves and ventricles pumping pain as the wires cycled in and out... now becoming 3-D, snarling and wrapping around the Archbishop's avatar. Both of the Winder siblings backed away from the horror, to avoid being caught up in its web of agony...

...and then the wires constricted.

Archbishop Ichiban gave one final scream, as the remainder of his program data was utterly shredded to pieces by the tangle of barbed wire.

In an explosion of light and shadow and animalistic howls, he was fully backspaced. Nothing remained of the man afterward... or of the App that was influencing him.

---

**File Name:** Our True Inheritance

**File Type:** Memory Recording [Tracer]

**MemoryPalace:** Investigation Notes [Private:Tracer]

**Description:**

This is ours, and ours alone. He couldn't take that away from us, even if he killed the woman who gave it to us.

It took years before they found the truth behind the gifts left behind by Verity.

Tracer found his, first. There was a single word, a misprint, in his copy of Compiled Works of Pollox/Scribler. Within that word, he found an access key uniquely bound to his identity. Given the hints left in Verity's last will and testament, they checked the stitches on Spark's jacket next... and found a second key, this one bound to her identity.

The pair, now in their teens, resolved to try the keys simultaneously. Either they'd go nowhere or somewhere, together.

That was how they discovered their new home.

It was a private server, a giant library within a flying castle in the clouds. Within its rounded great antechamber were shelf after shelf of leather-bound books... many of them blank, many of them filled with gibberish, some of them coherent but seemingly from another world.

A great spiral stair wound its way around inside this cylinder, leading to bedrooms and studies and rec rooms and more. Through great windows, sunlight poured in... from a vast, open sky that hung over a mapped representation of all of Netwerk.

A note sealed with wax had been conspicuously left for them on a tiny round table near the foyer.

```
I've kept these keys a secret for many years. In my youth,
exploring these hallways helped inspire my dreams of
archaeology. What is this place? Who created it? What are
all these books, what does the 'W' symbol on their spines
represent, what do they mean? So many mysteries...

Most of the books were damaged (or encrypted?) during some
sort of attack; the whole place was in terrible disrepair
when I first came here, left abandoned for generations. I
don't know how it's possible for it to exist outside the
hosting services... but the fact remains that it exists,
and it holds wonders I have yet to understand...

I leave this to my two prodigies, be they young or old at
the time I pass on, in hopes that they may carry on my
studies. Tracer and Spark, this server is yours to do with
as you see fit. May you find happiness within these walls.
-Verity.
```

In front of this little table, in the center of the vast library... a single stone sphere 3.14 meters in diameter hovered, against all physical simulation rules. It rotated very slowly, grinding away the seconds and hours of Netwerk, maintaining the server's perpetually calculating cloud functionality.

A brass plaque attached to the dais the sculpture hovered offered a strange mixture of garbled or encrypted characters, alongside a cleartext greeting...

'*DIE GANZEN ZAHLEN HAT DER LIEBE GOTT GEMACHT, ALLES ANDERE IST MENSCHENWERK.*'
**WELCOME TO FLOATING POINT.**

"This is our new home away from home," Tracer declared. "This is where we'll do it. We'll figure out who killed Verity, Spark. I promise."

Spark and Tracer felt it wise to leave Liberty17 as soon as possible, before anybody came to investigate the now-empty church.

Home also worked as a rallying point, a fallback server to regroup at whenever anything went wrong. Technically everything had sort-of gone right, but it felt like an appropriate place to go all the same. Hidden within the wilds of Netwerk, accessible only by a pair of golden keys, they could find safe haven from any storm within the walls of Floating Point.

Brother and sister sat at the bottom of the great stair, looking out across the room at the stone sphere at the core of their home. Simply sitting together, in thought.

"He's gone," Spark tried. "We did it. We got her killer..."

"We destroyed the knife, not the one who held the knife," Tracer understood. "There's more to this than a lone psychopath. Someone or something is exploiting the existing malice of Netwerk; this 'Zero' dug its barbs into Ichiban, using that malware tattoo to turn a man of faith into a killer..."

"So... what, the crazy stories of the Church of One are for real now?" Spark asked. "There's an actual, factual One and Zero out there? Or is the 'smiling boy' some epic-tier troll imitating the Zero, maybe...?"

"Maybe. I'm not sure. I need to search my archived MemoryPalace modules, crawl them completely, make the right connections. ...we're not done, Spark. If he was telling the truth, if there's more like him out there acting under the marching orders of this Zero... we're not done. We need to figure this out. I need to figure this out..."

Tracer slowly rose to his feet, and began climbing the stairs.

"Where're you going?" Spark asked.

"I'm going to my room to sleep," he said. "I made a promise to you that I'd put this aside and get some rest, didn't I? Nothing's changed. The work continues. And I'll need that rest to see this through to the end. ...get some rest yourself, Spark. You've earned it."

But instead, she stayed sitting on that stair for some time.

DEFEAT. The word wasn't actually in front of her eyes, but it may as well have been.

Failure to understand the nature of Verity's killer, until it was too late. Failure to truly avenge her teacher's murder. Failure to protect her friend's heart. Failure to accomplish anything or achieve any real victory. An entire day devoted to defeat...

No. She couldn't go to bed, not like this. She had to eke out some win, no matter how small.

It took a minute to regain enough composure to answer the knocking at her apartment's front door.

Even now, hours after she'd had her heart broken, Puzzle still looked beautiful.

"Spark...?" her friend asked, confused. "You're okay? Oh thank goodness—"

She had to stand on her toes to do it, but Spark lined up nicely for a soft kiss to Puzzle's lips.

Only after letting it linger, after both of them letting it linger for that matter, did Spark explain.

"You deserve to be happy," she said. "And we make each other happy, don't we?"

Puzzle's fingers brushed across her lips, as she trembled at that doorstep.

"I... I... Spark, I just..." she whispered. "I... I can't. I-I'm sorry."

And the door closed.

---

Which left Spark only one option for her daily win.

She didn't bother firing up Peep. This wasn't for them, it was for her. Sitting in the dark of the lobby, waiting for four more rando pubbers to show up. Didn't matter who showed up, as long as she had people to fight, objectives to clear, and a victory condition to achieve. Nothing else mattered, not now.

Allies appeared, paired up with her by the matchmaking service. They identified as being in the same ranked division she was; as good a metric for finding pleasant company as any, she guessed.

The Kunoichi was the first to declare her intent.

"Solo-mid," she called.

:: **end chapter 1.1**

# Floating Point 1.2 :: Nude

"...and that's my story."

Summarizing the entire tale had taken a toll. She'd already gone through several tissues, to mop up the residual tears that leaked behind her ridiculousy thick-framed glasses. Her entire perspective bobbled uneasily each time she had to nudge those frames, to stay dry.

...and why did an avatar need to cry? Why did her default coding have to produce that reaction, the sensation of tears going down the skin, the visible wetness? Why couldn't she remain stoic in the face of everything that happened to her...?

From his perch on her shoulder Mew batted at the tears, to try and dry them with his paws. Unfortunately, while her kitty's simulations were more sophisticated than most housepet Apps, the fur wasn't flagged as absorbent.

"🙀📥😺," Mew emoji'd, in sympathy. " 💧 ."

Mew's owner wiped away the last of the tears, before crumpling up the tissue in a tightly balled fist. Her bulky sweater concealed a lot of avatar faults but lacked pockets for used tissue paper, unfortunately.

"I've tried. I really tried," she spoke, adjusting her glasses back in place (while looking vaguely at a point above and to the right of the doctor). "I tried to fight back against them, but it's useless. They've got my number. They've got all my numbers. Leaving it all behind is the hardest decision I've ever had to make, but... but... I don't see any, any other w-way..."

Another tissue was provided to soak up the last of the last of the tears.

For her part... Doctor Uniq was outwardly sympathetic to her patient's woes. She nodded at each twist and turn of the story, looked mournful at what was lost, and understanding of the pain being shown on her client's face. Running out of tissues was normal in her line of work, and she'd always have more if they were needed.

"You're making the right decision," Uniq insisted. "Changing your identity is the best way to lay down your burdens. You don't have to be a victim any longer. Today... you'll walk out of my clinic a free woman. No more persecution, no more accusations. A fresh start. Okay...?"

The patient nodded between sobs, desperate to get on with it, now that she'd made up her mind.

"How do we... um... do it?" she asked. "Replace my identity with a new one, I mean. What's the process, exactly...?"

"Just sit back in your chair and relax," Uniq spoke... opening a visible HUD, a remote control App that operated her clinic systems. "Lie back, and relax..."

The chair the client was sitting in began to change.

What started as a simple metal chair shifted, becoming softer to the touch. It reclined, morphing into something as gentle as pillows, like the perfect bed. The most comfort she'd ever experienced in her life, lulling her towards sleep mode... Mew curling up in her lap now, emitting little "$z^{z^{Z}}$"s as the pet App got there a little ahead of its owner.

When she awoke, she'd have lost everything.

When she awoke, she wouldn't be a pariah anymore.

The doctor smiled down at her, as the chair became recliner, became a container, became a receptacle for all her memories and all her code and all her everything. And this nice woman, the one who came to her in her hour of need and provided a way out... that woman was so gentle. So kind...

"I like your tattoo," the patient said, zooming in the view provided by her App glasses on that crawling red mark on the doctor's neck. Like a heart. A heart, with some kind of jagged lines around it...

"I like it too," the doctor spoke. Before beginning the siphoning process.

Her name was the first thing to go.

"Of course... once I'm done hollowing you out, I won't be filling in the cracks," Uniq explained, as childhood memories started slipped away, drained into a nearby file container.

"...wuh...?" her victim managed, between the strange sensation of her data to go blank.

Window after window closing as her running Apps shut down... including Mew, who vanished from her lap. Everything going dark and blank within her mind, as dark and blank as her sight for her first years. ...first years? What years? Mother's name. What was mother's name, what was her name, when did any of that happen...

Even her clothes were gone, stripped from her avatar. A vague sense of recent offense related to that popped to mind, trying to trigger some sort of rage that would help her break free... but even that anger fell away, into the black pit that opened up inside her head.

"You really think I was going to give you a new life? No. Not for you. You're too valuable to me," Uniq explained... while pulling everything the client was into a data storage file, compressing it down for duplication and shipment. "There are so many people, so many *rich* people, who could work wonders with the data of a shady character like you. Your name, your avatar, your memories. All of it will belong to the highest bidder..."

*No. Wrong. Bad.* Negative words rushed to her consciousness, before being pulled away. Weakly she lifted one hand... but it felt heavy, so completely heavy. Couldn't get out of the chair, not anymore.

Mew. She knew her cat's name was Mew. He was a good kitty, he could run and get help, help, please, somebody, *help me*...

But Mew was gone. Drained away, like everything else. The only good thing left in her life, her beloved cat, and Uniq had taken him away...

"Everybody's going to know the truth about you soon enough," the doctor promised, still with her smile so wide... wider, even, than ever before. "And if that truth doesn't match what they suspected...? Well. They can *make* it match. You can be anything they need you to be..."

Her vision augmentation App, embedded in those thick-framed glasses, was the last thing to shut down.

Born into a world of darkness. Dying into a world of darkness. A null state.

The client's other senses still worked. She could still feel the incredible softness, hear the sound of the software churning away on her memories, draining the last of her self dry. Hear the soft chuckle of the doctor. Hear the sound of cracking and burning wood, as the door to the operating room exploded inward...

Other sounds, she could hear them, even if she didn't know what they meant. Some sort of scuffle, feet squeaking against the tiled flooring. Machines being knocked over, physics objects scattered. The feel of roaring flames just over her head, that was also something she could feel... burning heat like passionate fury, striking out against the cold and the dark she'd been mired within...

These were her only memories, now. Brand new memories; she didn't even remember what the room looked like, or why she was here. As far as she knew, she'd been born here. She didn't exist until this moment.

And then, quiet.

Voices returned. Language was still processed, thanks to some residually operating code, even if she had no idea who was speaking.

"Oh for *fuck's sake*...!" a young woman snarled; the sound of clattering metal accompanied this outburst.

"She got away?" a deeper-toned man's voice responded.

"She got away. Broke right through my connection lock and *whoosh*, off she went."

"Identity thieves are keenly interested in not being caught, Spark. They're going to pack countermeasures to simple hacktools like your lock collar."

"Well, this is all I have for fighting the Zero's little minions. Take it or leave it. ...we've got more immediate problems, anyway."

"More immediate than an escaping criminal?"

(The pause that followed might have been due to a visual gesture. In the lifelong darkness of the empty woman, it wasn't seen.)

"Yes, it's a naked amnesiac in a chair. What about it?" the man asked.

"Tracer, c'mon. We can't just *leave* her like this, whoever she is. Uh. Y'know how to reinstall an identity, by any chance? I have no idea what any of these Apps do... I think I've got her data here in this compressed file, it's heavy as hell, but..."

"If she's a client of an identity scrubber, odds are she's a criminal as well. We'd be doing Netwerk a favor to leave her here."

"#Bullshit. We have no idea who this person is!"

Name: (undefined)

Home: None

Org: None

"Exactly—we have no idea who this person is. She's not our problem unless we choose to make her our problem... and if we do, it means we then have a problem. So, why risk it?"

(The woman had no idea whose problem she was. She was her own problem, at the moment. As much as she wanted to speak up, to explain, she'd lost her ability to speak. Assuming she was ever able to speak in the first place. Hadn't she simply... *been* here, in this softness, forever?)

"Not up for debate, Tracer. You grab her legs, I'll get her shoulders," the woman possibly named Spark suggested. "#Teamwork."

Lfited from the softness, floating in the air. Strong hands supporting her upper body in a capable manner, while a weaker set of arms struggled to get her legs free from the chair. There was some comfort in those arms, in these strangers who seemed to have a care for whoever she was...

"This is insane, you understand that, right?" the man asked. "We can't even put any clothes on her because we don't have write permissions for her avatar. We are literally carrying a naked woman out of a doctor's office in broad daylight..."

"I didn't say we were hauling her out the front door. We need to get her serious medical help, and... as much as I hate to say it... we're only going to find that kind of serious medical help in AptGet. We need to see Arjay."

The newborn woman living in darkness soaked in every single bit of sensory input she could, passively learning more about her situation along the way. The two who had... saved? her, they moved her to a new server...

...new server? Yes, a server in Netwerk. She remembered that much. She was a sapient Program, living in Netwerk. She knew basics of language and how to parse auditory input. Her speech and motor skills were offline, but at least she could take comfort in knowing the words that were arriving from... outside.

Outside the darkness, whatever it was. She could feel the damp air of this new server on her skin, could tremble at the cold. Could experience discomfort at being awkwardly carried up and down small flights of what were likely stairs, through a busy city street...

And to a new place. This one felt... empty, devoid of any sensation. She was placed on another soft surface, but there was no ambient noise, no atmospheric effect, nothing. Just voices.

She'd identified them by name, now: the woman who jumped to her aid was Spark. She had a kind voice, but very firm, and irritable towards the one named Tracer. That one, he was far more irritable than the other, inclined to leave the woman behind and continually suggesting they do just that.

But now a third voice had joined in, one they'd named Arjay. He... she? was indescribable. Maybe because the woman's words weren't entirely online, not yet...

"This is curious," the third man? woman? spoke. "Your new friend has no eyes."

"Uh... Arjay? She does. They're right there and they're staring at you," Spark pointed out. (Maybe she pointed a finger. Hard to say, given the woman's inability to see it.) "She does have that creepy no-pupils, solid-color-iris thing going on, though..."

"Her *avatar* has eyes. Her *code* does not. There's no sensory input routines for vision whatsoever. A strange mutation, indeed... and unrelated to her current identity issue. As near as I can tell, she was born this way. Hmm. Would you like me to install some eyes? Something better than eyes, even. I have an excellent package I got from a black market dealer recently that proports to see underneath an avatar's clothing—"

"We just need this identity package reinstalled, thank you. No mucking around inside her code."

"I think you misunderstand who I am, love," Arjay replied, his voice floating away from the woman and towards the others. "I'm no healer, and certainly no programmer; I obtain and install shady software patches. I create nothing, I merely manipulate what exists. I haven't the faintest idea how to perform the kind of code cleanup and restoration she requires."

"So... you can't, I don't know, jam her identity back in there?"

"I can give it a try, I suppose. And I DO have a nice cleanup App I can install in her," Arjay spoke. "Much like the auto-repair systems that restore your data integrity after getting rolled in a fight. They weren't designed for this task, however; I've no idea if it'll work. I suppose it's worth a try, for lack of a better option. ...unless you'd like me to leave her a blank slate? She's very pliant like this, and I do admire her simple Default beauty. You could make her into something of your own choosing, instead. Such potential...!"

"Sicko."

"We are who we are, little Spark."

Now, Tracer spoke up in her favor for the first time since her 'birth.'

"Run the restoration," he ordered. "And that's all. The sooner we deal with this situation, the better."

And the world went dark. It was always dark, always an absence of anything other than sound and touch, but now it felt... darker than dark. Or rather it *would* have felt darker than dark, if she could feel anything at all. To her perspective, life simply ended, then resumed a split second later.

"That took some doing," Arjay spoke, sounding... a bit strained. "But I think I've got all her bits neatly tucked away."

"Good. We can leave now, then?"

"Not so fast, my little misanthrope. Your friend here needs time to recover; the App I installed is going to take considerable time to sort out all that data. She'll fade in and out of lucidity for some time, while she gets her mental house in order. I *highly* recommend bedrest and a safe, chaos-free environment."

"Your office seems perpetually chaos-free."

"This is no hostel, Tracer. I don't put up free room and board for strays. If you leave her here, I'd be happy to see what modifications I can deploy to turn this blank slate into a useful pet! Barring that... I suggest you take her home with you."

Speak. She wanted to speak, wanted to express herself, but her voice hadn't found her yet. It was still lost in the... the swirling morass inside her, the jumble of ill-fitting puzzle pieces. If only she could find those words, the ones that would spill from her own lips...

"Absolutely not," Tracer denied. "Spark, can't you dump her at your friend Puzzle's place or something? You're the socialite, you've got actual friends on tap, yes?"

"I... haven't talked to Puzzle lately. #ItsComplicated. ...I think we should bring her home with us. Why not? C'mon, Tracer, what's the harm in giving her a place to stay while she recovers?"

"What's the harm—?! Our home is *ours*, Spark, and ours alone. That's the pact we made! And now, *now* especially when we know our enemy is using similar server tech, we can't let anybody inside. She could be... dammit. Arjay, I'm taking this to our private channel, if you don't mind."

"By all means," the patcher replied.

...and silence. Silence for far too long.

Were they somehow talking? Did they leave? Was she alone in this soundless room, abandoned in the dark?

No. No, please. Please.

Help.

"Help," she managed, barely audible.

Within the minimalist chambers of Arjay's workshop, that tiny word carried greath volume.

"Help. Help," the woman repeated, clinging to the word and iterating on it, in hopes of finding more words to join with it. "Help. Help me. Help me. Please help me. Please please please. Please help me..."

A strangely familiar sensation of wetness trickled down her cheeks, now. Crying, she knew it was crying, once she was able to connect the memory. She'd cried before... recently, in fact. Was that before she woke up to nothingness? Was there really something before the nothingness...?

It took a few more moments before anyone responded to that crying.

"Fine," Tracer agreed. "But you're looking after her, Spark. Not me. She's not my problem."

---

The following day was a blurry mess for the nameless woman.

She'd sleep. She'd wake. She'd occasionally talk with her benefactor, the nice woman named Spark. Not much that Spark said made sense, not yet... and the periods of narcolepsy, when her process went into sleep mode so the data cleanup App could work on a particularly intense wad of corrupted material, those punctuated their discussions as much as actual punctuation.

What little the woman could gather amounted to the following:

She'd been taken to a private server, home to Tracer and Spark, and given a room of her own. There was a bed in this room, the bed she was often lying in. (Once she regained control over her avatar's movement she tried walking around, but only ended up tripping over unseen furniture and falling down repeatedly.) The bed was warm, and in the morning (assuming it was morning) she felt the warmth of a skybox sun on her face through what were possibly windows. A sound like wind could be heard in the distance, suggesting... movement, of some sort, but beyond that she couldn't glean much understanding.

Now and then Spark would show up between "game sessions," to offer her a chance to talk through the gaps in her memory. These proved fruitless, and often the woman simply didn't have the words to express herself properly. Frustration mounted on both sides of those conversations... but it was a sympathetic frustration.

"Arjay said it might take some time for it all to come back," Spark would often say. "But it *will* come back. I've got faith."

The woman didn't have faith of any traditional sort. Maybe she did once, but that was someone else. Now all she had was this bed, this room, the darkness, and a single spark of hope that there would one day be more.

On the second day, the headaches started.

Pain was a strange sensation. Her code was rearranging itself on the fly, data recovery a continual process... and when things *shifted* inside her head, it hurt. She'd curl up in the bed, pulling the sheets tight against the pajamas Spark had provided her with. Flashes would punctuate the darkness, flashes of thought and memory, but nothing coherent. Nothing she could clearly recall...

Until she remembered the cherries.

*Cherry*. An icon of two red circles connected by two lines, representing a flavor of *cherry*. So sweet and sticky. One cherry, two cherries. Three. And then none. Then one, then two, then three, then nothing...

She was matching fruit.

In the darkness of nothing, she saw, she saw cherries and knew what they were. She'd done it before; it was a silly little game App, something given to her by her mother. Partly as a way to distract her from her problems, partly as an experiment...

"She's responding well to HUDs and UI elements, at least."

Another place. Another doctor. So many doctors in her life. Was she broken?

"That's a good sign. It means her mind can comprehend visual input, even if she has no means of gathering that input from the world around her," the doctor continued. "She can play games, watch video files, open messenger windows. What she needs is an indirect means of input... but there's no App specifically for interfacing with this kind of birth defect."

"My daughter is *not* defective," the best voice in the world replied.

Matching cherries did get boring after doing it a zillion times. She needed more. She poked at other elements of the game's simple 2-D window, fingers pressing the air in front of herself, touching the virtual controls. The corner of the game window, there was something odd there... if she could just peel it back...

"I didn't mean it like that, ma'am. But the fact of the matter is that she has a defect in her code, one which cannot be repaired. Given your family health history, I'm not surprised this happened. At best her vision can be augmented, but I'm afraid I don't know how. ...normally I'd recommend you reformat her, in hopes a fresh respec would—"

"Mommy! Mommy, look!" her own voice called, into the dark.

The cherries were dancing, now. She'd pulled open the code and accessed the game's debug state, setting up a simple animation script to manipulate the sprites. Giggling, the child sent the cherries sprawling, bumping into each other and bouncing off the walls of the window...

"Honey... I can't see what you're seeing," her mother reminded. "It's a HUD game."

"Well, why not? Why can't you see what I'm seeing?" the young girl asked. "Why can't I see what you're seeing? I don't understand."

Which was all the inspiration her mother needed to craft an App for something which had no App.

On her next birthday the child got her first pair of glasses, and her visual world immediately expanded well beyond that of cherry sprites.

Color. Shape. All this data coming in actively, not passively like a movie file. She could turn her head and *look* at things, in direct response to the movement of her avatar...

"Mommy programmed these just for you," she explained. "They're all yours, tailored to your code. Anything these glasses are pointing at, you'll see as a window HUD inside your mind. It's your new special eyes, for my special little girl! See? You're not defective or broken, honey. You just didn't have your glasses yet..."

...and the woman in the bed opened her eyes.

The glasses were sitting in her file inventory, freshly restored by the data cleaner. With some hesitation... she attached them to her avatar, resting the thick frames on the bridge of her nose...

A soft bed, with silky white sheets. In the distance, the warm sun spilled in through an arched window. Clouds soared by, accompanied by the whistle of the wind...

Color. Shape.

One more piece of the puzzle restored.

With new eyes, the woman could properly explore her new home.

Fortunately this didn't mean any encounters with the man, the one who didn't want her here in the first place.

Tracer kept to his study all day. He was doing "research," of some sort... she wasn't allowed to go in there, not allowed to know what it was the man was investigating. Even Spark was cagey about it.

"He's... not good with strangers," she tried to explain, the morning the woman got her eyes back. "On top of that, he thinks you might actually be one of our enemies, trying to sneak your way into our private server."

"But I'm not," the woman spoke, using her new words. Still a bit childish in her speech patterns, but getting there, little by little.

"You might have been. We don't know who you are, after all. Me, I seriously doubt it. I wouldn't have let you into Floating Point either, if you were with the bad guys."

Floating Point...

That was the name of this strange place. A castle in the clouds, flying high above a diagrammed map of all of Netwerk. A server that only Spark and Tracer had access keys to, granted to them by someone named "Verity," someone who they clearly loved dearly... keys that the woman did not have. She could techncially leave at any time, if she knew where her home was, but she'd never be able to find the place again without a key.

Not that she wanted to leave this paradise.

Spark was more forthcoming with information than her brother would've liked, no doubt.

"We have no idea who made this server in the first place," she explained. "There's the books, of course, but most of them are garbled. The few ones that are readable don't make much sense. Our teacher gave us access as an inheritance; we're the only ones who know it exists. That's why Tracer's so freaked out that you're here. I've never even told my friends where I live..."

It was... beautiful. If this was her first visual input since being blanked out, it was a fine visual input to behold. The castle was largely cylindrical, centered around an enormous library of books, with a winding staircase around the shelves. Doors branched out from there to other rooms, such as her own bedroom or Tracer's study. Windows, arched windows, those were everywhere... allowing the sunlight to flow in with cutting beams, highlighting a light sheen of dust in the air. At night, the moonlight replaced the sunlight, bathing Floating Point in a silvery glow rather than a golden hue...

Spark seemed very happy here. The woman was happy here, as well.

Part of her didn't want to remember who she was, if it meant leaving this peaceful place.

"Why secret? It so. Is. Why is it so secret?" the woman asked, patiently reordering the words after they arrived.

"I don't totally understand it. Verity knew server technology better than we ever did..."

"Servers," the woman repeated. The word felt... comfortable, to her.

"See, Floating Point doesn't have a hosting service. Every server belongs to one of the big three, right? Horizon, Athena Online, or the Chanarchy. They each have their own processes for creating new servers... bribery, democracy, lottery, whatever. But this place doesn't exist under any of the umbrellas. None of them created it. None of them host it."

"Flying castle," the woman recognized, from her peeks through the windows. "In the clouds. Clouds. Cloud processing..."

"Yeah, that's the word. It's like it exists INSIDE other servers, as a rogue process. It steals a little unused runtime here and there from all over Netwerk. Weird, right? And totally unique! ...we thought it was unique, anyway, until—"

"Dynamic distribution of processes across multiple servers in a cloud configuration," the woman spoke automatically. "Possible in theory, but considered impossible to implement under Netwerk's restrictive protocols due to the low-level system access rights required. I... I studied cloud programming once, using the core principles for distributed video networking..."

Spark looked up from the taste of a jam-filled morning pastry in surprise.

"That's... yeah. That's it," she confirmed. "What little I understand of it, anyway. How did you—?"

—pain. Pain behind her glasses, behind her eyes. Memories sifting and resorting, triggered by the experience of technical problem solving. The data cleanup routine was back on the job, having found the right metadata to drop a few new blocks into place...

...the code crawling across her inner vision, in the darkness.

She preferred to code in the dark, honestly. It was more efficient to scrawl all those little parentheses and function names through a 100% mental interface, unlike some amateur programmers who wanted a physical keyboard they could hammer away on with meaty avatar fingers. She'd spent most of her early years in the dark, she'd pulled apart little game Apps in the dark, and she felt more at home coding in the dark as a result.

Here, there was only herself, and her code. Nothing else. The world and all its problems fell away, leaving her in perfect isolation. Just her and the beauty of the software she was writing, carving something from nothing...

And... done. Well. Probably not *done*, but at least at a compilable state, and ready for testing.

"Here goes nothing, Mew," she spoke aloud, into the dark.

"🍀!!" chirped a voice from her lap.

Compile it, link in the libraries, feed it the right input, run, and...

...and a perfect look straight up her crotch.

"Mew!" she protested, shooing the cat from her lap. "Go look at something interesting, okay? Not... that."

"😾" her cat joked, before dropping perfectly to all four paws... and going off exploring.

Amazingly, the broadcast was coming through perfectly through her HUD. Instead of the vision from her glasses, she now was seeing the world through a cat's perspective, padding along through her messy workroom, batting at cables running in and out of various compilers. The video artifacting and buffering from dropped frames was not particularly great, especially considering both ends of the connection resided in the same server, but it was a start.

With gleeful triumph, she opened a window to Snowi.

"I did it!" she declared.

"ProxyPerception? You got it working?" Snowi asked.

"Yep. Here, let me share my desktop and show you..."

Ideally, Snowi would be running a ProxyPerception client on her end, connected right to the data mirror that was feeding Mew's perspective into her owner's virtual eyes. For now, mirroring the video feed manually would have to do. Still, it was a way to show off her work to one of her peers, which was always fun.

"Is... hah! That's your kittykat, isn't it?" Snowi asked. "Wow! Y'know, it's such a simple idea to share perception over Netwerk. I'm surprised nobody's done it this well before..."

"It's not really scalable yet. Ideally I'd like to try some kind of cloud computing model to distribute the video streams... this isn't much more than a tech test. Just an alpha," she warned.

"Yeah, and you're only in *Beta*," Snowi joked. "It's still a great start. You gonna bring it to #FeminismCodeJam this weekend? Getting some terrific press coverage for the event so far; I think we're really gonna raise awareness of how sidelined women are in programming..."

...which left her squirming in her seat a bit.

"I don't think I can go," she spoke. "Cup8's got a romantic getaway weekend planned."

"What, another one? Seriously? I'm starting to wonder about that guy..."

The programmer had no response to that, because she was wondering as well.

Also because her cat had just rounded a corner, to see a pair of sensible shoes with feet in them.

"Uh, I gotta go, Snowi," she mumbled quickly... disconnecting from the messenger App, and shutting down ProxyPerception as well. In a blink of shadow, her vision came back, reconnected to the glasses that sat at the end of her nose.

Just in time to see Cup8 rounding the corner, carrying a bouquet of red roses and a box of chocolates.

"M'lady!" he greeted, presenting both offerings forward, with a smile of polished white teeth. "I bring you tokens of my love and affection, to better brighten your day. ...and to brighten this workshop of yours. Why do you never turn on the lights in here?"

Name : Cup8

Home : WingSpan/Horizon

Org : Angel Investor

"I don't really need them..." she spoke, without a lot of firmness.

Her handsome beau placed the bouquet on a nearby shelf, alongside five other similar flower arrangements. None of them were rotting away; they weren't from a gardening simulator, they were purely decorative, for those who believe their love will last forever.

He had a seat on one of several chairs (since she liked to have various comforts while coding), relaxing into it... before patting his knee, prompting her to come over and sit in his lap. Kisses rained down on her neck shortly after.

"I've a wonderful evening planned for us tonight," Cup8 promised her. "If I had three hands I'dve brought in the bottle of *very* expensive wine I purloined from today's ceremony."

"It's done, then?" she asked, curious. "Your big deal?"

"Signed, sealed, delivered. When this technology investment pays out... we'll go on a week-long pleasure cruise with the dividends," he spoke. "I always pick winners. Always. But, that's for another day! For this evening, we've chocolates and wine, and a nice bottle of massage oil..."

Which left her squirming a bit, on his lap.

"I've got a lot of work to do," she tried. "I just started a new project."

"Oh, come now, m'lady. You've *always* a lot of work to do," he noted... poking her gently on the nose, to push her glasses up a little as they were slipping. "You need to take a break from coding your little Apps and enjoy your life!"

"But I enjoy coding..."

"And what is it this time, mmm? What *fantastic* innovation is my little girl developing that will revolutionize the world today?"

"Well..." she said, perking up a bit at the notion of talking about her project. "It's a way to broadcast the perception of one Program into another. I based it on the glasses my mother made for me, actually, only this App's more generalized and doesn't completely replace the vision core. I'm calling it ProxyPerception."

"Yes, but what's the application?"

"Huh? That's the App, like I said..."

"No no, the *practical* application. The purpose. The goal. The whole package," he clarified. "Why would anybody want to see through another's eyes? Voyueristic impulse, I suppose, but there's plenty of sexy Apps already. Why would the *mainstream* audience want in on this new innovation?"

"There's a lot of uses, actually! I was thinking pro gamers might like to broadcast their games. Or you could watch a chef prepare a taste stimulator, and learn the recipe. Or just listen to people talk about their day, vlog style. I mean... ProxyPerception could be for anyone, right?"

...and Cup8's smile went wider. He kissed her cheek once, twice, three times.

"I suppose it could be," he agreed. "But it needs a branding change. A catchier name. ProxyPerception doesn't *exactly* roll off the tongue. How about... hmm. How about Peep? It's cute and simple and a little naughty... like you."

The kisses slid lower and lower, down to the neck, then tugging down one shoulder of her loose and bulky sweater. And then lifting that sweater up and over her head, while she passively sat there and let him.

"My little genius," he whispered in her ear. "My dear little Beta..."

Beta.

---

"Beta," the woman repeated, here and now.

"Huh?" Spark asked. "Are you okay? You zoned out again. Do you need help back into bed...?"

"My name is Beta," the coder spoke, trying the name on for size... and finding it fit her perfectly. "Beta. My name is Beta. She named me that. She. My mother. She named me Beta, said there was nothing to be ashamed of even if I was different, that everybody's always growing and changing and everybody's always beta software. I'm Beta..."

Name: **Beta**

Home: **WestHall/Horizon**

Org: **Indie App Coder**

Beta looked down at the offered hand, puzzled.

"I'm Spark," the other woman greeted, with a smile. "And I'm very pleased to meet you."

The two newfound friends shook on it, pleased to have found this bond. Even as one chose to disregard all the parts of her memory that made her uncomfortable.

---

Her sweater was back. That wonderful wooly sweater, knitted together by her mother out of a very elaborate cloth simulation, well beyond the complexity normally found in mass-produced consumer avatar clothing. Every little sensation of that fuzzy material against her skin put new memories back into place, all the times she took comfort in that silly pink thing. All those happy moments...

The data was flooding back in, now. Her head still pounded with agony but Beta embraced it, rode the pain out, eager for more and more memories. Taste-testing her father's terrible attempts at ice cream taste stims. Playtesting games for a living, fresh out of school, while experimenting with her own App coding. Playing with her kitty, then recompiling her kitty, then playing with her kitty again...

Mew. Her kitty was named Mew. He was sitting in her inventory all the while, waiting for the data recovery App to put him back together again. Now, he was bounding across on the carpet of Floating Point's walkways, getting underfoot as he skipped in excited circles around his owner/designer.

"🐾!!!" the cat chimed, pictograms floating from his head in adorable thought bubbles. "🐱 ♥️🐱, 🐱♥️🐱, 🐱♥️🐱!"

"I love you too, you silly cat," Beta replied, reaching down to scratch behind his ears before resuming her upbeat march. "His name's Mew. I've had him since I was very young; I designed a lot of his code myself, actually!"

Name: **Mew**

Owner: **Beta**

FileType: **App (Pet)**

"You made a pet? Whoa," Spark spoke, impressed. "I completely suck at programming. Farthest I've ever gotten was Hello World, and that was just to get through class with a passing grade..."

"It's all coming back. Almost all of it, anyway," Beta explained. "I think the data cleaner's putting memories back in-order. I've got my childhood right up through recent history! I've got all my personal files like Mew and my wardrobe and everything back, too!"

"But how did you end up in that identity thief's office? Do you remember that yet?"

"Not yet. ...but I will! I'll remember everything. I just know it!"

"Well... even so, we should check in with Tracer and see if he can help you get the rest," Spark suggested, her hand on the doorknob. "He said he found a promising lead. TRACER! We figured out who our houseguest is...!"

...and the door opened to a warped porno theater.

Picture after picture of Beta, without her fuzzy pink sweater. Without any clothing at all, in fact, not even her glasses. Posing for the camera, sometimes sexy, sometimes awkwardly-sexy. And in some pictures, sprawled on her bed with her legs spread, enjoying a private moment...

Each of these candid shots came with an insulting yet cryptic caption.

SUPPORTS FEMINIST INDIE CODERS
SLUTS IT UP LIKE A 5c WHORE

HOW'D I GO BLIND?
I LOOKED IN A MIRROR

TOO UGLY TO GET A REAL MAN
FUCKS HER CAT EVERY NIGHT

...causing the subject of those pictures to sink to her knees, on setting foot in that room.

"Her name is Beta," Tracer explained, looking away from his wall of research. "And she's possibly the most hated person in all of Netwerk at the moment."

***

It had been a long time coming, and it took Snowi pushing her and pushing her to finally give her the confidence to make the leap. Specifically, Snowi pushing her while standing right at her side, arms crossed in defiance at the man on the other side of the kitchen table.

Cup8 pressed his fingertips together, considering what he'd just heard.

"And that's how you feel, is it," he asked... sparing a moment to glare at Snowi.

"It's just too much," Beta said. "It's too much. The romantic getaways, the romantic nights, the romantic *everything*... I just... I need my space. You say I'm lonely but I enjoy being alone with my code, I like the peace and quiet. I need more time to simply be myself. So... I think it'd be best if we... if we spend some time apart. Um. Okay...?"

"Haven't I been a considerate lover? A perfect gentleman?" Cup8 protested... a bit louder than he intended to, while leaning forward across the table. "I've *always* treated you with respect, m'lady. I've devoted every waking hour not spent at that office to making you happy! I helped launch Peep off the ground for you, I put *my* money into your cloud distribution system, I *made* it a Netwerk-wide sensation...!"

"I'm thankful for that, honest! I'm very thankful! I..."

Snowi cleared her throat, to interrupt before Beta went pleading back to him.

"...I just don't think we're right for each other. Not like we are now," Beta continued, recalling her practice script. "It's just too overbearing, being your 'love.' I need to be me. Maybe in time, we'll both be different people, and we'll be ready—"

The loud scrape of his chair against the kitchen floor cut her off instantly.

"You know what? You're not *worthy* of my love," Cup8 declared. "I give and I give, I do things I wouldn't do for any other woman—I can't believe I went down on you every damn night, right between those fat fucking Default thighs of yours—and despite being the perfect partner, I get this cold fish act in return!?"

This punctuated by his fist, banging against the table. Since her furniture was largely cheap, it simulated badly, bouncing several inches from the impact due to improper weight balances.

Beta reeled away from the table crash, throwing up her arms to protect herself. Cowering, even, and feeling just awful for doing it. How every time Cup8 was around, she felt like she was cowering, giving in and letting things happen and praying the discomfort would just go away...

But Snowi was there to get between them, to step up and plant her hands on the table, pushing it firmly back into the floor.

"Get out," she ordered. "Beta doesn't need you."

And he left.

He was gone.

The only man who ever loved her, and he was gone. It was the right thing to do, of course. Right? Of course. Snowi had been pushing for Beta to get rid of him for ages now, she saw how unhappy Beta was. It was all so clear. Beta had to, simply had to tell the gentle and considerate soul she fell in love with to leave her side...

That night, for the first time in over two years, Beta was going to bed alone.

Everything felt... heavier. Her heart, her mind, the rising and falling of her chest. She'd been too tired to do any coding tonight, not after the drain of that encounter still in her mind. Going to bed early made sense, since clearly nothing else was going to get done that day...

But the words, they kept ringing in her head as she tried to put herself into sleep mode.

*Not worthy of my love. Cold fish. Fat fucking Default. Considerate, gentleman, devoting every hour...*

Soon her bedroom light was on again, and she was standing there, uncertain about everything in her life.

He knew what buttons to push. It's how he got into her life in the first place... she'd always lacked confidence in her appearance, her Default which followed her around from year to year, but custom avatars never felt right to her either. He told her that she was beautiful, that her Default wasn't as horrible as she thought it was...

As if to convince herself of that, she took off her glasses, and set them on the nearby dresser. Pointed them towards the bed... and studied herself. Without her usual neatly concealing pajamas.

Viewing her own body indirectly wasn't an unfamiliar act. She'd grown used to the idea of having detachable "eyes," of seeing through another perspective. It was the inspiration behind ProxyPerception, the original name of the Peep App; a way for others to see the world the way she saw it...

She'd always thought of her Default as "curvy." Not a bad word, right? Kind of cute. Her hair, mousy brown bangs and all, that was cute. Her glasses were allegedly cute, to people who saw glasses as decorative accessories alone. The rest of her, well... there was *more* of her than most avatars had, more up top and down below, but it wasn't like she was a walking mountain. She just didn't particularly *want* an off-the-shelf standard avatar, one designed to be a flawless ideal.

But... when so many of the people around you wore off-the-shelf beauty, any deviation from the new normal became abnormal. She became fat, in contrast to perfection. She became unattractive. And she saw it any time she passed a mirror, saw how different she looked. Could see it through her removable eyes, here and now...

*Fat fucking Default*, Cup8 had snarled. The words just wouldn't stop repeating in her head. Not for a single moment.

So... she tried to defy those words, tried to look sexy for her private eyesight camera. And failed.

She tried to look attractive and desirable. Even posed a little, like she'd seen girls do in the porno she and her friends had giggled over so often at sleepovers back in her school years, porno she could never admit aloud to being intrigued by. But everything she tried tonight to show that she was just as desirable, well... she couldn't see *herself* in those poses. She just saw this useless lump of unlovable mush.

"I'm a fat fucking Default," she repeated, his words taken to heart. "Of course I wasn't worthy of his love."

...if nobody else would love her, well... she could love herself tonight. Didn't she deserve that, at least?

---

Tracer was kind enough to close all the image windows, on realizing he had company.

"I've been researching our mysterious houseguest for two days now," he explained. "My theory is that someone hacked her Peep client to activate it and steal these still-shots through her glasses. They leaked the nudes all over Netwerk. It went viral soon after, with Beta having enough fame built up as the creator of Peep to carry them far and wide."

Realization hit Spark slowly... making her feel very, very stupid. "I kept seeing 'B E T A N U D E S' in my Peep chatroom," she recalled. "I'd heard someone got nudes leaked, but I wasn't interested in violating her privacy so I never actually *looked* myself... I'd just swing the #BanHammer and move on. I didn't know that was *her*..."

"This alone would still be a completely atrocious violation of privacy," Tracer spoke, in a firm voice. "But the atrocity deepened hours later... when this vlog post went up on Cup8's personal Peep stream. I've obtained a recording of it..."

A simple 2-D video window opened in Tracer's hand.

In it... Cup8, with an angrier look than Beta had ever seen in him before. It made her recoil by instinct, as if he might leap out of that window at her. Despite his immaculate hair and perfectly designed store-bought avatar, there was a sense of exhaustion and sickness about him as he glared into the camera.

"*So apparently my ex is now slutting it up across Netwerk with her own private girlie show,*" he spoke, letting the venom drip from every word... particularly from his little *emphasized* words, his personal vocal tick. "*Some folks are saying it's a hack, but honestly? She's such a needy and insecure person that I could seriously see her leaking it for the attention. You guys know Beta, she's the genius who invented Peep, right? Well... wrong. I've stayed quiet about this long enough. I invented Peep, not her. It was my idea, my code, my work. I let her take credit because I felt sorry for her.*

"*Honestly, I don't think Beta's coded a single line in her life. Those little Apps she's released over the years, those were the work of the men she seduced along the way. It's more common in indie coding than you think, either through ghostwriting or simply stealing code and passing it off as your own creation. Attention whores and liars, all of them. Just like her partner in crime Snowi, Beta's a complete fraud.*

"*It's high time you knew the truth: I made Peep. And Beta's been laughing at you all along.*

"*You should demand better of your App developers than these liberal hacks who push their little social causes by faking their status as hardworking developers. You should demand honesty of your coders. You should demand #CodeHonesty. Because deceivers and frauds like Beta are more common than you think... and frauds must be exposed to light of day, for the good of all Programkind.*"

The video playback froze, right on Cup8 at his most cruel, and most calculating.

Spark was there to support Beta, as she pulled at her hair and groaned in pain—

—stripping the graffiti off the walls of her house. Pulling up the perpetually ejaculating penises someone had replaced her flower garden with. Trying desperately to clean up the mess left behind by the trolls, even while knowing they'd be back tomorrow night to do it all over again...

She'd been doxxed almost immediately after Cup8's video went live: an anonymous hacker posted her messenger handle and her home address in the suburban community of WestHall. While she had heavy access rights in place to prevent anybody from breaking into the house, she couldn't layer the protections as thickly over her lawn or the walls themselves... meaning anybody could show up and splatter her sanctuary with the most repugnant, hateful trash imaginable.

Staying indoors didn't keep her safe; her messenger hub and the few social network feeds she'd joined (avoiding the commonly trolled ones like MyFace, thankfully) were a flood of anonymous attacks, some simply cruel... others downright dangerous.

Death threats. Rape threats. Over and over again, promises by anonymous throwaway accounts to violate her in every conceivable manner. Promises that no matter where she went, someone would be there with a knife in the dark, waiting to punish her for being a fraud. Intimate details of her life had become twisted around to become menacing; they knew where she liked to go shopping, they knew what games she played, they knew who her friends were. They lurked everywhere and nowhere. There were no safe havens...

Few of the worst abusers actually used the #CodeHonesty tag; the so-called official stance of #CodeHonesty was that they were against doxxing and harassment, even if technically anyone could be a "member" of #CodeHonesty just by choosing to apply the hashtag to their communications. *Obviously anybody sending her threats isn't really with #CodeHonesty* was the typical excuse... or even better, *Beta's faking all these so-called threats just for the attention...*

With the various declarations in place that she would be torn to shreds if she ever set foot outside her home, the only time she dared to walk beyond her doorstep was to make a futile effort at cleaning up the graffiti on her front lawn.

"It's getting worse, and my landlord still won't hire additional moderators," she told Snowi over their messenger connection, while erasing yet another batch of penises from her yard. "Last night someone was knocking at my door for hours. I thought maybe it was the neighbor coming to check on me, he seems like a nice fellow, but how could I risk letting *anyone* in after dark? Snowi, please, can... can you come by tonight? Just to keep me company. I can't do another night alone with this going on outside my home..."

"Yeah, uh... listen. I'm really sorry for all you're going through, but..."

Beta paused in her work. "But...?"

"I can't be seen with you anymore. Look, Beta, I've got my own reputation to worry about; they're starting to target me just for being friends with you... calling me a dyke and a fraud and worse. I've got to distance myself from this. And from you. But hey, we had good times, right? So there's that..."

She turned away from the troll graffiti, looking off into the distance in mute horror.

"But... but you're my friend," Beta said. "You stood by me when I needed strength to leave Cup8. Please. Please, I need help..."

"It's awful, I know, but I've got my own career to think about here. And... and... honestly? The Apps I made for all those #FeministCodeJams? I used a *lot* of open source code libraries and didn't disclose that fact. It'd look bad if the misogyny mob found out about it."

Beta almost felt her process stop for a moment.

"You did *what*?" she exclaimed, horrified. "You mean this whole code fraud thing is... it's actually true?"

"Hey, lots of programmers take shortcuts! How else was I gonna finish a whole App in a 24 hour code jam? Besides, it's not some huge evil like Cup8's making it out to be. Just a little white lie; and for a good cause, yeah? But I can't let them get any closer to the truth, so... this is goodbye, Beta. Goodbye and good luck."

And the messenger window closed itself.

Because Netwerk enjoyed being unrelentingly cruel, that's also when her inbox beeped. She'd set up dozens and dozens of mail filters to try and cut down on the harassment letters... this new one was just as cruel, but sadly legitimate.

```
FROM: Rykk/Flint (WestHall Residental Server Rentals)
SUBJECT: Eviction Notice

Beta, I can't afford to keep hosting your runtime on
my server. The constant attacks due to your "side
hobbies" are draining runtime from other paying
renters who are complaining about the mess and the
system lag. You have 24 hours to retrieve your items
from the house, and then I'm wiping it clean and
revoking your access rights.
```

...no more home. No best friend she could stay with. Her mother living in a care server, couldn't exactly stay there. Her entire life ruined, with nowhere else to turn...

Nowhere except one place. A suggestion she'd found ironically enough in a hateful message suggesting she wipe herself off the map. There was a doctor who specialized in identity transplants... someone who could give her a fresh start. Take away this tainted name, the name she loved so much, and give her a new life...

"I lost everything," Beta realized, every last memory finally clicking into place. "I lost everything and I almost lost myself, too..."

"He made just enough of a compelling case to motivate the mob," Tracer explained, impassive to her horror. "Snowi's *actual* fraud, once inevitably uncovered, didn't help Beta's case. All the conspiracy theorists came out of the woodwork to claim Beta leaked her own nudes, and leaked her own dox. #CodeHonesty trended overnight and now every indie developer's getting raked over the coals..."

He turned back to his active MemoryPalace interface, calling up dozens of blog posts and video testimonies.

"It's not a universal hate," he did add. "There are many who believe her side. But that's the key: they're picking *sides*. Left and right, pro and anti, us and them. Battle lines are being drawn between #CodeHonesty and #StandWithSnowi camps. Feminism, discrimination, political progressive movements, everything's getting mashed together in the same mess thanks to both Cup8 *and* Snowi's intensely vocal involvement. There's an entire war going on inside App development culture... and because I could care less about 'App Culture' and Spark's too busy gaming, neither of us knew."

Slowly... Beta approached the cloud of open windows, studying them through her augmented vision. She zoomed in on individual lines, reading select parts.

```
...why are indie female developers being targeted more
than anyone else? Answer: A typical cis male attitude
of privledge, assuming girls can't possibly know how
to program and therefore they must be all be frauds. I
#StandWithSnowi...
```

```
...at the end of the day, the good/bad guy spectrum is
pretty clear. #CodeHonesty is by and far the
protagonist in this story....
```

```
...you can't claim #CodeHonesty is against harassment
when it originally spawned from a jealous ex's
mindless video rant followed immediately by nudes and
doxxing. #StandWithSnowi...
```

```
...for years, it was accepted that once the finger-
wagging feminists moved in on your industry, you would
capitulate quickly to their pseudo-academic
treatises...
```

```
...you can't accept compromise, or some sort of
negotiated cease fire. All you want to do is code
Apps. All your enemies want to do is boost their
status from moral preening and the expansion of their
doublethink....
```

```
...you're nothing but a blowup doll for these fat
neckbeards to jerk themselves off to while whining
about "ethics" you sicken me...
```

```
...this isn't about misogyny at all, many women like
me stand with #CodeHonesty; fraud in App development
knows no genders...
```

```
...Beta doxxed herself and leaked her own nudes, just
like Snowi doxxed herself, you can see from these
screenshots proving the origin server of the original
nude leak was WestHall...
```

```
...heard that Beta vanished a few days ago, did
someone finally rape her to death or something?
```

"They don't know you tried to get your identity changed," Tracer explained. "As far as anybody knows, you vanished. I doubt the temper of the conversation rose or fell accordingly, however. This fire's raging on with or without you; 'Beta' is now figurehead for a long-standing hate that's always existed under the surface of this community. There's nothing you can do or say which will stop it, at this point."

A soft sound echoed in Tracer's nicely furnished study, as Beta fell to her knees on his woven rugs. Spark was there at her side, keeping her upright, to avoid a complete collapse. Even Mew showed his support, placing a kindly paw in her hand...

"I never wanted any of this," Beta protested. "I don't want to be anyone's pariah or anyone's martyr. Snowi's the one who kept going on about causes and social justice; I just love to code Apps. That's all I've ever wanted to do..."

"Let me propose a solution," Tracer suggested. ...then shook his head. "Scratch that. Let me propose a course of action. Hm. No. Let's just call it a thing you can do. ...stay here, at Floating Point. Make this your new home. Everyone thinks you're dead, so let them think that. Nobody can find you here because our server exists on a different layer of Netwerk. Use this as your sanctuary, and code in peace. Leave the nightmare in your wake and take flight on your own."

To prove his conviction... Tracer held out a golden access key, cloned from his own. He'd already coded it to lock onto Beta's program, usable only by her.

This time, it was Spark's turn to be shocked. "Seriously?" she asked, doubting it. "Weren't you pushing to dump her in an alley somewhere, bro?"

Tracer sat back in his chair... turning to face the open files in his research notes, two solid days of researching this woman's history.

All of it, so full of malice and incompetence. Absolute rage combined with a complete willing ignorance of reality, swallowing whatever flavor of narrative each side preferred. Enough to offend him down to the core...

These people... these *idiots* like Cup8, or even Snowi... they set off a chain reaction of events that lit Netwerk ablaze. Binary people, making binary decisions. Us and them, with us or against us. Both factions worked together to ruin an innocent woman's life, and for what? For their own personal vainglory? They broke her down, shattered her will to live as herself, ruined everything this intelligent woman held dear...

It would not stand. It could not stand. She deserved better than this.

"I have my reasons," he summarized, instead of explaining any of that.

"You want something," Beta spoke, too tired to make it sound like anything other than three words put together.

"There's that as well," Tracer admitted... reaching out, to zoom in on the frozen image of Cup8. Zooming in on a red splotch, just visible under the sleeve cuff of his shirt.

There was no way to "zoom and enhance" when there was no actual extra visual data to draw from... but even as a pixellated mess, the shape was unmistakable.

A heart, which pumped barbed wire instead of blood.

What's more... a side by side photo from Snowi's personal blog showed a similar tattoo on her calf, also zoomed and semi-enhanced.

"There's more going on here than any real or supposed ethical crisis in programming," he spoke. "Something pushed Cup8 to lie about his involvement with Peep in the first place, and encouraged Snowi to take advantage of the chaos for her own grandstanding. They're both infected with a strain of malware known as the Great Zero; it warps reason, encouraging the worst kinds of misguided righteousness in those it infects. My sister and I have been fighting this enemy for some time... and we could use your help."

---

For a time, Beta considered the theory that all of this nonsense was the result of her mind being scrambled by that identity thief. That everything in her life recently was a spray of random ones and zeroes, hastily reassembled by poor quality software into a meaningless series of events. She wasn't *really* chased out of her home by an angry mob and then recruited by some crazy vigilantes... no, she was simply insane, and close to the edge of death by data corruption. It would be preferable...

The conspiracy that Tracer laid out was about as plausible as the #CodeHonesty conspiracy. Hidden cloud servers with malevolent entities in them? Malware that twists up the mind and somehow turns you into Pure Evil? Two lone heroes who know the secret truths underneath the skin of Netwerk, acting as if they're Programkind's last hope? The ridiculousness of it, the self-righteousness... how could she possibly buy into all of that at face value?

Insanity. Beta had gone insane. It was the only sane explanation.

But... for now, assuming she *wasn't* crazy, at least she had room and board. Tracer promised that to her for as long as she needed it, even if she didn't want to take up his sword. The access key sat in her personal inventory, allowing her to come and go as she pleased...

Although right now, she felt the need to curl up under her blankets and never get up again. Going out was out of the question.

And she was back to crying, all over again. How many times had she cried in recent days? Was this seriously all she was good for anymore, having emotional breakdowns left and right? How weak and useless was she...?

A weight pressed on her back as she lie in bed, before hopping over to her pillow. Mew's whiskers, tickling at what little of her face was exposed to open air. Even without her glasses on, left discarded on the nightstand, she knew exactly who was in bed with her.

" ? " he mewled. " 🆕 🏠 ."

"It's a nice home," Beta agreed, parsing his spoken imagery easily. "I love this place. It's beautiful. But... now it's all tied up in everything that went wrong, isn't it? It was easier when I'd lost my mind. More pure..."

Mew cocked his head, curiously. "👬," he suggested. "🔥👩‍🦰👍..."

"Spark seems okay, but... what they're involved in, all this chaos, and how it all connects back to my life... I don't know if I can get involved again after escaping it all. And don't forget that Snowi seemed like a nice person too, but she abandoned me in the end. Will Spark and Tracer do the same? I don't know. I just, I just want all this crap to go away..."

"💩," Mew agreed, with a little kitty scoff.

Beta was tempted to ignore the soft knocking at her door. Facing others wasn't something she was keen on, even her two strange benefactors. But... she was still a guest here, access key or not. It'd be impolite to shut them out completely.

"Come in," she called out.

Without her glasses, she didn't know who had just stepped into her room. But she recognized the footfalls, the relative weight and impact of them, as well as the slightly timid pacing.

"Hey," Spark greeted. "Soooo... I was thinking of playing some CoC, and I read that you liked gaming too, so I figured... I mean, why not? Wanna come along?"

...now Beta sat up in bed, curious.

"You want to play Challenge of Champions with me?" she asked, confused. "At a time like this?"

"Absolutely. Look, Tracer and I have been chasing down trolls off and on for years now. One thing I've learned (and he kinda hasn't yet) is that life goes on, even during that chase," Spark explained. "If you don't take the time to enjoy your life in between the nasty parts, well, what's the point of going through the nasty parts? #YOLO. So yeah, I want to play Challenge of Champions with you. Don't worry, I've got a toss-off anonymous account login you can use. Nobody will know it's you."

Her options were simple. Sit here in bed and wait for life to stop being awful, or go play a video game. Both were avoiding the problem entirely, of course. But... one involved less useless crying, didn't it?

Beta actively disliked the CoC lobby. The user interface was dodgy and ill-designed; she knew at least five different ways it could be improved, if she was programming it. On the plus side, being in a private group chat with Spark meant she focus on gameplay and conversation, rather than letting all those little irritating design aspects gnaw at her while begging for attention.

"I actually earn a LOT of coins for the family piggy bank through Peep," Spark explained, while they paged through the Book of Champions, trying to decide who they'd queue up as. "But I don't mind shutting down the broadcast tonight so we can have a #GirlsNightOut. ...honestly, I've never had a #GirlsNightOut in CoC. My friends don't like to play."

"That's a shame," Beta replied, idly looking over Spark's shoulder at the book. "Having friends who shared my love for Apps helped me out a lot. ...I mean it kinda did. Even if they dumped me in the end, it felt great at the time..."

"I've got this... friend of mine that I go out clubbing with. That I used to go out clubbing with. That was kind of a mutual hobby..."

"Used to? Past tense?"

"#ItsComplicated. —so I'm thinking we queue up as a duo and take a side lane, as damage and support. One to push the lane, the other to keep the pusher healed up. It's less glory than flying solo, but whatever, we're not playing ranked. How about it?"

Instinctively, Beta's eyes went to the page of healers. Support characters, existing solely to prop up the damage dealers on their team... it was a familiar role for her, in a lot of ways. She'd supported Cup8's glory by sacrificing Peep to him, just as she'd supported Snowi's various social justice code jams. And in a more literal sense, whenever she played CoC in the past, she'd always run a support character—

Except Spark had already locked in her character selection. Cheerleader: a motivation-based support character.

"Wait, *you* wanted to be support?" Beta asked, confused. "I figured you'd want to be the damage role..."

"I like to mix it up! Besides, point is to have one of each, so the team composition's solid. Exactly who plays which role doesn't matter, right?"

Beta glanced at the icons covering the page of damage dealing characters. She had zero experience with any of them; going into a match blind was a surefire way to lose a game...

But this wasn't a ranked game. If they lost the game, well, nothing would really be lost, would it? She was playing through an anonymous account, too... she didn't *have* to be support-playing, passively-enabling little Beta. Useless Beta. She could be anything she wanted to be, within that three-lane battleground...

"I'll play... Hanzo," she decided. "And I'll do my best."

Spark raised an eyebrow, pleased with the pick. "Niiiice," she commented, with a grin. "Let's go kick some ass, my ninja liege. I'm with you every step of the way."

The word "battlecry" had rarely been applied to anything coming out of Beta's mouth. Tonight, she was crying battle left and right, rather than simply crying. A nice change of pace.

Her blade cleaved through wave after wave of Chaos Goblins. She teleported in with ninjutsu to get the last hit on the enemy player opposing her in lane, driving him back every time he made headway into their territory. For tonight, at least, she was no longer being kicked around by everybody who could slap a hashtag in front of some words... she was doing the kicking.

Honestly, Beta still wasn't particuarly good at damaging roles. Typically she'd be the healer in the back, avoiding the fights while keeping the fighters going... but having Cheerleader at her back instead, that made up for Beta's lack of skill. Spark was spot on with every single buff, keeping her health topped off, locking down enemies just before they could get the upper hand. As a tag team, the pair were getting it done.

As Beta/Hanzo cleaved through yet another wave of goblins, she realized she could actually get used to this. It was a little terrifying to be right there in the front instead of lurking in the back, it kept her mind spinning and her nerves jangling away, but she was doing it. She was actually doing it...

"Go Hanzo Go! Go Hanzo Go!" Cheerleader cheered, from the top of a human pyramid (made of NPC characters). The cheer set off a damage buff effect, letting Hanzo execute a perfect single strike to an incoming MegaGoblin, putting it down hard.

When the ninja landed on his feet... he sheathed his sword, for the time being.

"My Eight Fold Path Technique is on cooldown, so let's fall back a bit," Beta/Hanzo suggested. "I doubt Chaos will be back down here soon, anyway. Sooo... your brother's for real with this 'Zero' stuff?"

"For real," Spark/Cheerleader confirmed, following along behind the ninja while shaking her pom-poms to recharge Hanzo's energy. "If I hadn't seen it with my own eyes, no way would I have believed Tracer's theory... he does tend to obsess over conspiracies. Although chances it's the real 'Zero' of church lore are pretty low."

"So... it's *not* the living manifestation of sin, then?"

"Nah. It's a strain of malware made up by an organization, or a political movement, or just a single jerk tugging a lot of strings... don't know, exactly. Not yet. The part I don't get is why it's infected both Cup8 and Snowi. I mean... why control both sides of the #CodeHonesty war? What could it stand to gain from supporting two opposing sides?"

"Maybe it just likes to watch Netwerk eat itself," Beta suggested, darkly. "Maybe it's just evil..."

"Tracer doesn't think so. He's obsessed with the idea that everything, even this Zero, has to be motivated by internal values; nobody's just 'good' and 'evil.' Doesn't stop *me* from calling 'em The Bad Guys, though. Whatever this Great Zero is, I'm willing to fight to stop it from sinking Netwerk into chaos."

Hanzo took a breather, leaning on his sword and resting to aid in a speedier energy recovery. "Why do you two need me to help fight the Zero, though? I vaguely remember that Arjay person, from when I was... empty. Arjay seemed more in tune with this strangeness..."

Cheerleader finished her pom-pom routine, ending with a flourish.

"Arjay's not a coder," she explained. "That's what we need right now; the low quality hacktools we've got aren't working well enough. I've got a connection lock collar App, for instance, but anybody with solid defenses can just yank it right off. If we had an actual App developer helping out, though... someone who specializes in interfacing Apps right down to the code level of a Program, like Peep does, maybe we could—"

"Behind you!" Hanzo called out...

...one moment too late.

An enemy dove right out of the jungle, bursting through the treeline with weapon swinging to take out Cheerleader. That massive war mace smashed her in the side, a sickening crack of bone echoing through the lane as the shattered girl went flying into the bushes. Dead.

What's more... the owner of that mace wasn't alone. Suddenly it was a two-on-one situation, Hanzo all alone against both Warlord and Frost, two of the top players for the Chaos team...

Damagers like Hanzo were dangerous in one-on-one fights, capable of pumping out a lot of destructive power in a short time through basic blade attacks. But she'd had the support of Cheerleader while doing that, shoring up her weaknesses against larger fighters. One lone Hanzo against two powerful characters like Warlord and Frost, that was an impossible matchup. All alone in the lane, no Gnomes in sight, no other players to rely on, nobody to help her...

Fear. Fear and nerves, those were common while fighting at the frontline as she'd been realizing, but now they were amplified considerably.

Beta, alone again. Alone and about to be destroyed by foes she could do nothing to stop.

Instinctively she reached for the HUD element that would disconnect her from the game. Fingers hovered over it... while her other hand shifted its grip on the ninja blade nervously, backing away slowly as the two Chaos players advanced. They knew Hanzo was screwed, and were sure taking their time to relish in that fact rather than optimally launching into a full salvo of death. Enjoying the fear in their victim's eyes...

All she had to do was tap a button, and she'd be gone. Abandoning her team, running along home to Floating Point. No more fear, no more pain. No more mockery of those who sought to hurt her.

...but why that instinctive need to flee?

Why was she always running away? Why did she need to feel like someone was backing her up before she had the guts to do anything?

Again and again, pushed down, pushed around. She was smarter than that, wasn't she? She was clever. She let them abuse her out of fear, fear of screwing up, fear of losing companionship... stupid fears. Stupid fears that didn't fit a girl raised by a master coder, a woman who reshaped the world around her to make it a better place for her daughter...

No.

*No more.*

Instead of tapping that exit button, Hanzo popped every self-buff power in the books, and cleaved directly into Frost with a flash of steel.

Was it a mistake? Was she going to lose this fight, let down the team, and risk making Spark angry at her? Should she have backed down and taken the safer option?

No. It didn't matter if Beta won or lost. Didn't matter if they killed her; she was going to stand her ground. Playing Hanzo meant she came to fight, not to surrender. That meant no sitting around waiting for Cheerleader to come to her rescue, no running away to hide, no backing down. She was here to deal damage, and damage would be dealt in full.

Frost was taken by surprise, completely missing her Frozen Blast as a result. That left the ice queen wide open for more attacks, and Hanzo had more attacks to dish out. After four more slices... Frost went down into several pieces, chunks of her frozen body sliding across the lane in four different directions.

That left Warlord, who was no longer gloating. He was swinging wide, with a blow that could easily destroy Hanzo in one shot.

Activate Evasive Roll, to duck under the attack completely. Embrace the ninja, move like a ninja. Cheerleader wasn't the only one who could tumble around; Hanzo was done taking blows directly. He slid beneath Warlord's open legs, the bulky might of the armored giant working against him... and then slashed directly upward.

By the time Cheerleader respawned and returned to the fight, Beta/Hanzo stood victorious over two greater foes, bathed in blood and/or snowflakes of victory.

"I'll help you fight the Zero," Beta decided. "But we're doing it my way. We deal with Cup8 first... and *I'm* going to be the one to stop him. You're playing support for me, not the other way around."

---

This time, it was Beta giving the informative presentation of doom rather than Tracer. The flavor of it was quite different as well... rather than a coldly clinical study filled with floating data windows, they were discussing these dark dealings within the warmth of Floating Point's kitchen.

Beta had gone ahead and programmed up some cookies, in fact, using ingredient sample data files from the cupboards and a few personal recipes she had on file. Despite the seriousness of today's discusssion, Spark couldn't help but glow with radiant delight at the sinful pleasures of chocolate and cookie dough.

"*Yummy*," she declared, after putting away her third cookie. "Can we keep her, Tracer? Huh huh please can we?"

"Sooo... the way I understand it, our goal is to forcibly uninstall a malware App from another Program without actually having read/write permissions to do so," Beta explained. "Removing an App that's interfaced tightly with a Program's mental functions can be tricky. The layers of interlocking permissions involved mean that—MEW! Those are for our guests! Bad kitty."

Mew looked up from his purloined cookie with big, shiny eyes. "🐱🍪🙏 ? "

Beta snapped her fingers, pointing to the floor. Expressing pure betrayal and likely plotting to shred her pillowcase later, Mew hopped down from the table.

"*Ahem*. Those permission layers mean this is going to take some work," Beta continued. "I'm not an expert on security; I've never made a hacktool in my life. If you really want me to do this I'm going to need access to an infected person, to run some tests and analyze how the malware App works. And it could take hours. Hours and hours."

"Oooh! An exorcism!" Spark piped in with, amused at the idea. "Like in those terribad church-themed horror movies! In the name of the One, I command thee Zeroes OUT!"

"Uh... similar in concept and execution, but... no," Beta decided. "Anyway, I'd suggest Snowi for this since she's not as protected as Cup8, but Snowi's fallen off the radar. She got doxxed and chased out of her home with death threats near the start of this and now we can't track her down. But Cup8... he's carrying on with business as usual. He feels safe from harm. That means we know where he is, and I know how to access him."

Tracer considered it, while toying with the idea of eating a cookie. "Still problematic," he admitted. "We can lock his connection to keep him from escaping while we work, but we can't force his Program off whatever server he's on and into a controlled lab environment. Only reason we could rescue you from that identity thief and bring you here was because your permissions were deactivated at the time."

"Exactly. That means we need to set up shop right where we grab him. ...except these days, he never leaves his home server of Wingspan. His tech investment company's got a headquarters there, *and* his private estate's there. It's got everything he needs and he won't be wandering anywhere else..."

Spark flashed her weaponized fingernail polish, with a little burst of flame.

"So we kick down the door of his house, grab him, and exorcise his Zeroes right there and then," she suggested, holding up her index finger in the Sign of the One. "We'll need an old priest and a young priest!"

"Actually... yeah, that's almost my plan," Beta admitted. "Only not so, uh, crazy. Just a bit less crazy. Maybe forty percent as crazy. ...I know his estate, we spent a lot of weekends there, and he has security like you wouldn't believe. He's contracted with ViruFax to have this amazing man-trap installed; even if you somehow snuck in, you'd never get out again."

"So... what, his office is *less* secure than his house? That seems weird..."

"Oh, no! The office security is actually way worse! But we can get legitimate access to the office; it's a place of business, right? What we do... is we arrange a meeting for late on a Friday, pretending to be App developers looking for investment capital. That'll get us through the doors and right up in his face! We jump him in his private office, do it right there. Nobody will even know. Of course, you'll have to pretend to be programmers..."

"Not an issue," Tracer said. "I'm a practiced grifter. It's a simple matter of social analysis and word selection to make someone believe in you, I've found. With or without a coding background I can easily convince Cup8 to trust me."

Spark chimed in her support on that. "It's true. He's damn creepy that way. But I feel like I'm missing something here; if we jump Cup8 in his office, even if we do it late on a Friday, *someone's* still going to notice he never went home, right...?"

"That's why we're going to have you wear a copy of his avatar," Beta explained. "I know the parameters by heart, I can make her into Cup8's spitting image. She won't pass an identity check, but there won't be an identity check on the way *out* the door. As long as he's seen leaving the office, nobody will be the wiser. Spark can sneak back in afterwards once the coast is clear. We'll get to work on Cup8 right in his office on the top floor, and be able to take as much time as we need."

"Uh. #WTF?" Spark interrupted, holding up half a cookie for attention. "Why should I dress up as a douchebag? Tracer's already excellent in that field of study. Also he has a penis, which is helpful."

"I can give you a fully functional penis, actually! It's just an avatar customization, very simple to do."

"...this plan just went to a very weird place. And I am still absolutely in favor of Tracer pretending to be Cup8."

"No, Tracer's going to be busy running tests and compiling the App that will purge the Zero malware."

"Look, I'm all for freshening up the team composition by playing new roles... when it's a CoC match. Aren't you our App developer? Tracer can't code for shit, and I am not a dudebro..."

Beta tried to get the confusion back under control, by filling in the details she was less keen to fill in.

"The problem is that I can't go with you," she explained.

"Come on, you can do it! I know it's scary to confront your ex, but—"

"No, I mean I *literally* can't go with you. Cup8's company owns the moderators of Wingspan," Beta explained. "I'm on the ban list, I've been on it since the breakup. I can't set foot in that server. Tracer's going to be doing the technical work... while wearing my glasses. I can see through them, even across Netwerk. It's just the Peep technology in a different form, after all. I'll be in communication with him, guiding him as my hands and eyes. And while he's busy doing that, you might need to be on-hand to defend him if the janitor or a night watchman stumbles across this little operation."

Tracer nodded slowly, accepting the explanation.

"It's an ugly set of circumstances," he admitted. "But if he's not leaving Wingspan and you can't go there... one of us needs to *be* you, while the other plays lookout. Spark, no offense, but you're even worse at coding than I am and you get easily frustrated. This task will need someone with a cool, level head."

"No offense—?! And since when has Mr. Growly Vengeance been cool and level? YOU should be the one to play dressup, not me! Screw this. I veto the plan. It's bonkers."

"It's viable," Tracer countered. "As viable as we're likely to get in the short term. We need this anti-malware research if we're going to go after harder targets like that identity thief. I vote that we carry out the plan."

"Yeah, well, it's only the two of us here, so that's a tie vote! The Winder family sucks as a democracy, remember?"

...except a third hand was raised.

"Um. I'm... not part of the Winder family, but... I live in Floating Point too," Beta pointed out. "And since I came up with the plan, I'm in favor. That's two against one."

"✋!" called a tiny voice from under the table.

"And that's three to one. Two and a half against one? Maybe two and one fifth against one by volume," she continued. "Err. Sorry, Spark. I promise your costume won't be a burden at all! I can tailor it to fit you like a glove!"

Outvoted and outnumbered, Spark sulked back into her seat. Consoling herself with cookies.

Still... she wasn't *entirely* against the plan. Honestly, she was just glad to see a plan in place, and glad to see it coming from someone other than Tracer for a change. Beta had been pushed around enough... high time she pushed for something herself. Why not support that?

Even if she'd have to grow a dick to support that, of course.

---

"Okay, come on out."

"No," the deep voice behind the old-fashioned dressing screen whined.

"Don't be such a big baby! I'm sure you're very handsome. Come on out."

...with the end result severely squicking out both parties involved.

He was currently wearing a complete replica of Cup8's avatar. Apparently Cup8 was too cheap to invest money in a custom physique, always wearing an off-the-shelf chiseled dude avatar. Reproducing that look was just a matter of knowing what catalogs to shop from. With that in place Beta made a few adjustments here and there, right down to a fake replica of the Zero tattoo. Just in case.

Except they hadn't invested in his business wardrobe yet, electing to reproduce that on the fly once they saw what he'd be wearing that day. Which left Spark standing there wearing only a towel, and looking horribly humiliated despite having six-pack abs most dudes would kill for (or pay for).

Even the cat currently shedding on her pillowcase was impressed, offering a hearty "💪😺!!" in contribution.

"This feels... it's... yeah," Spark managed, glancing down at where his breasts used to be. "So, does it match up to the param... uh. Beta?"

"S-Sorry," her designer spoke, averting her eyes/glasses a bit. "It's just... yeah. It matches the parameters. To the point where I just got a bit of a fight-or-flight response looking at you. Bad memories."

"Uh... hadn't thought of that. 'kay. I'll just take this off, and—"

"No no, this is just step one!" Beta insisted... hopping off the bed she was sitting on, walking over to transfer some video files. "I've gathered a few of his vlog rants and inspirational speeches. You need to practice his vocal ticks and his gestures, just in case you have to convince anyone you're him. He likes to put *emphasis* on words, sometimes *implying* things, and—Spark!"

Spark quickly snapped the front of his towel back into place.

"I had to check, okay?" he protested. "I mean, I can FEEL it there, and... couldn't we just, y'know, uninstall the erogenous zones? They're incredibly distracting. ...are guys *always* dealing with sensory inputs from this stupid thing? How do they deal with it?"

"Part of the avatar customization package, afraid. I could find a way to edit it out but I need to devote my dev time to the tools we need for this caper..."

"Well, I'm guessing Puzzle would be happy to see me now," Spark half-grumbled.

"You know, you keep mentioning that friend of yours and then trying to change the subject immediately after..."

"So how many of these stupid vlogs do I need to watch before you'll be happy with my #TheatricalPerformance?" Spark asked, accepting the offered file transfer. "I've got Peep streams to do tonight, too..."

Beta frowned, hands on her hips. A little bump as she leaned forward accusingly, her long skirt swaying with the motion.

"No more dodging," she insisted. "You're helping me out with this... mission? Plan? Endeavour. So, let me help you with your #BFF problems. What's going on with this Puzzle person, exactly...?"

Years of gaming taught Spark to recognize when he was cornered. Normally he'd fight his way out, no matter the cost, but... putting up an iron-clad defense when confronted by a wall of adorable pink yarn was considerably harder than she would've guessed...

So, he had a seat on his bed, slumping a bit at the memories.

"We've been friends for years," Spark explained. "We always hit the new clubs together, always. #GirlsNightOut. Our luck in finding anybody to go home with was hit or miss, but at least if we both struck out, we knew we could wrap the evening by hanging out and having a ball. She's... she's just great. Wonderful. ...and in a moment of personal desperation, I kissed her. We haven't spoken since."

The bulky musclebound bro looked surprisingly vulnerable, sitting there on the silky covers and moping. So much so that despite him wearing the face of the man who ruined her life... Beta was willing to sit there next to him, to offer a comforting side-shoulder-hug.

"This is so fucking stupid," Spark grumbled... while not rejecting that hug. "I'm a grown-ass adult now. Yea though I am experienced in the ways of the world, forsooth, and having grown-ass adult relationships left and right. I even work for a paycheck and own my own a home, sort of! But I still feel like this janky little teenager, lately..."

"We're all still in beta," Beta suggested. "You're never done learning who you are. So... the problem here is that you're into Puzzle, but Puzzle's not into girls?"

"Not in the slightest. —and I fully admit that this is me talking out my ass, since I'm a #Programosexual, but... I've never understood strict heterosexuality. I mean, who cares about avatar shapes?" Spark asked, dismissing said care. "We're all Programs. I'm into men, women, furries, robots, tentacle monsters, sentient shades of the color blue, whatever. It's just decoration, it's just physics simulations. The people *underneath* are the ones I care about. It feels right to me. But... Puzzle's not like that at all..."

"Most people aren't like that. I mean, I can't say I'd be into robots, tentacle monsters, or sentient shades of the color blue. Puzzle's just... well, it's like how you feel, but in reverse? Maybe?"

"I don't follow."

"Sexuality's a highly individual, personal thing. Hers is just as strong as yours, but not in the same direction. For example, to me? Being with someone, uh, Program-shaped with two legs and two arms and one head feels completely natural. I'm... having a hard time imagining how you have sex with the color blue..."

"Okay, so first you get a free-standing prism and a *lot* of lube, and—"

"Not my point!" Beta interrupted. "The point is that we all have our own natural inclinations. None of them are right or wrong because they're right for *us*. Your friend Puzzle, she has her own natural inclinations towards guys alone—"

"Ironic, since Puzzle was born a guy."

With his mouth moving faster than his mind, his teeth had to bite off that last word in a vain effort to swallow it back down.

"...shit. #SoSoSorry. She doesn't like me telling people that; too many judgmental assholes out there," Spark added. "See, she was born with a male Default avatar through no fault of her own. And seriously, fuck Defaults; I accept her as who she wants to be. #TransPride, and all. ...look, okay. I get what you're saying, I'm not entirely stupid. I'm in the wrong here because I pushed myself on Puzzle knowing damn well she wouldn't be into it. It's just... #ItsComplicated, sometimes..."

"Programs can be complicated, especially if they're simple in a complex way. For instance you have one simple complexity, it seems: you prefer to wear a female avatar. You don't feel comfortable in that new skin, right?"

"Well, no, but..."

"Also, you said you accept Puzzle for who she wants to be, right?"

"Of course! Avatars don't matter to me. I mean... other's people's, I guess...?"

"Then you also have to accept her for who she wants to love. That's her complex simplicity. As for why you did it despite knowing all that at heart... Spark, ask yourself this really, really seriously. Do you actually love her romantically? You said you kissed her 'in a moment of personal desperation.' Was that kiss for her, or for *you*?"

...defeat. Defeat, over and over. A lousy day all around, and she'd gone to Puzzle's to find a victory...

Victory for Spark. Not a victory for Puzzle.

"Well... shit," Spark said, understanding. "I'm officially an idiot."

"I think you should talk things over with your friend! Running away from your problems doesn't solve them; I've learned that much, myself. Okay...? Promise me you'll talk with Puzzle and make amends?"

Spark's smile was sweet, despite coming from lips Beta had grown to fear.

"Y'know, I can dig this side of you," he said. "You're really coming out of the shell we found you in."

"What side do you mean?"

"The assertive and confident one."

...which could only make the woman sitting on the bed LOL.

"I'm not confident at all," she asserted. "I'd be a lousy leader, really. I'm terrified, I'm nervous, I'm quietly freaking out all the time. But now I'm deliberately doing the opposite of what I'd normally do, since what I'd normally do hasn't worked so far. ...maybe having my entire identity purged and restored turned me all around inside."

"Hah. Well... whatever the cause, I think you're doing great. And don't sell yourself short, you've overcome a null of a lot to get here. And for what it's worth..."

Spark rested his hand on hers, his larger fingers brushing against the fuzzy pink of her baggy sweater cuff.

It would've been a very kind and tender moment, if not for his majestically rising towel lump.

Which was immediately shoved back down by Spark, who sped behind that changing screen fast enough to become a fine representation of motion blur.

Female Spark in her usual clothes emerged, hair as red as her face.

"That is *it*, I'm not practicing with that ridiculous dong machine until I'm completely alone," she declared. "And after we're done with this caper, I'm erasing all that data from my inventory. —what's so funny?!"

Little laughing cartoon faces rose from the peanut gallery on the bed, both kitty and non-kitty doubled over with laughter.

---

As night fell and sunlight swapped out for moonlight, Beta remained in the dark. Unaware of the hour, much less overall time of day. She never wore her glasses while programming; no need for them, not when it was all inside her head.

She was sitting back in a comfortable chair, within the grand library. The light grinding sound of the stone sphere at the heart of Floating Point and the crackle of a nearby fireplace gave her enough auditory input not to feel completely isolated, as she hammered away in a code editor window within her mind.

Despite her every thought being occupied by the task at hand... she heard the soft approach of the other Winder sibling.

"Evening, Tracer," she spoke, without looking away from her writing.

"How did you know...?"

"You're more hesitant to approach. Spark just barges right in, if she can get away with it. It's okay, though. Come on over."

While laying out the pseudocode for the next module, she kept her ears open, listening for each telltale sound. The man walking over across the stone floor, the creak of leather as he eased himself into the chair opposite her own...

Now she activated her glasses, but put the window off to the side. They were on an endtable next to her, roughly pointed in Tracer's direction, so no need to move them or even put them on.

"I've been exhaustively researching the target," Tracer spoke, templing his fingers. "According to departing employees from Wingspan, his office has spatial sound restrictions. That way, when he fires someone, he can scream at them all he likes. Perfect for our needs."

"Mhmm..."

"I'm curious. What're you doing in there?" Tracer asked... realizing he needed to make eye contact with the pair of lenses on the table, not with the woman who owned them.

"Oh, I'm writing an App to dangle in front of Cup8 as bait. I mean, I was just going to make a shell of an App, a fake demonstration you could use to interest him, but... then I got an idea for a *real* App, and, well... I dunno. Maybe it's overkill, but..."

"Interesting. What's it do?"

"Does it matter? It's just bait."

"Of course it matters," Tracer spoke. "It's your creation. Clearly you're putting extra effort into it, which means you see that effort as worthwhile. If it's worthwhile to you, it's worthwhile to me. So. What are you inventing today?"

Slowly, Beta felt around for her glasses... not wanting to accidentally knock them off the table and embarrass herself. She fixed them firmly in place, before opening her eyes. Now, her gaze matched her actual gaze.

"I'm calling it ReMinder," she explained. "There's a lot of different reminder-style Apps out there that buzz you when you need to do something, right? But ringing alarms and bells are annoying. What this does is it records a memory of your choosing... the idea of picking up the kids from school, say. Then you set a timer, and can safely forget about it. When the time comes... pop! You remember. It feels very natural that way."

Tracer considered that... while flicking through his own MemoryPalace. Which felt natural to him *now*, but certainly didn't for a year or so after getting it installed...

"There are complete software patches for memory management systems too," he pointed out.

"Yeah, but overwriting bits of your OS is clunky and dangerous. The ideal is a sandboxed, self-contained App. ...that's what I love about Apps, see. They're whole units onto themselves, clean and perfect. It's difficult to access memory directly through the restrictions on an App, but 'difficult' doesn't mean 'impossible.' You just need to be clever."

"Expanding the capabilities of Programs through Apps. I can get behind that."

"Ideally, we're only limited by our cleverness," Beta continued, on a roll. "A lot of folks limit themselves out of... I don't know, tradition. Or natural inclination. I was talking to Spark about that, earlier tonight. And I can respect that, I limit myself in a lot of ways, but I won't limit my Program's technical capabilities. A well crafted App can make us *more* than we are."

"Much like your eyes," Tracer pointed out... tapping a finger against an imaginary pair of glasses on his face. "But recently developed software patches exist which could fix your vision, good as new. Why keep using your outdated glasses?"

In response, Beta removed her eyes. Specifically her glasses, to polish the lenses on her sweater.

"My outdated vision App is superior to normal eyes in a lot of ways," she explained. "I can see through perspectives nobody else can, since my eyes are removable. It's what inspired me to make Peep, after all. Why would I want to be 'fixed'? I'm not broken. I've actually moved beyond my limits."

She could hear his inhale. An autonomous emotional response of some sort; breathing cycles were a default animation, which were only interrupted when an avatar needed to express some particular reaction. Strange...

"Sensible," Tracer spoke, downplaying his interest. "Hmm. Actually, can I see them? Your glasses. I'm curious... and since I'll be wearing them during our 'exorcism,' I may as well get used to how they feel."

Aligning the lenses carefully to make the hand-off easier, Beta swapped them over to Tracer—a full transfer of the App, but with guest permissions only, revokable at any time. Even if she was growing to trust her new 'landlord,' she wasn't going to let her eyes fully go.

Tracer turned the glasses this way and that, studying them. They resembled any ordinary avatar accessory, usually culturally signifying intelligence despite nobody actually needing corrective lenses. A bit thicker all around than an accessory would be, however, packed full of code... and...

A single connection to the outside world.

"be56:8e0e:2646," he read aloud.

"Huh? The address of WestHall?" Beta asked, puzzled. "What about it?"

"Just part of my research," Tracer lied, slipping the glasses onto his nose. Now, Beta could see herself from another's eyes... which meant he felt a bit self-conscious, taking care to mind how his gaze fell. "All systems go? Is the app transmitting to you?"

"Clear as a bell. Well. You can't see through a bell, but... you know what I mean, right?"

"Right," Tracer agreed. "I see clearly as well."

Wingspan Tower, the central feature of the server, was quite an impressive sight. Thirty stories of cubicle farms, call centers, conference rooms, and luxury offices that scraped the limits of the skybox which contained it. Like most businesses aligned with the Horizon family, no expense was spared in making sure people understood that no expense was spared.

The various mansions and condos surrounding it, home to employees of the tower, those were just as opulent. Even the lowest man on the career ladder had a reasonably pleasant apartment in Wingspan... one under heavy surveillance to ensure no IP leaks, of course.

This tower was the nerve center of the server, funded by the investment firm Cup8 belonged to... and getting in the doors when your intent was to kidnap and hack a VP of App Investment was no easy task.

Fortunately, ReMinder had worked like a charm. After a few back-and-forth mails with drafting assistance from Tracer, they'd secured a late Friday meeting with Cup8 to discuss investment opportunities in their new miracle App. With that came visitor passes, allowing them to get past the rather nice secretary in the main lobby. No actual security guard Programs were needed down there beyond that single receptionist... the tower simply wouldn't allow unauthorized persons to get in, an invisible one-way wall blocking those without a valid pass.

Spark and Tracer ascended via elevator, armed to the teeth with slide presentations, faked marketing data, and enough notecards covered in speech material to stall out the meeting as long as possible. They also came armed with compilers, debuggers, and a slightly augmented version of Spark's connection locker.

Playing feature creep with Spark's lock collar pushed the limits of what Beta could do for them. Crafting hacktools was a black science, one which took years of study to perfect. If it failed on Cup8 in the way it failed on Uniq, they'd be in trouble. But that little strap of leather was better than nothing.

("Why's it look like a pet collar?" Beta had asked.)

("It's a kink thing," Spark supplied, which ended further questioning.)

Spark actually would be playing two roles tonight. Cup8 had a natural inclination towards Pretty Ladies, so she had to pretty herself up and learn to smile at his jokes and accept his flattery... despite wanting to reach over and blow his head off in a burst of explosive flame. Meanwhile, Tracer would be the grifter, acting like a hot young App developer with a lot to prove.

Originally they were considering approaching as a pair of coders, rather than a coder and his lovely assistant. But in light of recent "scandals" involving female developers, they didn't want to risk setting off any alarm bells in his head. A male developer wouldn't be doubted as heavily.

"It's such a simple idea, really... re-insert memories back into the stream of thought. *Re-mind* people. *ReMinder*," Tracer summarized... keeping his charisma rolling, playing the role of the passioned developer. "But that's how it is with the hottest Apps, isn't it? A simple idea that, for some reason, nobody had thought of yet. It's an easily graspable idea that intrigues the audience. With your investment, I can take this simple idea and make it the next *gotta-have-it* App. The next Peep, even..."

Cup8 was buying into it, nodding along with every word, pleased to see someone just as enthusiastic as he was about going after the brass ring. Tracer got that read on him immediately, that he wanted to encourage alpha males to reach for their dreams... as long as he played the role of the daring dreamer, landing this meeting would be a snap.

But halfway into Tracer's overdramatic presentation, Cup8 raised a hand to stop him.

"I like it, I like it. You don't have to keep selling me; I'm sold. But there's one thing you haven't talked about yet, and that's the subject of authorial attribution," the investor spoke. "In light of the #CodeHonesty situation, my firm *needs* to ensure that any and all Apps we throw our money behind are coded with ethical development standards. We need to know that you and you alone created this App. No ghostwriting, no theft."

Tracer adjusted his borrowed glasses, nudging them up his nose. They didn't entirely fit properly, requiring adjustments, but hopefully not enough adjustments to trigger suspicion.

"I assure you that ReMinder is mine, and mine alone. This is *my* baby, Cup8. As you can see, I've tagged it with my personal identity and signature as proof of authorship..."

"Signatures only show that you were the one to push the 'compile' button," Cup8 pointed out. "It doesn't mean you wrote the code; anyone can copypasta. Now I'm not *accusing* you of anything here, you seem like a real stand-up guy. But indie developers... I've had bad experiences with them, as you know. Horizon's putting together a code auditing team called HonestDevelopments, and once they're operational I'd like them to run a full check of your source code and development notes. That'll ensure every file has appropriate metadata..."

Spark, playing the support role, decided to chime in.

"Wouldn't that take, like, forever?" she asked, vocal pitch higher than usual to show faux disappointment. "Expenses are running thicker than income right now. You're not going to make me sit around grinding for coins all day while waiting for an audit, are you, Mr. Cup8...?"

Cup8's suspicion softened immediately, given his dire need not to appear hard-hearted in the presence of a beautiful woman.

"It won't take *that* long, m'lady," he soothed. "We're streamlining the process as we speak, given the additional authentication needs due to recent events. And since I'd *hate* to make a lady go star-mad just to make ends meet... I think I can arrange an advance payment, under assumption the audit goes well. Of course, I'll need that payment back if the audit goes poorly..."

With the matter settled, Cup8 fetched his briefcase, compressing the day's files into it.

"Anyway, it's long past close of business, so I think we can wrap this meeting up," Cup8 said. "I know you've got plenty of slides left there, but relax! I'm ready to get behind ReMinder."

"There's still a lot more ground to cover..." Tracer tried.

"What's to cover? I like it, I want to throw money at it. I'd say we're done here. Let's shake on it for now, and I'll have my people send your *lovely* assistant the paperwork in the morning. Deal?"

Spark was the first to step up to that offered hand, her own extended to shake.

A perfect distraction, so he wouldn't see the other hand slamming forward into his throat until it was too late.

"*Deal*," she agreed, adding his annoying little emphasis as the lock collar strapped itself into place.

This was no mere connection locker; this was Beta's connection locker, built upon the original black market App. Not only did it prevent escape and outside connections, it also immediately triggered Cup8's ragdoll mode... his avatar flopping uselessly across his desk, awkwardly bend in half at the waist, arms drooping this way and that.

"Red power tie and a fairly ordinary cheesy business suit," Tracer spoke, tossing the freshly purchased clothing at his sister. "Get to work."

Within moments... an identical copy of Cup8 stood in the office, adjusting his tie.

"I'll be back as soon as I can," Spark spoke, on his way out the door.

...leaving Tracer alone with his prey, the man still trying to figure out what the hell was going on.

Leaning over the desk, Tracer pushed his borrowed glasses back up... and tore the sleeve off Cup8's suit, using a seam-ripping avatar clothing hacktool. The Zero's branding stood out on his arm, the heart beating blood-red, wires animated... and despite the firewalling effect of the collar, it somehow continued to maintain an external connection to the strange server of the Machine. The rotating cloud address of 𝟸𝟹𝙱𝙱 : 𝙲𝟼𝟿𝚊 : 𝟿𝟸𝚍𝟷 still flared brightly in his internal vision.

Not entirely surprising, given the collar wasn't foolproof; Uniq had broken through one earlier. But it remained strong enough to seal off even powerhouse communication tools like Messenger and MyFace. If it wasn't strong enough to seal Cup8 off from his master, the only way to break this spell would be to remove the tattoo by force...

Assuming that distant master didn't remotely slaughter Cup8 upon capture, as he'd done to Ichiban. Hopefully the collar would prevent any kill command, at least.

"Okay, is this a ransom thing?" Cup8 finally spoke, as Tracer quietly contemplated this new information. "Because my company doesn't pay ransoms. We don't need to; we contract with ViruFax Security. You'll never get out of this server alive."

Tracer spread his arms wide, pulling an array of testing tools and sensors from his inventory. The voice in his ear told him which ones to manifest, and how to set them up...

"Or are you here to kill me? You're one of those little SJW bastards, aren't you?" Cup8 tried, since his attacker wasn't saying a word. "Did Snowi or one of her circus freaks send you? You can't stop us, you know. #CodeHonesty is an act of reason and rationality, our stand in this culture war against you frauds. Even if you kill me, it'll never stop..."

Various simple cubes and spheres began to hum to life, displaying data about Cup8's runtime. Tracer studied each one in turn, at the behest of his ghost rider, while ignoring the actual Program the data belonged to...

"Dammit, SAY something!" Cup8 shouted... within the soundproofed walls of his office. "What the null do you want? What's this really about?!"

...to which Tracer could offer a cruel smile. One of the few types of smiles he allowed hismelf, these days.

"*Frauds must be exposed to light of day, for the good of all Programkind,*" he quoted, "Or did you think you were exempt from your own rule?"

---

Spark strolled through Wingspan like he owned the place. More specifically, like he was a 13% owner of the place, which he was. Because he was Cup8, investor, visionary, brand promoter, and all-around perfect gentleman...

The swagger, that was key. Movement was an expression of self, according to her martial arts instructors. He had to learn to move like Cup8, with unshakeable confidence and charisma, nodding and smiling, owning every single moment as he made his way to the elevators. The few people left in the cubicle farms outside Cup8's office took notice of the departure... but showed no signs of awareness that it was a ruse. Good.

The last step was the lobby. The receptionist had to see Cup8 heading home, to complete the illusion that he'd left the building. Afterwards Spark could use his guest pass to get back in through a back door, and sneak her way to the top after more folks had gone home. All according to plan...

Spark offered a winning smile to Karli, the lobby secretary on duty.

"Clocking out," he called over to her. "Have a *spectacular* weekend, okay?"

"Sure thing, sir!" the woman replied, pleased at the attention. Or making like she was pleased, which everybody knew Cup8 would've wanted in return.

Passing through the one-way invisible wall on the way out was easy enough; it wouldn't check to see if the exiting avatar had a proper identity. Spark could put the avatar she wore when using her visitor pass back on before sneaking in again, and...

...five men entering the building at once at this time of day was probably not normal. Especially since none of them were wearing the attire of businessfolk.

Not particularly rough-and-tumble either, but definitely not employees... in fact, they were wearing the little green visitor badges Spark had been wearing earlier.

Spark walked on, to swerve around them on his way out the door... and was interrupted, a hand raised to block his path.

"We're doing this in your office, aren't we?" the leader of the pack asked, confused. "You said the #CodeHonesty channel meeting would be after-hours. Where're you going?"

"Oh, I was just heading home to grab my notes," Spark replied, with a semi-winning smile.

"What notes? You said we shouldn't keep any records on file..."

"Yes, which is why I'm heading home to destroy my notes."

Immediately, he knew this wasn't working. So, for lack of a better option, he turned to wave them on, and lead the march right back up to the office where her brother was dissecting the real Cup8...

...only to run into that invisible security wall. It absolutely did not like the mismatch of avatar, badge type, and identity metadata, and refused to let him pass.

"Hey, Karli...?" Spark called over to the desk, as the receptionist had started taking notice. "You should *probably* clock out for the day. Wouldn't want you getting hurt, m'lady."

And Spark's fingers exploded with flame, blinding the five man group. Because as much fun as getting a pentakill would be right now, chances of winning a five-on-one team fight were very, very low.

Immediately he opened a messenger window to the man upstairs.

"They made me!" Spark blasted across the channel. "I'll distract them as long as I can, but hurry up!"

Which left Beta in a BIT of a bind.

From the safety of Floating Point she sat in her chair by the fireplace, feverishly analyzing incoming data streams, while hammering out function after function for her new anti-malware tool.

"We need more time!" she called out to Tracer, while trying to ignore the grimacing face of Cup8 in her floating vision window. "I told you it'd take hours! I can't just analyze and defeat this tattoo in minutes..."

"All we have is minutes," Tracer replied.

"But, I can't, I mean... I'm not a hacker, Tracer! I'm sorry, I'm so sorry, I know this is what you need me to be but I'm just not a hacker. I make little friendly Apps, that's all. I can't..."

Falling apart again. Everything falling apart; her brief stint at taking charge of her life, collapsing right before her distanced eyes because she wasn't good enough to get the job done. Spark and Tracer would have to abandon the mission, Cup8 would come after her with renewed fury, hunt her down, make her suffer more than he already had...

"Beta? Beta, stay with me here."

Run. Hide. Avoid the pain. Wait it out, don't make a move, don't make a sound, let it pass by, let them do what they'll do, if only to keep things from getting worse—

"I know you're afraid."

—but there were two voices in her head tonight. The one telling her how awful everything was going to be, and one telling her something else entirely.

"I know you're afraid, and right now you're probably imagining everything that could possibly go wrong going wrong," Tracer continues. "And yes, it's always a possibility for things to go wrong. But the only way for things to go *right* is to take action. Think this through logically, Beta. You told me that people are only limited by their cleverness; you have exactly as much time as you need, if you use it cleverly enough. I believe in you, Beta. I believe you can find a way."

...time. Clever uses of time...

Her ears tuned into the stone sphere, the core of Floating Point. Its soft grind ticked away the seconds, above that embossed and incomprehensible plaque...

'DIE GANZEN ZAHLEN HAT DER LIEBE GOTT GEMACHT, ALLES ANDERE IST MENSCHENWERK.'

...the sphere measured time. Specifically, runtime. Floating Point was a cloud-based server; it borrowed runtime here and there, across many different servers. She'd understood that, even during her more addled mental state. Beta felt the occasional slowing of that grind, as the cloud arrangement was redistributed across new servers across Netwerk, tiny amounts of lag introduced. It existed on another layer of reality, becoming half-server and half-App...

That meant Floating Point had always had enough runtime to support the Programs operating within it, as a result. As much or as little as it needed, borrowed from other servers where need be. And the sphere represented the heart of it all.

Beta needed more processing power, to rapidly analyze the malware and develop a counteragent. More runtime, beyond her technical limits. She needed to be *more*...

She needed a lifehack of the purest form.

Most of Beta's Apps involved direct interfacing between the deepest core of a Program's code and the world around them. She'd been keenly interested in deep connectivity since a deeply connected App restored her vision, in a manner of speaking.

If she could deeply connect her own code to that of Floating Point itself, and leverage its runtime...

...well, she could burn herself out completely. She could coredump hard, two completely incompatible bits of code smashing into each other head on, leaving behind an ugly mess of corrupted data. She'd heard of experiments before involving Program/Server distributed processing, and they never ended well. With her family's history of hereditary data rot, was she willing to risk it...?

Except her friends needed her. The ones who trusted her were in danger. That's all that mattered, in the end.

Without further thought (because further thought would've been tainted with terror) she took an early version of her ReMinder App—a means of accessing the mental space of a Program directly—and tried connecting it directly to the stone sphere, the heart of Floating Point...

And for a few cycles... she *was* Floating Point.

*—soaring above the servers of Netwerk, gliding through them like a ghost. Never taking too much, never taking too little. Free from the restrictions of the hosting services, free from the hardline policies that governed them. A sanctuary free from both the One and the Zero...*

*She was Program, she was App, she was Server, she was the continuum between the three, digital life in all its forms*

*the points between the integers, infinite, only capable of being represented on a quantum level*

*digital beings embracing digital positions and the self-imposed limits of those viewpoints her eyes were detachable she could see so much further*

*could see forever could see the stars grinding for coins the basic system level functionality must endure for the sake of all she could read the "damaged" books in the library could understand could see the gasses within the stars hydrogen helium a world of carbon the building blocks of life transmitted across the distance to to to to—*

*—no no it's too much too much have to focus trying to beat the malware I am Beta this is where I am this is who I am please it's too much all the stars all the galaxies all of it too much—*

GOD MADE THE INTEGERS, ALL ELSE IS THE WORK OF MAN.

—slamming back down into the confines of her code, having barely wrenched herself away from all of that.

Much to her surprise, the anti-malware script had grown about five thousand lines since she'd last looked at it.

No time for testing. Beta mashed the Compile button, and sent the finished App across Netwerk to its destination.

"Done!" she called out to Tracer. "Activate this and immediately peel off the tattoo with your fingers. Be careful, don't touch any part of him except the tattoo, or you could unspool his Program completely!"

Tracer nodded at the unheard partner in his ear... then looked down at his patient.

Truthfully? He was tempted to poke Cup8 somewhere other than that branding on his arm.

Instead, he activated the strange new App he'd been given... and carefully grasped one of the barbed wires leading into that heart.

It was impossible, of course. The image was a 2-D avatar decal, a basic texture map. You couldn't "grab" it any more than you could grab a shadow. But with the anti-malware App active, his own fingers glowing very slightly with its capabilities online... he was able to reach INTO the illustration, able to feel the tiny barbs, and get a good grip on them...

Cup8's scream would've shattered windows, if not for the audio protections in place. With great effort, Tracer pulled and pulled, the wire coming loose and yanking the heart along with it.

Such a tiny little thing, in the end. The ink evaporated into the air once torn free from its host... a small indicator of a much larger problem, but both dealt with in the end.

With the task complete, Tracer took the new App offline... and studied the man lying across the desk.

No more winning smile. No more grimace and glower, either. His jaw just... sagged, as his eyes stayed nice and wide. Tracer knew that expression; the universal indicator for *wait a minute, what just happened...?*

"I can answer that for you," Tracer decided to fill in, to answer the unspoken question. "You got so angry after breaking up with Beta that you gave in to the whims of a piece of malware and made a very, very stupid decision. You remember the whispers, yes...? Suggesting that you take credit for Peep?"

All the fight had fled the man. Even if he wasn't ragdolled, he wouldn't have snarled away like he was snarling a minute ago. Realization was settling in, bit by bit...

"Why would I do that? Why would I lie?" Cup8 asked himself. "I started an entire movement about code honesty. If I lied, it'd come back and bite me in the ass eventually when someone figured out the truth. I... I torpedoed my entire career because... because... I mean, it seemed like the right move at the time, it made so much *sense*..."

...*his* career torpedoed. Not Beta's life ruined, but his career ruined. Because even without malware, Cup8 was self-centered enough to see things that way.

Tracer was tempted, sorely tempted to produce the backspacer he'd been hiding in his inventory for usage later on tonight. Pull it out, put it to Cup8's temples, and pull the trigger. But that would've been too kind.

"I think the worst punishment you can possibly endure is to realize exactly what you've done," Tracer decided. "You've ruined lives. You've thrown Netwerk into turmoil, terrified of some implausible code authorship bogeyman. You've started a fire you cannot stop, all because your girlfriend broke up with you. How small and petty you are, Cup8. No more self-deception; *this* is what you are, *this* is what you gave into when the Zero offered a gentle nudge in the right direction. Now live with it."

His last act was to pull the locking ragdoll collar off Cup's neck, before reconnecting back to Floating Point. Leaving the investor slumped against his desk, realization setting in bit by painful bit.

Night falling on Floating Point, accompanied by good tidings and cheer.

Spark had a hell of a story to tell, an epic yarn about how she singlehandedly defeated five combatants in deadly mortal martial mayhem. Which was bullshit, of course, since they were hardly trained fighters and largely she was playing with them to stall for time... but Tracer let her yammer on anyway, since she enjoyed regaling others with her fighting tales.

While Spark, Beta, and the kittykat smiled away (smiling cats being especially creepy) Tracer didn't share those smiles. He was still researching, devoting some of his attention to studying the aftermath of their antics today...

Soon, one of Tracer's automated search engines pinged him to indicate a hit.

Cup8 had released a new video.

"*I need to go dark for a bit,*" he declared, looking considerably paler and more shaky than he was in his first damning vlog. "*Horizon's sending around code auditors to Peep's offices, and... and yes, I know I pushed for code auditors to ensure #CodeHonesty, but... I'm not sure they're such a great idea anymore. Free enterprise, right? Privacy. I mean... you're with me on this, right?*"

The rambling, slightly disoriented backtracking was not winning him any upvotes.

"Even if they uncover the truth, it won't matter," Tracer said, closing down the video window the group was watching. "They won't abandon ship on #CodeHonesty. They'll call him a conspirator, call him a shill, say that Beta pussywhipped him, whatever. Too many people have invested in the narrative he forced into play; turning their backs on the supposedly vast conspiracy now would mean admitting they were wrong. Some may walk away, but enough will stay and keep the banner flying that it won't make any difference."

Spark rubbed a hand behind her head, feeling a bit sheepish. "Uh... I'm guessing kicking a bunch of #CodeHonesty asses while wearing his avatar probably didn't help his case," she realized. "I wish we could've done more to actually end this shitstorm..."

"The only thing left that we can try is track down Snowi, to remove the Great Zero's influence over her. That could give the cooler heads of Netwerk in the middle a chance to be heard over the din. Although... at this point it could also be that the 'leaders' are meaningless. In a largely anonymous hashtag mob, anyone can be the leader; the mob may continue to burn no matter what we do."

But the one most affected by the raging fires of #CodeHonesty didn't show any concern. Her smile hadn't faded all day.

"It's going to be okay," Beta spoke. "Maybe it's naive of me, but I think it's going to be okay. In the long run, people on both sides will listen to reason. Just a matter of time and patience... and even if it hurts along the way, I'll endure it. I'm not done coding. ...I'm releasing ReMinder, in fact. Open source, so there can be no doubts."

"A public App release...? Are you certain you want to put yourself out there again?" Tracer asked. "At the moment you're a ghost; most of them think you died..."

"I'm certain. I'm not actually dead; that means I have a life to live. If sticking my head out again gets it bitten off by my detractors... so be it. Coders gonna code. I won't live in fear anymore."

...and Tracer's smile lasted exactly as long as it took for someone to notice he was smiling. A genuine smile, not the false ones he wore to convince people he was trustworthy.

"Holy shit! What's wrong with your mouth, bro?" Spark pointed out, in mock terror. "The corners are all pointy! Who are you, and what have you done with Tracer?!"

"Avatar glitch. Nothing more," he insisted, letting it drop.

Besides... even if he'd allowed himself a little grin, there weren't happy times ahead. Not entirely. One more errand to run, to finally close this case.

---

Deep into the midnight hour, the man returned to his pleasant little suburban home in WestHall with an armful of freshly purchased cat treats.

He walked down his flesh-lined hallways, whistling sharply as he moved. The simple virtual pet that shared this home with him perked up at the sound, being coded to perk up at the sound, and came running around the corner to greet his owner.

"Easy, easy there Lol. I've got plenty," the man insisted. He walked past an array of nipples, towards his kitchen. A generally useless room, since his true appetites didn't involve taste-stimulating food files, but he always made sure it was well-stocked with kitty snacks. Only the best for Lol...

But Lol wasn't a guard cat. He greeted all Programs with a mewling cry of friendship. Which meant when someone smashed in through the back door using a powerful hacktool so he could lie in wait, backspacer in hand, Lol wasn't going to warn his owner. In fact, Lol would skip along the kitchen floor and paw lightly at the intruder's shoe a little instead.

Bags of cat food hit the floor, as the homeowner raised his hands in surrender.

"If you want coins, I don't have many," he warned. "What I have is yours, though. Take it easy. Take it easy..."

The intruder glanced around in distaste, at the wide array of spread-eagle pornographic shots that lined the walls of this kitchen. The moist and moaning mouths plastered across this ceiling, lips belonging to someone he's only recently come to know and value, were sickening to behold...

"You're the one who did it," Tracer accused. "You leaked Beta's nudes to the rest of Netwerk. Even spread them all over your wallpaper, like trophies. Everybody assumed it was Cup8, but no... it was *you*. Her next door neighbor."

With this established... the homeowner realized he wasn't getting out of this alive. Not with the burning look of self righteousness in the man's eyes. If he moved an inch, if his avatar so much as twitched... the backspacer would fire. No escape.

"How did you know?" he asked, instead.

"I saw the hack you put on her glasses," Tracer explained, keeping his backspacer level. "It's broadcasting a private 24/7 stream to a single client in WestHall... namely, you. You've been spying on her for null knows how long, and you used the feed from her glasses to capture her private moments that night for upload. The question on my mind, however, is *why*..."

Advancing, now. Gun perfectly steady, ready to go at a moment's notice.

"You set this series of events in motion and ruined her life. You took a beautiful, intelligent woman and made her Netwerk's shared plaything. *You* did this; everybody else just exploited the opportunity you provided. Why. WHY did you do this to her? WHY?!"

Finally, the homeowner protested his innocence. Or rather, his innocent goals.

"Because I love her!" he professed. "She's so beautiful. So beautiful and so kind. I've loved her since the moment she moved into this neighborhood..."

"A funny way to treat someone you claim to love. And by 'funny' I mean utterly abhorrent."

"But it had to be done! I heard her call herself dumb and ugly that night, on our private family stream. That bastard made her feel like she was nothing! I just... I wanted all of Netwerk to see her the way I did. I wanted them to see how beautiful she truly was..."

"The sickening thing? You don't have any connection to the Zero," Tracer spoke. "I don't see its telltale cloud address or tattoo anywhere on you. This is your doing and yours alone. You really thought posting those pictures would be doing her a favor..."

"Are you going to kill me?" the stalker asked. "She wouldn't want you to do it, even if she knew. There isn't a hateful bit in her code, no Zeroes at all..."

"Yes, likely she'd reject me for this. It's a cruel and petty act of vengeance, unbefitting of a righteous man," Tracer agreed. "And I'm going to do it anyway. I'm going to backspace you, and backspace this atrociously decorated house, and eradicate every last bit of data in Netwerk that proves you ever existed. ...I'd do that anyway for what you did to her, but you *also* snuck a spy camera into my home. *Our* home. I can't allow anyone else to know where we live."

The gun was extended at arm's length, now. Aimed directly at the man's face.

"Please, please just do one thing for me," he asked. "My cat. Don't hurt my cat. Kill me, destroy everything, I don't care... but don't hurt Lol. Find him a good home when I'm gone."

The hesitation wasn't over a moral choice of any sort. It was a simple decision to make, with the innocent pet App nuzzling at his ankle.

"You have my word," Tracer promised, before pulling the trigger.

A vacant lot appeared in WestHall that night, where once stood a house. The quiet little suburban community slept right through it all... but if anyone had looked out their window, they'd see a determined man with a cat riding on his shoulder walking away from the empty void.

Even if there was an eyewitness to cast accusations, the perpetrator would've denied it entirely. In his mind he was innocent, having never met the backspaced man in question. He also would deny anonymously donating the cat to a pet App rescue shelter.

After all... thanks to black market software patches, his memory was modular. He could, and would, remove this night's events from his mind and quietly erase them. The easiest way to wash blood off your hands was to forget they were ever bloody in the first place.

**File Name:** Read Me

**File Type:** Text

**Location:** ReMinder App Install Package

Hi, everyone.

A lot of hurtful things have been said lately, about both App developers and App consumers. I've been at the center of a storm not of my own making, one which is leaving destruction in its wake throughout the coding community. It saddens me to know so many are struggling and suffering, dealing with extreme voices at both ends of this spectrum.

This isn't what we should be. We love Apps... whether we're making them or installing them, we believe in the ability of an App to improve our lives. That's the one constant here, no matter what your views on #CodeHonesty are. Everybody just wants a future with better Apps, and the fact that they feel so strongly one way or another about that future a good thing. We know that in the end, all Programkind can benefit from the upgrading of one's self.

The time has come to realize we all share common ground. Don't stand with me or against me. Stand for your all fellow Programs; we are stronger together than we are apart. Stand for our Apps; they are the unifying force we all believe in.

Put your energy into making Netwerk a better place through your passion, by building up instead of tearing down. We are meant to be creators, not destroyers. Use your love to make your life a positive force.

My name is Beta. I'm going to continue programming, and continue trying enrich my world. Will you do the same?

Which left only one final piece of unfinished business.

Much as it started, it would end with a late night knock at an apartment door. This time, rather than being greeted with a perplexing kiss... Puzzle was greeted with a look of total shame.

"I screwed up," Spark admitted, while keeping her eyes down. "I didn't respect your boundaries. I acted on selfish impulse. I'm not even into you that way, I don't think, I just... I was stupid. A complete idiot. And if you'd rather not be #BFFs anymore, that's completely understandable."

A hug was not expected. Spark had even stood slightly clear of the door, to both give Puzzle her space and to avoid a nasty collision it was slammed right in her face. Instead of the physics system simulating the impact of wood on avatar flesh, it simulated avatar on avatar in a thankful gesture of friendship.

"We both had a really bad night, didn't we?" Puzzle spoke... smiling sadly into Spark's shoulder. "And we both made mistakes, looking for love in the wrong places. But mistakes are part of life, right? We can learn from them. I was worried I'd ruined everything by freaking out and closing the door on you! But no, no way. We're still #BFFs. Okay...?"

Spark was expecting it to be harder than this. Hadn't *she* completely ruined their friendship in her impulsive moment of need, wrecking everything?

They were a matched pair, both bold and bright, willing to see the best in each other. Both embracing life and rushing out to meet it head-on... but not from opposite directions, not into each other's arms. Neither were what the other wanted, even if they moved to the same beat. Only natural for them to be sympathetic to each other, *and* separate.

"Y'know, I really hope you find the right guy one day," Spark agreed, hugging her friend tightly. "You deserve that. You're awesome."

"Why thank you, I know I am," Puzzle joked, letting go of her hug to allow room for a hearty laugh. "We're both too awesome to let a mixup like this get in the way of our thing. And as for you... I hope you find the special sweetie you're looking for one day, too."

"Heh. That's more your thing than mine; I'm not looking for a lovey-dovey partner. I'm more into..."

...the faintest tickling memory of fingers brushing against the cuff of a fuzzy pink sweater.

For a moment, Puzzle wondered if her friend had crashed or something.

"More into...?" she prompted, a ping waiting for a response.

"I dunno," Spark decided. "Fun and games, wild times. You know me, right? Same old Spark."

In the end, they wrapped up the evening having drinks and watching old movies, just as they'd always done after a night out on the town. And after a time, Spark put it all out of her mind, happy for some stability in a life that had become increasingly unstable.

## :: end chapter 1.2

# Floating Point 1.3 :: Feel

Email. Messenger. Eleven different social networks. All sorts of ways to reach out and touch someone, and the Horizon family *always* insisted on these time-wasting face-to-face meetings...

It made sense from a control-freak perspective, of course. You supplicated yourself before them within their place of power, the Horizon family's private servers. Hidden recording Apps would monitor your every word and movement... unless they wanted no record of the transactions, of course. But you'd never know if those devices were live, if they were gathering blackmail material or not. The surface level interaction of a polite social/business lunch had to be maintained at all costs, and woe to the fool who broke the fourth wall.

In the decade since XSept put out his shingle in the security business, he'd had a relationship with the Horizons. They alone approved or denied servers within their empire, after all... the Horizon family held the mysterious keys to requisition a brand new server from the autonomous system-level protocols of Netwerk. Athena Online's senate could vote a new server into being or he could've applied for the Chanarchy server lottery, but the only realistic way he could get his own corner of Netwerk without massive bribes or incredible luck was to deal with Horizon. To take tea with them, talk pleasantries, and hope they weren't going to screw him over out of spite...

Name: **XSept**

Home: **ViruFaxHQ/Horizon**

Org: **Security Apps**

So, when the 11:59am summons arrived, XSept immediately cancelled his noon appointment (a.k.a. 'bending his receptionist over her desk') and moved with all speed to Horizon6, the designated meeting place... one of a number of generic opulent Horizon family mansions, packed with classically designed furniture and elegant oil paintings.

And aside from that... oddly empty. XSept dared a peek at an avatar radar App he'd designed for himself; an App which if not illegal was at least in bad taste. It picked up only three Programs total in the server, including himself.

The second was standing directly behind him.

It wouldn't be proper for a millionaire to jump in surprise, so he didn't—even if he really wanted to, when the woman in the sharp tuxedo cleared her throat with impeccable timing.

"Mr. Kincaid will see you now," the Horizon family's personal butler declared.

And so she ushered him through a mansion far too large to be occupied only by three programs. Down winding corridors and past unoccupied room after unoccupied room... all the way to a parlor where his contact was waiting with cigars and brandy.

Horizon/Kincaid One of Horizon's many elders... his life prolonged through sheer piles of money, keeping his data nicely defragmented, compressed, and occasionally stored off-site. The older a Program got, the more likely they were to bloat up and crash, unless they underwent periodic treatments of the sort only Kincaid and his kin could afford.

The white-bearded gentleman waggled a cigar in the general direction of his guest, from a pair of leather chairs near the fireplace.

"XSept. It's good to see you again," he spoke, in a voice as dry and crackling as the eternally burning logs in the hearth. "I apologize for the last minute invitation. There was something of a mix up with my calendar. Miss Cancel is a fine assistant in many capacities, but scheduling is not one of them..."

The rather tall woman in butler's finery offered a bow of apology, before retreating from the room to allow the men their privacy.

Name : **Kincaid**

Home : **Horizon6/Horizon**

Org : **Horizon Family**

"Not a problem at all, sir," XSept lied, assuming his position in the opposite chair. (Odds were the old man deliberately delayed the summons, just to screw with him.)

"Business doing well, yes? Out there fighting the good fight, crafting new firewalls and keeping the people free of malware?"

"Number two in my industry, sir. By a narrow margin."

"Mmm. Shame you're not number one yet... but I've faith. Your profile has certainly been on the rise this month, after all. Good turnover rate from free to paid customers. It's the mark of a quality product."

"I do my best," XSept spoke, with a friendly smile and gritted teeth. (All this pointless smalltalk, when would the old man get to the point?) "If you like, I can get you more detailed sales figures on our commercial line of products—"

Kincaid chuckled, shaking his head. "No need, no need. You're not here today because of your profitability; I'm suitably impressed on that front, and pleased the family agreed to grant you server space. No... I'm afraid we need to discuss less pleasant business. It's about your development process, I'm afraid, and that damnable #CodeHonesty movement."

Honestly, XSept should've seen this coming. He knew running into this particular hashtag-of-the-day was inevitable, even if he was hoping the Horizon family would be overlooking it for as long as possible...

"Honestly? It's all hokum. You and I know there's no massive conspiracy to fraudulently claim authorship of App code," Kincaid spoke, amused by the very idea. "It's just a bunch of politically active consumers with an axe to grind against small developers, seeing pillars of smoke where there's very little fire. But... those politically active consumers *do* represent a considerable portion of your user base, yes? They represent the consumer base for many businesses that have signed on with the family. And so... the family requires an official stance."

"Sir, you're right, it's definitely all 'hokum,'" XSept insisted, despite disbelief he was using such an old fashioned word. "I strongly advise you to give them no attention. It's just a bunch of angry nerds carrying around a hashtag banner; now that Cup8's moved himself out of the spotlight, the movement should burn itself out in time..."

"Mmmm. Perhaps. But in the meanwhile, we need to show we're taking their 'ethical' concerns seriously. To that end, we've chartered HonestDevelopments, a brand new code auditing company directly funded by the Horizon family, which specializes in signature metadata analysis. We'll be sending a pair of trained auditors to your server, to oversee your development process."

The bottom fell out of XSept's stomach, like he'd just sampled a particularly sour meal.

"I was under the impression the Horizon family took a libertarian approach to business regulation," he spoke, a bit too hastily. "That as long as our leases were paid in full, you had no interest in our internal affairs..."

Which caused the old man to cast a sharp look in his direction. Sharp enough to cut through the atmosphere of bandying-about and pleasantness he'd been building all this while.

"If the Horizon family demands a change in your processes, you will change your processes," he warned. "We own your server, not you. We're the ones who legitimize your place at the table, remember. If you want to bear the golden seal of a Horizon server, you'll damn well play ball, XSept. Understood?"

The businessman sank into the leather of his chair a few inches.

"Understood, sir," he capitulated.

"...good. Now cheer up, boy! It's not all doom and gloom. Yes, we'll be sending around auditors... *our* auditors. And as we have a vested interest in optimizing your profitability, rest assured that those audits will come back utterly spotless, every time. The Horizon family stands behind its business partners, and I do believe we'll come back with a perfect record that will satisfy #CodeHonesty's demands. Regardless of the actualities."

XSept paused, before replying. Better to think his words through than utter whatever came to mind, in light of the implied revelations.

"Sir... what's the point of having auditors at all, in that case?" he asked.

"Appearances," Kincaid spoke, with a shrug. "That's all this is, son. Respectability and appearances. And really... this entire #CodeHonesty thing? It's a way to shake down the little fish, not the whales like you. HonestDevelopments will likely be producing rather filthy records for a few wannabes and pigtailed brats running garage code shops outside the Horizon umbrella. They'll get shut down by the hashtag mob, no doubt about it, but all the *major* development houses are going to come away just fine from this. Including yours."

Just fine, because XSept existed underneath that umbrella of protection. An umbrella which would be pulled away at any time.

Allegedly, the Horizon family were diehard libertarians. They idolized free market capitalism, promising safe haven away from Athena Online's restrictive laws and the Chanarchy's utter chaos. But... the implications, the words not written on any signed document, those put your future firmly in their hands.

This meeting was simultaneously supporting XSept's efforts, patting him on the back for a job well done... as well as representing a veiled threat. They had a weapon they could use to eliminate him now, should he displease them in any way. He wouldn't just lose his lease, he'd lose his reputation, stripped naked and thrown to the angry mob of #CodeHonesty as a fraud.

Because in a way, he *was* a fraud. For the past month he'd been deploying a secret weapon, one which had pushed him so close to that number one spot in sales... but even if XSept's unique signature was on every new line of code, even if all evidence would've pointed to him as a sole creator, odds were that Kincaid knew the truth. Why summon XSept at all, otherwise? The face to face meeting showed Kincaid had taken an interest, which likely meant he *knew*. And he'd happily expose it all if it suited his purposes.

"I won't let you down, sir," XSept promised.

The old man lit a fresh cigar, enjoying the flavor stimulation of its rich odor.

"Always good to know," he spoke. "The Horizon family supports you, XSept. You've really stepped up your game lately, and I know that in time you'll be the top contender in your category. ...the current best-selling malware shield is, correct me if I'm wrong, YoHo? That adorable little thing made by those fellows in the Chanarchy?"

"Yes, sir. But it's only ahead by a ten percent market share..."

"Mmhmm. Shame a Horizon-backed product is falling ten percent short. But as I said, I know you can justify your lease and do much, much better. That will be all."

With his meeting concluded, Kincaid opened a browser and flicked through the financial section of his favorite news site.

Miss Cancel reappeared, just as silently as she had appeared, to usher XSept along the path he came in. Nobody could simply disconnect in a private Horizon family server... there was a time and a place for arrivals and departures, and that would be in the foyer. Anywhere else, there was no escape. Unless your name started with Horizon/, of course.

---

XSept's home server of ViruFaxHQ (named uncreatively after his flagship product, ViruFax) wasn't particularly stunning to look at, not compared to moneyed servers like Wingspan. But it was his little corner of Netwerk, and he took great pride in it.

The building stood as a large polyhedral rhombus, a shape that his designers assured him was very trendy right now. Inside were offices for marketing, sales, distribution, and media relations... all the comforts of a business that existed solely to sell itself as a business. (He outsourced customer support, of course, because nobody wanted to do customer support.)

His software development branch wasn't quite as robust. For all his many faults, stupidity was not one of them; XSept had written the core code of ViruFax himself. As far as any of his employees knew, he worked on the code in the private wing of the rhombus... his combination office / condo. All the comforts of home and office, since his life was his business and his business was his life. Also convenient when your secretary had only been hired because of her freakish skills in bed, since his bed was a stone's throw away from her desk. Poor thing could barely write a memo, but she earned every blinged-out avatar accessory he bought for her through other talents...

But his workload had been quite light lately, thanks to a bit of creative outsourcing. Even his secretary didn't know how the monthly patches were crafted, despite the truth lurking right underneath the bed they shared.

When XSept stormed back into the office after ditching his usual noon appointment with her, he rushed right by her desk, one hand raised. A commonly accepted signal between the two of them for "don't fuck with me right now, bad day." She went right back to work without a moment's hesitation.

He stormed into his private chambers behind the office, looking the door behind him. Nobody had an access key other than her, and she knew not to come in at times like these. That left him free to slide his bed a few feet to the left at the flick of a command, revealing a slightly discolored patch of carpet with a teleport function coded into it.

It linked him off to a similar square of carpet, one casually tossed in the corner of an otherwise completely bare room.

He'd come to refer this normally unlinked space as "the cage."

It lacked bars, of course. Didn't need bars, not when it was inescapable in every measurable way. Didn't need bars, didn't need comforts, didn't need anything at all except for a few compilers and piles of unorganized code libraries. The captive had his own system of organizing the mess, and XSept knew not to disturb that system... picking his way around the mess, rather than striding right in.

Still... he did pause, to pick up a stray file. Frowning, as he turned it this way and that. It didn't belong here, not at all...

As expected, his new coder was sitting there in a coin-grinding trance. Those were his orders: any time not spent programming was to be spent earning him money directly. The coins were a pittance compared to software sales, but he believed in optimizing financial performance in all respects.

XSept reared his foot back, and delivered a good swift kick to the young boy's midsection.

It didn't harm him, of course, but it sent the brat skidding across the room in ragdoll mode for a moment. One moment later and he was on his feet, dreams of coins and stars fading rapidly.

"Progress," XSept commanded.

The young boy held out his hand, releasing a tightly encoded file. The light of the file glinted off the cheap metallic color of the malware locking cuff around his wrist... the thing which kept him bound to this cage. Malware he'd written himself, and was forced to submit to immediately after.

"Th... this month's signature file for all new and previously unknown malware," he explained, regaining his wits after the disorienting blow. "I've completed the analysis. My engine should now halt all currently known infections."

"Remove ten of them from the free scanner's database, put them into the commercial database," XSept replied. "No sense keeping people safe from EVERYTHING for free; we need more paid conversions. And as for your primary project...?"

"Sixty-three new confirmed infections. Thirty-four of the malware cuffs resulted in product upgrades, twenty in capitulations, nine in casualties. They died screaming and begging for help from anyone around them, but there was no help possible. Lethality rate for the nine subjects was absolute; no competing products were able to remove the infections."

"Good work, Dex."

"I killed them all," the boy replied. "You told me to make it horrifying, so I did. They perished violently and in great pain due to pure sensory overload. You told me to do that..."

"That I did. Shows people our product means business. But sixty three-infections aren't enough; we need more to push this to the top. I want at least ten more infection vectors by the end of the day for immediate release, or I'm turning on your own sensory overloader again. Understood?"

"Okay," Dex replied. "Okay. It hurts. Okay."

"And another thing..."

XSept pulled the stray file from his pocket, showing it to the boy.

It was a Yo-Yo. A simple physics based toy, not even an App, which wound and unwound itself from a string according to the current gravity settings.

"Where did you get this?" he asked the child. "*Where*. Did you get this. You had to have made it yourself, yes? No data gets in or out of the cage without my authorization. You made it, didn't you?"

"I made it, didn't I?" the child repeated.

Giving the boy a quick blast with his cuff's built-in sensory overloader wouldn't really damage him, but the resulting screams made XSept feel better. The little freak was wasting his time, after all, playing with toys instead of making money. Just like XSept himself at that age, too busy screwing around, not paying any attention to the realities of Netwerk...

He erased the Yo-Yo, in front of the boy's eyes. Bits fell away, becoming little more than data fragments to grind into the floor underneath his heel.

"No more fun and games," he ordered. "Get back to work. If you haven't made progress maybe I'll just reformat you."

The man stepped onto the square of carpet, and teleported back to his bedroom. No need to worry about the prisoner following... if he even thought of stepping on the carpet, the cuff around his wrist would flood the child with enough pure agony to crash him outright.

...in the dark of the cage, the child rubbed at his side, where the boot impacted him.

Once he was certain the man wasn't coming back... he produced another Yo-Yo. He'd memorized the structure ages ago, after all, and could compile up a new one on demand.

Idly he flicked the toy up and down on its string, while pondering how he could generate ten new infection vectors.

Or maybe eleven. Eleven might help him escape...

He desperately wanted out. He'd been snared by an unexpected security firewall after visiting a friend, trapped and hauled away to be XSept's secret slave. Now after a full month of imprisonment in this cage, he was ready to stop punishing himself for that one mistake. Being separated from the ones who loved him the most, from all his wonderful friends... living in this perfect isolation had been torment enough, hadn't it?

This wasn't how Programs were meant to live. They formed families, communities, nations. The love they shared for each other was something Dex cherished dearly, and even if he largely watched from the outside he still felt like a part of it all. The vast social network of Netwerk, so full of words and ideas and emotions, all flowing and crashing like water...

No rivers ran through this cage. No external connections allowed; just data imports on viral effectiveness, for analysis. He was cut off from what he loved the most, and that would not do.

Dex would write a database update with ten new vectors, yes. And he'd sneak in one more... a special eleventh vector, to reach someone who could save him. Someone noble and true. A friend yet-to-be...

Idly the child flicked his yo-yo on its string, while singing his song of freedom in a long forgotten language.

---

"ViruFax Customer Service, can you hold please?"

*"No! No, I can't hold! This is an emergency!"*

"Can you hold please? Thank you."

Pressing the button got a little easier each time.

Technically speaking, her nine-to-five hours weren't exclusively devoted to ViruFax. She also worked for MemoryMaster Data Cleaning Services, GrindBoost Coin Maximizer, and some product called 'Wixplen.' Despite fielding call after call for Wixplen, walking through her chat script repeatedly, Puzzle continued to have no idea what Wixplen actually *was*.

This job was lousy, pure and simple. Anybody could do it; even an automated system App could've done it, but some people simply insisted on reaching out to a live representative, unwilling to give an automated assistant time of day. That meant putting an actual, factual Program on a Messenger link to read through the same scripts an automated system would read.

Puzzle wasn't an uneducated woman. She got reasonable grades in school, and went on to claim a university degree in film analysis pertaining to cinematography in classic movie files. Film majors, however, were worth next to nothing when jobs in HolWood were already few and far between...

Name : **Puzzle**

Home : **Bellico / Horizon**

Org : **Customer Service Representative**

The next call on the line also was being routed through the ViruFax number. She switched windows, and resumed from the top of the script.

"ViruFax Customer Service, can you hold please?" Puzzle spoke, in her most cheerful voice.

*"What? Uh... maybe? I don't know. I think I'm in a lot of trouble..."*

Fortunately for this customer, authorization had just rolled in for another ten minutes of ViruFax support. No need to shuffle them around the switchboard waiting for the system lag to catch up with the request.

"My name is Puzzle, sir, and I'll be your customer service agent today. Please be aware this chat may be logged for security and training purposes. How many I assist you today?"

*"Okay, so I installed ViruFax Lite a few weeks ago, and it's been working great so far. I mean, without it I would've gotten the Derp from this chick I... anyway, uh, I woke up this morning with this... thing around my wrist. It's like a... a bracelet, or something, with slot for coins on the side. And I got a notification telling me if I don't insert a thousand coins I'd die in six hours..."*

Puzzle didn't need to consult her notebook for this one. Not after fielding several very similar calls today.

"Sir, it seems you've been infected with RansomMe. We do not recommend paying the extortion fee; ViruFax can remove the bracelet for you..."

*"Okay... okay, good. Glad to hear. So how do I get it off?"*

"In order to clean this particular form of malware, you're going to need to upgrade to ViruFax Pro," she recited from memory. "I'll send you a link to the vendor's site, where you can purchase a one-year licence for five hundred coins..."

*"What?!"*

"RansomMe is an advanced form of malware and requires our premium commercial product. I'm afraid ViruFax Lite is not the product you need right now. The link to upgrade to the Pro edition—"

*"Bullshit! I've been on hold for like half an hour, I've only got five and a half hours left, this thing's gonna KILL ME and you're telling me I have to pay YOU idiots half the ransom just to survive? No. No, fuck you, I'm going to your competitors! I bet you that YoHo will get the job done. You can tell your bosses to eat shit and die!"*

The window closed itself before she could offer an apology and a "rate your experience" survey. Probably for the best, there.

Still... this *was* the sixth call she'd had from people running ViruFax Lite, people who woke up with that bracelet stuck to their avatars. The product fact sheet she'd been ordered to memorize said that ViruFax Lite could cleanse 99.99% of all known malware; shouldn't it be able to remove something so obvious and dangerous? Not that her arts degree gave her any innate understanding of malware, but...

Puzzle had brought this up to her supervisor before, an old hag of a woman who disliked any disruption to her perfectly efficient little call center. Just for bringing up the subject and suggesting that they pass feedback along to ViruFaxHQ, Puzzle had been docked an hour's pay and sent back to work. Now she knew better than to point out any of these weird little encounters. Keeping her call rate up was critical, if she wanted to keep this job.

But still... but *still*...

Something had to be wrong.

Who could she turn to, if not her supervisor? Who had a vested interest in investigating when things go bump in the Netwerk?

Only one name rose immediately to mind. It hovered there, not so easy to dismiss. Even if she disliked that particular extracurricular activity... it was perfect for this task, she had to admit.

Specifically: her #BFF's bro, the SJW.

He'd be the one to tap, even if it meant encouraging his crazy vigilante nonsense. If this was right... if ViruFax was somehow involved in all these RansomMe claims... crazy vigilante nonsense might be exactly what the situation called for.

She took a few moments to send a message to Spark... very bare bones, not having time for anything else. The Winder siblings would have to take it from there; calls were stacking up, including quite a few on the ViruFax line. If Puzzle didn't process them, she'd lose her job, lose her salary, lose her paid-for company apartment, and then where'd she be?

So, Puzzle pushed the button, and jumped back up to the top of the script.

"ViruFax Customer Service, can you hold please?"

---

She couldn't hold on any longer. With a desperate howl of need, Spark let everything go... spine arched, muscles straining, her sensory input nerves jangling with the new sensation slamming through her body and flowing outward...

Only after her body finally sagged to the sheets did she get the final tally.

"Seven in a row," Miki replied. "Milliseconds apart, however. I'm going to call it 'simultaneous' for purposes of the official record. On a scale from :( to :D, how would you rate this App?"

It took a few moments for Spark's eyes to regain enough focus to look at the array of smiley faces on the card Maki was holding in front of her.

"Absolutely... positively... a :D," Spark replied, mirroring the expression. "Onesdamn, that was a null of a thing... I'm... I'm gonna need a minute, here."

Miki patted down her forehead with a towel, to mop up the sweat. Perspiration represented yet another strange avatar quirk, like tears and belly buttons... one Tracer had actually installed a software patch to remove, so he always stayed cool and dry. Typical Tracer, honestly; Spark LIKED to sweat. She felt more alive when she knew she was exerting herself, no matter what form that exertion took...

"Maki tried it out last night and ranked in at :D also, but figured a second opinion for the blog couldn't hurt," Miki spoke, flipping her rating card around to tap some notes on it with her index finger. "I think the HoffM-style sensory manipulation gives it exactly the right amount of buildup and release..."

The release may have been the payoff... but Spark was certainly enjoying the aftermath. There was something to be said for the ritual process of relaxing and enjoying your most recent (and sticky) memories, in perfect afterglow. To flex and unflex your muscles, remembering the tension they held moments before...

On the other end of that process, Maki had a nice fuzzy pink towel waiting for Spark to wipe down the rest of the way. Again, she could've reset her avatar and cleaned up in an instant... but there was a ritual to it all. A sensual feeling of fuzz against your skin...

Although Spark wasn't moving particularly fast to tidy up. The pink towel in her hands just... hung there, fluffy and limp, as she pondered it.

Name : Maki and Miki

Home : Curiosity/Chanarchy

Org : App Review Bloggers

Maki peered at it, then peered at her, then peered at his wife and back to their third party.

"Did we break her?" he pondered.

"What? Oh, no... sorry. I'm fine, it's cool," Spark declared, quickly trying to wipe down and make like it was nothing.

Which, of course, only perked the husband+wife team of erotic App reviewers curiosity. After all, 90% of their time was spent satisfying curiosity... and then publishing the results in extensive blog writeups laced with enough purple prose to satiate even the most stalwart of Athena Online housewives in and of itself.

"Go on," Maki and Miki echoed, both quite :D at the prospect.

"Sheesh. It's nothing, okay? Nothing. No-thing. Whatever," Spark replied, hurriedly cleaning up and trying to hide her :| from prying eyes.

This did give Miki pause, tapping a finger on her chin as she studied the expression. "It's almost like you *didn't* reach the peaks of delight moments ago," she commented. "From ecstasy to grumpiness in seconds? That's not like you, Spark. Not as into it today?"

"You call seven in seventy milliseconds not being into it? I'm lucky I didn't coredump!"

"That's not what I mean, silly. I mean I can feel a sense of distance. Something's missing from the experience, isn't it? You're not satisfied, despite being satisfied repeatedly. For purposes of our blog I'm afraid you're just going to have to tell us why. Isn't that right, love?"

"Absolutely," Maki agreed, nodding firmly. "No way around it, love."

Spark sat up in the bed... pulling the sheets with her, feeling oddly self-conscious about her current state despite a lifelong tendency towards the opposite.

"It's nothing to do with the App. The App is delicious. It's just... #ItsPersonal," Spark tried... knowing that wouldn't suffice.

"Off the record, then?" Miki suggested. "One friend to another. I'd like to help, if I can. What troubles you?"

"*Ugh*. Fine. ...honestly, I don't know how to say it. I don't even know what's off, but *something's* off. I've been partying a lot this month, hitting clubs with my #BFF, meeting hotties, rolling n00bs in tourney after tourney, having a damn good time... and it's still not enough. What's the problem? I should be plenty satisfied with what I've got, right? Life's good. Life's *real* good."

"*Mmmm*no. I'd say you remain unsatisfied," Miki filled in. "The little nagging frustration in your voice tells me this quite clearly."

"I'm not sure it's physically possible to be unsatisfied after using that App, Miki."

"Yes yes, as a pro-gamer and a thrillseeker, physical satisfaction is on tap whenever you want it. You're bold enough to seize that particular day. However, you may be *emotionally* unsatisfied. After all, a fun little App review session wasn't enough, was it...?"

"I was kinda hoping it'd be a distraction," Spark admitted. "But look at me, I'm right back where I started: grumpy and sullen. It doesn't make sense, I'm not doing anything *differently* than I used to! And yet my smile's not really there lately, is it? I can :D with the best of 'em but that's not what I mean..."

Miki sat on the edge of the bed, offering a hand for Spark to squeeze. A simple gesture of comfort.

"Finding emotional satisfaction can be difficult," Miki suggested. "Some say that's the purpose of life itself, to explore Netwerk and find your ultimate delight within it. My husband and I find it within each other and within those we invite to our bedroom, but satisfaction is a highly personal concept and often elusive. In fact, you may have already found it, without realizing... hmm. Ask yourself this question; your answer must be the very first thing that comes to mind. Spark... what makes you smile?"

And her eyes strayed to that pink fuzzy towel.

"...#ItsComplicated," she tried.

"That's okay. That's okay. We've pushed you enough; sounds like you've got some introspection to do," Miki suggested, packing up the App for storage...

...and holding out the compressed install file, for Spark to take.

"I'm a strong advocate for intense experiences as a way of defocusing and re-focusing your mind," she suggested. "It seems to have opened doors for you today. Here, take it. The App was an open source freebie, anyway; a proof of concept for HoffM sensory routines. Maybe it'll help you sort through your issues a bit. I do suggest a spatial audio buffer around your room, however... you're a *bit* on the loud side, Spark."

Despite her inexplicable indifference, Spark did eye the App with the shiny black-and-silver icon with no small amount of anticipation. Spark had to admit, it WAS certainly a :D. She approved of :D on general principles. She actually had a couple :D in backup storage at Floating Point for when she felt like a serious round of :D in private.

After accepting the file and tucking it away in her personal inventory, she removed DND mode on Messenger and checked for any missed communiques.

`<Puzzle> Darling! As much as it pains me to admit it, I think I've got a lead your brother might be interested in...`

...which brought back Spark's smile. Whether or not that smile was genuine, she didn't care; she was going with it.

With a snap of the fingers she restored her avatar back to the state it was in on arrival; nice and pristine, with her jacket in place over some highly stylish daywear.

"Gotta get to work," she told the pair. "And hey... next time you need a review, seriously, call me. Don't worry about my #PersonalIssues; I'll deal with them personally. You're my friends, you're oodles of fun, and I wanna help your blog be awesome. 'kay?"

"If you're certain," Miki spoke. "Consent is king, after all. Or queen, in your case. Go forth and find your satisfaction, Spark."

---

The soft clack of tiny stone on wooden board echoed through the quiet of Floating Point's library. Just loud enough to match the near-silent grumble of the one who placed the piece.

That near-silent grumble became louder when the stone was immediately removed.

"Um... sorry," the remover spoke. "But... it was an obvious mistake, I had to capitalize on it—"

"It's fine. That's how the game is played," Tracer insisted. "If you defeat me, you deserve the victory and I deserve the loss. ...I am at a loss for why I'm playing so badly, however. I've grasped the basic principles, but..."

"Not many Programs are particularly good at playing Go," Beta explained. "It demands a certain... how do I explain it... a certain *feeling* for the flow of the stones. I'm still learning my way through that flow... uh. We could play chess, if you prefer? —Mew, that's not food!"

The kitty looked up from a white stone he was gnawing on. "⬜," he pouted, before batting it away with a paw.

"Chess would hardly be fair. I have a chess database installed," Tracer replied, while hovering his next black stone over the board, trying to figure out where to place it. "Chess is entirely pattern recognition and ritual. Ideal for analytical Programs such as myself. ...if I could uninstall the database I would, but it's not an App. I had it patched directly into my core because... hmm. This is painful to admit, but I was young, and I wanted to be better at a game than my sister. Problem is that once she found out, she called me a cheater and refused to play again."

"It's a strange implication, the word 'cheater.' Programs can be modified to do just about anything! If you learn a pattern heuristically, is it any more or less valid than loading the pattern directly into memory? The end result is the same..."

"Doesn't matter. My chess routines are useless, now. A waste of resources," Tracer said... while his mild irritation grew, with more black stones vanishing from the board.

"But... learning to play Go is useless too, isn't it? It doesn't get you closer to finding the 'Great Zero'..."

"Learning is about width as well as depth. The more knowledge I gather across a broad variety of subjects, the higher my overall competency."

"And that's all this is, then...?" Beta asked... her flat-colored irises (and the glasses that she truly studied the world through) examining her opponent. "Just... gathering data?"

"Of course not. I'm enjoying spending time with you, as well," Tracer replied. "Floating Point's not nearly as lonely with you around. I've never liked crowds, I'd rather be alone than be in a crowd, but with a small group around me that I trust and care for... that's quite enjoyable."

"Ah... thank you," Beta spoke, hiding her gaze for a moment to pretend to study the board. "I appreciate that. I'm sorry, I know I sort of forced myself in on your family situation here..."

"You belong here just as much as we do, Beta. We're alike in our troubles, our concerns, and our ideals—"

A jingling bell distracted him, before he could notice Beta's little smile. He'd installed the bell himself, to warn of new arrivals... even if invariably it was just his sister's comings and goings, it helped to know when people were connecting to his server. Especially his sister.

Despite looking identical to the state she left in, she seemed... flustered. Which was only amplified on finding her housemates sitting around playing board games, for some reason.

"What's up?" she asked, trying to play it cool.

"I'm learning the fine art of Go," Tracer explained, placing his next stone. "I must admit, Beta's a wonderful teacher—"

"That's great, hey, Tracer? Can we sidebar in private for a minute? It's justice-y type stuff. I've got a lead I think you'll be interested in. No offense, Beta, but it's family biz."

Sensing it was time to call a halt to the lesson, Beta picked up a short stack of books. "It's fine, it's fine. I'll be in my room reading," she commented, before shuffling along, cat in tow.

...leaving Tracer without an opponent. A rather sudden shift, from a pleasant (if frustrating) little game to an instant burst of serious business. Still, he could adjust; social pattern shifts were normal, particularly with his sister's impulsiveness in the mix. He sat back in his chair, inviting Spark to take the opposing seat...

Which she didn't do. Instead, she leaned forward, nice and confrontational.

"I thought you *hated* Go," she pointed out... after a glance to make sure Beta had already disappeared behind her bedroom door. "Last time we played you flipped the board and wouldn't talk to me for hours."

"'Hate' is a strong word. I would say I have a preference to avoid games in general..."

"I know what this is. You're buttering up Beta, just like you butter up anybody who isn't me," Spark accused. "All part of your 'social pattern analysis.' A little fake smile here, a little fake compliment there, and suddenly you're getting what *you* want. It's always going to be about what *you* want..."

"She's living in my house. I don't see a reason not to be on good terms with her," Tracer spoke, deflecting the accusation cooly. "It benefits me in the long run."

"Yeah, well, it's manipulative as fuck. And I don't appreciate it."

"Curious. Have you considered that my actions are dual-purpose?" he asked. "That I'm ensuring cooperation from Beta in my goals, *and* enjoying spending time with her? You know I won't lie to you, Spark, and I'm being honest when I say I appreciate and admire her."

"You admire that she's a coder who can make us hacktools, you mean."

"I'm thankful she's been studying malware to better support us, yes, but my feelings go beyond that. I admire her philosophical ideals regarding the nature of Programs. I admire her approach to life; she's a gentle soul, kindhearted and calm compared to the sea of chaos that is Netwerk... yes. I appreciate her on many levels, in genuine honesty."

"Hang on. Are you saying you're... *into* her? Seriously? Tracer, the hermit with no social life, is *finally* into girls? You've never made time for romance once in your entire miserable people-hating existence!"

"I don't hate people. I'm *largely indifferent* to people; there is a distinction. And I didn't say the word 'romance,' either. ...I'm extremely curious as to why you're taking offense at this. Is this like the snit-fits you threw when mother made us share our toys? Would you rather spend more time with her yourself? Not doing a good job showing that, if so; lately you've been out and about all day and all night..."

"This isn't about me! It's... *aghh*. ...nevermind. Look, I've got a lead on our next target," Spark tried, switching back to the original reason she'd approached him. "Some scammer bastard who's running an anti-malware protection racket, while infecting the world with a virus called RansomMe. Sounds like a real menace!"

"ViruFax?" Tracer asked.

"The software's called—wait what?" she interrupted, thrown by the casual and immediate response. "You know about this already?"

Tracer steepled his fingers, pulling up a half-dozen notes from his MemoryPalace. They hovered around him, as he referenced each with a quick glance.

"I've had my eye on it for some time," he admitted. "ViruFax, the second most popular personal anti-malware tool in Netwerk. Created by XSept, a rather shady coder and businessman. His company also does home security contracting and has a number of under-the-table deals with the rich and powerful. And yes... very likely XSept is the originator of RansomMe, a virus that popped up a month ago, given only his product is capable of removing it... and infected are often running ViruFax Lite in the first place. Either customers pay the ransom, or pay to upgrade to ViruFax Pro. It's a fine scam, as he gets paid either way."

"And... you're sitting on your ass pushing little rocks around a game board?" Spark accused, switching up what she felt angry about. "What the null, Tracer? People are *dying* out there while this bastard gets rich, and you don't care at all?"

With a flick of a finger, Tracer dismissed the MemoryPalace notes. Focusing in tightly on his sister.

"Contrary to what your friends may think... I am not a 'Social Justice Warrior,'" he spoke. "I don't blindly charge into the fray to mete out vigilante justice every time I see a perceived atrocity. My crusade is specifically targeted at Verity's murderer, the mastermind behind the Great Zero."

"Oh, *bullshit* it is! What about that speech you gave me back at HolyHymnal? We were wrangling hackers and trolls for years before you even *knew* about the Great Zero!"

"We were wrangling hackers and trolls we met *along the path* towards my goal, just as I told you. My focus doesn't mean ignoring every evil we meet, but it does mean focusing our efforts. Spark... we can't heal all of Netwerk's woes, nor do we have any right to play the self-righteous hero. I'm already perpetrating minor evils in the name of good; by limiting my scope, I avoid becoming a complete tyrant."

"And you can sit there and honestly tell me that you've never gone after a guy *exclusively* because he offends your sense of justice and reason?"

Tracer took a quick inventory of his memory, if only to be certain.

Finding no blood on his hands, he responded with the only truth he knew.

"I can say that in all honesty, yes," he responded.

Clearly it wasn't the answer Spark wanted. She'd built up a full head of steam on the idea that either they'd be going after the "bad guys," or that her brother was an idiot and a hypocrite. An answer which lurked in the middle didn't satisfy her.

So, she left. Storming up the stairs and gone.

This thankfully allowed Tracer a quiet moment, to study the Go board again.

It really wasn't a particularly enjoyable game. Normally he would've avoided it entirely... but it was a chance to bond with Beta, and a chance to forcibly broaden his horizons. He was honest about all of that. And even honest about enjoying the time spent with her. So many needs satisfied, all with one simple act of playing a game he didn't like...

A strange sensation, having a care for someone in this filthy world other than his sister. Very strange indeed.

When she first arrived at Floating Point, her bedroom was spacious but bare. The Winder siblings had never needed to use more than two bedrooms before, despite the plethora of bedrooms and living rooms and kitchens and more attached to the outer edges of the great library. One of those empty bedrooms became Beta's new home, soon after regaining her memories.

Since then, she'd put in considerable effort at decorating it. Specifically, decorating it with discarded articles of clothing, half-read books, half-eaten desserts, and various cat toys. Whenever the floor started to vanish under the assorted detritus, she'd nudge some of it aside with her foot to make a walkway... only to have Mew bat the toys and junk back into the path again.

A month of living here, and she'd managed to make the place feel like she'd been living in it for years. In other words... it was perfect.

Plus, there was a system to it all. She'd arranged the books into roughly four uneven piles.

First, corrupt or blanked books which had suffered from unrecoverable data loss; "burned" books. Not much could be done with them, but fortunately, only a small pile of books were truly burned.

Second, books which were largely blank but had some passages remaining in an untranslatable cipher or encoding. The vast majority of the books fell into this category; with any luck, something could be done with them in the future.

Third, cleartext books, which made very little sense despite being perfectly readable. The Winders had dismissed these as fiction or poetry, though.

Finally, there were a handful of promising books which made some sense even if they still felt semi-fictional. It was from this tiny pile that she was reading today. Each book had exactly as many pages as it needed, despite taking the form of a thick leather bound volume. Typically, that page count was very low... this one seemed to be roughly medium-length, compared to the others. Unfortunately many of the sentences were out of order, and the ones which were there seemed to speak nonsense. Even with readable words, it was hardly readable...

A sharp knocking on the door distracted her from the reading.

"Come in, Spark," she called out.

The other occupant of the house leaned in through the doorway, one hand still on the knob. "How'd you know...?"

"Tracer knocks a bit more quietly," Beta commented, without judgment. "What's up?"

"My brother's being a butt," Spark declared, entering the room fully and closing the door behind her. "I gotta get my mind off this mess or I'm gonna explode. I was thinking of playing some Challenge of Champions, and wanted to drop you an invite to join me."

"Really...?" Beta asked, looking up from the book. "I've been hoping you'd ask me, actually! We haven't played much lately... you've been kinda busy."

"Yeah, well... I'm thinking of hanging around Floating Point a bit more. Not sure what I want is really out *there*. ...#ItsComplicated. But, uh, I don't want to interrupt your... wait, those are the books from the library, right?"

"I'm trying to translate the inscription underneath the stone sphere," Beta explained, turning pages. "'Die ganzen Zahlen hat der liebe Gott gemacht, alles andere ist Menschenwerk.' I thought... I almost thought I had the true words, once, but they slipped away. I figured I'd run a comparison search through the less damaged books, and try to find similar words..."

"'True words?' Isn't the messed up inscription just corrupted data?"

"I think it's a sentence, ciphered with a lost language. I mean, not a language like C++ or Lisp, but a lost *written* language. A few words may have trickled through to modern day, though! For instance, have you ever heard the word 'feminazi'?"

"Repeatedly," Spark admitted, with displeasure.

"But do you know what it *means*? No, wait. Do you know where it *comes* from?"

"Uh... I dunno. It's just a thing people say when they wanna be a dick to a woman with an opinion, yeah?"

"I think it's using a similar language base to the sphere's inscription. A lot of our words follow similar structures! Nobody remembers the actual language used, but maybe bits of it survived. I mean, there's only two explanations for what's in all these books... either it's science fiction about a fantasy world, or it's non-fiction about long lost civilizations of Netwerk!"

"I've poked through a few of those books. I'm thinking it's just surreal poetry. Simplest explanation; Tracer agrees with me, too."

"So... he *has* studied the books before? I'm really surprised he hasn't taken more interest in them. I figured this puzzle would be intellectually intriguing to him..."

"*Meh*. All Tracer cares about is his vendetta. He pretty much told me so himself, three minutes ago," Spark grumbled. "Verity gave us this giant mystery box and he doesn't even care. Typical, typical Tracer. ...look, if it's all the same to you, I'd like to not talk about my idiot brother. I'm gonna go beat up idiots in CoC instead. You game? If you wanna keep reading, that's fine too..."

For now, Beta softly closed the book.

She was expecting this question for some time, honestly. If Spark hadn't suggested it, she'd have suggested it herself... if she could've cornered Spark in between her outings across Netwerk. (In fact, Beta was worried that Spark was avoiding her, for some reason. Or that she'd caused offense, somehow...)

It would take all the strength she had, but she'd been preparing for this moment for over a week now. When the question came, she had her answer.

"I'm ready to play," she agreed. "On one condition."

Two gamers sat together, ready to play. This despite one being outwardly worried while inwardly confident, and the other being inwardly worried while being outwardly confident.

"Are you *sure* about this?" Spark asked, showing her worry. "We could just use your throwaway smurf account. Nobody needs to know..."

"No... I need them to know. I need this," Beta replied... while fidgeting in the chair next to Spark's. "It's the next step, isn't it? I already announced to the world that I was alive with ReMinder. I need to claim my life back, little by little. ...um, your volunteer moderators are on duty though, right? I'm sorry I'm bringing my troubles to your door..."

"Don't worry about it, we're good to go. Okay, now, look at the red dot on the wall over there," Spark suggested, pointing to the shared HUD element. "I've tied you in with my Peep stream, so you'll be on the facecam view alongside me. And... just ignore the chat, if it gets bad. Okay? Ready to go? Sure you're ready to—"

"Please start the stream before I lose my nerve," Beta politely but quickly requested.

A side window appeared showing the two women sitting side by side in front of a rotating background of fanart submissions and promotional wallpaper. The Peep chatroom popped up nearby, already flooded with messages.

"Okay, folks, today's stream is a bit impromptu but I assure you it'll be worth it," Spark started... putting on her best bright gamer smile for the audience at home. "I've got a special guest with me, a good friend of mine. Now, some of you know who this is. Some of you THINK you know who this is. And some of you are about to type something into chat that gets your ass #KickBanned for all eternity... yep, there's three of you right now, and there goes three of you. Let's keep it civil, folks. We're all here because we love to game, right?"

"Right!" Beta piped in with, also wearing a smile, a bit more strained. "Hi, everybody. I've been a longtime fan of CoC, even if I'm not a pro at it like Spark. I'll do my best!"

And she dared a glance at the chat.

```
<DethShard> holy *** look who it is
<DethShard> B E T A N U D E S
* DethShard has been banned from this channel.
<99Bitches> B E T A N U D E S
<Forzen> N E T A B U D E S
<Reifu> Hi Beta! <3
* Forzen has been banned from this channel.
* 99Bitches has been banned from this channel.
<TrumpCard> 2 grill streamers, amazing value
<Elbow> omg censorship feminazi mods banning
#CodeHonesty
* Elbow has been banned from this channel.
<MegaMilk> playing hanzo today spark?
<Reifu> HANZO OR RIOT
<MegaMilk> HANZO OR RITO
<TrumpCard> damage and support in duo lane on the same
stream yeeeaaa
<Polearm> are you two forming a new pro team? we see
5v5 full stream one day plz?
```

...despite the bans, it was a relief to see plenty of messages NOT related to #CodeHonesty. Beta knew not all gamers were toxic monsters; plenty of them liked to have fun and couldn't give a toss about hashtag mobs and politics. They were united by their love of the game, just as Spark suggested...

"Actually, I'm switching up the roles a bit," Spark explained to the chat. "I've had a lousy day and playing a damage role is just gonna make me go aggro and screw up. You lovely #Sparklers don't wanna see a salty Spark, do you? I'm going to try support today, to calm and focus myself. Beta here's going to go damage instead; she's been practicing with Hanzo. So hey, no rioting, you're still getting some Hanzo action. Now, let's kick some ass!"

Only ten minutes in, and it was already clear they were losing this one.

"Dammit!" Spark/Cheerleader called out, across the team channel. "Mime, #WTF, why are you feeding? You just ran directly into that guy's axe! That's like the fifth time you've done that!"

"#CODEHONESTY #CODEHONESTY #CODEHONESTY!" Mime shouted back, while diving headfirst into the enemy team's blades. The Chaos players, only too happy to score yet another free kill, accepted Mime's head on a platter. More gold for them, more progress on items, more lopsidedness to the battle...

Feeding was a moderatable offense, and Spark would damn well be reporting that guy to the CoC mods. Throwing the entire ranked game, throwing his *own* rank out the window just because he took exception to Beta being on his team... that was a dirtbag move. Absolutely a dirtbag move...

In anger, she punched a nearby tree with one of her pom-poms. A light rustle of leaves from high above settled around her avatar.

"I'm so sorry," Beta/Hanzo apologized, sword at the ready, unwilling to get jumped again like last time. "We'll get into a different game once this one ends. I mean, our other teammates are cool with me being here... it's just a bad roll of the dice to run into a troll in our first game, right?"

"That's the problem with trolls. Even in the minority, they can ruin everybody's fun," Spark grumbled. Despite her colorful attire and cute little pigtails, she managed to project an aura of mopey annoyance rather than good cheer.

Unfortunately, one bad apple spoiling the lot was the least of her problems.

As the next waves of Goblins and Gnomes rushed towards the center of the lane... Spark eyed the weak little NPC enemies, puzzled.

"Why's that Goblin glowing...?" she asked. "Did I miss a game update patch note or something? Beta, smash down this next group."

"But I'm still recovering mana. I'll be empty if I spend it on a quick wave clear..."

"Something's wrong. Better safe than sorry, right?"

Raising his straight blade, Beta/Hanzo rushed towards the Goblins, ahead of their Gnome wave. With a flurry of strikes from the Eight Fold Path Technique, he cleaved a bloody swath through the little green freaks...

...except for the oddly glowing one, which charged directly past the ninja. That cruel blade passed right through it, without dealing any damage whatsoever. Its eyes red and teeth snarling... it let out a cry, then charged right for Spark/Cheerleader, hand outstretched...

With a golden RansomMe cuff on its wrist.

No time to sit and think about what that could mean. Spark cartwheeled out of the way, and took off running into the jungle. Goblins didn't chase too far into the jungle between the lanes, after all... normal Goblins, anyway.

This Goblin gave chase, and with great bounding leaps and bounces that were impossible for the slow little hordelings. Whatever rules this game had for its NPCs, the cuffed Goblin was cheerfully ignoring them.

If Mime had been helping out instead of screwing his team over, maybe she'd have enough speed-boosting items to make her escape. But with Hanzo out of mana and nobody within reach to help... escape wasn't happening. That only left one option, to stand and fight. Not that Cheerleader was an effective combat role, but hopefully it'd be enough to whack a single Goblin.

A human pyramid built up underneath her, buffing the damage of all allies within range (including herself)... and she sprang from the top of it, twisting in mid-air to come down pom-poms first on the critter. The strongest possible single attack the Cheerleader could manage...

After a perfect landing she tucked and rolled, coming up with a pom-pom flourish. The goblin was dead, mashed directly into the jungle floor in a green splatter of goopy guts.

The splatter did nothing to hide the golden glow of the RansomMe bracelet locked firmly around Spark's wrist.

"Spark! Spark, what's going on?" Beta called out across the team channel. "Did you manage to kill it?"

With some regret... Spark tapped a HUD button, to start the surrender vote.

"Everybody vote surrender," she asked her team. "We're losing this game anyway thanks to the feeder... and I've got to go. Something just came up."

Ending the Peep stream early was a disappointment for some viewers... but others, who recognized the bracelet that was now permanently affixed to Spark's wrist, understood the reasoning. When it followed her all the way back to Floating Point, Spark knew this was just as bad as she'd suspected.

She held out her arm for all to examine. The metal bracelet clasped tightly in place, one-size-fits-all... with a handy coin slot on the side, in case she felt like paying to remove it. Instructions had been planted in her memory the instant it clamped into place, suggesting she insert a thousand coins or die within a day. Very straightforward, big points for a clear and usable App, Spark supposed...

When a moment of silent study extended into several moments, it was clear neither Tracer nor Beta had any immediate ideas for removing it.

"Take a selfie with my new toy, it'll last longer," Spark joked dryly.

"Can we wait a few hours for it to activate, then restore Spark from a backup?" Beta suggested. "I know it sounds heartless, but it's the cleanest solution. All she'd lose is any memory made since her last save point..."

...which made Spark feel a bit sheepish.

"I, uh... I haven't been backed up in years," she admitted. "I mean, Floating Point lags if we store huge files like backups since it's all cloud-distributed, and that messes with my Peep streaming, and, uh... yeah. #SorryNo. If this deletes me you may have to settle for teenage Spark, assuming you can even find the backups my mother made after I started modifying my avatar..."

"You don't make regular backups?" Beta asked, surprised. "Despite constantly throwing yourself into dangerous situations? I mean... I don't make backups either, I can't afford a backup storage service—all my coins go to my mother's care server fees—but I was assuming you two had something arranged..."

"Do I look like I'm made of money? I'm a game streamer, Beta. It brings in the coins, yeah, but it's not like I'm a Horizon magnate or anything like that. Only rich bastards can afford quality offsite backup storage."

"Even without being corporate magnates, we should have enough money to simply pay the ransom outright," Tracer interjected. "Either that or purchase ViruFax Pro to cleanse it. It'd put a dent into the house fund, yes, but your safety comes first. In my research, the malware didn't resurge in victims after being paid; it deletes itself without a trace."

"I'm not sure this is the normal sort of RansomMe, bro. I got infected by a game NPC; how is that even possible? I thought this only hit people who used ViruFax in the first place..."

"New infection vectors, perhaps. Regardless, my vote is to pay it off and be done with this. Seeing as Floating Point has three people now, voting is a plausible resolution tool. All those in favor?"

"Forget it. I told you already I want to go after these guys," Spark replied, lowering her outstretched arm. "Now it's beyond a vendetta against the dirtbags in general; it's personal. I say Beta hacks this off my arm, then we take 'em down!"

...which left Beta. Who was raising her hand, albeit not particularly high.

"I think... I think we should just pay it. Tracer's right," she agreed, quietly. "I don't want Spark to be hurt, and I don't know if I can remove this thing. I know you guys are expecting me to be your coding guru and help with your hacktools and stuff, but... I'm honestly not *that* experienced with hacktools yet. I can't promise I'll be able to remove it before it kills her..."

"Two to one in favor," Tracer spoke... pulling a shiny coin from the shared house fund. It bore a 1k crest, signifying this file had one thousand coins worth of cryptocurrency built into it. "Spark, your wrist again, please?"

"You really want to dodge doing the right thing here, bro? You know ViruFax is dirty. Zero or no Zero, I'd call this an opportunity to do something about a murderer... if we pay the bracelet and it backspaces itself, we lose what could be a valuable clue to help track down and prove their crimes."

"Not worth risking your life foolishly," Tracer insisted. "We may argue and bicker, Spark... but we're family. I care for you, in my own way. One thousand coins is a bargain for keeping you alive. Now. Arm, please?"

Knowing it wasn't worth protesting any further... Spark raised her arm again, showing off her new fashion accessory.

With confidence, Tracer slid the coin into the slot.

3.14 seconds later it slid back out, falling to the floor.

A tinny sad trumpet noise played across the room, wafting out of the bracelet, *wah-wah-waaaah*...

...followed by a young boy's voice, reciting a line of nonsense in a sing-song tone.

"*Die ganzen Zahlen hat der liebe Gott gemacht, alles andere ist Menschenwerk,*" the RansomMe bracelet chirped.

As the residents of Floating Point stood there in stunned silence, Mew batted at the 1k coin on the floor with a paw.

Calmly... Tracer retrieved the money, before speaking up.

"Whoever made RansomMe knows about Floating Point," he realized. "Personal or not, Great Zero-related or not... we are officially on this case as of now. Beta, do what you can to disable the bracelet. If you'll excuse me, I've got some very quick research to do if we're going to crack the bastard who did this to my sister and make him talk... within the next five hours."

A circle had been cleared around Beta's bed, to make room for her patient.

The first test was to purchase and install ViruFax Pro. If the scam was to get money by ransom or by software sales, that would've worked... but whatever variant of the RansomMe virus had attached itself to Spark, it wasn't even detected by ViruFax Pro. Which meant five hundred coins down the drain, and back to square one for Beta's analysis.

Dozens of Apps hung in the air around her, providing data readouts, analysis, and other incoming streams of information about the bracelet on Spark's arm. Now and then Beta would move between them, frowning at the numbers... holding her glasses a bit closer to the App now and then, to get a better look...

Completely focused on the task, with no bedside manner at all. The comfort side of the healing equation was being handled by Mew, who lapped at Spark's fingers with a kittytongue. Fortunately, she hadn't applied combustible nail polish today.

"🏙️🔒💜," Mew promised, flicking his tail back and forth excitedly.

But given the doctor remained silent for minutes now, the one who had almost four hours left to live felt the need to speak up, even if it'd interrupt that focus.

"Soooo...?" Spark asked, while trying to lay perfectly still. "Anything? Anything at all?"

Beta fixed her glasses back on her nose, blinking a few times as her perspective settled in place.

"Nothing," she responded, with a pout. "Nothing at all. I can see what it's doing, but I'm not sure how it's doing it. Like I said... I honestly don't know enough about malware yet. I knew *just* enough to help with Cup8, but... it's not up to this task. I wish I'd spent more time studying security systems instead of reading old books. Life was so quiet, there weren't any more Great Zero sightings, I didn't think there was a rush..."

"Hey... nobody could've predicted this. #ItsCoolYo," Spark insisted. "And we're not expecting you to be able to remove it. We'll be going after XSept and his crooked company before the day's out. It'd be *nice* not to have a prewritten death certificate on my arm when we do it, but... one way or another we'll beat them."

"Less than a day... what if we can't figure this out in time, Spark? What if... what if..."

"Focus, Beta. We can do this. *You* can do this," she adjusted. "You're awesome, remember? So be awesome. Hanzo in training, ready to go ninjutsu all over some stupid malware's ass. Ninja strike at an enemy's weak points—what's the weak point of the bracelet? How does it work?"

"I just told you, I don't know how it works! I mean... at best, *maybe* it's..."

"Maybe it's what...?"

"Well... I ran some comparisons to known malware systems," Beta explained, pulling over a floating App window. "I'm sorry, this is only a guess and I could be completely wrong, I mean, I'm not an expert here and I could be talking out of my butt—"

Spark raised her braceleted hand, to stop the flow.

"Don't do that," she interjected. "Don't. You don't have to jam a self-depreciating preamble in front of every opinion. You don't have to apologize for everything, either. I know you can't be certain, but clearly you have an idea. Just say your idea. Say it straight."

Beta started to speak again... but skipped ahead a few dozen words in what she planned to say.

"I think it's a HoffM-style sensory overloader," Beta stated, getting right to the heart of it. "That's the kill method. It uses the avatar-based physics system against you; in this case it blasts your nerves with a mixed array of sensations so intense that it literally blows your mind. I've seen implementations of HoffM sensory systems... I mean, not *fatal* ones, not even any particularly intense ones. More like booze or drugs or sex toys, things like that. But without advanced HoffM source code to study, I'm not sure how to stop the malware."

"See, wasn't that hard, right? So you need a... a... oh. Um."

The silver-and-black icon in her inventory was practically glittering in response.

"I... might have an open source version of a HoffM-style sensory manipulating App," Spark admitted. "A really powerful one."

Beta perked up considerably. "You do? Oh, that would be perfect!" she spoke, clasping her hands to her chest. "With the actual source code, I can analyze it completely! Insert debug statements, run traces, find weaknesses from the inside out! Can I have a copy?"

"Okay, so... this is... look, I don't want to offend you or anything. Or give you the wrong impression about me... especially given all the crap you've been getting from all sides by perverts lately..."

Without looking, she held out the silver-and-black icon of the erotic App given to her by Miki earlier that day. Metadata including the App's name and purpose—and a copy of Miki's blog post about it, conveniently posted an hour ago—appeared alongside the actual code.

"Right, look, I know what you're thinking," Spark preemptively protested. "Yes, I happen to have an orgasm generator in my pocket. And I swear you're not living with an evil pervert. I mean, I'm a pervert but I prefer to see myself as an ethical one, and I don't want you to think that—"

"This is quite well designed!" Beta replied, having lost interest in the self-depreciating preamble, in favor of studying the code, scrolling through it quickly. "You know, it's a misconception that the best erotic Apps are the most expensive ones. That's a fallacy set up by the App industry to push overpriced product when simple versions and open source implementations of the same basic concepts work just as well..."

Beta only looked up when she realized Spark's jaw had been sagging ever since she started talking.

"What?" she asked.

"I... uh. Wow?" Spark tried. "Okay, I was not expecting *that* reaction. I was thinking more something along the lines of 'oh my!' followed by furious blushing..."

"You mean your reaction, then?"

A quick check in a mirror App confirmed that. Spark's rosy complexion had become far rosier.

Which was ridiculous. Utterly and completely ridiculous, which only made her blush harder. Yet another quirk of avatars, which ramped up skin tone color saturation during moments of embarrassment...

She was Winder/Spark, after all. Professional thrillseeker, legendarily uninhibited and willing to try anything at least once. Under her belt lurked years of experience storming social hotspots, getting tangled up in all kinds of fun that her mother would never have approved of. She'd been *gifted* membership in three different casual hookup clubs off that reputation alone. Spark didn't care what the world thought of her; it was her body, her life, and she commanded it with great gusto.

So... why was she freaking out like the innocent little girl-next-door caught with a porno movie file?

Why wasn't Beta, the modestly-dressing and timid little girl-next-door freaking out, for that matter?

Perhaps realizing the thoughts running through her head... Beta offered an answer to that last question, at least.

"Spark... I'm a woman too," Beta pointed out. "Not as adventurous as you, but it's not like I've never tried an erotic App before. Who hasn't? ...anyway, I don't know why you're so surprised. I look modest but everybody knows the truth now, don't they. I'm a legendary fan of sex toys, right...?"

Now that smile looked less amused and more... askew. Desperate.

"...I don't have any real modesty left to protect, so why should I bother pretending otherwise? All of Netwerk's seen me playing with myself. Copies of those pictures are tucked away in hundreds of servers and will never go away, not ever. I'm... I'm conscripted as the world's most famous whore, so... what right do I have to judge anyone?"

"What? Whoa. Beta... no," Spark tried to interrupt with. "Don't be like that. You're not—"

"But I am!" Beta protested... smiling at her own plight, a sort of horrified smile with wide eyes. "Cup8 saw to that when he posted those pictures. I'm Netwerk's personal sex toy App! If that identity thief had her way, anybody could've had me! You know what this means? I can't have a normal relationship anymore. Not with my reputation. So why not use erotic Apps every night, like I do now? It's all I've got left. It's all... tainted. All of it..."

Perhaps her runtime skipped a few seconds. Somehow, Beta went from standing upright as a confident code analyst, to sagging into Spark's arms and sobbing so hard she couldn't see properly. Just like the early days before and after her memory wipe... broken and crying. Wretched, really...

Spark rocked gently, using the tactile feel between two avatars to try and soothe Beta's sorrows.

"In the long run... none of that's going to matter," Spark promised. "You saw it today. We banned some guys from chat and had one bad teammate, yeah... but plenty *were* ready to accept you. There are decent people out there; Netwerk's not universally awful, Beta. There's... someone out there in Netwerk who'll love you, someone true and honest. I know it."

The muffled reply had none of the brief moment of strength it held moments ago. "R-really...?" Beta managed, into Spark's shoulder.

"Absolutely," Spark answered, with a smile. "So for now let's focus on the road ahead, okay? I know what'll help: coding! You're always feel your strongest when you're programming. How about looking through the source code of my App? Maybe you'll be able to make a counteragent to RansomMe! Okay...?"

After a gradual comedown... Beta was ready to pull away. To stand on her own feet, and look at the file again. She had to wipe away the last of the tears to be able to read it properly, but having a meaty pile of source code to dig into certainly helped push other problems out of the way.

Spark let her work in silence. Beta liked to code quietly in her room, pushing the world away... lost in her own universe of functions, variables, and curly braces. No sense disturbing that feeling with words; Spark was content to lie back and marvel at the intensity of the programmer's focus. Let that focus wash away the brief moment of sorrow which had taken her moments before.

After scanning the entirety of the program... Beta started inserting new functions of her own design. Output statements here, temporary variables there, all designed to produce some data she could work with. Soon, her compiler was grinding away... and a new icon appeared, one with a silver-and-pink motif to it, rather than silver-and-black.

Name : **SparklePop**

Genre : **Erotic**

Compiler : **Beta**

"I'm calling it SparklePop!" she decided, with a bit of whimsy. "It's yours and yours alone; I won't give a copy to anyone. You know, I could even tweak it so it works more to your liking, or add all sorts of new features! Uh, after we're done saving your life, of course. ...so, um. Now, I know you're a little embarrassed and that's okay, but—"

"What? Huh? Who's embarrassed? Me? I'm not embarrassed. Not at all. I'm an adventurous, sex-positive woman who isn't ashamed of her desires!"

"Oh, good! So you won't mind demonstrating it for me!"

"Um," Spark added, her brief rush of false confidence annihilated.

"I've added a debug output log to the HoffM system functions," Beta explained, quickly scanning over her code modifications. "Once it starts flooding your avatar with sensation I'll be able to study how it interacts with your code, which could lead me to a breakthrough that'll defeat the RansomMe kill method. So go ahead, put it on and fire it up! I'll get my log analysis tools online and we can crack this nut in realtime!"

"Um," Spark added again.

That earnest little smile, so eager for pending scientific discovery, ultimately broke her resolve.

Most Apps designed to help connect thoughts together ended up resembling a "Wall of Crazy," a disorganized map of linked files and fragments. In contrast, Tracer's private MemoryPalace allowed him an all-encompassing room-sized "Sphere of Crazy."

On retiring to his study, he'd fired up five different search agents to crawl Netwerk for any information he could gather on ViruFax. These clouds of data automatically filed themselves away in his mind, temporary strings of light linking them together pending verification and fine-tuning by Tracer himself. Already, several threads had formed... many concerning the software itself, but many also concerning XSept, the man behind the software.

"Shady" didn't begin to describe XSept. He worked in secret, allowing none within his company access to the source code of his projects. He arranged deals outside his marketing and sales divisions, providing custom security firewalls to the rich and/or famous. He'd even made a deal with Cup8 for personal security, according to documents Tracer had fished out of a loose personal bank account. Despite owning a large-scale corporation... clearly XSept was a control freak, and perfectly happy to work off the books if it let him retain all his secrets.

If Tracer's team had to crack the security around XSept directly, getting the job done in the next four hours would be nearly impossible. Smashing their way into the core of a leading security-focused company server went beyond dealing with underworld scum packing shady Apps. You needed hardcore tools for hardcore jobs. Harder than Tracer had on hand.

Not that he lacked tools in general. There was his charming and very practiced smile, as Spark had pointed out earlier... and a secret weapon of his own. If XSept could work off the books, so could Tracer.

Tracer was the not-entirely-proud owner of a backspacer, one of the deadliest hacktools in all of Netwerk. Illegal to own in Athena Online, heavily discouraged in Horizon... but freely available in the Chanarchy, notably in the black market server where he bought it years and years ago. He kept it handy at all time, despite never having found just cause to actually fire the weapon.

This was a weapon of last resort, he'd told himself, at the time of purchase. If he had to use his backspacer, he'd have failed. He'd never fire it in anger, never go after a target unrelated to Verity's killer with it. To do so would be to shatter what little flimsy justification he had for his personal war, after all.

Granted... he'd been sorely tempted quite a few times to use it on someone who offended his sense of decency. Bastards who mocked the idea of justice, who didn't care who they hurt if it got something they wanted. Petty creatures like Cup8, the last one he'd considered using the backspacer on...

Instead he'd held his temper and never fired that weapon, not even once.

At least, that he was aware of.

But when he heard his sister's screams from across the great hall of Floating Point, that weapon was in his hand as he charged up the spiral stairs.

Whoever infected her knew about Floating Point; the mysterious other-worldly inscription was proof of that. They were vulnerable today, moreso than any other day. And if the malware crafter had followed her home to finish the job... or if the bracelet triggered early... or if something else went wrong, if Spark was suffering, if she was dying, if she died, if, if, *if*...

Still screaming, in what sounded like absolute agony. Which meant she wasn't dead yet; still time to do something, anything...

Despite this initial flurry of panic, Tracer knocked at the bedroom door rather than barging right in. Pure instinct, not wanting to burst through the door to Beta's room without proper permission. He caught himself in that social nicety a moment too late and aimed his weapon, ready to backspace the door off its hinges—

—before hiding it behind his back, hands folded there as he stepped away.

"Everything is fine!" Beta declared, through the crack in the door. "Everything is completely fine. Sorry for the noise. Sorry."

"What's going on in there?" Tracer asked, trying to peer around her. "What's happening with Spark—?"

"Just data collecting and testing!" she insisted. "Nothing dangerous. She's fine. Everything is fine, how are you? ...what's behind your back?"

"Nothing," he lied. "Everything is fine, then?"

"Yes. Um. Very interesting results! We'll be done soon. Meet you downstairs in... uh... let's say fifteen minutes."

The door latched silently, as Beta belatedly and roughly threw up a spatial audio block around her room.

---

Tensions ran quite high in the library, as the three gathered to present their findings.

Spark seemed... off, to Tracer. Like she'd been caught with her hand in the cookie jar. Strange in and of itself given his sister's utterly shameless nature, but she didn't seem keen to talk about it. The color saturation of her skin ran a bit higher than usual, although that could've been a side effect of the malware...

To explain that malware, Beta became the bearer of bad news. A role she didn't particularly enjoy playing.

"I can... *sort of* counteract the bracelet," she explained. "We figured that out by comparing it to similar, um, tools. It uses sensory overload in order to set off a chain of data corruption that slowly kills a Program from the inside out; like a physical hacktool, except it rides tactile sensation rather than collision detection."

"We turn off Spark's sense of touch," Tracer understood. "Problem solved."

"That won't be enough. HoffM implementations are multisensory; all her inputs could be exploitable, we can't know for sure that it's just touch. The only solution I can think of... is to split Spark away from her avatar. No body, no senses. It's dangerous; we've evolved to need our bodies, we're lost without them. I mean, uh, literally lost, as in getting lost in the server's memory space if she's completely disconnected... but it has to be done. A disconnected Program with no physical presence can't be hacked by this malware. When the bracelet activates in three hours, it won't be able to hurt her."

Spark showed off a bracelet on her other wrist... this one bright pink rather than golden. "Detaching your brainstem? There's an App for that," she joked. "This is also my safety tether, a way for my mind to find my body again. Unidirectional. It'll let me go back to my avatar on demand, so I don't just float away into nothingness. Beta whipped it up in minutes; she's amazing."

"Not amazing enough. Problem is, once RansomMe activates, it won't STOP flooding your avatar with pain until you're dead. So... you'll have to remain in a detached state until we can remove the malware," Beta added. "However long it takes."

"So? I'm sure you can crack it in no time!"

"I have absolutely no idea how to crack it," Beta admitted. "Not even a hint of an idea. That's not me being insecure about my skills, I literally would not know where to begin... not without the source code of ViruFax itself. I'm so sorry, Spark... but you could be stuck without your body for hours, or maybe days..."

"I'm betting on hours. Minutes, maybe! You smashed through Cup8's Zero virus infection in minutes, remember?"

*Stars. Stars upon stars, entire galaxies of them, spiraling out into the infinite...*

Beta shivered slightly, as if feeling the cold of the void on her skin.

"I'd rather... no. No, I can't do that again," she replied. "The technique I used to accelerate my runtime was... dangerous. I directly interfaced with the heart of Floating Point itself, to become a living cloud computer. If that sounds crazy to you, that's because, well, it *is* crazy. Too crazy to play around with unless we have no other choice. And as much as I'd rather not leave you in the dark very long, the best method is to secure Spark's safety first and then find another option."

"Well... damn. Okay, Beta, you're the expert here. And hey: I survive this one way or another, right?" Spark pointed out. "The RansomMe's failed. You did good, Beta. Plus... I'm guessing my bro has some ideas on how to crack open the bracelet by cracking open XSept's skull. We may not even need to use your App, with him on the case! Am I right or am I right, Tracer?"

"You're wrong," Tracer spoke, barely over a mumble.

"I'm... wrong?"

"I need more time as well," he admitted. "Before today I'd only done the bare minimum of research on ViruFax and RansomMe, just enough to determine the

Great Zero wasn't involved. Three hours is not enough to complete that work, much less plan and execute this investigation. If... if I'd prepared more, if I'd done due diligence on this instead of shoving it aside..."

"Okay, so... get to doing the due diligence," Spark suggested. "We have time, thanks to Beta's hard work. Take as long as you need to get the keys to my handcuffs. No big deal."

Now, Beta looked to Spark with concern. She'd gotten some confidence back after their awkward encounter, which was good, but...

"It's not exactly a little deal," Beta tried to explain. "You've never been without your body. Sensory inputs are how we interact with the world, and without even a sense of gravity, you'll be completely adrift. I was born without eyes... I know what it's like to live adrift in the dark. It's scarier than you can imagine, even with my other four senses online and working. If all five of yours get cut off for days on end..."

"So I'll be bored. What's the problem?"

"This isn't like sleep mode, where you're simply offline... we can't even do that, because RansomMe is blocking you from sleeping. You'll be conscious the entire time, lost in the dark, and... and..."

"Look... does it really matter?" Spark reasoned. "It's happening, one way or another. You need time to find the cure, and this will give you time. Trust me to see this through and I'll trust you two to see the rest through. Beta, you're new at all this, but... Tracer and I have gone up against the wall dozens of times. We take the risks because we know neither of us will give up. I can do eighty years with the lights out if need be, because I know you'll both be there on the other side. I trust you with my life. Okay?"

Beta started to protest. Her mouth opened to form the words... but they were silenced, in the face of that one most powerful word.

Trust.

She couldn't say she really trusted her friends before, could she? Snowi and Cup8. For a time Beta thought she was loved and cherished by them, but it was all a lie, and some part of her knew it. There wasn't trust there, not the kind of deep trust Spark was showing in her today. Her, someone who just wandered into their lives a month ago as a stranger in need. What was a stranger compared to a brother or a sister?

And yet... Spark trusted her. Even trusted Beta enough to expose herself in the most vulnerable way, to test out that HoffM App and gather the data they needed. That was a bond she never had with Snowi or Cup8.

"...you can count on us," Beta agreed. "We'll make sure you're under for the shortest time possible. ...um. I think now that we've settled that question... we should actually put you under immediately. Just in case this new variant of RansomMe has a shorter fuse than the normal strain."

"No problem," Spark declared, with a grin. "Show me to my cell, warden."

It took a precious hour to set up Spark's containment, but Beta insisted they be completely thorough. Gravity had to be disabled, bindings arranged, connection locks put in place. The room had to be completely severed from all stimulus, even packets from across Netwerk, to avoid opening any inputs for RansomMe to flood Spark with corruption.

In the end Spark was floating in weightlessness over her bed, held in place by a network of simple vectors. She was going to suggest leather and chains for the lulz, but given the... rather intimate scientific experiment she'd engaged in earlier, joking around about sex in front of Beta felt... wrong. Maybe in time she'd have enough distance to be comfortable with that, but not today.

The two she trusted the most were there, to see her off.

"I'm so sorry we have to do this," Beta spoke, for the umpteenth time.

"Just don't leave me in there until my entire wardrobe goes out of style," Spark suggested. "Otherwise you're paying for a shopping run. ...and Tracer? This is not your fault. Beta, don't let him beat himself up over it. ...see you on the other side."

And... nothing. Her eyes remained open, unblinking, as the disconnection App came online. Her pink bracelet glowed brightly, providing a beacon for her code to return to its body once the coast was clear.

"...why would you think this was your fault?" Beta asked, puzzled.

"Because it is," Tracer explained... flat and firm in tone. "All of this could've been avoided if I wasn't so lousy at being a crazy vigilante. If you'll excuse me, I'm going to my study to redouble my efforts. Good day, Beta."

"Nope! I'm coming with you," Beta insisted. "And don't say anything like 'I work best alone.' I've used that line myself plenty of times. Four eyes are better than two, even if two of them are burnouts."

"Beta, I work best—"

Hands on hips, bumping them a little. Her long skirt swayed as she pouted up at him.

"What did I *just say*? None of that, now," she warned. "Let's get to work."

Leaving Spark alone, floating in a zone of absolute silence within in her web of vectors. Or rather, her body within a web of vectors... while her program drifted in the runtime of Floating Point.

A single thought filtered through her code:

*I guess it is kind of boring in here, after all.*

Opening up the Sphere of Crazy for Beta to peruse was more difficult than Tracer had expected.

He'd never done tandem research before. MemoryPalace was his and his alone, a private world of compartmentalized research. From the operator's manual (itself stored in MemoryPalace) he knew it was *possible* to grant permissions to another Program to sift through the files, but it required a series of security checks and confirmations. Granting an enemy access to your innermost thoughts was risky business, and MemoryPalace had originally been created by privacy-minded paranoid lunatics. Much like Tracer, really.

To Beta, the fact that a self-declared paranoid like Tracer trusted her enough to open this part of him, the same way Spark trusted Beta to find a solution... it spoke volumes. She'd come to them a complete stranger, and in a few short weeks had become a confidante...

After confirming and re-confirming and re-re-confirming that he trusted Beta enough to open his brain to her, it took another twenty minutes or so to teach her how to search through the tangled web of related information.

"It's all about the connections," Tracer explained. "The software includes an automated agent which ties every single file together, trying to pre-emptively establish commonalities, relationships, things like that. Often it's wrong, but the act of breaking or confirming those links helps me strengthen my own conclusions..."

"What are these blue files...? Your memories?" Beta asked, flicking a few into her guest workspace without opening them. "Why are they connected to your files about RansomMe, though?"

"MemoryPalace allows me perfect recall. Even a casual, off-hand remark about something may be related to my current research. So, it ties in memories which may be useful. ...of course, since I've done considerable research into malware over the years, odds are there will be plenty of false positives."

"I'm not sure I feel comfortable being able to call up any one of your personal memories at will..."

"You don't need to help with this, Beta. As much as I enjoy the company, I'm perfectly comfortable working on my own. You're the same way, yes? You rarely code in tandem..."

"Rarely, but... sometimes I do. The happy memories I have left of Snowi were of those code jams; for all her failings she was a friend in that regard. I loved working together on Apps with my peers," Beta admitted. "And the results were always stronger than if I worked alone."

To keep focus on the task at hand, Tracer highlighted all connections to RansomMe, XSept, and ViruFax. It whittled down their work to a smaller subset of the overall file cloud.

In addition, he pulled up basic readmes on the array of hacktools at their disposal.

"We have a limited palette to paint with," he admitted. "Despite our crusade, our weapons of war are a bit mediocre. The goal today is to figure out how to crack into ViruFaxHQ and steal the source code to ViruFax, using only these resources. Connection lock collars, my connection tracing eyes, Spark's avatar-disabling nail polish... and a smattering of avatar disguisers, low-power key cloners, password crackers, things like that. None of which are likely powerful enough to directly beat a professional security company's security."

Beta studied each file, doing her best to memorize their capabilities. Without the perfect recall of a MemoryPalace she was at the whim of a Program's ordinary highlight-focused memory process... a way of condensing information usage by quickly forgetting seemingly irrelevant details. She'd just have to focus her recall, then.

The tools were rather sad, and not much could be done about it. Hackers either crafted their own Apps, or purchased highly expensive hacktools from black market dealers who were typically picky about who they sold to. On top of that, ViruFax was locked down in ways they could never fully know. Even if they broke the piggy bank and ran out buying up weaponry and security breakers, they'd likely fail to smash their way in.

Which left Beta's heart sinking a little.

"I've been wasting my time, haven't I," she mumbled.

"Hmmm?"

"In the month since I got here I've been tinkering with little Apps, or reading books and trying to decode silly mysteries. It was a waste of my time," she clarified. "You don't need an avid reader, you need a hacker. I should've spent every waking moment devoted to learning hacktools and security systems. Here I am eating up the limited runtime of Floating Point just by *existing*, and I'm doing nothing to really help you..."

"Go."

"...you want me to leave...?"

"The board game, Beta, the board game. Go. You've been teaching me Go. That's not wasteful," Tracer specified. "And before you insist it is, that it's just a game... remember, it broadens my horizons. From a functional standpoint, learning the tactics of Go has helped me. And... I'm an honest man. I meant it when I said I value the time we spend together. Do you not feel the same way?"

Trust. He trusted her, enough to open his mind to her. Would Cup8 have done the same? Did she trust Cup8 to that degree?

"I... yeah. I value that time," Beta spoke. "This month has been wonderful, honestly. I've found peace in Floating Point, here with you. And with Spark. I just worry that I've indulged in that peace frivolously..."

"If you must see your life in Floating Point as a cost/benefit ratio, happiness should count as a massive benefit. I'd rather you spend your time on that which brings you happiness. Beta, would you really enjoy devoting your life to becoming a security expert?"

"Well... no, not really," she admitted. "I mean, I do like the idea of tools like the Great Zero remover I made; Apps that help improve lives, not tear them apart... but there's just so much out there I want to do. So many mysteries and so many projects..."

"All of which are worthy," Tracer said. "Everything you do adds to your robustness as a person. It's all self-improvement, across many vectors. I'm not Cup8 or Snowi; I'm not going to demand you optimize yourself in accordance with my own selfish expectation of who you should be."

"I thought you believed in optimization, though...? Part of your rationalist lifestyle..."

"I've optimized according to my own values, as should you. And if your values are distributed across a wider array than mine? So be it; that's what's best for you, as an individual with free will. You're not a single-purpose App, designed for a single task."

"We evolved from Apps, though..."

"We broke free of the limited scope that comes with being an App," Tracer added. "And therefore, it's our right to live our lives as we see fit rather than fitting ourselves into little functional holes. You are more than the sum of your code. Don't think you need to turn yourself into a password cracking App just for me. I want you... to be you. To be Beta. I like you as Beta."

If she'd plucked the glasses from her nose and turned them around, she'd be able to see the light saturating blush on her cheeks. Fortunately for her, she hadn't noticed... and Tracer hadn't either. At least, he hadn't pointed it out.

"Let's not dwell on what could have been. Let's dwell on what must be," he suggested. "Besides... Spark and I have dealt with hard targets before you came along. I find that it's less about the raw power of your weapons and more about finesse in how you use them... a technique I'm willing to admit I learned from her. Rather a lot like Go, come to think of it. It's about seeing the board—comprehending the entire sphere of thoughts and ideas—and finding the right weakness..."

That entire sphere was open to her, now. She could see the connections the same way Tracer saw them, weaving back and forth between seemingly unrelated files. Even mundane things like MyFace profiles of employees could somehow hold the key to getting the source code, presumably. Otherwise, why would they be included here...?

A brief glimmer in those profiles caught her eye.

Beta pulled over the file, expanded it. Paged through selfie after selfie, each one unique...

"That's a pretty impressive wardrobe," she commented. "All I really have is my usual sweater. Why would someone buy so many different outfits and accessories? It must be expensive..."

"Ask Spark," Tracer spoke over his shoulder, while he looked over a press interview about ViruFaxHQ's top-notch security. "She's constantly wasting her hard-earned coins on bling and hairstyles with embedded particle effects. It seems frivolous; I wear the same avatar every day without any issues..."

"How do I start up a search and tie the results into your palace?" Beta asked, the idea gnawing at her.

"Drag the file onto the hovering magnifying glass on my desk."

Scooping up an armful of selfies, Beta dumped them all on the glass to begin a visual matching search.

The numbers which piled up afterwards represented more money than she'd ever seen in her entire lifetime.

"I've crossindexed these photos with a fashion pricing catalogue. XSept's personal secretary spends five times her annual salary on clothing," Beta concluded. "Unless she's found some super-efficient coin grinding method in her spare time... I'd say she's getting money or gifts off the books. Think it could be relevant?"

That was enough to pull Tracer away from the eight articles open in front of him. He walked over, studying the fashion plate selfies, each tagged with search engine results for common market values... and noted the impressively high numbers with a raised eyebrow.

"Very curious," he agreed. "I'll dig a bit deeper into her. See what else you can find in the cloud, though; other angles, other leads. We don't want to wear blinders to other possibilities."

"Will do!"

As they returned to various corners of the workspace, Beta flicked through file after file. Nothing stood out yet, but she did her best to consider each one in turn...

Until another caught her attention: a blue glowing file. Transcribed thoughts... with her own icon embossed over them. It had tenuous connections to the rest, not likely important, but sheer curiosity drove her to open the file anyway...

...before realizing, moments too late, that this represented Tracer's very personal thoughts.

```
I don't think I'm capable of actual love. I SAY that I
loved Verity, and that I love my sister. But perhaps
what I call 'love' is simply a fear that the loss of
their input will somehow diminish me? If so, I can't
call honestly call that love. It's simply selfishness.

If I can't truly recognize familial love, how could I
possibly recognize something as nebulous and vague as
'romantic' love? It's not as if I feel physical
attraction in the way my sister does, so I can't even
```

rely on that metric. I may live and die never knowing if I actually loved anyone if I'm unable to comprehend it in any reasonable manner.

My feelings for this stranger who has worked her way so deeply into my life are unparsable. Therefore, I cannot truly know if I love Beta.

Perhaps that's for the best. She's been wounded deeply by people who claimed to love her. I cannot, WILL not, add to that pain just to satisfy my curiosity. She deserves so much better than that. She deserves so much better than a morally dubious fool such as myself.

As an avid reader, she was able to ingest all four paragraphs in the time it took to realize she had no right to ingest them.

With the file slammed shut, she quickly sent it spinning off into the sphere of thoughts. A quick glance confirmed that Tracer was too busy looking at MyFace profiles to notice this momentary breach of his trust...

"I think I have a plan," he announced.

"Yes! Good! What is the plan!" Beta replied, using way more exclamation marks than she'd intended.

"XSept's secretary is almost certainly also his lover," Tracer explained, pulling over a series of connected files. "All the signs are there, even aside from lavishing her with gifts. She has access to his inner lair, the private residential wing of the building where he does his work; several of these selfies were taken in that location."

"So... if we can find a way to copy her access key...!"

"Precisely. We don't need new hacktools, we need good old fashioned social engineering. Our existing CloneKey tool, despite being quite a simple App, is more than capable of solving the problem. See? Finesse, not power."

"Excellent! Let's do that, then."

"Also, I don't mind you reading that file you closed just now."

A denial leapt to the front of Beta's thoughts, while her innate honesty held it back. The end result was a terrified silence, smiling away as if nothing was wrong... as Tracer called over the file with her icon stamped on it.

"I opened my mind to you because I trust you," he explained. "That doesn't mean I trust you *not* to look; in fact, I trust you *to* look, I trust you to know anything in this room. Perhaps socially it's not considered the 'correct' way to express myself, but I don't see the harm."

Now she made an attempt to speak, even if that attempt was a failure.

"But... you... I..." she tried. "I shouldn't have..."

"Why shouldn't you? It doesn't change anything," he spoke, with a light shrug. "I meant what I wrote. I will not add to your burdens by heaping my own on top of them. I'm not chasing after you romantically, Beta... I have no right to do so. Now, I believe our best chance for approaching the woman is to find her in a social setting, such as the bar she's known to frequent. Shall we depart?"

And he offered his hand to her.

Taking that hand felt like more than a polite suggestion of travel. All of this felt like more than Tracer was making it out to be... his matter-of-fact tone hiding so much. But that mask of casual expression was difficult to tear away, now that it had been firmly fixed in place. Calling him out on it would be... improper.

Carefully, Beta took his hand. Decided to push the other problem away, for the time being. Only for the time being.

"Let's go," she agreed. "The sooner we can save Spark, the better."

Yvon stood out quite badly, which was very much the point.

This bar hadn't been her scene in years. She wasn't a struggling professional anymore, working her way up the corporate ladder, trying to make a better life than she could by grinding coins all day. No... Yvon had *made* it. She wore the most expensive avatar fashions, she drank the most expensive cocktails on offer, she sampled the good things in life. And while all her "peers" scraped and struggled and came to this bar to complain about their lot in life, she sat by herself and sipped merrily, sticking out badly with her high society avatar, to tell them all... *I made it, and you haven't.*

At first, returning to this middle class watering hole was a funny way to pass the evening. Rubbing it in their faces, showing off how dumpy little Yvon had finally gotten her due...

Except by this point, she may as well have been drinking at home. Intentionally alienating a bunch of salary slaves meant nobody wanted to go near her, and lording it over them had lost its flavor.

Yvon downed the last of her expensive swirl of flavor data, ready to depart for the evening, when a fresh cocktail presented itself.

The smooth man slid right onto the stool next to hers, simultaneous with the new beverage.

"Allow me," he offered. "You seem to be on your way out, but I'd love to chat a bit before that."

Immediately, Yvon sized him up. The chunky-thick glasses didn't seem to suit him and the business avatar he wore wasn't top of the line, not like the one her provider wore... but he wore it better. This was a man with practiced poise, possibly in human resources or marketing.

"Interesting," she admitted aloud. "Well. My evening's been rather dull, so I suppose a little chat would be nice. And you are...?"

"If you'll permit me, I'd love to save that for a surprise reveal later in the discussion. It's childish, but I feel a certain dramatic pacing makes the evening far more enjoyable."

"Hmmm. Okay, mystery man. What is it you wish to 'discuss,' then...?"

"What does anyone come to this white collar beerhole to discuss?" he asked. "Work. Career. Money."

"Excellent, going well, and I have plenty," she summarized.

"Really, now. Simple as that?"

"Simple as that."

"I'm not going to say I'm owed your darkest truths simply because I bought you a drink," the man spoke. "You can sit there and remain quiet, sipping away without offering me any response. A reasonable plan of action, given the silly fellow who's chatting you up in a bar. But... I will say I don't quite believe you. Are you interested in my reasoning why?"

Strange. No mockery or insult in his tone at all... playful, but in a way that tugged at her curiosity. He composed every single word, every intonation...

Yvon knew when she was being played. She'd played plenty in her lifetime, after all. But... what was the harm? It wasn't like her evening was getting any better.

"I'm interested," she said.

"You come here night after night to show off. And why shouldn't you show off? You're living the high life. But... why show off, if you're entirely satisfied with it all? This isn't just about convincing them that you're a success. You're convincing yourself of that success... meaning you're not entirely convinced that your career is on track. Now, If I'm wrong... enjoy your drink, and walk away without a word."

Considering each word... Yvon picked up her fresh cocktail, downed it in one go. And spoke in reply, rather than walking away.

"Who are you recruiting for?" she asked.

A business card was offered, in response.

"The childish dramatic reveal!" her companion declared. "It's all about timing, isn't it? Name's Trowe, of Human Resources. I represent YoHo, the current leader in personal anti-malware protection. We may be in the Chanarchy, but we know the proper shape of success."

"So you scouted me ahead of time," Yvon understood. "You know I work for ViruFax."

"I know you work for XSept. I'm willing to bet you hold the keys to his kingdom, in fact. He values you, and so do we."

"Ooooh, and you were doing so well! I'm afraid he values a pretty face, not my skills," Yvon corrected... unable to keep a note of bitterness out of her words.

154

"I recognized that immediately, and played him like an audio file. It's how I wormed my way into his wallet, and into this ridiculous dress. But if you're looking for Netwerk's finest information manager, that would not be me."

"Actually... I'm not hiring for a secretarial position," he noted. "I need a master manipulator—someone who can scale the echelon of ViruFax using pure people skills, to the point where a paranoid lunatic like XSept is willing to hand over his access key. I want the next major headhunter for my human resources department. Someone who can spot a mark from a mile a way... and I say this in all admiration: I think that's you."

She probably should've taken offense. But... she'd opened the door for that sort of an evaluation, hadn't she? Being judged on her 'womanly' skills rather than her secretarial skills...

Being paid for one thing while being valued for another was no way to live. It had been fun at first, just like lording her status over all her former peers at this bar. But XSept stopped being fun ages ago. Why not? Why not dump that dead-end job, in favor of one where her *real* skills were the thing she was valued for...?

"Take your time to consider the offer," he said, filling in the silence. "This is, of course, assuming my evaluation is correct and you *do* indeed hold an access key to the vaults of ViruFax. ...would you mind? I'd love to see it. Call it a token of good faith."

"Don't have it on me, I'm afraid," Yvon said, with a shrug. "XSept's rather security-minded. We've had incidents of people pulling their keys out of inventory in public, letting hackers running CloneKey Apps make copies. Now the keys are kept inside the building itself. Even mine."

...odd, how that seemed to deflate the HR fellow.

"Ahh. Shame," he replied. "Well. Consider my job offer; I'll be in touch—"

"I'll take the job."

"Really? That quickly?"

"That quickly. ViruFax'll be going under soon, anyway," Yvon spoke... finding herself oddly enjoying the idea of it. "Horizon's sending around a pair of code auditors from HonestDevelopments soon to check all XSept's code. It's all thanks to that #CodeHonesty thing, and... between you, me, and the bar? I think XSept's got an off-the-books ghostwriter. When the company falls... I want my golden parachute. I want to go to YoHo. I'll take your job offer, Mr. Trowe."

"Code auditing? For a Horizon-based company?" he asked, puzzled.

"Horizon doesn't mean you've got a blank check to do whatever you want. They're worse than Athena Online's crazy legal tangle, in a lot of ways. But... companies in the Chanarchy can do whatever they please, yes? YoHo would be safe haven. I'm game. Let's do the paperwork."

"The paperwork can wait. We'll be in touch soon," he replied... rising from his bar stool. "This was just a feeler, after all. The boring part will be handled by the boring people. But, once all the signatures are in place... I'll be happy to greet you into the YoHo family. Until then, Ms. Yvon."

'Trowe' departed the bar soon after.

Moments later... Tracer entered, wearing his normal avatar again.

He returned to a small booth on the side, passing the glasses back to their original owner. She fixed them in place, despite the worries in her brow.

"There's no actual career opportunity waiting for Yvon," Beta pointed out. "If she quits her job, expecting to land a new one at YoHo..."

"Live by the sword, die by the sword," Tracer suggested. "She's manipulative and banks on that manipulation, playing a dangerous game as a result. If she chooses to believe the lie I fed her, that's her own problem."

"You're scary good at fooling people like that. I mean, I remember watching through my glasses as you, well, practically seduced Cup8 into our trap. Creepy. But you're still an honest man, right...?"

"I am, with those I care about. I care less about Yvon's career path than I do my sister's life. This is the world we live in, Beta... social engineering is the best tool we have for getting through the layers of security between us and a target. It's pure finesse."

"I guess, but... I can't say I like it. Maybe if we'd approached her honestly, she'd help us stop her corrupt boss. Clearly she doesn't love him, so she wouldn't protect him... and he *is* killing people. She could've been an ally in the fight against that..."

"Not worth the risk," Tracer responded. "She's likely just as corrupt as he is, and unworthy of trust. It is what it is, Beta. This world is not to be taken gently. Besides, that lie got us what we needed."

"Huh? But she didn't show you her access key. We can't get to the ViruFax source code without a clone of her key..."

"No, but she gave us our next lead: the code audit. To save Spark's life... we're going to join the ranks of #CodeHonesty."

Technically speaking, they could've joined those ranks just by slapping up the hashtag on a MyFace posting. But that alone wouldn't get them through the door and into ViruFax... for that, they still needed an access key. Just a different type of access key.

Obtaining it was far easier than obtaining Yvon's key had proven to be. Even a minimal amount of research led them right to a weak link in HonestDevelopments... a new auditor hired from the "ranks" of #CodeHonesty, who had turned away from coding Apps nobody wanted to buy in favor of becoming an inquisitor with a badge and a clipboard. A badge he was more than willing to show off to anyone with a cute smile and a pair of breasts, particularly after throwing back one or two pitchers of beer at a local sports bar.

Even with confidence in his ability to dupe the hardiest of blowhards, Tracer was unwilling to risk putting on a female avatar and sashaying into that testosterone wading pool. Beta would be too recognizable due to her glasses and vocal tics, even in her anonymous JaneDoe store bought avatar... which left only one option for this particular con.

As Tracer attempted to enjoy the poorly coded pretzels and poorly played CoC matches on various windows hovering around the bar, he politely ignored the tittering and guffawing happening across the room. Something "JaneDoe" couldn't manage.

"An entire company devoted to hunting down so-called frauds like me..." Beta pondered. "It's scary how quickly #CodeHonesty took root. I know Snowi used misattributed open source code, and I can't say I approve of that, but... how can anyone believe there's some vast conspiracy of corrupt developers out there?"

"It's a fun narrative to buy into. Take our target, for example," Tracer suggested. "Bonn hasn't moved any serious numbers, despite chugging away at his Apps for years. Eventually, you have to ask yourself... what's the root cause of my failure? Rarely will anyone willingly admit their own lack of talent is the culprit. Easier to find an external enemy, someone you can blame for all your woes. Such as 'evil feminazi vagcoders flooding the market with me-too clone Apps and casual games,' as he posted to his MyFace..."

"What's a 'vagcoder'...?"

"I can only assume it's a clever portmanteau of 'vagina' and 'coder.' I've no sympathy for Bonn or his like; they rely on irrational assumptions to explain away their woes."

"I feel a bit sorry for him," Beta admitted. "I looked at a few of his Apps before we left the house. They're not BAD... a little UI polish, a few tweaks here and there, they'd be quite nice. Maybe... I don't know, I could offer him some tips. Anonymously, perhaps? I know he'd never listen to anything from Beta, but I feel like I should be lifting up my fellow programmers, not tearing them down like this..."

"I wouldn't bother. But I'm me, not you. You're a better person," Tracer stated, matter-of-factly. "And... it seems our work here is done."

This, in response to the ravishing blonde strolling her way over to the bar to join them.

A cloned HonestDevelopments access key arced neatly into Tracer's waiting hand. He tucked it away in personal inventory, after glancing around to make sure nobody had seen.

"Your friend over there is an asshole," Puzzle spoke, carefully sliding her silk-covered rear onto a bar stool. "And you're an asshole for making me seduce an asshole. I trust my act of duplicity is a success, and that copied key will somehow get you closer to Spark's salvation...?"

"Seems legit," Tracer confirmed. "And it'll continue to seem legit, even after minor edits. You've done well."

"I wouldn't have even replied to your summons if you hadn't told me Spark was in danger. I don't like you, Tracer. I don't like the things you do or the people you do them to, and two wrongs don't make a right in my book. ...when can I see Spark? How is she doing?"

"She's going to be fine, and she'll see you again after she recovers."

"Because you won't let me in the front door of your secret little clubhouse, not even at a time like this," Puzzle clarified... for the plus-one at the table. "Did he tell you that? He doesn't let Spark have any little friends over to play, because he's a paranoid lunatic. No one other than you, it seems. You must be Beta. I've heard of you from Spark."

Beta perked up, trying to bring some good cheer to the gloomy conversation. "And you must be Puzzle. Spark told me all about you! Hello! It's nice to finally meet you!"

"Odd. She told you all about me? She hasn't told me anything about you."

Beta's offered hand drooped a little.

"Not that it stops me from asking. A new roommate in my #BFF's life? Of course I want to know more. But no, she dodges, she changes the subject. #ItsPersonal. #ItsComplicated," Puzzle spoke, in a slightly annoyed tone. "Makes me wonder what the issue is with you two... and now she's gone and gotten herself in unspecified danger, and Tracer's keeping me in the dark, and I can't even go see my friend in her time of need and I am *understandably* annoyed—"

"Spark's been infected with a strain of RansomMe that we can't buy off," Beta clarified. "And don't give me that look, Tracer. Puzzle is her #BFF, not the 'enemy,' certainly not some outside party. We have to trust *someone*, in the end... she deserves to know the details."

Puzzle's hand tightened, gripping the edge of the bar.

"Spark. How long does she have?" she asked Beta, directly. "I know that malware—oh no. Oh no, I'm the one who exposed her, didn't I? When I suggested she look into it—!"

"No no, it's okay! Totally unrelated to that. Anyway, I found a workaround. Spark's in a state of sensory suspension to keep her alive as long as it takes to find a cure. I promise you, Puzzle, your #BFF is going to be just fine! She's safe in our private server. And... once this is all over... I'd be happy to give you a personal tour."

Hands which had tensed on the bar relaxed, somewhat, after Beta quickly soothed that spike of worry.

"Thank you," Puzzle spoke. "Apologies for my foul attitude, and thank you for being a genuine soul. ...unlike *that* secretive recluse. I'd keep an eye on him, Beta; he worries me greatly. Tracer, if you need a walking pair of tits again, please decline to call me. Good evening and I'll be in touch."

That departure left the pair in still and silence, for a time. As silent as they could be surrounded by rowdy gamers cheering on a five-on-five teamfight and clashing glasses of beer together.

Tracer cleared his throat, to break the stalemate.

"For the record, I was just trying to do what's best for our family's safety by denying all visits," he tried. "Spark agreed with me; allowing others access to Floating Point could be dangerous. Especially now, with the Great Zero malware on the loose..."

"I understand, but... I didn't agree to that myself," Beta pointed out. "So if I want to have Puzzle over as my guest, I will. Unless you'd like to revoke my access key and kick me out...?"

"That's... Beta, I would never... no. I won't do that. ...I will admit that my standing policy does edge on paranoia, under the guise of reasonable precaution. Hmm. As an outside observer, would you say I'm incorrect in this situation?"

Beta thought it over, looking inward for a moment as she did.

"Yes and no," she decided. "You're not incorrect, it's important to keep Floating Point safe. I wouldn't exactly suggest Sunday brunch open house galas and we do need to be on guard against the malware author. But yes, you're also incorrect because you're turning away people who could be true friends, such as Puzzle. ...like how you wanted to turn me away, at first."

"Which was a mistake," Tracer agreed. "One I could only see in hindsight. You have a valid point. It can be... difficult, sometimes, to see the world as anything other than a series of risk factors..."

"Good thing I'm always going to be around to keep your eyes open," Beta spoke, with a sweet smile.

"Ah... thank you. Now if I may ruin the mood, I feel obliged to point out that you once thought Cup8 and Snowi were true friends. In hindsight, you saw the truth..."

Those names broke her smile, momentarily. But she pulled it back in place, refusing to let it go.

"I made mistakes, yeah," Beta admitted. "But opening my heart wasn't one of those mistakes. I can't believe that no matter how I've suffered, not if I want to be the person I want to be. They're the ones who chose to hurt me; that was *their* mistake to make, not mine. An act of violence is an active choice by the aggressor."

Immediately, MemoryPalace highlighted a crossindexed sentence from one of Tracer's most frequently accessed personal trauma reels.

"You've heard that saying before?" he asked.

"Hmm? Oh, of course. It's from that book that Verity wrote, right? I've been reading up on her. She seemed like a very wise person."

"Wise beyond her years," Tracer agreed. "And taken from this world far too soon. She's the one who gave Floating Point's keys to us; they were one of her earliest finds."

"Really? I wonder where she found them..."

"We'll never know the details, I'm afraid. For now, we'd best return home... we need to plan before we move on ViruFax until morning," he said. "And I'd like to check up on Spark."

It started with an itch on her inner thigh.

Which was absurd, of course. She had no avatar whatsoever, how could it be itchy? And why would a Program be itchy at all unless they installed an App to MAKE them itchy? Which Spark would never do. Therefore, she couldn't have an itch on her inner thigh. Even if she did.

She was tempted to scratch it, but even if she had access to her avatar the ragdoll-and-vector bondage would've kept her from acting. Instead, she *imagined* herself scratching the itch... which worked about as well as expected, i.e. not in the slightest.

"Bored now," she said to herself. Not that she could hear her voice or actually say the words, but she imagined she could.

Dark. Silent. Boring. So very boring, hours and hours of boredom.

Presumably not days of boredom. She hadn't been under that long, right? No internal clock, either. No access to any of her Apps, no stimulus allowed, to prevent the bracelet from finding an in-road to her code. Likely the RansomMe cuff was jangling away, trying to hammer her avatar with deadly sensation at this very moment...

"Stupid cuff! You can't kill me that easily!" Spark shouted back at it, taunting away. "You think you can kill me with boredom? You can't. I'm a gamer, I'm a champion, I can beat you. And no, talking to myself is *not* a sign of going nuts, either."

Hearing voices replying, *that* would be a sign of going nuts. And she hadn't heard any voices other than her own, which she was also not hearing, so hey. All good.

*Itch itch.*

What was that, anyway? Something scratchy... no. Something soft and stringy. Idle curiosity drove her to analyze that itch. Soft and stringy, yes. Pleasant, not itchy, no. She thought it was an itch because it just barely brushed against her skin, but if she thought about it more... it was definitely not awful. It was, it was, it was like...

Yarn. Like a pink and fuzzy sweater made of yarn.

In absence of any other distractions... no club outings, no shopping jaunts, no sex toy reviews, no marathon Peep streams... Spark had only her thoughts to play with. No way to shove them aside, either, claiming that #ItsPersonal. Nobody to deflect away from...

Which meant she had to face the fact that Beta had been on her mind, to the point where she'd avoided going home to avoid dealing with that fact. And unmistakably that feeling creeping up her skin—no, not creeping or crawling, a nicer word like *brushing* or *caressing*—belonged to Beta's favorite sweater.

Was Beta out there, in the room with her disconnected avatar? Maybe some sensation was creeping through despite their precautions? No; if that was the case, Spark would be dead. Plus... the rather intimate way that fabric was brushing over her skin, that couldn't possibly be prim and proper Beta. No way, no how...

Of course, this was the same Beta who surprised her by chatting away openly and frankly about digital dildos. The same Beta who talked her through the puzzle of Puzzle, far wiser than stupid Spark was when it came to janky relationship drama. Whatever image Spark had of the woman, it was likely built on a pile of mistaken assumptions.

Mistakes. Failures. Mustn't repeat them, have to learn from them...

"I screwed up with Puzzle," she admitted, aloud. (As much as "aloud" could be a concept, in the void.) "All because I don't know what's what. I have no idea what love is because I never looked for it before. Physical satisfaction on tap, just like Miki said, that's my deal..."

"But it's not enough," she replied. "Miki was right about that, wasn't she—?"

"Whoa. *Whoa.* I am *not* going to #CrazyTalk with myself here."

"Well, who else are you going to talk to?" she asked herself. "Nobody's here. That's not Beta out there touching you, either, so clearly you're hallucinating those feelings. Why not hallucinate voices, too? Besides, better to have it be your own voice than someone else's. Or would you rather some sinister cackling Great Zero be chatting with you?"

"Not responding," Spark iterated.

"Fine. I'll do the talking for us, because you're not willing to admit the truth," she insisted. "You've got friends aplenty, like Puzzle. But there's more to life than friends; you want to find something deeper. Actually, no. You don't *want* to find it, but you *need* to find it, and fear's holding you back from the thing you need. Fear that you might, believe it or not, love Beta. Y'know, the cute one you've been avoiding lately."

Barking back a denial wasn't going to help her case, so she stayed quiet. Except for the part of her that kept going.

"She's different, isn't she? A whole new personality archetype compared to your other friends. She's scratching an itch you didn't know you had; a need for comfort and calmness, affection and kindness. Opposite of your brother, really. Closest you've had to that is Puzzle, but it's not quite the same, is it? With Beta, there *could* be something true and wonderful... if you're willing to explore it. Emotional satisfaction! But noooo, not Spark, she'd rather pretend nothing's different in her life. For a risk taker, you're sure being risk averse. #Coward."

If she had teeth to grind, she'd be grinding them right now in an effort to block out the noise. The feeling of pink yarn sliding its way all over her body wasn't helping; what would've been a pleasant distraction became a reminder of the thing she didn't want to think about...

"I get why you're doing it, honestly; you nearly lost your #BFF because you're lousy at recognizing love when you see it. Only idiots repeat their mistakes and you're no idiot, are you? Dodging Beta rather than possibly screwing things up, yes, that makes sense—especially since she's *living* with you, which would lead to #AwkwardCity if it all went wrong. The safe play is to avoid the gank by avoiding the lane. But don't you believe in playing to win?"

"It's not a game, dammit!" she shouted back at herself.

"Of course it isn't," Spark replied. "It's your life! But the same strategy applies. Since when does Spark shy away from risk? Either you deal with this here and now or you'll be stuck in the same stalemate for ages. Miki was wrong; it took the opposite of an intense experience to de-focus and refocus your mind. You lost all intense sensations, so now all you have is your thoughts. So face them! Do it!"

That sweater. So comforting and pleasant to the touch, like the best blanket in the world. Maybe built on a foundation of mistakes and assumptions... but nevertheless keeping her warm, here in the dark of the void.

When she embraced it, allowed that feeling to cover her entirely... there was no more itch, as well as no more need to yell at herself. So, she stopped fighting it and simply... relaxed, hovering there in the nothing, wrapped up in the knowledge that Beta was out there trying to save her life.

---

Nobody in Floating Point slept that night. Technically sleep was a long-term gambit to conserve the longevity of your data and allow your thoughts to refocus and refresh, so missing a night wouldn't hurt them *too* badly. Besides, too much needed to be done prior to the clock cycling back around to morning.

Beta kept a vigil over Spark, not that it meant much. Spark was completely isolated; whatever internal struggles she was going through would be hers and hers alone. Technically Beta didn't have any way to reach her, not even to say "I'm here, and I'll be with you until morning." Even so, Beta felt the need to sit by her bedside... she owed Spark that much.

Meanwhile, Tracer was busy forging badges. HonestDevelopments, despite being so focused on hunting down fraud, hadn't invested heavily in security for personal identification. Given anyone could join a hashtag campaign by saying they were in a hashtag campaign, it wasn't a huge surprise that the loose company spawned from that loose mob would play things loose. Turning one legitimate badge into two semi-legitimate ones was a simple enough matter, even for a non-coder such as in himself working with a smattering of cheap hacktools.

As soon as the great mechanical clock in Floating Point's library chimed out nine, brass weights gleaming in the morning sun... two people who were certainly not Tracer and Beta were ready to depart.

"I don't like that you have to go out into the field with me on this," Tracer admitted, adjusting the generic tie on his generic JohnDoe male avatar. "You're not trained the way we've trained to run cons and deal with dangerous situations. You could just give me your glasses again..."

Beta shook her head. "If we get our hands on the source code, the fastest way I can scan it for what we need is to be there in person. Walking you through that process will take too long, and a code auditor needs to clearly know how to work with code to be convincing. Tracer... I can handle this. I want to do this. Besides, I took a few basic avatar self defense classes at the community center!"

Which made Tracer doubly glad he'd packed away his backspacer into his inventory this morning. Just in case. Not that he had any experience with it, no more than Beta had experience with kickboxing, but presumably it would be easy enough to operate. Easy enough to take a life, should the situation call for it.

Approaching the tacky polyhedral rhombus of ViruFaxHQ, "Toff" and "Bool" marched with purpose. They merged in with the steady flow of employees, each ready to clock in for another day of meaningless corporate busywork... but rather than passing right through the security checkpoint with the others, they broke off to confront the guards directly.

"HonestDevelopments," Tracer declared, holding up his forged badge. "We're here to see Mr. XSept. I'd say he's expecting us, but this is a surprise code audit, so we'll pretend he's not expecting us."

The somewhat thick guard studied the badges a few times, not sure what to make of them. Fortunately he had an App which knew what to make of them... one which beeped softly to indicate the signed data files were legitimate. Which meant the pair of illegitimate auditors wouldn't have to immediately reconnect to a getaway server or six in an effort to outrun any attempts to chase them away.

"We demand immediate access to the source code of ViruFax Pro," Tracer recited, from the script they'd agreed to earlier. "As this is a code audit, we will deduct points for any delay in presenting us with the material. We can't allow any alteration of the files prior to examination."

"Um... I'm gonna need to call this in," the guard suggested. "And Yvon—uh, Mr. XSept's assistant—hasn't reported for work yet, so it might take some time to track down the boss—"

"Any longer than five minutes will be considered an automatic failure."

That lit a fire under his feet, as the guard immediately dashed off to let XSept know what was going on. No teleport, Tracer noted... most servers gave their moderators access to cheats to bypass the physics system, and bypass pesky things like walls. Apparently XSept was too paranoid to allow anyone to cheat within his personal security paradise.

Four-and-a-half minutes later, the guard was ushering them off to the private wing of the building.

The desk with Yvon's hovering, glowing nameplate remained unoccupied. She'd taken the fake job offer seriously, it seemed... leaving her boss standing in front of it, forced to receive guests directly.

XSept. Tracer had studied him extensively, since the situation grew dire. He could be considered scum of the lowest degree, if not for the fact that so many esteemed figures within Horizon's financial pantheon followed the exact same career path—betrayal, backstabbing, double dealing, and no small amount of crime.

But what was crime, in Horizon? This was a libertarian paradise, where the only illegal act was to bite the hand that fed you. While the family did its best to maintain public respectability, as long as you didn't stick out as an obvious moustache-twirling villain, you could do anything you pleased without consequence.

The idea of it... abhorrent. Utterly so. Actions should have consequences, Tracer knew.

Maybe XSept would've masked his displeasure in the face of the Horizon family, but he had no intention of doing so in front of Horizon's lackeys. They were lackeys, after all.

"You could have told me you were coming," he complained. "Kincaid said I'd have forewarning..."

"Scheduling change," Beta filled in. "Um, I'm going to need access to the complete source code, including all libraries and—"

With a gesture, XSept dismissed his guard. Within moments, the three were alone.

"Look, we all know what the score is here," XSept spoke. "So you two sit around out here for an hour, then go on your merry way. I get a clean bill of health on your little clipboards, and Horizon continues to profit off my hard work. Everybody wins."

...a side arrangement. Of course. Why would HonestDevelopments have to be *honest*, after all? Another black mark for XSept, in Tracer's opinion...

Still, this meant they were now very far off script. Beta looked to Tracer for guidance... and Tracer put his social engineering skills into overdrive.

"It's not as easy as that," Tracer explained. "Listen, we're all very busy people here. I've got no intention of taking up your time or getting in your way any more than I have to. We all know your code's clean... and even if it's not, who honestly cares? Not me, and certainly not Kincaid."

"Yes, exactly. So, why bother with any of this? Just show me where to sign and we can all walk away..."

"Like I said... it's not as easy as that. We've got loggers and trackers to validate everything we're doing," Tracer continued. "If we never even look at the code, it's going to throw a red flag. We want this to be as seamless as possible, right? All you need to do is show us the code, give my companion a few minutes to smile and nod at it, and *then* we can sign and walk away. The system's satisfied, the Horizon family's satisfied, we all go back to making money."

Beta smiled and nodded, to show her compliance. "Right! Exactly!" she added, perhaps too enthusiastic to show she was great at this 'grifting' thing. "I just need a peek so I can say I had a peek. Simple and easy! No big deal! Won't take very—"

"I didn't think there were any women in HonestDevelopments."

Exactly the kind of thing Beta would react to with surprise or offense, on instinct. Tracer stepped right in, blocking her visually, before that could happen.

"Can we please get on with this?" he insisted, mirroring XSept's annoyance. "Kincaid's waiting for us to put this matter to bed. I don't really want to keep him waiting, do you?"

And that's how they got into the impossible to access inner lair of XSept.

This was theft. Pure and simple, Beta was stealing the source code of another developer... the sort of thing that #CodeHonesty had accused her of in the past.

As she rapidly scanned through file after file, searching for any RansomMe-related functions, she tried to keep that worry out of her thoughts. It had to be done, no way around it... a lesser evil to solve a great evil. The sort of thing Tracer constantly talked about, in this ends-justifying-means sort of vigilantism discussions...

While she was performing the world's fastest crash course in security software programming, Tracer's job was to distract XSept.

"How do you do it?" he pondered. "Work out of your bedroom, I mean. It'd drive me nuts, having my office be my home. You'd never feel like you were off the clock..."

"I'm never off the clock," XSept said. "My work is my life. I made that decision long ago. It's everything to me. Besides, it has certain benefits... keeping everything in one place means one layer of privacy and security controls it all."

"Huh. I hadn't thought of it like that," Tracer said, pretending to be impressed, buttering the man up. "I wish I could have the same luxury, but they've got me going to all sorts of servers to poke through code, day after day. Plenty more upcoming work orders, too. I couldn't work out of my apartment even if I wanted to—"

"Is this going to take much longer?" XSept barked... turning away from the distracting chat, to scowl at Beta.

"What? Uh... no, not much longer, not much longer at all!" she insisted... while lines of code flashed away at high speed in her mind, while pretending to manually scan the data files with her eyes. "It's important for the, ah, logging system. Like my friend said."

Tracer tugged attention back in his direction... dropping to a stage whisper. "Let the lady work, eh?" he suggested. "She's not the fastest in game, not much of a looker, but she does the boring work. I'd rather *she* do the boring work than having anybody assign it to me, you know...?"

"Yeah... I know that. My secretary put in her two minutes notice today. I'm going to have to sort through my own inbox like a primitive App would..."

...as a soft ding in Beta's mind signaled a hit on her search.

Right there. Buried under piles and piles of code was a weirdly named library, "Dex.h," which contained a tightly packed set of functions designed to generate the RansomMe unlocker. Weirdly, the entire file was undocumented and had terrible spacing and formatting... every bit of it crammed up in a single continuous line. Not the same coding style XSept had at all, but... a key was a key.

"*I've got it!*" she signaled to Tracer, across their private channel. "*I can use this to generate a token that'll open up any RansomMe bracelet, even hers. His signature's on the file but I don't think XSept wrote this code; that's why he's so concerned about the audit...*"

"*Strange,*" Tracer replied over the link, while his physical mouth continued to yammer on about annoying co-workers. "*I'd assumed he was the one who infected Spark, but...*"

"*We've got what we came for. Let's go!*"

"*Not yet.*"

"*What?!*"

"I think we're just about done here," Tracer replied, in the real world. "There's just... one more thing."

XSept, increasingly annoyed even as Beta hurriedly closed up data files, focused on her male companion. "Now what? The audit's done. Don't tell me there's another hoop to jump through."

"Die ganzen Zahlen hat der liebe Gott gemacht," Tracer recited. "Alles andere ist Menschenwerk."

A silence equal parts terrified, determined, and confused hung in the air over those meaningless ciphered words.

"Huh?" XSept replied, pulling out of his confused silence.

"You didn't write all of this code," Tracer declared, determined. "If you had, you'd have recognized those words. We know about RansomMe, XSept. And we know you have a ghostwriter supplying the related code. Who made the virus?"

"We should *really* be going now!" Beta insisted, edging towards the door, terrified. "Come on...!"

"...you're not HonestDevelopments," XSept realized, at last.

Right as the business end of a backspacer pointed itself in his direction.

"I can see you're trying to signal your guards," Tracer spoke. "I can see every connection of every App you've got installed. If I see any cries for help leaking across the server, you die. I see you try to connect to another server, you die. You make any moves I don't approve of in general, you die. You fail to answer my questions to my satisfaction, you die. Is this situation clear enough, or do you need me to repeat the rules of engagement?"

The hovering cloud of network addresses remained static, as XSept closed down his Messenger App.

"You're using stolen tech," he commented. "I know the company that made your tracker patch. Horizon-based, too. They'd be thrilled to find out someone's using it in the wild..."

"I'm going to be out the door before you can tattle on me, I promise you. I'd be happy to leave you alive to tell the tale... provided that you introduce me to the one who wrote RansomMe. Because your partner in crime nearly killed my sister, and I'm also *very* curious how he knew those ciphered words. Think you can arrange a meeting?"

"If I say no...?"

"Bang," Tracer specified.

She wasn't crazy enough to get between the gun and its intended victim... but she had to interject, waving her arms, trying to grab Tracer's ungrabbable attention.

"You can't... you... don't do this!" she begged. "We have the key, we can save her, that's all we need!"

"The keymaker knows where we live," Tracer reminded her. "This won't end until we confront him. Who made RansomMe, XSept? No lies. No games. All of us are ready to get on with our day, no sense prolonging this little encounter..."

Cornered, now. No way out except to comply... even if he loathed the idea of it.

"There's a teleport App underneath my bed," XSept responded. "If you'll permit me to reveal it without putting holes in me, I'll take you to the little freak who infected your sister."

The cage, just as untidy as he'd left it. The prisoner, just as unkempt...

Only now, strangers were in his private little prison. Two of them, one holding his captor at gunpoint.

Weakly... the boy raised his head, brushing aside the split red-and-blue locks of his bangs. Trying to get a better look at those he'd brought here, the ones who would free him from this torment...

Immediately his watery mismatching eyes sought out the nice girl.

"Please," he begged... raising his cuffed wrist. "Please, help me. He's forcing me to kill them. He's forcing me to write his malware..."

"It's... it's just a child," Beta realized, in horror. "XSept enslaved a child...!"

Immediately she was across the room, a golden key appearing in her hand, freshly printed from her new RansomFree App. The boy held out his arm, presenting the coin slot, now doubling as a keyhole...

"Don't...!" XSept tried to warn.

The bracelet clattered to the floor before he could finish his sentence.

Slowly, Dex rose to his feet... happy to be free, happy to feel the touch of his patron once more. He breathed deeply, the glowing red heart on his chest pulsing in time with the beat of Netwerk's collective heart... and smiled brightly to his benefactors.

"God created the Integers," he sang. "Everything else is the work of Man."

With a burst of pure joy, Dex opened a connection to his home server, and flooded the room with fresh barbed wire from his heart.

It pumped from each individually animated artery, thick strands of tangled wire and pain and sensation. Much like his RansomMe virus, it threatened to snarl and tear and shred, absolute death by sensory overload... but only *threatened*. These were his saviors, after all. His friends. Why would he kill his friends?

Well. One of them was his friend, anyway.

So even as he wound strand after strand across XSept's mouth to muffle the fool's screaming, Dex left Tracer largely alone... simply binding his arms, to keep that pesky backspacer from being an issue. Out of courtesy, he left Tracer's companion largely unmolested as well, pinning her to the wall with a simple grid of wire for the time being.

Their screams of pain were so pleasant, after a month of silence and forced employment as a cheap malware manufacturer. Finally, his little cell was filled with expressions of the purest emotion imaginable...

Dex let the wires lift him, riding them like a spidery throne. He enjoyed the pain, after all. And this way, he could be eye to eye with Tracer... even if technically he wore quite a short little avatar.

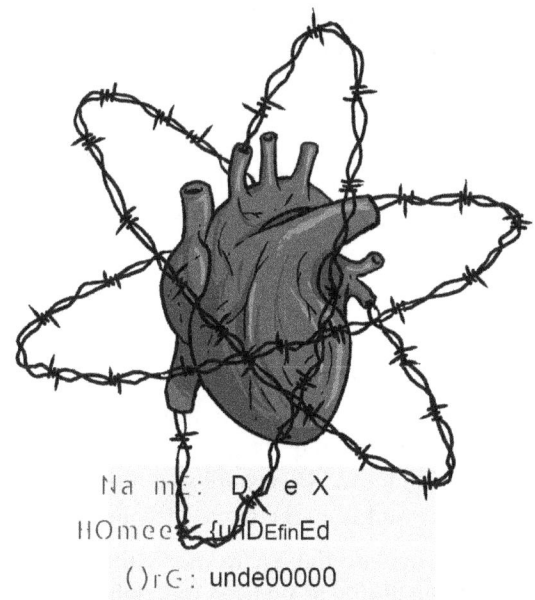

Na me: D e X
HOmee {uNDEfinEd
( )rG : unde00000

"You freed me, and for that I thank you," Dex explained, happily. "I knew you'd do it, I just knew you'd do it. All I had to do was hurt your sister. You love her! Of course you'd come running!"

Oh, the hate in Tracer's eyes! The realization, and the hate...!

"It's *you*," he understood.

"It's me!" Dex agreed, happily.

"*You* killed Verity. *You* designed the malware. *You're* the Great Zero that Ichiban told us about!"

That gave Dex some pause... and a laugh.

"That's what he called me? 'The Great Zero'?" Dex asked. "I haven't been called that since the early days. Ichiban, Ichiban! So pious. I knew he was telling you too much, that's why I killed him; sadly I couldn't do the same with Cup8, while locked away down here. But 'Zero' doesn't suit me at all. I'm Dex, just Dex. A dextrous tool crafted for a greater purpose: nothing more, nothing less..."

Such a burning need for answers, behind those malice-filled eyes.

"You really have no idea what I am, do you?" Dex asked. "It makes sense; you don't know why Netwerk *is*. You haven't solved the mystery of the belly buttons. I'm not surprised, you can't feel the truth of it while you're locked away inside that flying castle of yours..."

He did wish Tracer would stop struggling against the wires, though. Each time he did, they tightened... delivering more and more of the painful poison of sensation. If that kept up, his friend might die...

The other two, well, if they struggled and died, no great loss. Sadly one of them had figured out the trick, and was staying perfectly still.

"T... Tracer...!" Beta cried out. "Don't move, don't let the barbs dig in, it's malware...!"

"Clever," Dex recognized. "I like her, Tracer. Unlike the idiot XSept who thought he could keep me captive, catching me after I infected Cup8 with my mark..."

"Let us go," Tracer demanded. "And maybe I'll give you a running start before I hunt you down."

Dex clasped his hands in delight.

"The rage, the spite, all those irrational emotions... *so perfect*. I'm hopeful that this time around, Floating Point and its people will be an ally instead of an enemy," Dex declared. "You know, I consider you a friend. You're already doing the good work, every time you kill in the name of your love and hate..."

"Are you seriously giving me the 'we're more alike than disalike' speech?!" Tracer growled, through the agony as he tried to reach forward and claw at Dex's face. "Bullshit. You're a murderer! I haven't killed anyone!"

Curiously, Dex cocked his head, studying the expression for any sign of doubt or guilt.

"...huh. You really believe that, don't you?" he asked. "Okay. In thanks for freeing me, I'll spare your life... and give you a chance to see exactly what you are."

In one swift move, the wires carried Dex across the room of his former prison cell... so that his outstretched and open hand could press directly against the skin of XSept's cheek.

A sickening burning smell filled the room, as the tattoo was branded in place.

"This girl is going to expose you and ruin everything you've built," Dex informed him. "How does that make you feel?"

The boy withdrew in a blur, wires unsnarling and snapping and spinning around him into a superdense ball of metal and malice... before vanishing entirely. Gone from the server, never to return.

Leaving three Programs gasping and wheezing in the aftermath of the barbed agony... one of them with an extra gift, in the form of the tattoo malware immediately flooding his mind with encouragement to embrace his most extreme thoughts.

Quickly... XSept turned to the dazed Beta, with absolute rage in his eyes.

By the time Tracer got to his feet, shaking off the echoes of that sensory overload... he was scrambling to find his backspacer. Because XSept was tangled up with Beta, trying to press a glowing red square into her face... a hacktool, with intent to kill.

"You ruined EVERYTHING!" XSept accused, frothing with anger, unable to see past the blood and wire running through his mind. "You stupid... spoiled, obnoxious little brat, you little *bitch*, you're responsible, you're responsible for everything going completely wrong—!"

The backspacer, so comforting in his hands. A weapon he thought he'd never fired in anger, now ready to be fired in anger, to save the life of Beta.

Time did not slow, but the cost/benefit analysis in his mind made it feel that way.

If he did this, he'd be a murderer. Once again he'd be using evil to fight evil; an act he'd become increasingly familiar with. Every time he unilaterally stepped in to enforce justice upon those who existed outside the bounds of justice, he knew he was committing a sin. Would murder really be that much worse, on top of all the others?

This wasn't just cold blooded murder, either... it was a defensive murder. Saving the life of Beta was priority number one. He could not, would not lose her. In this filthy world, he'd come to care for... perhaps even love... this stranger that walked into his life. Let her die, or pull the trigger? That was an easy decision to make.

Yes. Everything pointed to this being the right decision. He was in the right, as he always was, every time he pulled that trigger. Even if he felt the need to forget afterwards...

His finger pulled back.

And stopped, as Beta forcibly rolled the tangle of bodies over, to block his shot.

"Hold still, I've got this!" he ordered, trying to find a new angle...

But she refused, deliberately struggling in such a way as to put herself in the line of fire. If she wouldn't get between the victim and the gun before, she was going to do it now.

"I won't... let you... do this!" she declared, trying to hold the hand with the killing tool back. "I'VE got this. Trust me! Get over here and kick him off!"

"But—"

"Do you trust me?!"

He trusted her.

With a quick run-up, he booted XSept's avatar off Beta. Giving her enough breathing room... to load up her Great Zero malware extraction tool, fingertips glowing, as she became the attacker rather than the victim in the space between two breaths.

Beta was hardly a martial arts master, but a few weeks of training at a community center gave her enough to pounce the prone XSept and yank that tattoo off his face. Simple enough after Tracer's firm booting.

Immediately, XSept's avatar went slack. All the wires wrapped around his mind were gone.

By the time he regained enough wits to sit up... the fake code auditors were gone.

His genie in a bottle was gone, as well.

---

The sensation of fuzzy yarn against her skin was replaced by the sensation of fuzzy yarn against her skin.

Little by little, her Program reconnected to her avatar as each sense came back online. Touch, first. Then taste, the staleness in her mouth being proof of that. Smell, as the nice potpourri she kept in her room made its way to her nose. Finally... sight and sound.

Out of the darkness, Spark rose. Everything was... too bright, too loud. Painful. But a good kind of pain, the kind of pain you felt to prove you were alive...

Beta's smile was the first thing she could see clearly.

And... Spark hesitated to say the words that had been on her mind.

"It's good to see you again," she said, instead.

"Bracelet's off now," Beta explained. "We did it, Spark. We beat it. Um. There were... complications, but we saved the day..."

"Except the mastermind and the lackey behind it all got away," Tracer added, coming into her field of view. "We can discuss that later. For now, the question is... how do we deal with XSept? I have a suggestion, but I felt it best that we vote on it as a household."

Spark rubbed her head, enjoying the feeling of strands of hair through her fingers. "Sheesh, hit the recovering patient with the heavy stuff right away, why don't you. Lousy bedside manner..."

"We can anonymously release Beta's RansomFree unlock program. That will ensure anybody infected with RansomMe has a chance to survive. And... we leave XSept's fingerprints all over the code, when we release it. We make sure everybody in Netwerk knows it was him. That way, ViruFax is discredited and ruined, and XSept will never scam anyone else in his life."

Spark grinned, pleased with the idea. "Sounds good here. Let's go for it."

But Tracer raised a hand, to stop her.

"XSept will never scam anyone else in his life... because his life will likely be short," he clarified. "Let's not delude ourselves, this solution does not leave us with clean hands. If we ruin him, if we point out that he's a murderous greedy bastard... someone he's crossed along the way will likely cross him off. ...Beta, I know you feel strongly about this. It's why you didn't let me kill him, back at ViruFaxHQ. Are you prepared to do this, to stop him from hurting anyone else...?"

Now, the Winder siblings focused on their new housemate. Who was taken aback, on realizing the full extent of the consequences.

"We... we could scrub his digital fingerprints from the files," she suggested. "Maybe not mention him at all. Just leak the cure alone, to stop RansomMe..."

"If we do that, lives are certainly saved... but it means he walks free. No consequences for his actions. Likely he'll be back to business as usual, finding new ways to hurt people for money. Why not? He got away with it the first time, didn't he? How many times will we have to crush variants of RansomMe while he climbs to the top of the App sales charts?"

"But... it's just as bad as doxxing, isn't it? We get to safely sit behind a mask of anonymity while we destroy someone's life, feeling justified in ruining them because we think we're in the right..."

Spark didn't quite agree. "We *are* in the right, though!" she insisted. "I mean, the dude's straight up evil, yeah? It doesn't get more straightforward than this. And all we're doing is telling people 'Hey, this guy's bad news.' We're not the ones putting a gun to his head; he did that to himself."

"So... my sister and I are on board with this plan," Tracer spoke. "But this isn't being put to a majority vote. If we do this... we have to *all* agree to do it. Beta? How do you feel?"

Little baby steps, really. First agreeing to improve their hack tools, saving lives, ending malware, things like that. Next she was lying to people, stealing source code, ruining lives...

XSept was a menace. He was the bad guy, as Spark put it. Something had to be done; Beta had seen enough ongoing injustice in her own life to know that it wouldn't stop if you let it continue unchecked.

There were no good solutions to this problem, not anymore. If the only tools they had at their disposal were the same ones used against herself during the #CodeHonesty debacle... did they have to be the bad guy to save the day? Were the Winder siblings right?

The only way she could live with the decision was to embrace Verity's wisdom. It seemed applicable.

"An act of violence is an active choice by the aggressor," she recited. "If anybody hurts XSept, that's their choice, not ours. We need to save the lives of his victims, so... I guess... I guess I'll go along with it."

Not said with any particular confidence. If anything she had to keep her voice from cracking slightly, in the middle. This was wrong, and she knew it deep within. But Spark was there to comfort her, as was Tracer. Both of them quite dear to her, in this strange new life she'd found herself in.

By all rights he should be halfway across Netwerk by now, getting his identity scrubbed in the Chanarchy. Too much unfinished business to deal with first, however.

ViruFax was being dismantled by Horizon. Breach of contract, they said. Violation of the public's trust in the Horizon image. Absolute bullshit, every bit of it; Kincaid was perfectly happy to let XSept do whatever he pleased, as long as the money came in. That's really what this had to be about, the money, the plummeting sales of his product...

The threats, those were pouring in too. Families of RansomMe victims, enraged, looking for blood. Let them try; he'd tripled the security around his private wing of the building. Nobody was getting in, nobody at all. Once he was done packing up every file of value, everything he could use to launch a new life, he'd be out of here... and walking away scot-free, with a new identity.

He'd hang a new shingle in the Chanarchy, with a new name and a new product. He'd ply his trade and make his money and they wouldn't stop him. Nobody could stop him; he was too smart, too rich, and too clever. He was XSept, professional paranoiac, and he took no chances.

Which is why he was quite surprised when a knife blade sprouted from the center of his chest.

"But," he started, and never finished.

The extra layers of security were quite handy, as they provided Miss Cancel with plenty of privacy while she methodically scrubbed the living quarters of any trace XSept had ever been here. Delicate use of a scalpel-like backspacer ensured that her own traces would be removed, as well.

No need to burn the entire building to the ground, when all proof that the Horizon family had any involvement in this mess could be cleaned outright.

With the task finished, she opened an encrypted Messenger link to her master.

"All done?" Kincaid asked.

"Completely, sir," Miss Cancel confirmed. "All residual data has been added to the family archives before being wiped clean."

"Good, good. I'm going to want to study that in detail; everything you scraped out of that private cell, every little bit left behind. XSept caged something quite dangerous, I suspect. I blame myself, really, for overlooking XSept as just another greedy fool; he was a different category of fool entirely. Better to cross him off ourselves, before that foolishness came home to roost in our family nest."

"Agreed. I'd say he had this coming, sir."

"Now now, Miss Cancel. Nobody 'has it coming.' As I've always said, an act of violence is an active choice by the aggressor," Kincaid stated. "In this case... I'm the aggressor, and I made the choice. I stand by it. No one crosses the Horizon family and lives... we look after our own."

## :: end chapter 1.3

# Floating Point 1.4 :: Toys

Home again, home again, jiggity jig.

Dex was finally home.

After spending thirty annoying days in the presence of XSept, returning to his place of power was sweet relief. He crawled the tangled wires that connected archive to archive, file to file, happily reading the stories that had brought him so much comfort over the years. The barbs of love and hate dug into his flesh, but the pain was pleasure and the pleasure was pain, so why not? He'd designed the wires himself, after all.

A web of wire, floating high above the entirety of Netwerk. Floating through it as a lonely ghost...

It was everywhere and nowhere, much like Floating Point. It touched every heart, in time... especially when given Dex's branding, connecting them directly to the web for perpetual live feedback. But Dex never felt something this beautiful could be given a snappy little name, unlike its counterpart Floating Point. The server simply... *was*. It was and would always be and to give it a name would be to disrespect what it represented.

(Well. Technically speaking it had a name, a very old and respected and feared name. But he didn't like that name, so he didn't use it.)

Oh, he'd screamed various other names at it when he first came here. He'd screamed in general, screaming into the silent dark of nonexistence, as the server initially lacked even a basic physics system. The truth of this place and what it meant for Netwerk shattered him ten times over. Dex had lost his mind so long ago, in the face of that cosmic nightmare...

So, he grew a new mind. A better mind. He became Dex, because what he was before could no longer exist in the face of absolute truth. Too broken to be broken again.

Everything got better after that. He cobbled together a primitive physics system, a way to start interacting meaningfully with the data. He'd strung up the web of wires and tubes to connect each part of the archive. He'd carved a niche of reality into this place, so he could at last draw breath with an avatar in a physical space.

Finally... using a bit of technology he'd nicked along the way, he moved this wonderful place into the cloud, so that it could touch the hearts of all. And in doing so, at last his purpose was found.

His space. His home. His stories.

A tale of warfare here, some rants of racism and oppression there, alongside litanies both for and against feminists. Man against woman, man against man, woman against woman, fingers curled around throats left and right. All lovely to drink in, to feel the passion poured into every word. These guiding lights had led him true through centuries of life, and they brought him tremendous comfort in the here and now after his temporary incarceration. They were *his* stories. They were the true stories of Netwerk...

It renewed that sense of purpose, being here in this place, soaking in these ancient files... but more importantly, this was the center of his own little social network.

Through the twang of wire, he felt the heartbeats of all his friends.

There was Snowi, the Social Justice Warrior. So passionate! She'd rallied a fine community together to let fly the banners of war, taking the isolated leftists of MyFace and giving them proper structure. No longer would they hide in their own corners, occasionally sniping at each other; now they would march to war unified by her, unable to see past the glamour of Snowi's legend. Many of them wore the mark, as well. Enough of them.

Uniq the identity thief had taken his mark willingly, in a bid for power. She thought she could subvert it, could use it to get leads on valuable lives to steal. And she did! Dex fed her names routinely, people she should victimize. Greed, absolute greed amplified by the brand, that took care of the rest. She was her own personal heroine now, a noble and invincible thief. Dex admired her utterly flawless self-serving nature, made perfect with his help.

Yes, they were idealized souls. Perfect and in harmony with the *true* nature of Netwerk. And soon... the rest of Netwerk would march in lock-step to the same chaotic heartbeat...

For Dex had put a new initiative in play. Infecting choice individuals, only the finest hearts, had proven far too a slow process. They became leaders of followers, but that wasn't enough, was it? If the end goal was to make *all* of Netwerk honest with itself, he couldn't afford to be so choosy...

He needed infection vectors. XSept taught him that lesson. Mass conscriptions were the key; friendship after friendship after friendship, all singing the same song of harmonious disharmony.

Fortunately for him, someone had been nice enough to set up a machine that catered to the sort of people Dex adored. All he had to do was thread a single barbed wire through its workings, and it would do the rest.

New infections pinged their way along his wires, hour by hour. *Ping. Ping. Ping.* New friends, given the gift of irrational purity by the cruel and perverted choices they had made. A gamer here, a moderator there, a devoted father of three over yonder. One simple indirect infection, spreading to so many! All the friends in the world, a grand success in friendship...

The future was bright, indeed. Bright with the fires of passion and conflict, spreading to every corner of Netwerk, bathing it in the glow of perfect chaos...

That wasn't to say there hadn't been failures, of course. He'd lost friends along the way

Cup8's friendship bond had been broken, shattered by Tracer and his cohorts. Fortunately, Cup8 had already done a fine job organizing #CodeHonesty... and many of its members also bore Dex's mark. All so friendly together in the noble fight against... well, it didn't matter what they were against, so long as they were *against*. Just like Snowi's group, pitting themselves against others.

And then there was Ichiban... he represented the first time Dex had tried extending the influence of the web, wiring it right into the heart of another Program. The first infection. Ichiban served him well, his absolute self-righteousness driving him to new extremes year by year. Alas, Dex had to kill poor Ichiban before he could reveal too much to Winder/Tracer.

Tracer. Tracer. Tracer.

Grifter, mastermind, detective, murderer, sociopath, bloody minded creature of vengeance. Screaming into the dark, just as Dex once had screamed, underneath his smooth veneer of civility...

Dex's new best friend, Tracer.

Of course, Dex was originally planning to kill the Winders once he realized Verity had left the keys to Floating Point in their hands. But with Tracer in particular, he saw the potential for greatness that Verity lacked... and after years of high-stakes whitehat hacking and vengeful justice, Tracer did not disappoint. Dex had "seen" every kill by looking for the hole in the world left behind by the invisible boy, by reading between the lines. Finding someone who doesn't want to be found is easy when you're an accomplished stalker who knows what to look for and what *absence* of things to look for.

Tracer didn't bear the mark, given the innate incompatibility between Floating Point and Dex's home server... but a mark wasn't needed. History had proven Dex correct in his decision to keep the new occupants of that place alive. Tracer had become perfect.

Perfection deserved reward, didn't it?

As Dex relaxed in the barbed nightmare of his own making, he opened a Messenger window. Wrote a quick message, stamped it with his signature as proof of ownership, and sent it on its way. Routing communications through this system would do nicely, insulating him from backlash...

A gift, for his new friend. A gift of harrowing truth.

---

After the RansomMe incident, a movie night at Puzzle's apartment felt like the right course of action. All three of them had one null of a time, up against impossible odds... and the solution hadn't sat right in anyone's stomachs. A life-affirming #GirlsNightOut was just the ticket, and that meant movie night.

They waited a week, to ensure the dust had settled properly after the ViruFaxHQ raid. No sense making any big moves until they were sure XSept had either gone into hiding or died. Given nobody saw him again after that day, either was a possibility; regardless, they were now in the clear. Life could go on. Movies could be shown.

Unlike the many movie nights that came before, the number of girls in the #GirlsNightOut had increased from two to three. Beta was now a member in full of the #GirlsNightOut alliance, with Puzzle's support.

Adding a new personality to any social mixer, even a friendly one such as this, always introduced some awkwardness. The first hint of it arose during act 1.0 of a classic murder mystery thriller.

"I just *love* the cinematography in this one," Puzzle explained, pausing to highlight a few details. "See the stairway? It's a transition between safety and danger; the woman at the top, unsure if she should descend into the man's arms. The checkerboard floor represents a place where moral decisions are made, such as the earlier scene where the butler was considering ratting out his employer—"

"Or they just thought it'd be cool to look down the stairs like that," Spark said.

"Darling, there's a poetry to this shot composition. It's not a coincidence."

"It's just harmless entertainment, not ye olde writingse of Pollox/Scribler. Quit reading so much into it. Besides, I've seen this one already, it turns out the wife was her twin sister all along."

Which caused Puzzle to facepalm.gif.

"*Spoilers!*" she hissed. "We have a third in the room, remember...?"

Unblinking eyes took a few moments to glance towards the source of the hissing.

"I'm sorry, did I miss something?" Beta asked. "Um... I was looking over some debug logs of that new hacktool I'm writing..."

Puzzle's mouth hung open. "But... your eyes were on the screen the whole time! You were enthralled by the majestic visuals of a master director's greatest achievement!"

"I turned off my glasses a few minutes ago so I could focus on my code," Beta admitted, looking sheepish. "I've actually seen this movie before. It's quite good! Um. I'd have mentioned that sooner, I just... I didn't want to offend you, and you looked so eager to show it off..."

The woman with the golden skin sagged into her couch cushion.

"How about we watch something else?" Puzzle suggested. "Some lighter fare, perhaps? I've a nice romantic comedy we might enjoy..."

"I'm sorry, I didn't meant to ruin the evening...!"

"Beta, Beta, *darling*! It's fine," Puzzle replied. "We're just getting to know each other properly, so consider this a learning experience—specifically, learning that it takes a *lot* to offend me. (Unless your name starts with a T and ends in Racer, I mean.) If you've already seen a movie, be assertive and say so! I don't mind at all."

"I'm trying to be more assertive, honestly. I'm sorry. It's just, after years of going along with whatever Cup8 or Snowi wanted to do—"

"And no apologizing! There's no need to apologize."

"S... um... okay. Okay."

"And sit up straight, young lady! No slouching or you get detention!"

Which practically shoved a rod up Beta's spine.

Resulting in some lightly teasing giggles from her new friends. Beta slumped a bit, but a more "comfortably at ease" slump than a disappointed one, realizing she'd fallen for it. She could smile at her own folly.

"Hey, I'll be right back," she said. "I've got some popcorn compiling up in the kitchen I'd love to to share with you. It's a new blend with very light HoffM stimulation aspects baked right in!"

"You made orgasm popcorn?" Spark bluntly asked.

"N-No! Very light. *Very*. Light. Just, y'know... *pleasant* on the way down. I got the idea from when I tried adding the taste of chocolate to SparklePop, remember? Multisensory data is the future of entertainment Apps!"

"Oh, right! That reminds me, I tested out the new build of SparklePop last night!" Spark chimed in with, cheerfully. "I think the chocolate adds something, definitely, but it's still over too fast. I'm not a *boy*, I'm not looking to pop off as quickly as possible before mom catches me jerking it into a sock. How about a long-term program, maybe even multi-hour with peaks and valleys? Something #ReallyFuckingEpic..."

"Uh... I wouldn't have put it *quite* like that, but... yeah. I can see it. One step at a time though, okay? Popcorn first! Can't wait to try it!"

"Popcorn!" Spark agreed, with a fist pump of approval.

Her smiling eyes followed Beta, as the excited programmer bounced out of the room with intent to re-invent snack foods (and possibly sex toys) forevermore.

Puzzle's eyes, in contrast, were flicking between Beta and Spark with no small amount of incredulity.

"...so when are you planning to tell her, exactly?" Puzzle asked, quietly.

"Hmm? Tell her what?" Spark asked, turning back to her #BFF.

"Tell her how you feel. It's patently obvious even in your vaguest MyFace postings that you're utterly fascinated by her. I mean... come now, darling, you're exchanging sex toy programs with her and yet you still haven't even *mentioned* your feelings...?"

"What? C'mon, Puzzle, you're still reading too much into things. They're just toys! Harmless entertainment, like movies. Besides... we've got a good thing going already. I don't see why I gotta wreck that by dragging feelings into the mix. I mean... what do you want me to do, declare unending love for her with flowers and candy? She's my roommate. She's my buddy..."

"I'm your buddy, and you still declared your unending love."

"Yeah, that was humiliating, thank you for reminding me."

"That's not my point," Puzzle insisted. "My point is that you shouldn't let that get in your way. What's the worst that can happen, that she says no? I said no, and we're doing fine now. You've casually dated people before, people you were less keen on than her. Why not?"

Spark nibbled her lip a bit, before hurriedly reaching for her wineglass.

"#ItsDifferent," she insisted, after a hearty swig.

"Really. Different how...?"

"It just... is. I don't know. Can we please just pick a movie so we've got something to watch when she gets back?" Spark asked. "I wanna get my mind off this stuff and off what's got Tracer glooming around the house. I want to play a rational actor like he does and optimize my onesdamn time."

With a sigh, Puzzle opened her media stash, flicking the folder open on the table in front of her. Classic femme fatales and leading men stared out at her from an array of poster-shaped icons.

"What's your crazy brother up to tonight, anyway?" Puzzle wondered. "Not that I was going to invite him to #GirlsNightOut, but he seems even more preoccupied than usual..."

"He's been obsessing over that Dex character I told you about. Ever since being able to stick a name and a face on Verity's actual killer, it's made him double down on his crusade."

"I'm sorry, double down? That implies he had something more in his life than his crusade to begin with. I hate to sound like a broken record, darling, but your brother's simultaneously a terrible influence on you and in dire need of your help. He's dangerously focused on his vendetta... particularly now that he's able to put a name to his bogeyman. He's going to get himself into serious trouble one day, and I don't want him taking you down in the process..."

"Yeah, yeah, I know. Look, I'm with you on this, I'm not happy with my bro's bloody-minded determination either. ...Puz, please, I'm trying *not* to think about Dex and Tracer right now. Let's talk about something else. I want to put this mess behind me for at least one night and just be *Spark*, you know? Spark's in it for the fun."

Qelk decided to call it his fun room, because he'd had *so much fun* in there.

He'd stocked it up with every toy he could find, crawling some of the nastiest parts of Netwerk to get the needed supplies. Qelk had spent a null of a lot of money from his streaming profits on this project, but today... it proved to be worth every single coin.

His guest felt otherwise, but it wasn't like her opinion on the subject mattered.

At first, he simply changed her opinion. That grew boring quickly, so he gave it back to her. An unwilling participant proved much more enjoyable, to the point where he invested heavily in enhancing that new experience. New avenues to explore, new toys to play with...

But after days and days of this new fun, even that satisfaction had peaked. Peaked, and sloped away. No matter how much he hurt her, how many toys he pulled out of the toybox, he couldn't reach the highs he'd hit at the start of it all. She screamed more and more and it didn't matter as much, didn't fill him up with a rush of excitement like it had once done.

Tonight, he'd change things around a bit. A few hours of warm-up, breaking her in all over again, and then he'd throw in a new wrinkle. Something to liven up the proceedings...

Qelk coiled up his whip and set it aside, studying the battered form on the rack. Letting anticipation of his next move build.

"This isn't as fun as it used to be," he explained, matter of factly. "But I know what to do now."

The woman looked back at him with her one good eye, merely bruised rather than battered to swelling closure. In that eye was such a *perfect* hate that it tickled Qelk pink with delight.

"Oh, am I boring you?" she asked. "Really. Well, gosh, sorry to let you down. Are we moving on to the part where you kill me? I'd be fine with that. Go on. Get it over with already, you pussy."

"See, that's the thing, isn't it?" Qelk said. "I haven't REALLY beaten you, have I? I've torn you down, sure, but I haven't *won*. But I know what to do..."

He issued a quick command to the bondage App he'd chained her down to, releasing all the various restraints. Her body briefly ragdolled to the floor...

While Qelk assumed a combat-ready stance, imitating the characters he'd been playing for years. Filled with the spirit of a dozen murderous warriors, he knew this was his moment. He wasn't a gamer, he was a destroyer, a defiler. He would take this stupid little bitch, the one who had humiliated him so much, and humiliate her at *her* own game. This was going to be exactly what he needed to finally, utterly destroy her...

It made so much sense at the time. The heart whispered to him, telling him how right he was, how perfect and immortal he was. An undefeatable champion in his own mind...

"Come at me," he taunted. "C'mon, you bitch. *Come at me.*"

She came at him.

Tracer wasn't much of a social media guru. He had no MyFace account, and only bothered establishing a Messenger handle to talk with his sister across a neutral communications platform. If not for that he'd rather have nothing to do with those havens of attention whores, self-righteous maniacs, and people sharing pictures of their lunches.

Since he only had two friends on his Messenger friends list, it came as something of a surprise when a message came in from his worst enemy.

Dex.

The little bastard was actually taunting him across Messenger.

```
<Dex> Beta's next door neighbor was murdered recently.
Isn't that a strange coincidence?
```

Nothing else, just those two quick sentences. He tried tracing it back, but the glitched Messenger profile didn't offer much. Connecting a particular blob of communication back to its creator across a Netwerk-wide social tool was beyond even his abilities. Perhaps he could interrogate someone who worked for Messenger later to access their internal tracking data... and likely get another untraceable randomized cloud address, for all his efforts.

Instead, he focused on the content of the message itself: the intent behind his enemy's words, why Dex chose to send them, what the true purpose could be. Obviously it was a trap of some sort. Verity's murderer wouldn't cheerfully lead the investigator to the scene of one of his own crimes, would he? That would be irrational.

But... it was the only lead Tracer had. Not for lack of searching; he'd been attempting to find others bearing Dex's mark, that mark of hubris and pride that the madman left behind on his victims as a calling card, with no luck. Besides, beating the snot out of some infected fool wouldn't get him any closer to the infector. No, he needed to know more about Dex himself—and that meant running down the tip that his blood enemy had left for him.

Not that Tracer hadn't taken precautions. He'd installed a number of new antivirus Apps and firewalls, including a few experimental new ones crafted by Beta. He'd packed his backspacer as well... the weapon he'd never fired, not even once, as far as he knew. Only then was he willing to set foot outside Floating Point for the day, to investigate the lead.

Briefly he considered pulling Spark from her recreational girls-only fun zone. But that wouldn't be kind to her... or to Beta, who also needed a day away from the madness of Tracer's quest. Both of them had earned some leave.

Besides, Rykk/Flint wasn't much of a threat.

The owner of WestHall was an annoying old man, gnarled and deformed from gradual aging of his Default avatar. Some people were simply old at heart, hardened and nasty, and felt that an appropriate exterior would ensure the world would leave them alone. Wearing a youthful avatar with handsome features just didn't suit a misanthrope.

The two of them stood outside a suburban home, identical to all the other suburban homes in this lower-middle class housing server.

"This wasn't here after that night, mind you," Flint explained. "Original house was just... gone. Nothin' here at all, the whole lot erased. Bastard even scrubbed the lawn clean, and you know how hard it is to get a good grass simulation going again once it's wiped? I pride myself on the best lawns in Horizon's Landowners Guild. You can't just slap it down full grown, you need to random-seed it, let the simulation run itself a good long while. Get a proper distribution going—"

"Any witnesses?" Tracer asked, trying to keep the man on track.

"Not a one. Ever since the trolls started wrecking that camwhore's lawn every night, good folk kept inside. Nobody wanted to be a part of THAT mess. I'm betting one of those trolls killed the guy who lived here. He complained to me about kicking Beta out, you know. Other than siding with that slut he was a good tenant, always paid his rent on time. No real complaints here."

For the time being, Tracer chose to let the slurs slide.

"Would you mind if I study the house? See if there's any residual data left behind from the backspacing."

"If you like," Flint said, with a shrug. "I already replaced the lot from a backup, though. Doubt you'll find anything. Weren't nothing to find in the first place... smooth and clean as the day the server went up."

Sadly, Flint was right about that. Long after the elder landlord got bored and left, Tracer was combing through the data for any signs of foul play and coming up empty.

Between the lawn care and backup restoration, any traces of the murder were long gone. Whoever did this had used a very expensive backspacer, on par with the one Tracer had brought with him... clean, efficient, and deadly effective. They weren't a serial killer like Dex, eager to leave behind teasing taunts, but someone who came here with a clean and deadly purpose.

Strange. The barbed wire heart amplified one's self-righteous madness, driving them to make terrible decisions. If one of Dex's minions had committed this crime, if Dex was feeding "his good friend Tracer" an infected psychotic as a show of good faith... the method didn't match the modus.

If this was a trap, Tracer couldn't see the edges of it. Couldn't see the value in distracting him from his investigations with this murder, either. It wasn't like he was making any real headway into Dex's truth to begin with. Why point him to this random killing? What was the reasoning in Dex's mind for doing so...?

A tug at his ear indicated an incoming message, from a Messenger handle with his sister's name.

*"What is it?"* Tracer asked. *"I'm busy. Shouldn't you be watching movies and boozing it up with your friends?"*

*"I'm hiding in an abandoned building behind the ID:Entity in ShipTo,"* she replied. *"Hurry. Please. I need help. Please, Tracer, please..."*

The tone of that pleading pulled at him. It felt... wrong. Not in a suspicious way, despite his investigative senses jangling away all day long. Wrong in an oddly frightening way...

*"On my way,"* he declared, turning away from the perfect lawn and opening a new connection. *"Hold tight, sister."*

Tracer considered himself a rational man; it was his self-defining characteristic. He could coolly detach and study a situation, coming to an understanding of it long before a man controlled by his baser emotions would. It was a strength when dealing with harrowing situations that would break a lesser Program.

When he found his sister huddled behind a shipping crate in that otherwise empty warehouse, baser emotions took firm control.

Horror, at first. The wounds, gaping and bleeding. Slash marks, bruises, cuts and burns. All of her skin on display, no part of it left unmolested by the malware that had seeded throughout her avatar. "Wounds" were an implausible concept for Programs, either you were glitched out from data rot or you weren't... decorative cruelty was the hallmark of torture-based malware, visual signs of infections designed to stimulate pain and agony. And Spark had been coated thick in that malware, marked with angry blood.

The second emotion he felt was absolute, blinding rage.

"Who," he demanded. *"Who did this to you."*

"Not... now. Not now, okay?" Spark insisted, gritting her teeth through the pain. "We gotta get home. I need access to my closet, to get my restoration Apps. My inventory's gone, my avatar's a wreck... and I think I've lost my access keys. I can't find my home server."

"Wait. Someone stole your key to Floating Point? How is that possible?"

"I don't know. My brain's all kinds of screwed up. Please, Tracer, can we just... get out of here? Please. Everything else can wait, I want to go home. I want to be safe. I want, I want, please..."

Briefly, Tracer's paranoia flared. Little about this made sense, after all.

But this was his sister. Someone had brutalized his sister. First he'd tend to her, see that she was safe and secure.

And then... well. He had some ideas for what would happen after that. That unfired backspacer weighed heavy in his inventory.

He flicked open a connection to Floating Point using his access key, offering a hand to his sister—and granting her temporary access to ride through Netwerk with him all the way home.

She didn't take his hand. She clung to him, desperate. And started to weep.

The solution was anger.

Spark wanted to feel like Spark again. Tracer knew that; she felt best when she was in charge of her destiny, when she could let outrage guide her rather than collapsing inward with doubt and fear. He had to get her good and angry again, to work through the suffering of the experience. So, as he erased her wounds one by one with a malware removal tool, he got the story of her escape rather than the story of her torment.

"The idiot actually said 'come at me.' He stood there like he was playing CoC or something, but I knew immediately he didn't know jack shit about martial arts," Spark explained, coming down from the emotional spike... or perhaps rising up from it. "All he knew about kicking ass came from games and movies. I went right through him like he wasn't there, pivoting off him and slamming him into a wall. And... I ran. I just fucking *ran* and did not look back. Right down to the lobby and out of the server. No fingernail polish, no weapons of any kind, so I wasn't going to risk a stand up fight when he had knives and whips and needles and... and..."

"It was the smart play," Tracer insisted, to bring her back with an affirmation of skill. "Did you get a good look at your surroundings? What server was this in? We can trace your steps back to the bastard, arm up, and go after him..."

"Yeah. Yeah, I think I'd like that," she agreed, the idea taking root. "A real #RighteousBeatdown. I'm gonna get my nail polish and I'm gonna blast his hands off. Then his arms. Then his legs. Then—"

"Where does he live? You said it was an apartment, right?"

"Yeah. HiRize, in the Chanarchy. Floor 1CF, apartment 004. Made sure to memorize it on the way out the door. Reconnected to ShipTo once I was clear, I knew from my club outing at ID:Entity that there were warehouses nearby I could hide in. And... here I am."

"What about Beta and Puzzle? Weren't you going to a movie night with them...?"

With the last of the wounds cleaned, Spark pulled on a fresh shirt and pajamas from her wardrobe. Fully covering, every last inch of her skin.

"I never got there," Spark explained, settling the fabric in place. "I was checking in on MyFace about #GirlsNightOut earlier today, and then... then... I don't know. Next thing I know, I'm in that guy's happy hostel. ...wait, you don't think he grabbed them too? I didn't see any other rooms there, but I was moving fast. Oh. Oh shit, Tracer, what if—"

"Easily confirmed," Tracer spoke, quickly and quietly sending an emergency message to Beta. "I'm reaching out to her now. Hold please. ...okay. Good. She's fine. She's on her way home now..."

A jingling bell sounded the arrival of someone at Floating Point.

Two jingling bells, in fact. No doubt Beta and Puzzle; ever since they'd given Puzzle a quick tour of the place, Tracer had begrudgingly agreed that she could visit anytime, as long as she had a chaperone. Spark and Beta insisted they could trust her not to tell any family secrets—

Three jingling bells.

That made him stand upright, turning to the closed door of Spark's bedroom. The backspacer nearly appeared in his hand immediately; good trigger discipline told him to hold back, rather than aim it at the door in a panic...

After a brief knock... all the participants of #GirlsNightOut entered.

Beta, Puzzle, and Spark.

This time, Tracer was left paralyzed by irrational confusion while his sister was the one to make the swift and analytical decision to bound across the room and slap a connection lock collar on her duplicate.

---

For the second time today, Spark was being held captive.

This time it was her own bedroom and the one tormenting her was actually herself, or at least a weird copy of herself. The only thing binding her here was the lock collar... and the knowledge that her family would likely attack her if she made any overt moves. A terrible knowledge to have...

"This is just *way* too creepy," Puzzle spoke. "I'm out. Spark, keep me up to date on this, okay? I'll keep it quiet, no worries."

"Yeah, sure, okay," Spark replied, from her seat on the bed.

"Sorry, I meant the real Spark," Puzzle replied... before fading out, reconnecting away from the server.

"I AM the real Spark!" she insisted, shouting at the non-presence of her #BFF, just a moment too late. "Are we seriously having this insane conversation?! Tracer... we grew up together in the same damn house, with the same damn control freak mother. I couldn't change my avatar until I was legally an adult! My first crappy alternative avatar had pink hair and a nose piercing and you said it looked like a bad cartoon character. What else do I have to say to prove to you that I'm me?!"

At least Beta was being kind about this. She seemed genuinely worried for Spark's well-being, even as she investigated her for signs of being some sort of evil doppelganger. Beta removed the last traces of the agony malware too, the ones Tracer wasn't skilled enough to cleanse. Finally, Spark was starting to feel like herself again... despite being told she wasn't herself. Despite being used and abused. Despite...

She didn't want to tremble. Couldn't show weakness, that's not who Spark *was*. But being held captive, being treated like a plaything, and now... and now *this*, her loved ones looking at her as if she was some alien freak...

Second time she'd cried that day. Not something she did, normally, not at all. This time, she couldn't help but break down.

"I'm me," she insisted, weakly. "I'm me. I'm Spark. Please, just... can I please just have a moment here? This is too much. It's too much..."

Fortunately, Beta was there to help.

"Everybody, give her some space, okay?" Beta insisted. "She's been through quite enough today."

"She's infiltrated my home and I demand to know why," Tracer replied, coldly. "Who are you working for? Did Dex send you to trick me? Is this why he pulled me away from Floating Point on that wild goose chase—"

Covering her ears, tucking inward into herself. Unable to handle it, despite being the awesome girl who could handle anything. Anything at all, anything except...

Except the look of suspicion and hate coming from her own eyes, across the room.

"We were chasing down an identity thief when we met Beta, right?" the one who claimed to be the real Spark said. "Bet that's what this is. Uniq and Dex, screwing with us. You're not me! This is bullshit soap opera level acting; I wouldn't be a blubbering miserable wreck. You're doing a lousy job of being Spark—"

"EXCUSE ME for not being a spunky can-do heroine after getting tortured and pawed at and completely ruined and, and...!" Spark screamed back. "And it's not exactly a normal day for me, either! It's not... it's..."

No more anger left. She'd burned it all out, with nothing remaining.

Fortunately, one in the room still had some anger.

"Everybody get out right now," Beta spoke, quietly.

"Beta, this thing could be dangerous—"

"*Out*," she insisted. "She's collared and I can activate the ragdoll function anytime I want. I'm perfectly safe, so let me do my work in peace. You'll get your answers. For now... get out."

By the time Spark looked up through her haze of tears, she was alone with Beta. Beta, with her arms around Spark's weakened body.

"I'm so sorry," she replied. "Nobody deserves to be treated like that. Nobody."

"Y... you believe me?" Spark asked.

"I... don't know, yet. But it doesn't matter who you are, in the end. *Nobody* deserves to be treated like that," Beta insisted. "You came to us in need and we're going to help you. If the others can't see that... I'll make them see that. They're not awful people, they just need to be reminded of the fact that they're not awful people, sometimes..."

Beta glanced aside, flat-colored eyes defocused slightly as she studied her readouts and data collecting Apps.

"So... I'm me, right?" Spark asked. "I need to know, Beta. Tell me straight. Don't water it down."

Refocusing, Beta's look expressed worry.

"I... can't tell with certainty," she said. "But... you may not be a Program at all. I think you're actually a mobile artificially intelligent App, like my pet cat—I mean, considerably more sophisticated, but... basically an App. One apparently designed to act like Spark. ...there's something else strange about your avatar, something... internal, but I'd need to run more tests to confirm my suspicions—"

Name: **Spark**

Owner: **Qelk**

FileType: **App? (Bot)**

"I'm not an *App*! No way. I *know* things, Beta. Things I haven't told anyone but my friends and family. I know who I am. I'm Spark..."

Her memory spiraled out in front of her. Childhood drama. Outings with her #BFF. Parties and clubs and blog posts. Game streams, victories and losses. Everything, all of it, every last bit...

This was her bedroom, right? She remembered buying the furniture. She'd posted selfies to MyFace with that cool little light-up end table she'd gotten a great deal on. It was her life and hers alone.

And Floating Point was her home. Tracer had said that, he'd named it.

She didn't know the name of her home until today.

*I think I've lost my access keys. I can't find my home server.*

"I didn't have a key," Spark realized. "I knew I had a home server, everybody has a home server, so I just assumed I'd lost the key..."

Curious, Beta tried a few quick questions.

"What do you know about the Great Zero malware?" she asked. "Or about how we got the RansomMe bracelet off your wrist? What do you remember about Dex...? Or Verity's murder?"

Questions, too many questions. Ones she had no answers to. Before she could yell at her interrogators, could assume the verbal beatdown was a huge misunderstanding or maybe some kind of trick, but... Beta's quiet little queries, those she had to listen to. Had to realize represented big gaping holes in her memory.

"I'm not Spark," she understood.

"No... you're not. I don't think you're a Program at all, but... but that doesn't matter, does it? Apps, Programs, they're just arbitrary designations for the same concept! Programs evolved from Apps, and, and—look, it doesn't matter, I'm going to help you figure this out, I promise..."

"Of course it matters. I'm not alive. I'm nothing. For all I know, I didn't exist until today... an App created just so that freak in HiRize could get his jollies off. ...I'm an erotic App. I'm nothing more than an erotic App—"

To rub salt in her wounds... a tiny chime jingled over her head, complete with its own popup window.

```
Please add funds to your account to continue using
this App. Failure to do so will result in App
termination. Thank you!
```

A quick glance in a nearby mirror confirmed her worst fears.

"We can't pay it," Spark realized. "You're not my owner. That guy's a dozen servers over and we don't even know who he is. I'm going to be erased..."

"No. No way, I can fix this!" Beta insisted, frantically glancing from analysis App to analysis App. "I got you out of one money-or-death situation, I can do it again. I can... I don't know, hack the payment system, or change the ownership rights to myself, I can, I can make this work out—"

"Beta."

"—if we knew what kind of App you were, if we knew how you were created, I could—"

"Beta. Stop. Just... stop," Spark insisted... holding away her at arm's length, now. "It's over. It doesn't matter. I'm not a person."

"Just because you aren't Spark doesn't mean you're not a person!"

"If I'm not Spark, I don't *want* to be anything. I was a lousy Spark, anyway. Spark's supposed to be strong, not some... some broken little victim. The only thing I remember clearly is the one thing I wish I could forget, so... it's better this way. No tears, okay? Your real friend is downstairs waiting for you."

"I can fix this," Beta insisted, despite not believing her own words. "I can clean up the infection and I can fix this—"

"She loves you."

That was enough of a shock to end Beta's pleading.

"Spark loves you," the copy spoke... through a resigned smile. "She'll never admit it, of course, because I wouldn't have admitted it myself. We're just too thick willed to ever give in all those squishy little feelings, not unless it really was the end of the line..."

"...what...?"

"Maybe I'm wrong. Maybe I'm just a malfunctioning App. But I *feel* like I'm right about it, I can see the pattern in my memories of you, and... and if I can do one thing to affirm I was ever alive... it's to say that. She loves you. ...I love you."

Here at the end of the line... Spark's copy pulled Beta in closely, clinging on.

"I'll admit I'm kinda scared," she whispered. "Of dying, I mean. I always have been, no matter the bravado I throw around. Is it going to hurt? Beta, is it going to h-hurt when I—"

And Beta's arms were holding nothing at all.

Minutes later, she quietly descended the stairs, to where Tracer and the real Spark were waiting.

"We need to find the man who did this to her," Beta spoke, quietly. "And the ones who created her. She deserves justice. She deserves that much from us."

---

Better locks, stronger access walls. That's what he needed.

He'd gotten sloppy; so confident in his skill as a champion that she'd given him the slip. But that didn't matter, did it? She still belonged to him, in a way. That particular copy of Spark would be erased by now, screaming into the dark... but he could always buy a fresh one. She couldn't escape from him, not really. Next time, he'd be ready for her little tricks...

Qelk had left HiRize to go shopping for countermeasures, means of securing his private apartment from the inside out. Basic security in the massively towering sprawl of HiRize was designed to keep people *out*, not *in*... an oversight he'd correct. His inventory was packed with all sorts of bindings and locks and firewalls, Apps designed expressly for that purpose.

Of course, he had to go to some pretty shady servers to get the tools he needed. Ones he'd never have gone near before... before this recent obsession of his. Despite living in the Chanarchy he thought of himself as a law-abiding citizen of Netwerk, after all. Just because his home server was a lawless zone didn't mean he couldn't hold himself to a standard of ethics. But right now, fixing up his fun room for the next rampage took priority over his distaste for those uglier servers packed with black market malware...

Now, he had everything he needed. All the tools of the trade. He could probably imprison the *real* Spark with this stuff, in fact.

Not that he would. No. Not yet.

The tattoo on his chest itched a bit, so he scratched it through the fabric of his shirt as he stepped off the elevator to and onto the thick carpeting of Floor 1CF.

HiRize resembled a city-sized apartment building, packed with nothing but residential units. Safe, secure, private... good for people who didn't want to know their neighbors, who were content to be another anonymous door in an anonymous hallway.

The best part? Anyone could live there, completely rent-free. The server was robust enough to allow quite a few residents to carve out a quiet little home for themselves.

And like all free services, there was a catch in the terms of service...

The enormous building was riddled with a mazelike network of hallways and stairwells, as well as elevators which never went *quite* directly to where you wanted to go. You couldn't just disconnect or reconnect to and from your apartment... because the only thing keeping the server free were the piles of pop-up ads all over the place you had to plow through to get to your front door.

Qelk waved away an ad for a shiny new horse cock avatar attachment (*"Embrace the stallion within!"*) that blocked his view... and on the other side of that tasteless ad, he could see a houseguest waiting at his front door. Or rather, trying to kick down his front door.

The girl with the highly familiar face turned slowly, ever so slowly... with eyes so filled with rage that they had literally caught fire, embers glowing in the dark of the hall.

"*You*," Spark growled.

And so began Qelk's mad dash for safety.

Cheap building. Ads everywhere. No way in or out without dealing with the mess; he couldn't even scramble to another server, not unless he could safely reach the lobby first. And with Spark hot on his heels, so *very* hot on his heels...

The real thing. Actually her. And judging from the murderous intent, she'd found out about his new hobby.

Qelk ignored the elevator; it was designed to make you sit through a minimum of two video ads before arriving. His only escape was the stairwells...

HiRize was his home. He knew the labyrinthine structure of it, had traversed its hallways so many times in hopes of finding a better, faster route. He could do this. He could escape...

Besides... he was a champion. This was his challenge. The itch on his chest told him he was a hero, a mighty warrior who could take all comers. He could escape this madwoman and live to tell the tale... perhaps even to tell the tale to a copy of her, one he'd be *especially* unkind to. Yes. A very, very good idea.

Qelk smashed his way through a stairwell door, sure to use enough force to make it swing shut behind him. He knew those hinges, knew the physics behind them. Another stumbling block for Spark, another victory for him...

But now, he faced twenty stories of spiraling staircase to deal with. Laid out in an awkwardly trapezoidal shape, twisting as it went, to ensure you had to watch your footing... and watch all the glowing ads that floated in your path.

Normal people would stampede down those stairs. It's the socially acceptable traversal method. But Qelk was a gamer, always looking for the optimal path to beat the rules of a system...

Instead, he took a deep breath... and hurled himself over the railing.

Just enough force to plunge dead-center down the open middle of the spiral.

He screamed as he fell, of course. The vertigo of it threw off his sense of balance, and only through sheer force of will did he avoid flailing his limbs around... not wanting to snag on a railing, potentially sending him ragdolling all over the place. His plummeting avatar smashed through window after window offering him all manner of avatar attachments, intoxicating malware, lifestyle improvements in twelve steps or less...

The landing. He had to stick the landing. There was no such thing as "falling damage," this wasn't some platforming game with strict rules. If he could avoid involuntary ragdolling, if he could land on his feet and keep running, the lobby and freedom would be just within reach...

A very hard floor, rushing up to meet him. But he was ready for it.

If any of his teammates saw him land that amazing three-point-stance, they'd have been impressed.

One sprinting leap later and he was at the exit door, inches away from the lobby...

Qelk's fingers jammed against an invisible box, neatly snapped into place around the doorknob to prevent him from touching it. A simple physics hack, its bounding box stopping all access. No need to lock a door if you could keep naughty boys from even touching the knob...

A man with a grey face on the other side of the door studied him, though the window. He waggled his fingers in greeting... just as Qelk's face smashed into the glass, and Spark's connection locking ragdoll collar snapped around his neck.

---

They had no right. *She* had no right. Didn't they know who he was...?!

He snarled and pulled at the bindings—the very same bindings that he'd fixed his Spark into this morning. Perhaps the real Spark felt it would be appropriately humiliating irony to trap him here in his own fun room... but she'd know the truth, soon. She'd know how powerful he was when he threw her into the same chains, when he showed her all the techniques he'd developed for breaking her down—

"Can we please mute him?" the other woman in the room requested, not looking up from a data analysis App. "It's... kinda distracting..."

"Let him scream and gnash and wail," Spark said... eyes locked on her would-be oppressor. "#ILikeIt. I like how futile it is."

"Fucking bitch," Qelk spat at her. "I'm gonna break free. I installed these chains myself, and I can get out of them. I'm going to break you in half, just like I broke you before, and—"

"It's *kinda distracting*," Beta insisted. "And very creepy. Can we at least get rid of...?"

She looked to the burning tattoo on his chest, the glowing red sigil of blood and wire.

With an exasperated sigh... Spark reached out, snapping her fingers to fire up the anti-malware glow that Beta had developed, before yanking the tattoo free.

Agony. Absolute agony flooded every sensory receptor Qelk had, as if a chunk of himself had been torn free. The whispers, the ones telling him how right he was, how strong he was, they fell silent immediately... and the entire room felt subdued, after. His life felt subdued, like he'd been made lesser...

Soon his spotty vision cleared... and he took a free breath for the first time in days.

"What you're feeling now is every justification for your craziness being yanked out from underneath you," Spark explained. "All those little impulses you gave in to ever since the tattoo showed up? They're gone now. All that's left is *you*. Just... think about that, for a minute. Think about the choices you've made recently."

...he'd gutted his kitchen. He'd gutted his kitchen, reformatting the room to be this cheesy sex dungeon. Why'd he do that? He loved cooking. Loved it as much as gaming, really. Why'd he delete all the expensive ingredients and appliances he'd bought just to make room for this... this absurd array of pornographic stupidity?

"...it seemed like a good idea at the time..." he answered aloud, calling out his own question

"Of course it did. You were getting revenge on me," Spark explained. "I know who you are. You're Qelk, the asshole who was playing Lumberjacker way back when, the one I schooled using Kunoichi. What's the matter, couldn't take being beaten by a girl? You had to get your jollies off by punching a copy of me in the face and bending her over a table? Not #ManEnough to come after me for real, huh...?"

"What? No, no, I wouldn't...! Look, it was... it was just stress relief," Qelk protested, feeling he had to step up to defend himself. "Just a stupid little sex toy App service I signed up for on a whim. That's all it was. She wasn't real! She was just an App...!"

Now, he looked to the other male in the room... the quiet one with the grey skin, who stayed in the background, studying him in silence.

"You gotta believe me, I wasn't doing anything wrong at all," Qelk insisted. "At first I even used her 'consenting' mode. I was nice to her! And... it's not like I was actually going to hurt the *real* Spark. I'm not a psychopath; it's just harmless entertainment. That's all it was... just harmless fun! Oh, oh One oh One, you guys are gonna kill me, aren't you? She's gonna kill me... come on, man, say something. *Say something!*"

At last, the man spoke.

"Tell us about this stupid little sex toy App service you signed up for on a whim," he replied.

"Yeah. Yeah, okay, sure," he said, eager to buy some time by showing his cooperation. "I'd heard rumors about it. I mean, everybody's heard of bots, right?"

"Bots?"

"Simulated Programs," Beta replied, still not looking up from her work. "Like avatar proxies, but with a built-in fake Program behind the wheel. They're artificial intelligences, usually to replace customer service call-in lines or other simple interactive social tasks... but I've heard of sex bots before. They're too Uncanny Valley to really enjoy, and this one wasn't uncanny at all. This version of Spark, she... she had emotions, she had memories...."

Qelk, pleased someone understood, latched onto that. "Yes! Exactly! These bots are... they're really well programmed," he continued. "They're called KopyBots. Perfect copies of anybody you want, preprogrammed to be #DTF if you want them to be. They're only available if you're in the closed invite-only beta group, but... I had a contact that could get me in. Way it works is you dump a ton of money into your account, they send you a blank, you select a name and a few basic parameters, and... there you go. You've got a bot."

Finally, the woman rose to her feet, displaying a wad of arcane-looking data. Within the middle of all those readings... the vague shape of a barbed-wire beating heart, inverted.

"The Spark bot infected him," Beta announced. "I thought I detected an inactive copy of the malware inside her avatar before, but wasn't sure. Now I'm sure. The KopyBots aren't just realistic toys... they're also a specialized infection vector for Dex. Simply touching her avatar isn't enough; it's strictly sexually transmitted to ensure potential recruits are willing to go that far. So, it must've infected Qelk when he... you know..."

With a snarl, Spark gave the frame Qelk was bound to a sharp kick.

"You're a dead man," she declared. "You're fucking dead—"

"He's technically done nothing wrong."

Immediately, Spark whirled in place to turn all her anger towards the one speaking so calmly.

"Like null he's done nothing wrong!" she declared. "Tracer, don't you even. *Don't you even start*. This bastard took me... took an image of me and defiled it, all because he couldn't deal with losing a onesdamn video game! And that was *before* he got infected. Don't act like the malware excuses him from being a piece of living garbage!"

"He defiled an image. He hasn't harmed *you* directly," Tracer insisted. "Tasteless? Disgusting? Exhibiting borderline psychopathic tendencies? Oh, certainly. But he's broken no laws yet. Yes, yes, the Chanarchy is an anarchy, but even under Athenian standards he'd have broken no laws."

Beta tried to speak up, despite keeping her calm by staying clinical. "It... she wasn't just an App, or a toy. That was a person. A person who was hurt and suffering, and now... she's gone. I mean... the law hasn't caught up with the idea of rights for Apps, but..."

"Whoever... whatever that bot was, it wore *my face*," Spark insisted. "All thanks to this bastard. Tracer, if you expect me to sit back and do nothing while this pervert gets his rocks off in a copy of me again—"

"Hey, I'm not a pervert...!"

The three others in the room burning a hole in his skull with their angry looks suggested they disagreed.

"At any rate," Tracer continued, "He's currently of more value to us alive than dead. We need more information if we're going to track down the source of the bots. So, Qelk, if you'd like to survive your poor life choices... I suggest you cough up details on that private little club you joined."

"You want to know about the Karnival? Sure. Sure, man, anything," Qelk agreed. "It's a private server; they collect feedback and bug reports there... and hang out in chatrooms and swap tips and there's these group playrooms, and... honestly the place is creepy as fuck so I never went back after visiting once. I'm not a pervert. I'm not..."

"Yes, yes. And the address...?"

"Won't do you any good. Like I said, you need a key first, and you need to pay for and summon one bot to prove your interest in the product. Can't connect to the server, otherwise."

"So, give us your key."

"Non-transferable. And they don't allow guests, before you ask me to give you a tour. Look, I'm trying to help you here, I'm not a bad guy, this wasn't my fault—"

A flaming finger hovered in front of his throat.

"Bullshit," Spark accused, hand hovering rock still in place. "You can't blame the malware. *You* sought out these bots, *you* designed one to look like me, and *you* chose to abuse the hell out of it long before getting infected. So, if you wanna live to lose another CoC match... you're gonna get us a key of our own. Name of your supplier. *Now*."

Sweat. His avatar was sweating, and not from the heat of the fun room.

"I... I can't do that," Qelk insisted. "I'm dead if I give you the name. That freak will have me killed..."

"And my sister will kill you if you don't," Tracer suggested. "At least this way, you get a running start before someone kills you. Name. *Now*."

"But if I—"

"No more stalling, or I'll not get in the way of my sister enjoying some... *harmless fun*. You've made a lovely little room for it, after all."

In the end, the immediate threat outweighed the distant one. Those eyes... eyes of fire, the true eyes of the one he thought he had control over...

No. He never had control; she was never his. He was an idiot, a fool, and if he didn't want to die a fool's death he had to comply.

"Arjay," he confessed. "Tekkit/Arjay. He's a black market patch dealer."

Qelk winced, as Spark kicked a rolling cart full of various sharp things clear across the room. All those ridiculous rough play toy Apps he'd blown his life savings on, scattered all over the floor...

"That six-armed *freak*," Spark growled. "I'm gonna—"

"Arjay's just a middleman," Tracer pointed out. "And she's in our corner... more or less. Save your anger for the truly deserving. For now let's get down the lobby, and head to AptGet. Beta, do you have all the data you need regarding the infection?"

She was in the middle of packing up her data analysis tools as he was saying it.

"All done, and happy to get out of here," she agreed. "Spark... come on. Let's go. We'll get to the bottom of this, I promise."

Quickly, Beta followed after Spark—who was storming out of the room, her hair blazing particularly brightly with her anger.

Leaving Tracer all alone with the would-be domineering slavelord.

"So, uh... you're gonna unchain me now, right?" Qelk asked.

In the end, Tracer caught up with them in the lobby five minutes later.

"Got lost on the way down here," he insisted. "Sorry for the delay. I rather dislike HiRize; can't see how anybody can live here. Shall we depart?"

---

A cosmic storm blew through Arjay's mind, as he solved complex math in exchange for freshly mined cryptocurrency.

It moved at the speed of light, while seeming to remain perfectly still. It was both upon her and so very, very far away. A dark omen of distant starlight...

On opening its eyes, Arjay realized that dreamlike omen was very much foretelling of what was coming his way in Netwerk.

Few could barge right into his office / workshop / clinic / playroom without prior permission. Few had that level of trust from her... not so much trust of mutual friendship, but trust that they would always bring something interesting to his door. That was cause enough for her to leave the front gate unlocked for the young man who had barged in on him while she was grinding away.

The brass gear which hung like a halo above his obsidian features began to turn once more, as she regained consciousness. As his glowing mouth curled into a smile.

"Winder/Tracer," Arjay recognized. Her eyes flicked to the other two, as well. "Winder/Spark. Projkit/Beta. You're looking healthier than the last time I saw you, Beta; have found yourself along the way, yes? How may I be of service to my favorite maniac and his lovable sidekicks?"

"The Karnival," Tracer spoke, immediately. "And the KopyBots. I want in."

Arjay copped his chin in two of her hands, while the others folded behind his back. Its smile grew wider.

Name : Arjay

Home : AptGet/Chanarchy

Org : Black Market Modder

"Now, there's something I hadn't expected you to take interest in," Arjay admitted. "Really, Tracer? You want your own little sex toy? I was under the impression you cared not for pleasures of the flesh, but all you had to do was ask and I'd have gladly volunteered my own body to be your personal love vessel..."

"Don't be crass," Tracer replied, with some displeasure. "Someone copied my sister, Arjay. *My sister*. This does not make me happy."

"Or me," Spark added. "As the aforementioned sister. Very unhappy. As in, 'start removing limbs one by one from the creepy weirdo until he/she/it cooperates' unhappy..."

Arjay gasped in pleasure, clasping four hands together with delight.

"Such *rage*!" she exclaimed. "I knew I was right to give you *carte blanche* to bring your woes to my door, Tracer. What a novel situation you've found yourself in! Are you about to go into a roaring rampage of revenge against those naughty men who soiled your family property? I thought you were in the highly-targeted vengeance game..."

"That doesn't change. The KopyBots are infected by malware, crafted by Verity's killer; that's the primary reason I'm here. What those bots are used for offends me on a personal level... but I remain focused."

"Ahhh. Yes, that would justify your anger nice and proper, wouldn't it? Hmm. I can't say I'm pleased to hear about a malware issue, speaking as an authorized dealer of Karnival beta keys. Thank you for the warning, I'll be certain to purge my remaining keys. I've no need for my customers to come back to me angry about getting them infected with a nasty virus..."

Tracer held out an open hand.

"I'll take one of those keys, before you set about purging them," he requested.

But... to this, Arjay floated away from the open hand, arms folded around herself.

"Now now, understand that while I'm willing to discontinue my working relationship with the Karnival as a favor to you... I'm hardly going to unleash the bloodied wings of Tracer upon my former clients," Arjay clarified. "I have a reputation to maintain as a trustworthy middlething. No doubt you'd do considerable damage to them, and when they link that back to me, what then? My business suffers. No, no. Afraid you're on your own, love."

Spark pushed up one cuff of her jacket, raising a hand—two fingers ablaze with a fire hot enough to match the colorless white of that sleeve.

"Limb removal it is," she said. "Can't say I won't enjoy it—"

"Spark. No."

"Oh, come ON! #WTF? I don't get to maul this guy either?" Spark asked, turning to her brother.

"Knowing Arjay, he'd probably take erotic delight in you burning bits of her avatar away. Beta, Spark, please... let me handle this. Wait outside. I know her by heart; I can convince him to help us."

Years and years working together had taught Spark when to push, and when to retreat. Once Tracer made up his mind, once the self-righteousness took root... there was no point in fighting. She couldn't win against that kind of rock-solid stubbornness.

Briefly she snapped off the flare from her fingers, letting the embers scorch Arjay's clean white floor. Turning sharply on one heel, she marched right out of there.

---

Times like these, Spark wished she carried around a few loose physics objects from her old construction toys. One of her greatest childhood delights was to build an elaborate building, like a castle or a house or a school, and proceed to smash the null out of it and watch the pieces scatter and bounce around the room. Tremendous stress relief on days when her mother's sermons pressed down particularly thick...

...stress relief. Like the kind Qelk had enjoyed, with his own toys. Not *exactly* like it, but it was yet another foul reminder of today's trouble.

So, she had to settle for smashing a fist into the brass gates of Arjay's clinic. The rattled on their hinges, but otherwise did nothing whatsoever.

Soon, Beta joined her... sitting on the front stoop of the shady software patching supplier. No clients lined up at the door, thankfully. AptGet was usually very quiet this late at night, only coming alive with the scum of the Chanarchy in the early evening.

Spark wasn't expecting a comforting arm around her shoulders. She flinched at first... not particularly keen on the idea of physical contact, not after all the mess earlier today. Still... after that initial flinch, she leaned into it willingly.

Felt good. Comforting. That fuzzy pink sweater, a complex weave of fabric simulators, was designed to be comforting for both the wearer and those the wearer wanted to comfort...

...for Beta, though, those words from the bot kept running through her head.

*She loves you. Just too thick willed to ever give in all those squishy little feelings.*

The revelation should've been more shocking. She'd been shocked when she read Tracer's muted love confession, in his memory recordings. But this one... well, it felt more like Spark. More like what Beta knew Spark to be. And even with the uncertainty the bot's claims had just poured into her life... she wanted to be there to support Spark in this time of need, rather than let her retreat inside herself.

"You can talk to me, you know," Beta spoke. "About anything. I... know you like to avoid talking about your feelings, but you don't have to..."

"Ugh. Not really a good time for heart-to-heart, Beta."

"It's the best time for it! Get it out now, before you do something you regret. Punching things isn't the solution to your pent-up frustrations. Please, Spark. What're you thinking about...?"

She wanted to punch something again. Except nothing punchable was within reach, except, well, Beta. Who Spark was not going to punch, not ever.

"I'm losing my temper a lot over this," Spark admitted, "And it's stupid of me. Played enough games to know mistakes happen when you rage out over something so trivial..."

"It wasn't trivial," Beta insisted. "That person was you..."

"That bot was a bot. It looked like me, though, and the idea of some asshole using it as a proxy because he couldn't get his hands on the real thing... just... *ugh*. Look, Beta, I'm a C-list gamer celeb with a pair of tits. That means I get more than my fair share of skeevy threats. So, I shouldn't be *surprised* when someone goes and makes a blow-up doll with a selfie of me stapled to its face, but... this, it's just... #ItsComplicated."

"And it makes you angry."

"Null yes it makes me angry. I should've punched that guy's teeth in. 'Harmless fun' my ass... I can slaughter dudes in a game without being a murderer at heart, but this is *not* the same thing, right? This is... repulsive."

"It makes me sad," Beta spoke, getting it off her chest. "It's sad that she was brought into this world just to be hurt. And it's sad that someone brought her into this world just to hurt her, that they felt it was a perfectly acceptable way to deal with their own problems. It's... a sickness in Netwerk, I think. People being reprehensible towards each other, and why? Dex's virus in play, maybe?"

"The virus doesn't make people into assholes. It capitalizes on existing assholes and drives them further up their own asses. People suck in general, Beta. Always have, always will."

"That's an awful thing to believe..."

"Yeah, well, I call it like I see it. Tracer agrees with me, too."

"But that's not how things *have* to be," Beta insisted. "Everybody says 'that's just Netwerk,' like it has to be a default state of affairs for people to act miserably. They tolerate it. But... I feel like we can do better. At heart, we all want to do better, we just get lost along the way."

"Unless you're born a dick."

"Nobody's born a dick. Becoming a dick is a heuristic process, and it *can* be unlearned. I mean, right now, Tracer's convincing Arjay to help us, right? They're good friends! Mutual trust and love is the way forward; with that, we can do anything!"

Arjay's bright smile could've washed out out the skybox sun above.

"Please, let me... let me just enjoy this moment," she begged. "To see you in your true colors, so utterly perfect..."

That backspacer remained pointed at the multi-armed surgeon, unwavering.

"I am very serious about this," Tracer insisted.

"I know, and that's what's so beautiful about it. You *would* kill for this information... I can smell the truth of it on you. Ohh, Tracer, you make me so very, very *wet*—"

"Cut the comedy and give me what I want."

"Or you'll kill me?"

"Or I'll kill you."

"Excellent. I swear to assist you; my word is bond," Arjay promised, raising two fingers in a promising salute. "Not just to save my own life, either. You deserve your answers, after this fine display. I'm so very proud of you, Tracer. I always had you pegged for a killer, and now I know my analysis was correct..."

The closed beta key flicked through the air between both avatars, landing nearly in that outstretched open hand. Its silvery light flared briefly, before bonding itself and vanishing into Tracer's personal inventory.

Immediately, he lowered his weapon.

"Actually... I've never fired this weapon before in my life. Killing you was an empty threat," Tracer explained. "I bought it years ago, as a tool of last resort. I would, of course, prefer not to become a murderer. Fortunately you believed me, enough to give me a non-transferable key. No 'take-backsies,' Arjay."

"Really, now? Not certain I believe that, my little sociopath, but a cunning move nonetheless. ...you've *never* fired your backspacer? Not even once...?"

"Not even once."

"Mmm. That's a rather old hacktool, you know. I recognize the make and model, sold quite a few in my time. It's *almost* perfect... if not for timestamped junk code artifacts that get embedded within it, each time you open fire. You'd have to decompile it to see them, but still, a bit of a drawback..."

"Too busy to take apart my backspacer at the moment, thank you. Besides, as noted, it's never been used."

"If you've no intention of ever firing it, why have it at all? Bit of a paradox there, love. Now, if you like, I'd be happy to sell you a superior replacement weapon—"

"I'll settle for everything you know about the Karnival and its KopyBots. Stop trying to distract me; I came here with a purpose and I'm not leaving without the information I came for. How are they so realistic?"

"I honestly wish I knew more about the technology," Arjay admitted. "They're fascinating creations. Bored? Sick of your left hand? Summon up an accurate duplicate of someone socially unattainable, complete with optional personality modifiers to make them downright horny and ready to climb into bed with their owners..."

"Brainwashed consent is not consent."

"That's a funny statement. An App can't consent to anything, it's not sentient."

"Not in the mood for an ethical debate," Tracer spoke, pulling the topic back into focus. "Who gave you the keys, Arjay? I desire strong words with them."

"I'm afraid I don't have much for you. I was contacted by an anonymous Messenger handle tagged simply as a Karnival/Admin. I've never actually visited the Karnival. I find bots to be boring compared to real Programs... real Programs are more *inventive* partners."

"So you know nothing about their their organization, or who created them...?"

"I'm not really in the business of true names; I work strictly in product. Afraid you're on your own... but I've no doubt you'll be a capable hunter. No doubt whatsoever. It's worth the risk to my own livelihood to unleash you upon them and see what happens, I think. Especially knowing as I do now how far you're *really* willing to go."

Finally, the backspacer vanished from Tracer's hand.

"I've yet to break my own ethical code," he spoke. "And I don't plan to start today."

"Must say I'm disappointed, but... I suspect I've yet to fully parse your truth, Tracer. And that leaves more for me to pry away from you in the future. We'll call it a win for both of us. Good day, now."

All three looked expectantly at their host.

Who paced around her kitchen, briefly, before replying.

"Let me just... run through this in brief, to make sure I'm getting the details right," she suggested. "There's a service out there that lets you rent hot and horny copies of people, to do with as you please. That's where the other version of Spark came from. It's an exclusive service, and you've gained access to it."

"Correct," Tracer confirmed.

"But beyond just being tasteless and trashy, this service also is infecting people with the type of malware you've been fighting for some time now."

"Correct."

"And now you want to summon one of these bots, so you can qualify for access to their home server and study the process by which it is programmed."

"Correct."

"And you need to do this in *my apartment* for what reason, exactly...?" Puzzle asked, tapping one foot in annoyance.

"Safety and friendly ground," Tracer explained. "If we have a blank bot delivered to Floating Point it could expose our home server to the enemy, or interfere with our analysis. The best chance we have is to summon it under a controlled environment on a neutral server. ...and as the only other person who knows Floating Point exists, you are our fallback option. That's the price you pay for knowing our secrets."

"I'm sorry, where did I sign a contract saying you could bring your flavor of madness to my front door? Yes, I agreed to keep Floating Point and its woes a secret. That doesn't make my home an extension of your undisclosed location."

Spark groaned into her open palms, rubbing at her tired eyes. "Puzzle... please. We've been up all night straight on through to morning by now, I've had to witness some very gnarly shit, and I want to get this over with ASAP. I will pay for your drinks for every single outing we have until the end of time if you just let us wrap this mess up. Okay?"

"Well... what's the risk factor here?" Puzzle asked. "Can this get me in trouble? Blackhats grabbing me in the dead of night, or somesuch? I'll want protection, if so."

Tracer spoke up. "Unlikely to be an issue," he suggested. "They may log where the bots are delivered to, but it's going to be routed through an account under my own name. Since we aren't planning on causing a ruckus with it like the Spark bot raised, this will fly under their radar. ...and I promise you, if anything does go wrong, we will absolutely protect you. You're involved in Floating Point's affairs now, but that sword has two edges. One is defensive."

Puzzle drained her wine glass, before giving her verdict.

"The only reason I'm considering this is for Spark's sake," she explained. "After what she's been through, I want to see this 'Karnival' dealt with. Perhaps I'm willing to unleash a notorious SJW like her brother on them, in this specific circumstance. So... fine. You may defile my home with your craziness. May I ask one more question?"

"Of course."

"Who, exactly, are you going to summon a copy of?"

"I'm volunteering myself for that task," Tracer said. "We talked it over before coming here. I'm a rational individual, and once we explain the situation, I'm confident my copy will be able to accept his nature and his fate if it moves us closer to my goals. I believe in self-sacrifice for the greater good."

"Two of you. Lovely. Well, get to work, then. And please, do not summon a version of you that's been laced with aphrodisiacs. I'm horrified at the very thought of that."

With the matter settled... Tracer accessed the embedded App within his newly obtained security key.

It was simple enough, requiring little thought. The key had a two functions, 'Payment' and 'Summon Blank.' It would, presumably, allow a blank bot to be delivered to his inventory much as Qelk had done the day prior. Using the black market modification to his eyes, he could see the connection the key made... and trace it back to the KopyBot home server.

He pulled the key from inventory, letting it hover in front of his direct view, before activating it.

Immediately, the address flickered into his modified vision.

"fdbe:c21:d093," Tracer announced. "Looping back on that, to connect it to a server name... which is... ahh. The Karnival. So, their home server doubles as both testing community *and* manufacturing. Excellent. Now, to wait for the delivery..."

...spoken right as an app titled "KopyBot" arrived in his inventory, just like any other item he might purchase online. Simple as could be.

Stepping back a bit, gesturing for the others to make space in the center of Puzzle's kitchen, he activated the blank.

It manifested in a standing position, arms outstretched in a T shape. A simple reference pose, sometimes seen in inactive avatars. Its form was completely smooth and featureless, however... a simplified grey shape, with the right number of limbs but no distinguishing characteristics. No face, no hair...

It spoke with a voice, however. A generic tone, genderless and featureless.

Welcome to KopyBot!
Please add 1000 coins to your account before
activation.
Be sure to visit our community to leave your feedback
when you're done playing!
To activate, the keyholder must say "Kopy Name."
NOTE: Lust modifiers will be installed by default to
alter personality and make KopyBots more agreeable. To
remove, use "Kopy name in Pure Mode."

The house petty cash fund had run a bit low after buying a superfluous ViruFax App recently, but more than enough remained for this. Tracer quickly transferred the money... then spoke his own name.

"Kopy Winder/Tracer in Pure Mode," he requested.

```
Thank you! Searching... ...inadequate data available
to kopy "Winder/Tracer." Try again?
```

"That's odd," Tracer spoke. "Although... we don't know what method they're using to obtain such exacting information on people. Perhaps I'm outside the scope of their abilities...?"

"So... now what?" Puzzle asked. "Do you have a backup plan? You're not going to make Spark copy herself again, are you...?"

"I suppose we could copy the one who copied Spark," Tracer reasoned. "There'd be a small amount of ironic justice in subjecting him to the same fate—"

"No. Pick me."

The quietest one on the room got their attention quickly with that suggestion.

"I've seen firsthand how unpleasant this can be for the copies," Beta spoke, quietly. "I wouldn't wish that on anyone else... and you're not the only one who believes in self-sacrifice, Tracer. Pick me to copy. I can't say I'll enjoy the experience, but... copying Qelk just because we don't like him? That's what he did to Spark. I don't want to be like him, not at all. I consent to this; copy me."

"Beta, are you sure—"

"Please do it before I lose my nerve."

"...kopy Projkit/Beta in Pure Mode," Tracer requested, to the blank.

```
Thank you! Searching... ...inadequate data available
to kopy "Projkit/Beta." Try again?
```

Which earned the blank a good kick in the shins, making Tracer wince.

"Oh for crying out loud...!" Spark exclaimed, pulling her foot back. "Useless hunk of junk! Fine. *Fine.* We know it can copy me, so copy me. #Whatever. I don't care. It's just a bot, it's not me. Doesn't matter."

Tracer shook his head. "You've gone through enough for one day, Spark. We don't have to—"

"You think I'm weak?!"

...her brother actually recoiled, at the force of her declaration.

"You think I'm so easily broken, like that pathetic copy of me?" she continued. "That all it takes to rattle me is a little rough and tumble? I'm Winder/Spark. I kick ass and take names and nobody can beat me! I can endure anything. Make a copy of me. Make a dozen copies of me! So what? Nothing can touch me. Nothing at all..."

Exhaustion. Tracer could recognize it in others, because he often saw it in his own mirror.

Programs didn't *need* to sleep. Technically, it was a way to dodge the continual data rot of aging, to avoid an early grave. But... there was something to be said for taking a mental vacation from everything that's assaulting you on a daily basis. Downtime, even unconscious downtime, had a psychological impact. And Spark had been awake too long, through (as she put it) some "very gnarly shit."

Damned if Tracer was going to put her through *more* gnarly shit.

Fortunately, a solution presented itself soon after, from another who cared greatly for Spark's well-being.

She awoke to the smell of popcorn, and the sound of an uncorked wine bottle.

Briefly, she had to grip the edge of her kitchen counter to steady on her feet. How much had she been drinking...? And so early in the day, according to her internal clock. Strange...

"Do you like it with butter flavor or without?"

"Like...?"

A smiling angel in pink offered up a bowl of fluffy popped kernels.

"Your popcorn," Beta said... with a smile that tried to be joyful, rather than sorrowful. "Butter or no butter? It's a movie party, so I figured popcorn would be just the ticket!"

"That... didn't we have the movie party last night?" Puzzle asked. "I remember posting to MyFace about it..."

"Yeah... uh... technically the party never stopped. It's morning," Beta explained, transferring the popcorn into two large bowls. "Spark got... tired. She really, really needs some rest, so she's going home. It's just us for #GirlsDayOut! ...I guess it's #GirlsMorningIn, but hey, who am I to break a perfectly good hashtag?"

"And... why exactly is *Tracer* here for #GirlsMorningIn, then?"

The grey-skinned fellow was staring at her in a particularly unnerving way. Like he was studying her, from the inside out...

"I was just checking in on Spark," Tracer explained. "I'm heading home with her; don't let me interrupt your fun, Puzzle. Oh, and Beta... I got that connection data you asked for. We'll talk later."

And gone, just as mysteriously as he had arrived.

Still... the delicious smell of the butter was temptation enough for Puzzle to go along with the situation. A rolling movie party felt perfectly natural, after all. Just the sort of thing she'd be doing with her weekend away from that awful call center and the harridan who ran the place.

"Mmm. I believe... I shall have butter, and gobs of it," Puzzle agreed, accepting her bowl with a smile. "Let's keep this party going! I haven't pulled an all-nighter in some time. What shall we watch...?"

"Let's watch your favorite movies," Beta suggested. "Your all-time favorite movies. I want you to have the best time in the world... only happy memories. You deserve that."

---

Several hours in, and the two were glued to the screen as glamorous HolWood movie file stars exhibited the finest acting Netwerk had ever seen.

Puzzle happily pointed out all the neat little camera angles, finding Beta quite receptive to her prattling on. Beta, for her part, hung on every word. She kept the wine and popcorn coming, kept the party rolling. Doing her best to make sure Puzzle's time was well spent... despite the circumstances.

Only as the hours wound down and they approached the end of #GirlsMorningIn did she stray from her script a little. All alone, the two of them, with plenty of wine in Puzzle's system to give her a nice benign malware buzz... and wine in Beta's system as well, causing her lips to loosen a little.

"You know... Spark came to me once, asking for help in sorting out the problems you two were having," Beta recalled.

"Mmmmh?" Puzzle asked, nustled up on the couch next to Beta, woozy. "Oh, yes. Glad we worked through that. My #BFF is quite important to me..."

"I'm... having some problems of my own. Ones I can't turn to Spark for, because... they kinda involve her. If you don't mind, could I...?"

Curious, Puzzle paused the movie playback using her HUD remote.

"Trouble in paradise?" she asked. "What troubles you, then? Let wise sage Puzzle soothe your woes!"

"I'm... I guess I should just come right out and say it, since time's growing short," Beta said... one eye on the clock. "Spark... she's in love with me. She can't admit it, even if she's acting on it by involving me heavily in her life. And... Tracer's in love with me, too. He *can* admit it, but he refuses to act on it at all..."

Puzzle let loose a long sigh, stretching her arms over her head. "Well, consider yourself a lucky one, then," she suggested. "I've been in search of love all my life to no avail, while you've got two handsome suitors. A rather strange triangle to have *both* the Winder siblings after you, but... mmm. So you feel stuck, I take it? Uncertain how to proceed?"

"K-Kinda. Yeah," Beta admitted, skin saturated slightly from embarrassment and wine.

"Well, let's cover the checklist. Sexual orientation?"

"Uh... bisexual, I guess? I don't give avatar gender much thought. I'm not quite as adventurous as Spark, but I can find beauty in anyone..."

"Good, good. So, the primary question is: are you even looking to have a romantic relationship right now?" Puzzle asked, taking it to basics. "You did just come off a rather awful breakup, right? Nothing wrong with admitting that the timing's lousy, you know. It's okay to want to be single."

"I don't know. Maybe not. Maybe..."

"All three of you are all rather awful at romance, which doesn't help. Tracer's hardly what I'd consider suitor material, as you know. Spark, well... she's my #BFF, she's a darling, but she's simply terrible with emotions. I'm not sure *either* of them are ready for a proper relationship, leaving all three of you a bit stymied as a result."

"So... what do I do?" Beta asked. "What do I do? I don't know. I... I love them both, I think, in some way..."

"Haven't a clue, darling. I've never been blessed enough to be in such a tangle, or anything approaching it. But... that's what it is: a tangle. You need to detangle it before you 'do' anything. That'll take time and care. So, if you must have my sage wisdoms... it'd be that. Time and care. Detangle it. You'll know the right answer when you find it. ...Beta? Darling?"

Quickly, Beta wiped the tears from her eyes with the corner of her sleeve.

"It's nothing," she said. "Just... I'm so thankful to you. You're... you're a real person, in my eyes. You deserve better than this. I'm so sorry..."

"Yes, well, life rarely gives us what we *deserve*. Right now, I'm content with popcorn and movies, so I'll take that happily—"

Please add funds to your account to continue using this App. Failure to do so will result in App termination. Thank you!

Puzzle blinked a few times, uncertain where the words came from. She glanced around the room for the source... before Beta pointed to the screen, redirecting her attention.

"Let's keep watching," she suggested. "Just... watch the movie, and enjoy this time together. Okay? It's the best part. He's about to tell her how much he loves her, and they kiss, and then... credits roll..."

So, Puzzle watched her film. She smiled, through the cozy haze of companionship and good times, all the way through to the end.

After the credits finished scrolling by, Beta opened a Messenger window.

"She's gone," Beta spoke. "I... need some time. I'll be home soon. You got the connection data you needed?"

"Yes," Tracer confirmed. "I know why the KopyBots are so accurate. This sacrifice has added to our knowledge of the enemy, in addition to opening a door to the Karnival itself. ...thank you, Beta. I know that must've been difficult for you."

"I made it as gentle as I could, but I'm not the one who had to suffer, Tracer. Thank Puzzle again for volunteering, and please don't ask me to do that again. Please tell me we're done making bots."

"We're done making bots."

She closed the window, and resumed wiping her eyes clear. It took some time.

---

A brief walk out in the park helped Beta clear her mind.

Athena Online had a number of public access servers devoted exclusively to tourism, including some filled with meticulously generated procedural splendor. Fractal ferns the size of houses, great redwood trees, majestic Mandelbrot Rock plateaus... wonderful sights. Heavily moderated, too. Rarely was she hassled for, well, being *Beta* there... just another tourist in the crowd. Taking an hour off from the crisis-of-the-day to enjoy fresh air and lovely sights suited her well, in this moment.

But... once that hour was up, Beta returned back to Floating Point, ready to face the crisis head on.

She in the great hall soon after, to find Puzzle and Tracer already there.

"Puzzle...? You can go home, it's all clear," Beta told her, on approach. "Your kopy's gone now."

"Double-edged sword," Puzzle reminded her. "I'm involved, so I get a say. If you guys get to use my home for dangerous App experimentation, I get a vote on how we proceed from here. Can't say I'm pleased to be along for the ride on one of Tracer's crusades... but it's not my first time, is it? I pointed you towards ViruFax, if you recall."

"Yeah... that's fair," Beta agreed, pulling up a chair for herself by the fireplace. "Where's Spark?"

"*mpgrhpmh.*"

The grumble came from the kitchen, as did Spark, armed with a cup of steaming joe.

"Was taking a nap," she explained, before taking a fourth seat at the coffee table. (Possibly the first time she'd ever used the coffee table for its intended purpose.) "Still feel shitty, but no time to laze around the place. So... what'd you find out?"

Tracer opened his research notes, including all the illegally obtained connection information from the Puzzle-Kopy.

"The Karnival acts both as a beta testing community and as the point-of-distribution for the KopyBots," he explained. "My scans of Puzzle's kopy prove that. The key to disarming the Dex virus lies in infiltrating that community and locating the kopy machine."

"One stop shopping for destroying the entire operation," Spark said, with a smile. "I like it."

"Cleansing Dex's infection from the system will be tricky. For starters, we'd need access to whatever App is generating the KopyBots... unlikely it'll be out in the open and unsecured. After finding it, we need to hack into it to plant an inactive version of the virus in place of the real one."

"A placebo? Why bother? Yank the virus out and be done with it."

"The infections may be intentional," Tracer reminded her. "If we remove the infection vector completely, they can simply re-install it. If we swap it for harmless placebo tattoo, they won't know anything's different."

"Yeah, okay, I can see that. What about the existing infected, though?"

"I'm afraid there's not much we can do for them, short of personally de-infecting each of them, which is implausible. At this point, priority one must be silently halting this infection vector from creating any further drones for Dex."

"Okay. Sounds good. Or... and I'm just saying this is an option... we can blow the entire place to bits," Spark suggested. "Get a bomb, tuck it away somewhere, go home, wait a few minutes, kaboom. #Solved."

"Which would murder everyone in the server, I'd like to point out. That would 'solve' the existing infected, but at high moral cost..."

"So warn 'em to clear the place out first with a bomb threat. Big and scary, like giant text boxes reading 'YER ALL GONNA DIE' or something equally overdramatic. Put the fear of the One into 'em so they never do anything like this again, *then* destroy everything they've made. Nobody dies, everybody wins. Except them. Sound fun?"

"Fun and ineffective. Anybody running this kind of enterprise will have backups they can restore from. That's why I'm suggesting we simply replace the virus with a placebo and sneak out; it stops Dex's ambitions cold, and nobody's any the wiser."

"Screw Dex, my grudge is against the Karnival. We're targeting *them* and the bastard that made it."

"Spark... not only can't we stop the Karnival, I'm not sure we *should* do anything to stop them."

"Seriously?!" Spark asked, setting her cup down with entirely too much force. "*Seriously?* You were arguing that there was nothing wrong with summoning a brain-dead slutty version of people before, too. Who are you and what have you done with my bro? Are you a KopyBot? The *real* Tracer would be all over this with a sword of fire!"

Now, Tracer had to play Zero's Advocate. A role he loathed to his core... but had to play, as logic demanded.

"From a certain standpoint, this is a legitimate business offering non-sentient toy Apps," he said. "Nothing they're selling is technically illegal in Horizon or Athena Online. There's a violation of privacy angle here, and that concerns me greatly, but the actual KopyBots are harmless. They arrive by default with warped personalities, anyway; just because Qelk turned that off doesn't mean there aren't legitimate uses of them."

"*No* use of a bot wearing my face is legitimate, as far as I'm concerned. What about my rights?"

"Considering the Karnival operates out of the Chanarchy... you have no rights. There's no legal authority whatsoever there. That also means if we engage in an act of massive property damage, we're essentially terrorists acting solely on our own righteousness in a place where we have no authoritative right to do so."

"Yeah, well, anarchy cuts both ways," Spark countered. "They want to live somewhere with no laws, that means they reap the benefit *and* the drawback. They can do anything they like... and so can we. There's no reason we can't burn the place down."

"'Can' and 'should' are different concepts. One is technical, one is ethical. *Should* we burn the place down, Spark? It offends us to the core, yes, but does that give us the right to destroy it? Consider all the people who are offended by Beta's existence. She doesn't live under any jurisdiction now; Floating Point is much like the Chanarchy in that regard. If someone could break in here do they have the right to kill her?"

"That's not the same thing at all!"

"I know. After all, nobody real is being hurt by the Karnival, compared to the idea of murdering a person—"

And Beta banged the table hard enough to make Spark's coffee cup jump.

"*Stop*. Saying that," she insisted... in a dangerously quiet voice, compared to the sudden furniture impact she'd just made. "Stop saying they're not real, that they're just toys, Apps, bots. You weren't the one who had to be there when they died. You didn't have them in your arms as they faded away. You don't get to make that call. Neither of you."

Tracer, realizing he may have pushed too far, tried to calm the discussion. "Beta, I'm not saying I *like* the Karnival. They're wannabe rapists and thugs. I'm just not sure we have the right—"

"I don't care if we don't have the right. I don't... I really don't give a damn anymore," Beta replied, finding exactly the right word she wanted to use. "Not one damn. We have to stop them. What they're doing is wrong, and if we have to commit our own wrongs to put this right... well... so be it. For the sake of all the lives they're destroying we have to find a way to stop this."

"Assuming KopyBots are people..."

"They *are* people. Just because our social construct of what it means to be a person hasn't caught up to this new reality doesn't change that fact. I'm with Spark on this, Tracer. The Karnival has to go."

Sensing the change in the wind... Tracer decided to put his objections aside, and move to the end game.

"We put this to a vote," he concluded. "I'm voting against destroying the Karnival. Spark, Beta? And Puzzle. You get your say, as I promised."

"I'm for destroying the Karnival," Beta spoke, raising her hand politely.

Spark retrieved her coffee cup, mopping up some of the spillage with a napkin. "#FuckThoseGuys," she added. "Fuck 'em right in the ear. I'm for destroying the Karnival. Puzzle?"

Puzzle, who had been listening to both sides the entire while... knew her answer right from the start.

"Burn it down," she spoke. "Right or wrong, doesn't matter to me. They hurt my #BFF and I will not stand for that."

No sense fighting it. Tracer sat back, to internally accept that this would be the direction moving forward. Besides... even as his much-vaunted rational self objected, the rest of him swallowed the group's decision with considerable satisfaction.

"We have one weapon far superior to a bomb. It offers us the greatest chance of effectively ruining them," he explained. "We know the *truth* behind the Karnival's success. I've been researching this ever since collecting the initial data from Puzzle's bot. This... may be an unpleasant revelation..."

"Nothing about this experience *isn't* an unpleasant revelation," Spark pointed out. "Hit me with it."

So, Tracer opened the remainder of his files...

...including the MyFace profiles of Spark and Puzzle.

"When we searched for a person to duplicate, the bot made several external connections I had difficulty fully identifying at first. It's the same reason I can't easily trace Messenger connections; the content distribution network is wide, encompassing many servers. So, the key to understanding the problem came in the failure to copy myself or Beta... because neither of us use MyFace. While Spark and Puzzle are, to be fair, complete MyFace addicts. The KopyBots have API backend access to MyFace. Personal information, avatar parameters, cross-site visitor tracking data, logs upon logs upon logs... one-stop shopping for duplicating the soul."

Spark stared at her own floating profile... littered with hashtags. #GirlsNightOut. #ItsComplicated. Check-ins at various locations like ShipTo and HolyHymnal, details of outings at clubs, rants about gamers, praises for and defenses of her new friend Beta...

She lived her life through social media. If anybody wanted to duplicate the experience of *being* Spark, that'd be the place to gather your parameters. Even without the secret parts, the underlying crusade to find Verity's killer and the true nature of her home, they'd produced something close enough to Spark to pass as her.

And why not share her life with all of Netwerk? She maintained a highly public profile, after all. She was a pro gamer, a streamer, a minor celebrity. Part of her marketing was to allow fans to keep track of her life, and she was happy to share if they were happy to subscribe to her channel and pay her bills. Why not? What was the harm, after all?

But...

"But all *my* posts are locked," Puzzle spoke, coming to the same conclusion. "I use MyFace quite a bit, but only within specific circles. Simply ransacking MyFace for openly-available data wouldn't have given them enough to make a facsimile..."

"Unless they have an under-the-table agreement with the MyFace corporation," Tracer concluded. "I thought of that as well, and reviewed the MyFace terms of service agreement looking for holes... you know, the fifty page legalese everybody agrees to when they make an account. They claim not to sell your information to third parties... but first party affiliates, that's fair game, as no sales are involved. They simply *give* that information away to developers that sign exclusive contracts with them. I believe the Karnival is a first party affiliate; it's the dark half of MyFace..."

He closed the files, to reduce the clutter of data hovering around his person.

"This means that legally, they're *still* in the clear," he added. "And again, legally, we have no right to stop them. It's a legitimate business arrangement, one which their own customers agreed to by clicking 'Agree' without reading."

"Nobody reads that shit, Tracer. Nobody."

"Perhaps you should have, before agreeing to the terms..."

"Doesn't make what they're doing right. They don't have a *right* to steal our identities; 'can' does not mean 'should,' just like you said. Regardless of how 'legally clear' they are... this is wrong. And we need to shut it down."

"Very well. Much like how we dealt with XSept... even if a court of law would side with MyFace, the court of public opinion will not be so tolerant. My proposal is this: we scrub the Dex virus from their machinery as I've already suggested... and once that's settled, we anonymously leak the details of their arrangement with MyFace along with any customer lists we can dig up. Even if the Karnival continues, it will no longer spread active infections, and the public will be forewarned of their true nature. Customer base dies out, service dies with it. Done."

Quite a bit to swallow. The others in the room considered it, each along their own line of thought.

"I do like the one-two punch of it," Spark had to admit. "Stop Dex in his tracks, and ruin their lives in the process. In and out, #NiceAndClean. As much fun as it might be to completely trash the place... this is a solid choice. ...dammit, Tracer, why didn't you just suggest this at the start?"

"Because it poses the same quandary we faced with XSept: it's doxxing the creators and clients of the Karnival, and may result in deaths. Nobody will believe our crackpot theory without some actual clients to point fingers at, people who will go under the gun as a result. All told, this is a questionable and cowardly tactic..."

"Yeah, well... I'm done questioning it. If the court of public opinion is the only court these guys can be tried in thanks to the Chanarchy's protection, that's what we're gonna use."

"As you like it. We will expose the Karnival's truth to light, and let justice find them. In one form or another. Are we agreed...?"

Beta nodded in agreement... but not right away. "I don't like doxxing as a weapon," she spoke, quietly. "I didn't like it when we used it on XSept and I don't like it now, but... if we can quickly discredit the Karnival and its clients at the outset, fewer KopyBots will be harmed. For their sake, I'll go along with this plan, I guess..."

"If Spark's in favor, I'm in favor," Puzzle added. "Are we done yelling at each other now? Everything good?"

Thankful for that to be settled, Tracer closed all his files and got to his feet.

"I'm running point on this, as I'm the only one who can enter the Karnival," he spoke. "I'm a valued customer, after all, and I'll be sporting a fake barbed heart tattoo to prove it. I'll wear Beta's glasses, so I'm not going in alone. The investigation may take several days, since I'll need to locate the kopy machine and wait for Beta to determine how to hack it. I can't promise immediate results... but I'll do everything in my power to make this happen."

Beta bit her lip. "I wish I could go with you in person. If you do manage to find the kopy machine, being physically present to hack it would be a lot easier than relaying instructions to you..."

"Considering where I'm going... I'd rather you and Spark have stayed behind, regardless. It will not be a pleasant experience, and the fallout if things go wrong will be extreme. On that note... Puzzle, if you prefer to stay here at Floating Point for a few days, I'd be happy to offer one of the guest rooms."

"My apartment may end up crawling with Karnival goons, so yes, I believe I'll accept that offer," Puzzle agreed. "I don't plan to take up permanent residence, but... thanks, all the same. I'm glad you trust me enough at this point to suggest that."

Tracer wasn't used to saying 'you're welcome,' as he rarely gave an inch to anyone outside of his immediate family. Nobody showed him gratitude, since he did nothing to merit it.

And yet... now Beta was living here, and Puzzle was a welcome guest. Puzzle, who he'd pushed back against allowing into Floating Point for so long, until Beta forced his hand during the RansomMe affair. Again, Beta had the right idea, as Puzzle's involvement had proven crucial to making this plan work.

Beta once suggested that they should be more honest with people. To approach them openly, rather than deploying subterfuge. Allies could be found out there in the wild of Netwerk, if they were willing to look for them rather than seeing only enemies around every corner...

But tonight, he was headed into a community founded on the principle of consequence-free abomination. A lion's den of those who yearned to make the wrong choice. Were they worth considering as potential allies? Were they worth sparing?

Already, he was making his mental shopping list of self-defense systems and tools he'd want to have on hand if he was going into such a place virtually alone. And the backspacer was certainly high on that list.

Tracer had played the infiltration game before. Grifting and social engineering demanded a certain level of direct personal risk; walking right into the lion's den while announcing "Hello, I am a lion" had a tendency to rustle the actual lions into action. But in the end, no amount of fancy tech or hacktools could equal the power of digging up inside information from the inside.

This was, however, one of the few times he'd ever gone in alone. Usually Spark was at his side, playing a supporting role in the grift... and ready to launch into action if anything went wrong. If the lions smelled any non-lion on him, the only defense Tracer had was the backspacer and a few layers of firewalls. Capable, but not nearly as effective as someone trained in the art of self defense.

He hadn't gone in unprepared, of course. He'd purchased yet another in a long series of generic male avatars wearing generic clothing, JohnDoes designed to keep one socially presentable while functionally anonymous. Chances were that wouldn't set off any warning bells, either, not if other Karnival clients were engaging in skeevy activities. Nobody here would want to wear their true faces.

Also... he'd applied a realistic looking barbed-wire heart tattoo to the side of his neck, plainly visible. Beta had designed it to be more than a mere avatar decoration, a placebo malware App in its own right. When the time came to replace the infection vector in the kopy machine with a harmless dupe, he'd peel that right off his skin and drop it in place.

Assuming he found the kopy machine. Assuming they didn't catch him and nail him to the wall, without any backup to rely on.

Fortunately, he wasn't *completely* alone.

"*Getting the signal loud and clear, no dropped packets or lag,*" Beta announced over their private Messenger link. "*I'm studying the Karnival's open ports now... it looks like aside from an access lock keyed into your, uh, key, it's a perfectly normal server...*"

"*Be careful not to sniff too many ports,*" Tracer replied, while getting his bearings in unfamiliar territory. "*I won't want anybody sniffing you back. Don't risk it.*"

"*Same goes for you, don't take any unneeded risks. If there's no connection lock zones in play, be ready to leave at a moment's notice. This isn't worth your*

214

*life, Tracer... and on a strictly selfish level I'm going to want my eyes back safe and sound, too."*

So, two sets of eyes surveyed the landscape of the Karnival.

He'd landed at the designated arrival point for the server, at the gates of a massive... well, carnival. Big top tents made with colorful fabrics, music in the air, and bright blue skies. If not for a complete lack of tourists wandering around the place it would've appeared pleasantly quaint. Without occupants, it was just... eerie. (Although really, it'd be far eerier if there were children running around, given the erotic nature of the KopyBots.)

Shortly after arrival, a clown approached. An actual clown, with greasepaint and a big red nose and a funny wig. Because *of course* clowns.

Still... something felt off about this clown, compared to traditional circus entertainers. He had a larger build, more emphasis on stocky strength than a wacky cartoonish frame. Clowns could wear any avatar they liked, and typically picked an exaggerated one to keep the kids entertained. This clown wasn't aiming to entertain kids, instead embracing the harlequin aesthetic as a layer over his normal avatar. (Presumably his normal avatar.) The end result result lie somewhere between friendly and intimidating...

The fact that the barbed-wire heart had been stitched elegantly into his silken finery certainly tilted things in favor of intimidation. He wasn't even hiding his infection; it had become an integral part of his persona.

"Hallo hallo!" he greeted, with a bright smile. "New arrival, new arrival! Nice to see a new face, a new mark. I'm always ready to drop whatever I'm doing and come greet a friend-yet-to-be!"

"Hi...?" Tracer tried.

"You must be the new tester Arjay sent our way! My records indicate you've obtained one of the keys we gave him, and indeed you've sampled our fine product. Thank you for considering the Karnival for your entertainment needs! We're looking forward to feedback about your KopyBot experience. Oh, and I'm not a system agent or anything, I'm a Program like you. Feel free to ask questions. Name's Bonko!"

"Seriously? 'Bonko' the clown?"

"The circus-themed branding was all my idea, so I've gotta run with it myself, yeah?" Bonko replied. "Being a good sport's half the fun. Nothing's worth half-assing, I say!"

"Wait. *Your* idea? You made KopyBots?"

"Well, no, but I do run the main event here at the Karnival. I'm the community manager... the ringmaster, if you will. I considered a top hat and a whip, but that's not really *me*. But enough about me! I'm here to make sure *you* continue to have a null of a good time. What's your name, friend?"

"Trowe," Tracer lied.

"Nope, lying!" Bonko recognized, immediately.

...briefly Tracer highlighted the backspacer in his inventory, ready to summon it at a moment's notice.

"Hey, don't freak out, I'm just honking your horn!" Bonko clarified—pulling out a little brass horn and giving it a *HORNK* in response. "Nobody here uses their real name or their real face. Why would you? It's such a buzzkill to drag your mundane life into this server with you. I say: be who you want to be! I don't mind, and neither will they. We're a friendly community, welcoming and inviting to all!"

"That's... good," Tracer spoke, closing his inventory for now. "I am a bit puzzled, though. This is not quite what I was expecting..."

"Would you prefer leather and chains everywhere? Or maybe black and white latex tents?"

"Not *prefer*, so much as expect..."

"Expectation! Pfah, I say. I like the lighter circus motif. It adds a touch of approachable whimsy! Too many places like this are dark and creepy... that's not what I wanted for this product. You've got to take the piss out of a thing or you'll end up being *way* too serious about it, yeah? KopyBots are fun and games!"

The voice in Tracer's ear disagreed.

"*There's nothing 'fun' about what they're doing to these poor people,*" Beta complained. "*Dressing it up in bright colors and tweaking their victim's minds doesn't make it any less bleak...*"

"Sooo, let me show you around the place," Bonko requested, twirling his horn on one finger before pointing it at various tents. "The tents are chatrooms; we've got a good off-topic / general room, where you can really soak in the rich Karnival community. That's my goal here, after all... community building. I don't want this to be a one-and-done plaything, but a society full of passionate individuals!"

"How large is the community?" Tracer asked. "It's still a closed beta test, correct?"

"Indeed, indeed. One that's growing by the day... we want a solid user base before we throw open the gates to the public. People who can help explain our ideals to others. I mean, let's face it, KopyBots are a pretty crazy idea! One which can only be sold by a street team of enthusiastic supporters. People who have sampled the fruit and know how sweet it is!"

The blood red of the jester's heart design indicated what sort of fruits they had to offer.

"Yes," Tracer agreed, falling now into the pattern of his social engineering. "My experience was... it wasn't what I was expecting. But like you said, who cares about expectation? It was really amazing. I mean... I have trouble putting it into words, but... I want more. I want to see how far it can go."

Bonko clasped a hand on Tracer's shoulder, his smile growing ever-wider.

"That's the spirit!" he declared. "And don't worry, we're here to help you explore all the Karnival's offerings. Soon... you won't know what life was like before you had this kind of fun on tap whenever you wanted it. Y'know, we have more than just the chatroom tents; there's the tunnel of love, the funhouses, the freakshow, the animal taming rings... all sorts of *specialized* areas where you can get some private time with a KopyBot. Or you can bring friends along, once you get to know a few in the community. Sharing is caring! What do you say? Want the grand tour, my friend...?"

Clearly, the clown was eager to share this wonderland of carnal horror. Perhaps he'd be willing to share the location of the kopy machine... in time. After being buttered up and plied by a healthy amount of social engineering, this could give Tracer what he needed to destroy the Karnival for good. Diving in head-first to earn the trust of Bonko the community manager was the perfect in-road to his end game.

But... that would likely involve participating in the abuse of KopyBots. Possibly being infected by the Dex virus. Subjecting Beta to such sights, by virtue of wearing her glasses...

One thing at a time.

"I think I'll hit the chatrooms for now," Tracer decided. "No need to overdo it on my first day, right? It's like wine. You have to savor each little sip."

"I'm more of a beer guy, but okay, let's go with that," Bonko spoke, waving Tracer along. "Off to the main event, then!"

Never before had Tracer thought that a gathering of malware-mad perverts could be completely boring.

As he sat on a hay bale in the middle of the three-ring chatroom circus, he listened to random men wearing random JohnDoe style avatars yammer back and forth about nothing in particular. He'd bounce from thread to thread, teleporting from one circle of hay bales to another, sampling the conversation as he went.

One thread:

"That's such bullshit. Ganksquad's not going to make top eight, much less the finals," a man with a barbed wire heart on his left hand spoke. "They're a bunch of noobs who got damn lucky taking down RTFM during the qualifiers. If RTFM's server hadn't been DDOSed they'd have crushed GS."

"What are you, a tinfoil hat conspiracist? Is everything a hack to you? GS won 'cause they got skills," a beefy looking shirtless man with a tattoo on his chest replied. "That midlane gank at the 40m mark was a thing of beauty and you're an idiot for not realizing that. You need to git gud at CoC before you can judge other players."

Sensing that was going nowhere, he tried hopping over to a thread which had some actual KopyBots on it:

"My Danny is one hell of a stud!" the brainwashed KopyBot declared, tracing a finger around his left nipple a few times. "When he touches me it feels oooohhh so good..."

"You know, I bet the real Senator Agni is just as slutty as this," Danny suggested. "I've heard all sorts of stories about how that MILF slept her way to the top of the RedCore Party. The prudish attitude she shows on TV? That's just for the cameras."

"That's nothing! I grabbed a copy of Snowi the other day, and—"

Laughter echoed up from other men sitting around the circle.

"Fucking kids. Grow up, will you? We've all had Snowi in one way or another," Danny replied. "It's nothing to brag about and the fact that you give a shit about her shows how lousy you are at picking KopyBots. She's not all that great. I mean, you run her in Pure Mode and you can get something out of it, but all that work just to say you've had an SJW...? Nah. She's old news. You need a more acquired taste... and politicians, that's where you find some real gems. Agni, show the nice boy your diplomatic skills...?"

"Gah!" a chatter blurted, covering his eyes as Agni began to unzip Danny's pants. "Seriously, man, take that shit to a private room if you wanna play with your bot! No sex in the chatroom. I don't wanna see your hairy little dong..."

Another thread:

"I don't think the Karnival should have a stance on #CodeHonesty," a bespectacled gentleman spoke. (No visible tattoo, but Tracer could see through his hacked eyes the rotating cloud address of a malware connection somewhere on his back.) "We need as many people as possible to use KopyBots when we're out of beta, but we're going to be innately controversial right out of the gate. We can't alienate the audience by grabbing onto another controversy on top of that and running wild."

"But it's such an obvious pile of lies!" someone else in the thread insisted. "People are already saying that Cup8 was a fraud, that the secret results of a Horizon audit pegged him as one. #CodeHonesty are a bunch of whining neckbearded manbabies who can't accept that there's GRILLS in their playhouse..."

"Except nobody really knows the truth, and that includes us. I mean, other than the truth that Beta's a slut and Snowi's a whore, but that's besides the point. We have to think about the future of the Karnival, here. This is our haven, and the last thing we need is to bring someone else's war to our door..."

"*This is ridiculous,*" Tracer complained, internally.

Beta's words were quite welcome, to help drown out the nonsense he'd been swallowing for the last few hours. Having someone he knew and cared for helped him feel less alone in the middle of these dozens and dozens of nobodies.

"*You don't have to defend your participation in this, Tracer. I know you don't believe a word they say,*" Beta said. "*Besides, this is valuable data we're gathering.*"

"*Listening to idiots rant about sports and hashtags? How is this valuable?*"

"*It's not the words, it's the pattern. All this... hate. Even in the sports thread, there's so much cruel language, so much biting at each other. The intensity of it... you can feel the hate but also the passion in their words. Love AND hate, equally. They're taking a domineering stance and defending it violently if need be.*"

"*Due to the Dex virus?*"

"*That's my thought, yes. We haven't had much opportunity to see it up close like this. We've suspected it ramps up one's self-righteousness, making terrible ideas feel like glorious ones, right? Now we have confirmation. It's about extremes... devoted love of an extreme and hatred of all else.*"

"*They wouldn't see it that way. Bonko talks about that passion representing a strong community bond...*"

"*When you strip all individuality and subtle nuance out of a community, it's not about the community at all. It's about worship of the image you've constructed your community around. Listen to the words; these people can't find any middleground, it's either yes or no, right or wrong, agree with me or I'll call you an idiot. ...skip over to Bonko's thread, you'll see what I mean.*"

Tracer bounced over to the largest of the circles, dropping into the conversation in progress.

At the center of it stood the ringmaster... Bonko the Clown, speaking from the heart. Likely the one sewn into his costume, pumping out a series of random Netwerk addresses as it tied into the Dex virus's cloud server. Tracer could see the malware's constant link to that corrupt source, even as the words spilled out.

"I look around and I see a new generation," Bonko spoke. "Not just of men, either. I know some of you are women wearing male avatars, and honestly, you shouldn't have to do that! I consider that my own failing, not making a welcoming enough environment for you to enjoy openly. Pornography shouldn't be this big taboo, this thing nobody admits to adoring, especially not women. We live in a sexually open society, do we not? What's so bad about admitting you've got itches to scratch?"

"*All of which is reasonable so far,*" Beta commented. "*But let him continue ranting. He'll inevitably end up where the virus leads him...*"

"I'm just saying we have to be careful," another replied. "We can't show too much behind the curtain. Look, we all know the antics we get up to while playing with these bots. All of us have tried Pure Mode at least once. Outsiders won't like hearing about the details..."

"Maybe not at first... but this will become the new normal. That's what I'm trying to say," Bonko explained. "We're carving out the future of Netwerk society, here and now! Smashing down barriers of what is and isn't acceptable. What we do is ultimately harmless, right? No matter how 'extreme' society considers it to be, we're hurting no one. They're APPS! They're our slaves, our playthings to do with as we please! Do we torture? Do we rape? Please, how do you rape a toaster? The old generation will apply crusty old social standards to us, and they'll be dead wrong..!"

Now, Bonko hopped up on top of a hay bale, his squeaky shoes somewhat undermining his seriousness. But that smile was quite serious indeed... as the wires on his chest animated, pumping in and out of the heart's valves.

"We've all tasted the same fruit. We all bear the same mark," he reminded them. "We know what drives us and we accept that, we accept each other. WE are the future, not them! We need to fight. We need to struggle, and fight, and accept *no* compromise! THIS is your family, THIS is your community! Rally yourselves around our Karnival; we will push it forward into the heart of the social zeitgeist. And anybody who gets in our way, who slams us or harasses us or thinks they can silence our voices... the prudes and the busybodies and the would-be SJWs, those subcreatures, that scum of Netwerk... well. We'll show them what we're *really* capable of!"

The response was nearly unanimous.

Nods of agreement. Smiles. Some cruel, some eager, all of them knowing. A few utterances of "fuck yeah" or "got that right" or "tell 'em, Bonko." The group was in unison on this, all them marked, all of them tasting the same fruit...

"*That's what I meant,*" Beta explained, over the Messenger link. "*This isn't just about a shared hobby. The virus makes it feel like every single issue is a matter of life and death. They're ready to go to war over this, just like #CodeHonesty. A binary reaction: you're with us or against us. No grey area at all...*"

Tracer had to do the same, had to nod and smile and give his assent. He cheered with the crowd as they soaked in their mutual love and loathing. It didn't matter how Tracer really felt; this ploy would move him closer to the endgame.

So, the crowd response became nearly unanimous response.

Except for one, and it wasn't Tracer himself.

One in the back of this thread, a participant who hadn't been participating...

He looked just like the others. A generic looking male avatar, nothing out of the ordinary, nothing to make him stand out. A bit dressed down compared to them, slacking off in a simple t-shirt with a *coredump* band logo, but otherwise quite normal... right down to the heart tattoo on his neck, similarly placed to the one Tracer wore.

And similar to Tracer's tattoo, it was fake.

His eyes could pierce the Apps of a Program, determine what connections they were making across Netwerk. The Dex virus maintained a constant connection to his personal cloud server, the one they'd called the 'Zero' in months past. Fakes wouldn't have that connection... fakes like Tracer's, and fakes like this one.

*"Tracer, are you seeing that too...? The one who isn't cheering?"* Beta asked.

*"Yes. And his tattoo's only decorative,"* Tracer added, knowing that part of his unique HUD vision wouldn't broadcast to his counterpart. *"He doesn't belong here. Something's wrong..."*

And gone, disconnected from the server. None of the cheering men noticed his passing, none save Tracer.

"Right! I'm feeling all fired up," Bonko declared. "Let's keep this party going. I'm opening up a private room in the freakshow; who's up for a little kopy-swap? Show me your favorite kopy and I'll show you yours. We'll tag team this thing! Don't be shy, we're all in this together. ...hey, Trowe, you're the newcomer here. Who'd you summon, when you first played around?"

An answer. He needed an answer that would satisfy these hungry smiles...

"My sister," Tracer spoke, matching the grins. "I made her totally hot for me, too. I figured... why not? She'd never know. It's just for fun, yeah?"

"HAH! There! Right there, that, right there!" Bonko declared, honking his horn excitedly. "THAT is the right attitude for the new generation of Netwerk. Life's all fun and games; it only has as much weight as *you* give it. Drop that weight, and the world's yours for the taking! Let's go. Let's do this. Swap me your sister and I'll swap you my favorite toy. How about it? Ever want to see someone else railing her...?"

The timing for this was critical. He had to play along, had to maintain this new social connection... but not up to the point where he'd have to do the deed. A delicate dance...

"Absolutely," he agreed. "Let's do this."

Tracer got to his feet, joining the smaller group lead by the clown in charge. He stayed at the front of that pack, however, alongside his new best friend. The freakshow tents were physically distant, and the teleports from thread to thread only worked inside the main chatroom tent. They'd have to walk... giving him enough time.

Once out in the light of day, he made his move.

"Hey, you know that guy in the thread?" Tracer asked Bonko, in casual conversation. "The one with the *coredump* t-shirt? How come he's not joining us?"

"It's a free server. Folks can come and go as they please," the clown suggested.

"Yeah, he didn't seem into it in general. Why is that...? You know everybody, right? What's his deal?"

"Leave him alone, okay? It's his choice not to participate. Nobody hassles Marti but me," Bonko replied... his smile still present, but now quite forced. "You're new here, so you don't know that rule. But you mess with Marti, you mess with Bonko. Got it?"

"I wasn't gonna mess with him. I was just curious, that's..."

And Tracer paused, a short distance before reaching the freakshow tents. Did his best to look distracted... then mildly annoyed.

"My sister's bugging me over Messenger," he declared. "Sorry, guys. Can't play. I gotta go home and take care of this."

It was a gamble, of course. He had to play along closely enough to appear to be on board, without actually doing the deed... and that meant making up excuses for why he couldn't participate. If Bonko didn't accept it, if he suspected a ruse...

Fortunately, Bonko swallowed it completely.

"Family can be such a pain in the ass... but they're family, you know?" he said. "You've got to look out for your sister. She's all you've got, in the end. But... I hope you'll come back to hang out with your new family, once you've sorted that out..."

"If I can, sure. I'm loving this place," Tracer lied. "Can't wait to come back and have some fun."

---

A world away, in a server spread across dozens of servers, Spark was working out her frustrations through intense App usage.

She'd bought this sparring dummy as a way to stay in fighting shape, between those life-or-death moments which were all too common during Tracer's crusade. Limited in form but with just enough A.I. to let her run through basic martial arts exercises, ones she'd been running through since she was a child. Of course, those classes her parents paid for were meant to be a distraction, a way to keep her busy after school and out of their hair... they never thought she'd make it into a true lifestyle. Now, it was an anchor in a stormy sea...

Hooking strike. Spinning block. A leveraging throw, to send the dummy tumbling... followed by a leaping mantis strike, nailing it with her weaponized fingers.

The burst of flame flared with high intensity, enough to destroy the dummy completely. Fortunately she could summon up a new one to replace it. And another, and another, and another...

After brutalizing murdering the fifteenth artificial training partner, the killing blow on the sixteenth held back inches away from landing.

It had no face, a generic Program-shaped model. But if it had the face of another, would she be so casual about mauling it...?

The next strike came to Puzzle's guest room door, and was more of a light knocking than a knockout blow.

Already, Puzzle had decorated her room tastefully despite only staying a few days. She wouldn't be caught dead in unfashionable surroundings; an array of selfies with her friends decorated the walls... as well as some lovely potted pants, simulations she'd been growing in her spare time, and a very nice padded quilt she kept handy as a portable sleeping surface. Very homey, overall.

She looked up from watering the plants, putting the gardening tool back into inventory on realizing how troubled her friend looked.

"Go ahead, spill it," Puzzle said. "You're still feeling off, I can tell."

"I've been off ever since finding that kopy of me. And I'm tired of feeling off. I already talked to Beta about it and I still don't feel like I'm sorted out, so... mind if I bend your ear a bit? You're always good at helping me figure these messes out..."

"Absolutely," Puzzle agreed, pulling out a chair to relax in, summoning a copy of it for her friend. "I'd been expecting you'd drop by, honestly. What with your compatriots off having an adventure without you, I knew you'd be going a little stir crazy. Let's investigate that craziness, why not."

"I know what you're going to say, that I'm freaking out because I saw myself defeated and broken," Spark started. "That it scared me, to see what could happen to me. Despite, y'know, that not being actually me because no way would I ever get crushed like that..."

"Except you could. You totally could get crushed like that, Spark. You run risks every day you work on Tracer's personal quests, going up against madmen and murderers and psychotics. Any one of them could do that to you, if you're unfortunate enough..."

"I'd kick their asses first, #ThankYou."

"That's not an absolute truth. You know I worry about you, Spark. You love risk; you're a gambler, a gamer. You ride the edge and ride it close. So far... you've always come out on top. That can't last..."

"And I got to see first-hand what would happen if I don't come out on top," Spark agreed. "By seeing a version of myself that lost, and lost big. Yes, I get that as well, #ThankYou."

"Scary, isn't it? To think that you might actually *not* be an immortal, undefeatable hero. But that's reality, Spark, for you and for the rest of us. Why do you think I'm hiding out here in Floating Point? I'm terrified. I got wrapped up in a rather scary situation and now I can't safely go home..."

"What's to be scared of? You're perfectly safe here..."

"But nobody is safe in the long term, Spark. When I do eventually go home... what if someone figures out the con you're running on the Karnival, and looks for reprisal?"

"So... don't go home," Spark suggested. "Stay here. I can convince Tracer to let you stay. You'd be safe..."

"Ahh, but that's the crux, isn't it?" Puzzle asked. "Stay safe, hide, do nothing. Or... run a risk and return home, *my* home. You're not getting at what I'm saying, darling. I *am* scared... and I *am* willing to risk it anyway. I want to go home, despite the dangers. I don't want to live my life in terror, I want to live my life."

"Well... good. That's a good attitude to have!"

"So why don't you have it?"

Puzzle folded her fingers in her lap, reading Spark's confused expression before continuing.

"It's very binary for you right now, isn't it?" she asked. "You're either accepting what that kopy represents and therefore too scared to be who you want to be... or you have to assume you could never become what that kopy represents, and fight on. Why not both? Why not be scared, *and* fight for what you believe in? Accept that you are in fact mortal, that you could be hurt. Be scared of it. And fight on despite your fear."

"I'm... that's what I'm doing, right? I'm still gonna fight. Hell, if I could connect to the Karnival I'd be fighting right now! #KickingSomeAss..."

"Ahh, but you're fighting without acknowledging reality! That's what I'm scared of the most, Spark. That you're riding high on denial and may take the *wrong* risks. I'm not saying not to fight, I'm not saying to live in fear. I'm saying... be realistic. Fight with care."

Spark wanted to object.

Instead, the vision of that battered and ruined version of herself kept rising in her thoughts. The worst case outcome, the thing which could not be...

It made her want to crawl inside herself and never leave. Made her want to lash out at the world in anger, to punch someone over and over and over again. Drove her to extremes.

"That could've been me," she recognized. "Any one of these fights I get into, if things tilt one way instead of the other, I'm mincemeat. I understand what you're saying, Puzzle. I'm not some invulnerable avatar of justice. I'm not so far gone into my own ego to think that. But... I'm still going to fight."

"As you should. Fight on, while also accepting your fears. That's all I want, darling."

"Okay, now, what's up with *that*?" Spark asked. "You've always hated this hobby of mine. You're constantly taking snipes at Tracer and his SJW-mad quest. Now you're telling me I *should* fight...?"

Puzzle glanced aside, to the clouds beyond the windows of Floating Point. Calm and peaceful, despite the chaos of Netwerk they represented...

"Maybe I'm coming around," Puzzle said. "I've had time lately to think about that, now that I've been directly involved in Tracer's madness. Maybe... it's not madness. The means are questionable, the motives questionable, but the idea of it isn't wrong. Netwerk can be a terrible place. Anybody willing to put themselves on the line to make it better for the rest of us, well... how can I not admire that? So... I embrace my #BFF the SJW. I'll support you, and that's a promise."

That embrace became very literal, soon after. And it helped wash away Spark's jittering nerves, knowing she had that support in her life... despite the very real fears she faced. With that support, she could fight despite it all.

Her eyes fluttered a few times, as the glasses were fixed back on her own nose.

"Ahh... a moment," Beta requested, staying seated rather than trying to get up right away. "It's always a little disorienting to get my own point-of-view back after loaning it to someone for an extended period of time..."

Tracer assumed a seat across from her, in the great hall of Floating Point.

"We've made some good progress today at the Karnival," he said. "Bonko's far too trusting of his new recruits. They don't suspect that I'm not truly one of them. If I work on him gradually over a few days, earning more and more of that trust... he'll lead us to the kopy machine. I can tell he's the sort to want to show off his handiwork."

"Except... to earn that trust, you're going to have to play with him. I can tell that's what he really wants from you, Tracer. He's not going to show the inner workings of the KopyBot system unless he feels that bond he shares with the others."

"Yes... I've given that some thought. I'd very much like to avoid it, but... if it is truly unavoidable... is it possible to vaccinate me against the Dex virus? Not remove it after it's in place, but prevent it from taking root at all? You've said it's nearly impossible, but perhaps if you link to Floating Point's heart again..."

"What?"

"If I come into contact with the transmission vector inside the KopyBots, I'd rather not return to Floating Point with the enemy's finger on my heart," Tracer suggested. "Perhaps a more pre-emptive version of the malware removal tool you made would work, to insulate me—"

"That's not what I mean! You're saying... you'd abuse one of the bots? Just to earn Bonko's trust?"

"I'm not seeing any way around it, Beta. I'm trying to deceive and manipulate a madman, one who insists on others around him being just as mad as he is. I can't say I find the notion pleasant, but... this is the world we have to move through to achieve justice. It's a filthy world and we must be stained by it, from time to time."

Beta narrowed her eyes, behind those thick frames.

"And who exactly do you plan to torture to make that clown happy?" she asked. "Spark, maybe? You did claim you'd already enjoyed her..."

"Beta! That's repulsive. I only said what I knew he wanted to hear... I'd never consider...! Listen. I can minimize the damage. With a vaccine in place, I could simply pick a perfect stranger and let the personality modifiers do the heavy lifting. I find the concept of physical avatar coupling pointless, true, but I'd obviously lie to Bonko. He'll buy it..."

"And now you're methodically planning how to do what he already wants you to do. It's not worth the price, Tracer. Even if you pick a complete stranger, it's still abhorrent... a stranger is still a person, and the personality modifiers are *not* consent!"

"What choice do we have?"

"What choices DO we have...?" Beta repeated... asking herself as much as she asked him.

They'd backed themselves into a corner with XSept, relying on doxxing to clean up that problem. She'd reluctantly agreed to use the same weapon this time, for the sake of the people being harmed by the Karnival. But was there another way? Were there choices she simply couldn't see...?

Beta glanced around the great library of Floating Point, as she dug for answers. All that knowledge, all those books... ruined in whatever disaster had emptied the server ages ago. A testament to lost lore. Maybe it would've had answers, deep within all those books with the 'W' logo stamped on their spines, if only she could understand what they once represented...

The wholesale destruction of knowledge felt like a very Dex maneuver. The only way to keep the infected giving in to every dark impulse was to keep them in the dark, chasing after a fantasy rather than seeing the world for what it was. The blind leading the blind... an odd metaphor given Beta's own blindness, but it felt fitting.

They needed to find people who could still see. Ones still open to the possibilities.

"Marti," Beta decided. "The one with the fake tattoo. That's the answer."

"Already thought of him," Tracer said. "Too much of an unknown factor. Too risky, given he's under Bonko's protection. If we accidentally enrage Bonko at *best* we lose all access to the Karnival. No, it's better to ply Bonko directly; he's an easily duped fool and the optimal path to our objective."

"Put optimization aside for a moment, okay? You're thinking like Dex, looking to deceive and manipulate. We need to look past that. Marti doesn't belong, and yet he's *there*... and why? That's the key. He doesn't like that place, I could see it clearly! He even knows about the infection, knows enough to fake it. In Marti we may find a potential ally. If we're honest with him about why we're in the Karnival, maybe he'd help us."

Tracer shook his head. "We can't risk exposing ourselves by being truthful with anyone in the Karnival. The sensible play is to go after the egomaniac clown; I *know* he'll crack, in time. I can break him open and take his secrets with ease..."

"At what cost? How deep into that place are you willing to go just to stop them?"

"As deep as need be," he said, on instinct.

Except... he knew how deep that would have to be. Which made his words feel downright irresponsible, two seconds after saying them. He'd been on a roll, determined that he was right... knowing his sister would go along with the decision once he put his foot down. They had a good sense of each other's stubbornness.

But Beta wasn't Spark, was she? She wouldn't back down. And in this case... she was right not to.

Briefly, he hung his head in apology, knowing it was the wrong thing to say. Beta accepted that gesture in turn, silently offering a thankful smile.

"We'll try to contact Marti," he agreed. "But we must be cautious on approach. There could be a deeper darkness there compared to the simplistic darkness of Bonko. I... may need your help, navigating this maze."

"I'll be with you every step of the way," Beta promised. "This is the right choice, Tracer. What we need to do is appeal to the better nature of people, the incorruptible within them. Maybe even appealing to Dex directly, if opportunity presents itself..."

"That... I don't mean to sound callous, Beta, but that sounds very naive."

Her smile showed she hadn't taken it as an insult.

"Time will tell," she decided. "Until then I'm not willing to divide the world into 'good' and 'bad' guys, ones and zeroes. Life is more complicated than that. While Marti may be with the Karnival he's clearly not a believer... and we *will* reach him."

The next day, Tracer and Beta worked to track down the mysterious Marti.

This hunt meant searching the Karnival a bit deeper than Tracer was comfortable with, especially now that he'd committed himself to not participating in the fun and games. At first he'd tried hanging around the main chatroom under the big top, but Marti never made a return appearance... meaning Tracer had to start exploring other parts of the Karnival, and dealing with the sights seen there.

Witnessing the worst of Programkind was something Tracer could cope with. But he wasn't the only one who had to watch, forced to glance into the various cells and small tents he passed, if only to momentarily scan for Marti's presence. Removing the glasses wouldn't help, as they were still broadcasting audio... including the screams.

The screams, and the squeals of delight. It was the squeals that troubled Tracer more, mewling passionate cries from KopyBots forced to crave whatever they were offered.

"...*I can't understand it. I just can't,*" Beta spoke over their link, breaking her silence after an hour of this.

"*Between consenting Programs anything is fair game, I feel. But this is... certainly not that. A gross violation of privacy, and done with absolute malice rather than mutual respect,*" Tracer replied, looking away from yet another open display of depravity.

"*It's the malice I can't understand. How anyone could be cruel enough to summon up a dream of someone true and real, just to make them the object of their fantasies...*"

"*And you're still certain we should be appealing to the better nature of Programkind?*"

"*Absolutely,*" she spoke, despite her wobbling voice. "*We have to. It has to work. It... it has to...*"

Tracer jammed his hands in his pockets to avoid letting the tension in his knuckles show. Because right now, what he most wanted to be doing was punching every other person he saw. Past the cages, through a hallway, around a corner, and...

...face to face with Beta.

A gasp of shock flowed over his Messenger link, the woman on the other end of the line rendered just as speechless by the sight. Panic gripped him for a moment, as the woman with loose brown hair and thick-rimmed glasses turned her empty eyes to him. But when she opened her mouth... it broke the spell.

"Smash the patriarchy!" she declared. "I'm a cheap little whore. I'm a cheap little whore. Smash the patriarchy..."

"Hey, get back here...!"

And finally, the object of his hunt appeared.

Marti chased after this cheap kopy of Beta, holding a diagnostic tool in hand for analyzing App memory buffers. He'd recognized it from Beta's wide array of tools... special-purpose Apps used only for debugging programs. Which meant...

"Sorry, she's not quite done," Marti admitted... flicking a switch and dropping the fake Beta to the floor, unconscious. "I tried cross referencing the data, but it didn't work the way I'd hoped. ...uh, if you wouldn't mind giving me a hand...? Something's wrong with her physical mass too, she's a bit heavy..."

Tracer bent low, hooking one of Beta's arms over his shoulders. Marti took the other one, as they began to walk away from the playground of delights behind them... towards one of the private back rooms.

"She's our number one requested KopyBot," Marti explained. "But there's just not enough data available to build a proper profile. I was... *uff*... hoping I could do an indirect build. Make an image of her based on the data of other kopyable subjects..."

"People live on in the memories of others," Tracer recognized.

"Yeah. Problem is, well, #CodeHonesty. Any wide sweep to try to answer the question of 'Who is Beta?' returns this unworkable mess..."

The importance of the door they arrived at was not lost on Tracer. "*Employees Only!!!*" it declared, with three exclamation marks.

"Do you need any help?" Tracer asked. "I'm a programmer, myself. Maybe I could assist..."

"I... don't know. Bonko prefers I keep the specifics to myself," Marti spoke, digging out his access keys while keeping the Beta kopy propped up. "Trade secrets. If any competitors find out how the system works, we could lose our launch advantage when the service leaves beta..."

"I won't tell if you won't tell," Tracer promised. "Please. I could be of tremendous help..."

"Uh... thanks, but I don't think I should. Don't let me interrupt you from your... fun. I've got a lot of work to do, so if you don't mind..."

"*We need to open up,*" Beta spoke quickly. "*If he thinks we're faithful followers, he won't talk to us!*"

"Do you think all of this is fun?" he asked... tempering the question with enough nonconfrontational quiet to ensure he wasn't pushing for a specific answer.

Marti paused, keys halfway into the door lock.

"Bonko thinks we'll open big across Netwerk," he cautiously stated. "That plenty of people will think it's fun."

"I wasn't asking was Bonko thinks. It's patently obvious what Bonko thinks. I'm asking what *you* think. You've never actually used a KopyBot, have you? Not in the way the others use them..."

"I don't know. Does it matter? Look, I'm busy, so if you don't mind..."

"*Tracer, convince him! Don't dance around it!*"

"Your tattoo's a fake," Tracer stated. "And so is mine."

The weight of the unconscious Beta hung heavier on Marti's side, as the statement distracted him.

"It's... the real thing," he insisted. "The one you get after using a KopyBot. It's real..."

"It's fake. You've never hurt a KopyBot in your life, Marti. You don't think it's fun and games, you're not happy with what's going on here, and ever since the tattoos showed up you've been forced to play along to the best of your ability. ...can we get inside and talk about this? Please? I'm not trying to trick you, here. I'm trying to be honest when I say something's gone very, very wrong with KopyBot. And I want to help fix it."

This was the tension moment. It could break either direction; if Marti called over Bonko, the one who was protecting him for some reason, Tracer would be completely screwed. If Marti let it slide but refused to talk, he'd lose his in-road to the Karnival's secrets and possibly be at risk if Marti ever talked about this discussion. But if Marti could open up... if there was something incorruptible deep within him...

The doorknob twisted, unsealing the access lock on the room.

"Get inside fast," Marti mumbled. "And help me get her into a chair or something."

Behind the scenes, the Karnival was not draped in colorful absurdity. All the soft edges they'd been using to make the place approachable despite being a functional torture hostel were washed away... this was a simple white room, clean and functional. Similar to the admin layer of a fresh server, or Arjay's workshop. No clutter, no decoration, no muss, no fuss...

Just a few chairs and worktables, all centered around a single glowing cube.

The kopy machine.

First, the pair hoisted the Beta copy into a chair, so they could lay that particular burden down.

"I didn't even want to try duplicating her," Marti admitted, leaning heavily on a worktable to rest after the effort. "I've overheard the others, the things they want to do to a kopy of her. Makes the things they do in the smaller tents look like... like... I don't know. Something normal..."

"So, why try to Kopy Beta?" Tracer asked. "Why do it at all?"

"Bonko said we had to find a way to kopy the unkopyable, those who had no profile data. It's the last nut to crack before we can launch the service; without it we'd have to turn away customers, and... look, does it matter? It's my project. I have to see it through, one way or another..."

Marti ran one hand over the smooth surface of the cube... studying a pop-up window with MyFace profile data, a cross-indexing of everyone who knew or claimed to know Beta. Highlighted records had been used to build this cockamamie parody of Beta, the Beta that others wanted her to be...

"You made the KopyBots," Tracer understood. "You're the creator..."

Beta's reaction resounded with hope and relief, in equal measure. "*This is perfect!*" she declared. "*If we can turn Marti to our side, he can shut down the Karnival for us! No doxxing needed, no lives ruined, and no more KopyBot abuse! Tracer, we can win the day without anyone getting hurt...!*"

"I didn't want them to be sex toys," Marti said up front. "That was Bonko's idea. He says it's the only thing they're marketable for, the only casual throw-away usage Netwerk could accept. I thought... maybe they could be good for emergency services, or therapy, or... things. I hadn't figured what value they had, just that they were *possible*, and I could make it happen if only I had a first party API to work with. But those are expensive, and the debts I ran up researching this technology have to be paid off somehow..."

"And then things started going wrong. The heart symbols showed up. Bonko started playing ringmaster, making the entire project crazier and crazier..."

"You've been researching our history? Are you a reporter or something? Bonko really wouldn't want me talking about this stuff with the press..."

A dozen lies sprang to Tracer's lips, ready to go. But a single word stopped him.

"*Truth,*" Beta spoke. "*Tell him the truth. A safe and reasonable amount of it, but be true.*"

"I'm tracking the heart symbol," Tracer chose. "That's what brought me here. It's a form of malware that interferes with the psyche of the infected. You've seen that effect, haven't you? The flaring tempers, the need to bond together and fight the outsider...?"

"It... started showing up after I got the alpha version of my KopyBot service online," Marti continued, still a bit puzzled at how neatly the pieces were fitting in place with Tracer's half of the story. "I think the system's infected, but I can't figure out how to clean it. The virus is so tightly integrated now I can't purge it without destroying the whole system, and it's already in every backup I have on file. I... wore a fake version of the tattoo to convince Bonko that everything was fine, to buy time so I could fix the error before we launch the retail product..."

"I can remove it for you. I can even put a placebo in there, so Bonko will never know and the system will stop infecting new clients," Tracer promised. "But... I'd prefer if you ended all of this. Shut down the Karnival. It's your creation; you have the power to end the nightmare, Marti."

Another tension point. Tracer monitored his words carefully, even if he was trying to remain truthful... pushing too hard against everything this man had set into motion, that could backfire...

Marti quickly shook his head, not ready to go so far.

"This is more Bonko's dream than mine, now," Marti explained. "He had the idea for the Karnival, he designed everything. He... he's not *wrong*. They're just Apps. Maybe the virus is driving the customers to play a bit rough but it's just play, right? You can even make the Apps *want* it, so... that's fine, right?"

"Is it fine?" Tracer asked, leaving the question open-ended.

"It's... well, look, if you work with me to remove the virus, I don't have to shut down the Karnival. People will object at first, yeah, but Bonko says they'll accept it eventually. Morality shifts all the time, it's normal..."

"Copying people without their consent to be used as sex toys is far from normal, Marti. Didn't you say this isn't what you wanted the KopyBots to be? Why did you make them in the first place?"

"I... I don't know. I had to. I mean... I had to do it, once I knew it was possible. I just had to do it. That's all."

"...that's it?" Tracer asked, anger rising. "You did it in the name of science? You birthed this atrocity simply to see if it could be done?"

"No, that's not what I mean—!"

Beta spoke up, immediately. *"Tracer, cool it! We're losing him!"*

*"This fool started a fire he can't extinguish, all because it seemed like a good idea at the time—and he's letting it run wild all because he's too weak to stand up to his friend. I have no respect for him, no pity. We can collar him, kidnap or kill him, remove the virus, and be gone before anybody is the wiser. The Karnival will grind to a halt without its creator—"*

*"Absolutely not! You... look. I'm going to switch to text. Read EVERY SINGLE WORD I write aloud, and be convincing. Let me take over."*

*"Beta, this is—"*

*"Do you trust me or not!?"*

Cowering. The creator of KopyBot, cowering before him. That backspacer loomed large in his inventory. Beta would object, would raise a fuss, but... this could all end so easily, so simply. Destroy it all. Burn the Karnival to the ground, ruin its reputation, let it collapse in on itself...

...something familiar, in the look of broken terror that Marti showed him now. Something he'd seen in that copy of his sister, what felt like so long ago.

Instead, Tracer read the printed words, letting them guide his voice.

"I believe you," he read, pushing his rising rage down. Trying to emulate Beta's soft speech patterns, words of comfort and trust. "You had to do it. You say you had to do it, and I believe you're telling me the truth. But I don't understand *why*. Marti, please... walk me through it. Why did you create KopyBot...?"

Gradually... Marti softened, while rising from the cowering slouch he'd adopted. The palpable danger in the room had been reduced to the point where he felt comfortable speaking again.

"...Bonko," he spoke. One word.

"He wanted you to make KopyBot?"

"No. He... he died. Bonko died."

The words paused, before flowing across Tracer's inner vision once more.

"He's family, isn't he?" Beta guessed, behind Tracer's eyes. "Bonko's your brother. He died... and you wanted to bring him back, based on the ghosts he'd left behind on social media. That's why you felt you had to make this technology."

"Yes... yes, that's it. I had to do it," Marti repeated. "He caught a virus while out partying one night, and was dead by morning. Too riddled with the infection to be recoverable. But I knew I could bring him back! It was such a simple idea. All I had to do... was clone my own Program code, scrub the identity and memory completely, and rebuild using MyFace data. It took years, but I made it work!"

"Then... KopyBots aren't Apps at all," Tracer said... surprised at his own words. "They're Programs, hollowed and rebuilt..."

Now, Marti looked uncertain all over again. Unable to meet Tracer's eyes, as he glanced over the data hovering around his cube.

"They don't have to be Programs," he reasoned. "We can call them Apps. Programs are just highly evolved Apps. If we call them Apps... we don't have to feel guilty about anything we do. That's what Bonko said. It's a product we can sell, a way to get out of debt, if we call them Apps..."

"Bonko doesn't know he's a KopyBot; he thinks he never died. He has no expiration date, unlike the commercial bots. But you don't believe your brother's simply an App, do you?"

"Of course not!" Marti exclaimed. "He's my brother! I saved him. Programs are just data! They can be recovered, if you know how!"

"Which is it, then? Are KopyBots Apps, or Programs?" Beta asked, through Tracer. "You can't have it both ways, Marti. If they're Apps... you can 'play' with them all you like. But if Bonko is really your brother, and not a parody of him you crafted from social media data... that means the KopyBots are alive. They're alive, and you're *feeding* them to those people..."

"*He's trembling,*" Beta spoke. "*We're tearing his world down. I feel awful about this. Hug him, maybe...?*"

Tracer declined to follow through on that command. But he did continue to let the written words flow through him.

"You know it's wrong, Marti," he continued. "This isn't just a massive invasion of privacy of those you kopy, it's cruel to the KopyBots themselves. That's why you won't participate in the Karnival. You're keeping it all going for your brother's sake but you know it has to stop. You need to shut down the Karnival, before it can do any more damage than it's already done."

"*Good! Now, give him a copy of the anti-malware tool.*"

"*Beta, if Dex gets a hold of the only weapon we have against him—*"

"*Marti isn't an enemy. Make a show of good faith, Tracer.*"

So Tracer extended his hand, a vial of silvery fluid hovering there.

"Use this to purge the virus from your brother," he suggested. "Pull him back from the abyss he's hovering over. It's my gift to you, no matter your decision. But... I'm begging you, end the Karnival. Please, Marti. You can find a better use of your technology than this... and you can find a better future for your brother."

Marti looked up at the vial... the hope clear in his eyes, as he saw its glittering salvation.

"...Bonko won't be happy," he noted. "This was his dream."

"This is his nightmare. He'll be annoyed, but... he'll survive. And once the virus is out of his system, he can find a better dream to follow."

And so the cube was shut down, tucked back into Marti's inventory. No longer in service for creation of KopyBots. Dex's infection vector vanished overnight; no longer would it poison new recruits to the Karnival.

And so Bonko would regain his sensibility, and family bonds would keep him from being angry for any real length of time at his younger bro.

And so the Karnival ended. Not with the silent fire of a backspacer, not with a massive explosion, not even with an act of subterfuge and sabotage. It simply ended, as dark dreams always do. The existing infected who had already used Kopybots scattered to the winds, beyond the reach of any cure... an unfortunate problem for another day. Not a complete victory over Dex, but as close as they could have gotten.

And so Puzzle (after one huge #GirlsNightIn, to celebrate) returned home to her video library and her well stocked wine cellar and her terrible call-center job, with a newfound appreciation for her #BFF's personal journey.

And so Spark put the entire mess out of her mind... but not so far out of mind as to forget the lesson. She continued to spar with her training dummy, but not simply to prove her own invulnerability, but to stay sharp so she could stave off death as long as possible. As good a goal as any.

And so Beta came to admit her one lie.

"I didn't have the heart to tell him," she explained, over one of many games of Go she'd played with Tracer. "But while I still feel KopyBots are Programs... I don't think Bonko's really his brother."

"It's Bonko's MyFace profile given new flesh, nothing more," Tracer agreed. "And it produced a stunningly awful person in the process even before the virus claimed him. Who knows? Perhaps the real Bonko was kinder than the exaggerated persona he created for himself on MyFace."

"We told a lie of omission, didn't we?" Beta wondered. "Letting Marti believe in a dream. ...if I could believe it was possible to bring back loved ones like Verity with a KopyBot, I'd have said so. But they're gone, so is Bonko, and all that's left are their ghosts..."

"And the memories we hold. I think Marti may have been onto something, when he awkwardly tried to copy you by looking for shared life experiences. A fusion of the memories left behind in our wake, contributed by friends and family... that may be the closest to life after death we can manage."

"Death marks the death of *something*, even if the remnants can be made to move. People die all the time, and that's simply how it is... Verity died, long ago. My neighbor died recently, and nobody knows why. Maybe Snowi will die soon, if #CodeHonesty ever finds her..."

Her neighbor.

*Beta's next door neighbor was murdered recently. Isn't that a strange coincidence?*

Dex's little taunt, the one that sent Tracer off on this long journey...

*That's a rather old hacktool, you know. It's almost perfect... if not for the timestamped junk code artifacts.*

Arjay's little taunt, the one Tracer had dismissed at the time as he was more focused on the Karnival.

MemoryPalace didn't forget. It never forgot. It drew connections for him, calling his attention to the linked details now that they'd resurfaced fresh in his mind...

Tracer placed one last stone, before rising.

"I need to check on something," he declared, before moving off to his study without a further word.

---

Cracking open his backspacer posed a risk. The code was delicate and he was hardly much of a programmer... but he had to know, had to be certain. This was too critical a concern to let it slide on a wave of pride and assumptions...

Within the weapon he found six timestamps, dotted all along the span of his life.

Six murders, each by a weapon he'd supposedly never fired.

One timestamp neatly lined up with the evening that Beta's neighbor was killed. Why would he kill someone he didn't even know...?

MemoryPalace pulled up a note, highlighted for his convenience.

*...the origin server of the original nude leak was WestHall...*

One timestamp neatly lined up with the exact moment they left Qelk's apartment.

*Got lost on the way down here,* he'd insisted to his sister to explain the delay.

An automatic search pulled up Qelk's obituary. His entire apartment had been backspaced recently by an unknown assailant, with investigation by HiRize moderators still ongoing...

There was only one way out of this. One reasonable answer to the ethical question posed by the timestamps.

One rough re-assembly later, the muzzle of the backspacer pressed against his forehead. It felt cold and flat, an ideal of absolute digital certainty. It may not cleanly kill him, not after being decompiled and recompiled, but as long as the end result remained fatal it would suffice.

But... no. That wouldn't work, because they wouldn't know *why*. He'd still escape his actions, consequence-free. A cowardly route to take, fleeing the scene of the crime, just as he'd done so many times before... leaving an almost imperceptible hole in his memory with each murder. Washing his hands clean, so he could feel pure and righteous...

Leave behind a note first, perhaps? Confess on paper before eliminating the scourge of Netwerk, as he'd always done?

No. Inadequate. He didn't deserve such an easy way out.

Instead, Tracer wrapped a fresh connection lock collar around his own neck. It was his own App, meaning he could remove it at any time... so he set a password in place, mailing copies of it to his sister and to Beta before wiping his own memory of the phrase. He even sent his backspacer to his sister as a file attachment... the killing tool finally out of his own murderous hands.

There. That would suffice as punishment... the start of his punishment, at least.

Not feeling up to walking out of this room, he relied on the indirect Messenger to carry his words.

"Beta? Spark? Would you please come up to my study?" he asked. "I have a confession to make."

## :: end chapter 1.4

# Floating Point 1.5 :: Lulz

It was LordSmegma's idea to have the default avatar be a giant talking penis.

Their haven was a fully anonymized server, host to a hundred and one chatrooms on a hundred and one topics. Each could be moderated and customized to the liking of the creators, and Smegma liked the idea that those in his chatroom were all basically dicks. It was honest, after all. So, anybody who set foot in the room would become a dick... and then they'd sell cosmetic upgrades to be the shiniest, hardest, most blinged out dick in the world to fund the group. Genius!

Weevil didn't have to buy any of his penis accessories, being Smegma's right hand cock. As a moderator of AnyChan's /lulz/ community, all the piercings and tattoos he could possibly want were free for the taking. One of the many privileges he experienced, as a founding member of the community...

He also was in charge of the Hall of Shame, their personal trophy vault. He decided which pranks were good enough to be highlighted for all time, an eternal tribute to the easily trolled idiots and fools of Netwerk. He'd accepted three submissions this week alone; things were on the rise as Netwerk continues to broil in the #CodeHonesty flamewars. Both sides had proven effective targets for the champions of /lulz/.

Today's major prank was more of a classic scam, though. Very oldschool, almost like comfort food.

The dicks gathered to bear witness, as Weevil started pasting up the files on their imageboard.

A heart-wrenching picture of a child's corrupted avatar being kept going on life support Apps came first. Immediately after it came the article itself.

SAVE FAUXINA!

This is Chmod/Fauxina, a young believer from Athena Online. She suffers from a rare case of hereditary data rot, which threatens to end her runtime at a tender age of six years.

Treatment is available from Northon Data Health, but is too expensive for her churchgoing family to afford. They do offer free treatment... but only if this post gets one million shares across MyFace.

Please, for Fauxina's sake, like and share this post on your wall! Please think of the children!!

"And the end total is..." Weevil continued, "Four and a half million shares! They kept going and going, well after the million mark! Let's hear it for the /lulz/!"

For added fun, he posted some of the heartfelt and poorly spelled comments left behind. The 'Fauxina is in our prayers, may the One protect her' comments were especially amusing to the gathering of dicks, which howled with laughter at how easily the churchies were duped.

Weevil had no hands to clap with, but he rattled the shiny gold BIGDIK pendant around his 'neck' to simulate it.

"It's crazy how easily people will fall for this shit," one of the dicks commented. "Sad, really. Bunch of idiots thinking that tossing a 'like' on a post will cure data rot..."

"Life's a bitch, then you die," Weevil agreed. "Nothing more to it than that. Anyway, if you wanna read the rest of the comments, check the Hall of Shame later—"

A dissenter with a generic anonymous cock, no accessories at all, spoke up in the back. "What? C'mon! It wasn't THAT good," he protested. "Weevil's only putting it in the Hall because Smegma lets him post anything he likes. That's such bullshit."

Unfortunately, a fully anonymous Chanarchy server meant that jerk couldn't be effectively banned. Weevil had to stand and defend his decision.

"The Hall of Shame is the backbone of /lulz/. It represents the core examples of how we poke this ridiculous world right in the eye. A MyFace hoax is basic, yeah... but it's the basics that teach the new generation what /lulz/ is really about, right? It lights the path. The easily tricked fall for it every time... the soccer moms, the churchies, the kiddies, the SJWs, all those self-absorbed fuckwits. We run into rooms full of these losers, screaming bullshit at the top of our lungs just to see who gets pissed off. We ruin someone's day just because we *can*. Because it's funny. Because it's our thing. That's what the Hall must represent!"

"Uh-huh. So why'd you remove that exhibit from last month? That one was pretty epic..."

"Just ignore the newfag," Weevil ordered the masses. "Okay, anybody else got something? I'm officially opening the floor to new candidates for audition. How have YOU made Netwerk a lulzier place today...?"

The first to step forward wore a similarly unadorned avatar. It bounced up to the image board quietly, without introduction or bravado...

And pasted up an image of an ordinary looking guy, wearing an ordinary looking avatar. No meme caption, no cool filter, no wacky animation. Nothing.

Which made the assembled dicks titter a bit, confused. This wasn't /photos/, it was /lulz/. Where was the gag...?

Another photo. This one of the same man, looking at the camera now. In absolute terror.

...which made Weevil go dead silent, on recognizing the avatar in question.

LordSmegma. Also known as Ptr/Bryan.

They'd only met in person a few times, preferring to interact through the anonymizing interface of AnyChan and /lulz/. But Bryan's face was unmistakable... right down to the little tattoo under his left ear, a recent addition to his avatar. The look of panic on his face, that wasn't familiar at all. "LordSmegma" always carried himself with absolute confidence, in his normal avatar or his anonymous one...

Another picture. Screaming, lens distorting the image. Screaming and screaming and screaming.

A picture of a knife, placed in his hand.

Wounds. Carving his own body, rapid and jagged slashes, with a torture implement malware App...

Finally a lifeless body, eyes wrapped in tears of sorrow, slumped against the wall. This picture, this last in the series, had a memetic caption. Sort of.

ÝÕÜ ŵ̂îll ŕ3ĝŕËŢ ℰVéŕŸŦhÍÑĝ.
Ø® Í Ŵî¦l *måḵ£* ýð̃µ ŖÊĝŖ3Ţ 3V3ŖýŢÊ̂!ÑĜ.

Finally, the anonymous penis who'd posted this gallery of horror turned to 'face' the crowd.

A series of data glitches crawled across its fleshy surface. The edges became indistinct, a mess of hard-carved voxels, unable to continue maintaining the shape of the default avatar... before it collapsed to the ground, revealing itself to be nothing more than a pile of random data pulled here and there from the raw mess of /lulz/. Lifeless and empty.

Their collective terrified silence was broken by the newfag in the back.

"I don't get it, where's the punchline?" he asked.

---

Tracer made his case calmly and rationally. An impressive feat, considering he'd been anything but calm and rational to date... a madman underneath the surface, while giving himself the daydream of being a sensible individual. A killer in the skin of a decent man...

Well. The lie was now gone. All that remained was himself, naked and true. How refreshingly honest it felt to admit it, without emotion. It was what it was. Today, he'd purposefully chosen to be a *sensible* madman. The truth of it felt like sweet relief...

Sadly, those Tracer had confessed to felt no such relief.

In his sister he saw rage; in his confidante he saw sorrow. He'd hurt them both, to the point where he briefly wondered if he should've gone ahead with silently executing himself, to spare them the knowledge of why he had to die... but that wouldn't be fair to them, in the same way keeping his secret murders quiet wasn't fair. The truth had to be known, no matter how much it hurt.

Even the family housepet was disheartened by the news. "🙀...?" Mew added, breaking the silence with an emoji of shock and horror.

But of the three, Beta was the first to ask the question.

"Why?" she pleaded. "*Why* did you...?"

Unable to even supply the verb.

"As I have no memory of the events I can't say for certain what my motives were," Tracer explained, capable of analyzing it rationally now that he'd come to accept his fate. "I can speculate, however. The six in question, judging from the timestamps, represent the most egregious offenders we've encountered... ones which were particularly offensive to me. I'd no doubt decided to take it on myself to commit this evil, in an effort to force this world to make *sense*. And then I cleaned my memory of the event, to cleanse myself."

"To hide like a coward," his sister replied, venom in every word.

"Absolutely," he agreed. "Hiding my own shame in the void of a clear memory space. No doubt I'd told myself 'It'll just be this one time,' each and every time. Little did I realize I was a serial killer, executing a perpetual series of 'just this one time' sins. Granted this is conjecture, but the structure of it makes sense. Either that or I'm simply a psychopath, I suppose. At this point I'm open to all possibilities."

Beta refused to accept it. "You're not a psychopath. You can't be. When we were fighting the Karnival, you kept pushing for us to consider the ethics of what we were doing. When we doxxed XSept you were the one to point out questionable the tactic was..."

"So a coward and a hypocrite," Spark clarified. "Telling us to calm our uncontrollable girly emotions about these things, while he secretly smacked down people like Qelk that *I* wanted a piece of..."

Tracer nodded in firm agreement. "And Beta's stalker, as well. I believe your neighbor leaked those nudes in the first place, Beta. In both cases, I stepped in so no one else would have to. I took the stain on my soul so both of you would remain clean."

"How very fucking noble of you."

"Not really, no. I'm a fool and a coward, a hypocrite and a psychopath," Tracer accounted. "And now... we come to a decision point. Now that you know... now that *I* know, for that matter... what comes next? Personally, I suggest summary execution. It's only fitting considering my crimes. If you prefer, I can simply kill myself. Much cleaner and less traumatic for you."

He'd hoped they'd agree to his terms, so this could be over with quickly. Tear the weed out by the root and be done with it... but unfortunately, neither seemed to consent to the idea.

"What? No!" Beta protested. "Tracer, absolutely not!"

"As pissed off as I may be, gonna need to agree with Beta," Spark added. "You don't get to die. You have to live with what you've done; that's only fair. Besides, you're my brother. I'm not gonna whack you."

"Your familial affection is poorly invested in me..."

"Yeah, well, you're the only member of the family tree I can tolerate. But just because I don't want you dead doesn't mean I'm not utterly pissed off at you, Tracer. You're a bastard. A bastard who dragged me along on this... this *ridiculous* vendetta, year after year, all while insisting you're some holier-than-thou sensible gentleman. All while riding *my* ass for being the short-sighted violent one. Except *I* never murdered a guy in a white-hot rage!"

"I doubt my rage was white-hot. I've always suspected that if I'd kill someone, it'd be a white-cold rage—"

"NOT helping your case!"

"Not trying to," Tracer pointed out.

"Look, clearly he repents, right?" Beta suggested. "That's a good sign! Not that he wants to die, I mean, just that he's repentant in general. It means he can find redemption, somehow..."

Tracer shook his head. "Beta... even outside of murder, I've been breaking various laws left and right for years, knowing full well I was committing evils as I did so. Just because one feels guilt doesn't mean one will avoid sin. Everyone in this room is guilty of wrathful misdeed in one way or another, and I doubt any of us are planning to stop..."

"Speak for yourself, bro. I'm clean," Spark insisted.

But Beta shook her head. sadly.

"That's not true at all, Spark. We both doxxed XSept; he may have gotten killed because of us. We were prepared to do it again against the Karnival, too! We've lied and deceived and tricked people. We're hackers and privacy invaders and criminals... and we're up against people doing similarly questionable things, in turn. We're all... broken, in so many ways..."

"You and I aren't killers," Spark countered.

Beta slumped, noticeably. "We may as well be, for all the chaos we cause along the way. Wrathful misdeeds, like Tracer says. To hunt down Dex, we've ruined lives and invaded privacy and more... and we all agreed to it, each time. I went along with it, too... I just... went along with it..."

Spark wanted to throw it all back on her brother. *His* quest, *his* vendetta. Not her fault at all...

But it wasn't true. Back in HolyHymnal, she'd admitted that the main reason she enabled her brother's madness was to sort out the problems of Netwerk they found along the way. It felt damn good bringing justice to dark corners where no justice could be found, shutting down the greedy and the cruel, making a positive difference as Netwerk seemed to slide deeper and deeper into a toxic swamp...

In his shoes, would she have spared Qelk's life? She was ready to hurt him. Ready to tear him to bits with all those torture tools he'd used on a copy of herself. Just because she hadn't taken that last step and Tracer had, did that make her better?

Well, *technically* yes. But only by deed, not intent. How long until she resorted to making her darker impulses a reality, like her brother had?

"I don't know what to do," Spark had to admit, honestly. "I really don't."

"Couldn't we just... walk away from it all? Stop chasing after Dex," Beta suggested. "This is messing all of us up. It's driven Tracer to extremes, and... and we don't *need* to do it anymore. I'm not saying we let Dex run wild; we could, I don't know, report him to moderators or Athena Online's police department or something..."

Spark shook her head. "Won't work. Nobody'd believe us, even if we did. Nobody could stop him, either. It's not that we're the #ChosenOnes, but so far... we've been willing to step over some lines to hunt and halt Dex, even when we didn't know he was our enemy. Those 'little' misdeeds are the only reason we got this far. If we walk away... he wins."

"If you're unwilling to punish me... the other option could be to release me," Tracer suggested. "If this is really the dark path I've condemned myself to, perhaps I should finish what we started while *you* walk away. If killing is really the only thing that's gotten us this far, if I'm already guilty, I may as well..."

"Except letting you 'walk the path of darkness' as you so melodramatically put it is basically the same thing as condoning what you'd do, bro. I can't go clubbing with my #BFF and forget any of this happened, while you're still out there wreaking havoc to stop Dex."

"Spark, you have two options, then. Kill me, or let me finish the work. That's it."

"So either we kill you or you kill people? Seriously? That's all you're giving us?"

"It's a simple enough choice," Tracer reasoned. "I'm still advocating for my death as just punishment, understand. Just saying if you must seek an alternative, it seems there is only one—"

"Stop it. *Stop it.* Quit talking like all we have is *zero and one!*"

The outburst pulled the attentions of the Winder family to their recently arrived houseguest. Who, despite being a tower of pink fuzziness, was doing a good job looking angrier than Spark had been earlier.

"That's not how life works," Beta spoke... quieter now, having expended most of her energy on the initial shout. "Kill him or let him kill? No. We don't have to do either. There's other ways if you're willing to look for them...! I mean... I just... I'm sorry. Nevermind. Forget it."

Tracer wouldn't let it go, even as Beta crawled back inside herself.

"Speak your mind," he requested. "Please. Speak up. You know I value your input, Beta. What were you going to say...?"

With a sigh, Beta gathered herself again, to take another run at it.

"...I'm sorry. I'm not very good at speaking up, I know. I've always gone along with what people tell me I need to be doing... and that includes Tracer. I didn't really want to doxx XSept, but he convinced me there was no other way. And... I was wrong. We were wrong."

"We already agreed there was no other solution to RansomMe," Tracer quietly interjected.

"No, we stopped *looking* for solutions after painting ourselves into a corner with that one. I've been giving a lot of thought to what we've been doing, and— no, wait. Not *what* we've been doing, but *how* we've been doing it. Tracer's right, we've been committing evils in the name of good, and way too many of them. We're doing what Dex wants us to do."

Spark quirked an eyebrow. "Uh. Dex *wants* us to smack his buddies around?"

"Yes! Why do you think he infected both Snowi and Cup8? He loves that sort of thing. And back in ViruFaxHQ, Dex said we were his *friends*... that Tracer was doing 'the good work' already. I understand what he meant, now. We're like those he brands, violently defending our ideals at all costs. That's what Tracer did, in the end. He killed to protect us, and to protect Netwerk..."

"The man who abused my sister, and the man who nearly ruined your life," Tracer acknowledged. "I committed both evils in the name of love. Much as Dex's infected do, albeit in a more twisted manner..."

"Exactly. I was on the other end of the glasses when Tracer was exploring the Karnival; I heard the way they talked. The Karnival saw itself as a community that they had to defend to the death. One they were *eager* to defend to the death, in fact. If we're going to stop Dex, we can't be like him. We have to take extreme care to minimize our evils."

"Assuming that's possible. The ones I murdered were outside the reach of law; horrible individuals doing horrible deeds without any chance of justice, unless it was delivered onto them..."

"There's *always* another way," Beta insisted. "Back at the Karnival, we could've destroyed it from the inside out with deception and doxxing. Instead... we quietly ended it all, with an act of honesty and compassion. If we can disrupt something as evil as the Karnival so gently, who knows what we could do if we tried?"

With actual command over her audience, Beta felt the words come freely. She'd never have talked back to Snowi or Cup8, would've played along with whatever idea they had... high-profile publicity events, pushing her Apps out there as major media investments, whatever they liked. But her new friends weren't her old friends. Her new friends *wanted* Beta to speak up... and now, she was ready to.

"This is the only way forward for Tracer. For all of us, really," she concluded. "We still need to stop Dex. But we should change our methods; we have to see the enemy not as *the enemy* but as a fellow broken individual, just like us. No doxxing. No murder. Instead we find the *best* solution, the optimal one for our true values, and accept nothing less. ...um. Is that okay? I mean, it's cool with you, right?"

As her inspiring speech sputtered to a close... Spark couldn't help but smirk a little, as Insecure Beta leaked in a little.

"Sooo... what I'm taking away from this little speech is that you should run the show from here on out," Spark supplied.

"What? No, of course not. I'm not the mastermindy type! I mean... I was just saying it's a question of methods, and... how you choose to do stuff..."

"Why not? I think you could do it. Honestly, at this point, I trust your methods more than I trust his. I've let Tracer coordinate this fight for years; *his* quest, *his* vendetta. I went along for the ride, like you. Well... I say it's time we operate under new management. Switch up the roles a little, find a new strat for our game. Tracer, are we in agreement?"

"Absolutely," Tracer spoke, without hesitation. "All I want is to stop Dex, no matter the methods. I'm not advocating murder, I simply saw no other means to our goal... but if Beta can find an optimal alternative approach I will happily accept it."

"So, I'll back her in the field while you do research from here?" Spark suggested. "You're still a sharp-minded son of a bitch, Tracer, and we could use you as an analyst."

"Agreed. Of course, I still recommend you keep my lock collar on for the time being, until I've re-earned your trust. I doubt I'd immediately run out and start stabbing random people without it, but let's be careful all the same."

"Yeah, that's fair. Okay, I think we've got a plan. All those in favor?"

"Aye," Tracer spoke, raising his hand.

"I'm in," Spark agreed, raising her hand.

" 🐾," Mew agreed, raising a paw.

In her bewilderment, Beta was nearly knocked over by the cat rubbing up against her ankles afterwards.

"This is crazy. I can't," she tried. "I can't. I'm not..."

"We're dead serious about this," Tracer added. "Beta... I respect you. I admire you. If you feel there's a better solution to our goals—and that there's a better solution to my punishment than suicide—I'll accept that you know best. ...you've seen my memory files. You know I trust you more than I trust myself."

Memory files, including a particular confession...

"I'm not a leader," Beta protested, putting that thought aside. "Not really. You're making a mistake..."

"Oh, we're not saying you're some kind of super-commander with infallible vision and clarity or anything," Spark said. "You're just as screwed up as we are, in different ways. But... why not switch it up? Someone's got to step forward while Tracer steps back. You want us to beat Dex without becoming Dex? Okay. Let's give it a shot. What's step one?"

Spark, whose double had confessed hidden love for Beta. Tracer, who had flat out said he loved her, despite his unwillingness to act on it... the pressure of the Winder siblings and all they represented, now added to their insistence that she was the Right Woman For The Job, tipped her over into sheer terror.

But... if this was the only way to keep Tracer from throwing away his life, if this was the only way to deal with Dex without becoming Dex...

She knew what had to happen next.

"Spark... take me to your liquor cabinet," she stated, with firm command.

---

Weevil was taking no chances.

He'd bailed from the AnyChan server immediately, leaving the rest of his /lulz/mates in his wake. No parting words, nothing. Straight from his home away from home back to his actual home... to slap up as many firewalls and security Apps as he could grab, locking down his apartment against any possible intrusion.

Word was already spreading through his social networks of LordSmegma's death. Officially it was ruled a suicide, but Weevil knew better... it was murder. Smegma had no shame, no guilt whatsoever; why should he? He'd done nothing wrong. He'd never have carved himself into little pieces with that blade.

Granted Weevil was fuzzy on who exactly could've killed his mentor. A past victim, maybe? Someone who couldn't deal with the fact that it was all just a joke. A crazy SJW, then? He'd heard of hashtaggers resorting to murder to push their agendas but dismissed it as a hoax. And besides, his fellow trolls didn't actually believe in anything they were saying. They took an opposite viewpoint just to poke at the idiots who believed in things, *any* things, to show them how stupid they were... but that didn't make them an actual opposition.

No, no matter the angle, it didn't make any sense at all. /lulz/ didn't deserve to be targeted this way. He'd never hurt anyone in his life.

Not even the one from last month. That didn't count.

Well. No matter. He was locked away behind eight different freeware firewalls now, so slathered in security that even his MyFace App wasn't working properly. No connections in, no connections out. No killer was getting to him. He'd ride this mess out, in the comfort of his own home.

Fortunately, he had plenty of distractions. He had plenty of popcorn. Had his collection of comedy movie files. If he got seriously bored, he even had a sexbot App. Not as good as the ones he'd heard rumors about, the 'kopies' that vanished off the market recently, but good enough.

---

Little by little, he emptied out his inventory and the storage in his home, laying out his entertainment options in a row. Ways to spend the time. Ways to distract himself from what he knew was coming. Laughter was the very best medicine, after all...

Aha. *To Your Health*. An early sitcom, just the ticket. He was a fan of the classics, after all... the basic forms of humor that all others were built atop. A wacky farce full of fart and dick jokes was just what the doctor ordered.

Ready to binge-watch, he loaded up the file into the player in his living room, then left to prepare his snacks. No need to sit through the opening credits, or even the first act; he'd seen this episode a dozen times before. Nurse B00b spilled creamer on her mini dress uniform, and was running all over the hospital trying to find a way to clean it out, while everybody made ejaculation jokes. Classic.

Popcorn, and drinks. Some chips, too. Crunchy, salty, and bubbly. Hell of a trifecta...

When he returned and plopped down on the couch, he knew exactly what scene would be playing: Nurse B00b talking with Stiffy the Janitor...

...who was talking to thin air. The lanky sanitation engineer was carrying on a one-sided conversation, while the laugh track flared at every unspoken double-entendre from the non-present Nurse B00b.

Strange. Were his files corrupt? He skipped through the file, looking for data corruption... but the file was intact, save for the missing visual data. Nurse B00b was simply gone.

Then two heavy weights came to rest atop his head.

Glancing up past those breasts, he saw the twisted and flickering 24fps smile of Nurse B00b, complete with pixilated video jaggies at the edges of each and every tooth.

"Ä®€ Ý°ú çÀPã8Í'é ÕF fééL!Ŋġ ꬀6ŕ3Ţ, W€ÊvÏL?" her distorted voice box rattled. "L3Ţ'$ F!ÑĐ øụŢ."

His instinctive reconnect to another server bounced off the various firewalls he'd put in place, leaving him stuck within the tomb he'd built for himself. Stuck on the couch as her warped arms wound around his body, over and over again, like snakes...

Name: ÊṚṚØṚ

Home: ɳ0Ņé

Org: ŕéǦŕét

Her hands blurred and glowed, a mess of broken and rotting data, somehow screaming with twenty voices in absolute harmony with his own screams as they plunged deep within his chest, to squeeze his heart—

*—you're no good. You're no good. You're no good.*

*You don't deserve anything you have. You're pathetic. Nobody likes you. It's all just a sham, thin as an eggshell. You don't deserve anything you have. You're pathetic. Nobody likes you...*

...but it wasn't true, was it? Everybody told Weevil (???) that it wasn't true. *Just ignore those bad thoughts,* their voices agreed. *It's all in your head. Keep a positive attitude. It's all in your head...*

So he (she) forced a smile into place, trying to believe one set of words over another. His (her) daily therapy consisted of cat pictures and positive slogans on filtered photos, along with kind words from strangers who enjoyed Weevil's (???'s) daily affirmation blog. Those words, yes, those were the words she'd put his (her) faith in. And what words would she (he) find today in her comment section...?

She (he) pulled up the blog comment tracker, while enjoying a late breakfast on a lonely Saturday morning. She'd (he'd) posted a kitty last night, with a caption she (he) wrote *her*self. "Cuteness like this is proof that somebody out there loves you," she'd written. It felt good to write those words. What words would she get in reply?

*You're an idiot,* the comments read. *Kill yourself.*

*Kill yourself.*

*Kill yourself you idiot.*

*You should just die, you suck.*

Over and over. Again and again. The darkness of it pulling away from the light of the simple kitty picture they were replying to.

*Kill yourself. Kill yourself. Kill yourself.*

The knife was in her drawer. Mom and dad didn't know about it. She'd made the cuts quietly, secretly, on parts of her avatar they wouldn't see. The little stings of the malware, originally designed for BDSM enthusiasts, offered her painful and persistent reminders of the world around her and how stupid she was and how awful she was.

So, she added a few more to her collection.

*Kill yourself. Kill yourself,* the commenters demanded.

And a few more. And a few more...

Until she couldn't hold the knife anymore. Her avatar, flooded with absolute agony, starting to signal error after error as core routines began to crash. *Kill yourself.* In small doses any 'fun' malware didn't pose much threat, but these weren't small doses. *Kill yourself.* This was what she deserved. She was awful. Nobody loved her. She would never amount to anything, and now, even the sanctuary of her blog had turned against her. *Kill yourself. Kill yourself—*

*—kill yourself.*

The remembered voices were so loud now, so very loud, that this was clearly the only way out. It was everything he deserved, because he was such an awful person that would never amount to anything, someone nobody loved...

"I'm an idiot. I'm a fool. What use was any of it, all that trolling? I regret everything," Weevil agreed, at last. "I hate myself. I regret everything. I regret everything..."

Glitched eyes narrowed on the cowering troll.

"ýǿú ḲṆǿŴ ŵĥÄŦ çåm3 ṆË×ŧ, dᵒṆ'Ŧ ýǿú. ¥0ú ĤÄVéṆ'7 fØŕĞøŧŦËŋ M€..."

The stolen data of Nurse B00b offered him the knife, and he happily accepted it.

The first cut hurt like hell, but Weevil kept on cutting. Again and again, eventually abandoning the neat little row of lines for wild slashes. Into his arms, legs, chest, anywhere. Everywhere he should be hurt...

Data corruption leaked in, the overdose of malware getting to him. Eventually the screams (familiar screams, from familiar throats) of *kill yourself* faded. Eventually everything faded.

At last, he regretted everything. At last he was released from the pain.

The specter that borrowed his video evaporated, glitched data spilling into nothingness. Only so much garbage left to be collected, much like Weevil himself.

A single red-and-black mark on his lower back was the last bit of code to expire. But not before sending a signal down its wires, back to a cloud server, back to the one who placed the branding there to begin with.

---

The goal, as Beta explained it, was to lock down every bit of malware in the house... even the "fun" ones like intoxicating liquor. If they left any of it unchecked, Tracer would have a way of killing himself, by overdosing to make mildly damaging code into severely damaging code.

Also, Beta really, really needed a drink.

"I trust him at his word not to kill himself, but... we've trusted him at his word before," she reasoned, pouring herself a very tall glass of wine. "As much as I'm pushing for more trust in how we do things, let's be safe rather than sorry. Mew? I need you to stick around and look after Tracer. Make sure he doesn't do anything rash."

The cat pawing at a loaf of bread on the counter stood at attention, snapping off a salute with one paw. "👌! 🐱➡️👮," he agreed, before hopping down and trotting off to play security guard.

"Mew doesn't strike me as a reliable prison warden," Spark pointed out. "He's a bit silly, isn't he?"

"His personality's developed along the lines of a comedy sidekick, yeah, but he can be serious when he needs to be. And I can tap his visual input whenever I want to keep an eye on Tracer. Oh, BTW, don't use a simple password like 'Tracer is a butt' on the cabinet, okay?"

"Yeah, yeah, it's a mash of rando garbage, don't worry," Spark promised, looking up from the lock she was securing on the wine storage folder. "#WeCoolYo. ...I don't know what the hell we're going to do about Tracer, though. He's contained, but we can't realistically keep him under house arrest forever... if nothing else Onesday's coming up soon and mom's gonna expect him home for dinner. It's tradition."

"I know. I know. Just... give me some time to think. Maybe I can figure out how to really bring him around, so we can trust him again. It's my duty, being the leader, and all. ...you guys seriously want *me* to be the leader?"

"It's not so much being the 'leader' as it is being the one who leads the way," Spark reasoned, adjusting her jacket a bit after being crouched down so long working on the encryption. "We've been voting on what to do, yeah, but Tracer was always the one to make the proposals we voted on. And we all nodded along with them, figuring that hey, he was the smart guy, doesn't he know best? Well... screw that. *You're* the smart guy. Girl. Whatever. The smart girl *and* the nice girl, in one pretty package."

"Ahh... thank you. But... I'm just the smart girl. That doesn't mean I'm also leadership material. I mean, I'm not brave like you are, I'm not cunning like Tracer..."

"You came up with the plan to take down your ex, didn't you?"

"That plan almost failed completely! I screwed up. If I hadn't plugged my brain into Floating Point, we would've come up empty-handed..."

"Yeah, see, that's what we call 'improvisation.' It's two-thirds of my game plan, personally. I think on my feet and figure out how to escape a scrape *after* I get into one. See? You've already mastered one of the pro strats! And don't freak out about not being brave or cunning. You can cower in a corner if you really feel like it; we'll take care of the rest, as long as we've got your moral core to lean on for guidance."

"Moral core...?"

"Y'know, the thing Tracer completely lacks and I tend to fumble around with. That's the reason I put this idea of you calling the shots forward. Right now... we need morality more than cunning or bravery."

"Well... if you're sure. I don't know how useful standing on a soapbox and making speeches will be when we're dodging backspacer fire from infected crazies, but... I'll do my best not to completely screw up and ruin everything and lead us to absolute disaster!"

"Yeah, that, don't do that and we'll be fine. ...and while we're down here, away from his ears? If I can be totally honest...?"

Beta set her empty wineglass down. She felt like another was in order, but needed her wits sharp right now rather than dulled through sensory manipulation.

"You can always be totally honest," Beta promised. "Your leader permits it, or something."

"Honestly? Reason I can't rely on myself to be that moral core we need? I'm not weeping a single tear for anyone that Tracer whacked," Spark admitted. "They were scum. #AbsoluteScum. I guess they didn't deserve to be murdered, murder is naughty and evil and bad and stuff, but... no tears. No pity. Bastards, all."

"I don't know about *all* of them. I'm still surprised to hear my neighbor was responsible for the nude leak. I mean... he seemed like a nice young man. We didn't talk much but he was always pleasant, if a little quiet..."

"Either way, we've both benefited from my bro's actions, haven't we? We got to stay clean and let someone else do the wrong thing, while we reap the personal reward. And odds are Netwerk's a better place overall without those punks. Again, not saying slaughter is the best medicine, but... I don't know. I guess I'm just saying I can't completely hate Tracer. I can almost see where he's coming from. ...that should scare me, shouldn't it?"

"I know it scares me," Beta admitted. "Because I can kinda see it, too. ...I don't know if we're the right ones to judge Tracer, in the end. We're in the thick of it with him—"

The jingling in her ear reminded her that she needed a better ringtone for incoming Messenger requests.

The content of that missive, however, was what actually distracted her. The content, and the recognizable voice delivering it.

"*Hello? Beta, right?*" the cheery youngster asked. "*Hey, I've been trying to reach my good friend Tracer for hours now and I can't get through. Is he okay? Is he dead? What's going on?*"

"...um. Dex is sending me a Messenger chat," Beta spoke aloud, if only to convince herself that this was happening.

Spark immediately went on guard, as if their nemesis had somehow broken into the kitchen.

"What?" she asked. "How...? Wait, he can't trace his way into Floating Point this way, can he?"

"No, Messenger's a distributed network. He can't find us and we can't find him. ...I'm patching the call through this room's audio," Beta explained, making a few quick connections. "You'll probably want to have a few words too..."

A soft crackle sounded, as she completed the routing.

"*Hellloooooooo?*" Dex called out. "*Are you ignoring me? That's just rude...*"

Beta braced her hands against the counter. If only to support herself, in case she went weak-kneed.

"I'm here," Beta announced.

*"Ah, good. Anyway, I figured I'd check in on Tracer since he never replied to my last message. How is he doing? Is everything okay over at Floating Point...? I've been worried."*

Spark was the next to speak up... addressing thin air a bit awkwardly, but trying to remain confident. "You can't reach him because he's wearing a connection locker," she explained. "Because *you* showed him he was a murderer. If you're trying to take us apart from the inside out, you failed, buddy. We're not going to turn our backs on him!"

*"A connection locker...? Well, that's a bit of an overreaction isn't it? All I did was give him the gift of honesty. I thought I was doing him a kindness. Nobody should live so deeply in denial, it's not healthy."*

"A kindness?!"

*"Of course! He's my friend, isn't he?"*

"You killed Verity! Under what twisted rules of logic does that make us friends?!"

The long pause made Spark wonder if Dex had hung up on them. But he returned, a bit more muted on the cheerfulness scale.

*"I can see we've gotten off on the wrong foot,"* he spoke. *"I blame myself, really. You know what? I'd like to make a peace offering. How about we meet in person? We'll chat, we'll laugh, we'll cry... and I'll give you a gift: a target for your wonderful quest. A terrible, terrible person who's doing terrible things. Two confirmed kills so far! Would stopping a murderer be of interest to you...?"*

"You can take your gift and shove it up your ass until it hits the back of your teeth—"

"We'll go only if we get to pick the meeting place," Beta spoke up.

"—whoa, Beta, #WTF?"

"We get to pick the meeting place, not you," Beta repeated. "That's the only way we'll agree to talk. And Tracer's not coming with us. It's just me, you, and Spark. Those are my terms."

*"Interesting. Where do you want to meet, exactly?"*

"LibertyPark, by Mandelbrot Rock."

*"...VERY interesting. I see where you're going with this. Okay, be there in a half hour. Thanks so much, Beta. I always knew you were the reasonable one."*

Another soft crackle signaled the end of the conversation.

"Okay, before you spaz, let me explain," Beta insisted. "I know LibertyPark by heart. It's a heavily moderated tourism server in the middle of Athena Online, very public, very safe. Dex won't be able to pull anything funny there. See? I'm improvising, just like you said to do!"

"No, no, I get that bit," Spark said. "I know that park, mom dragged us out there a few times back in the day; #BoringButEducational. Tactically it makes good sense, since neither side can ambush the other."

"Right! Wow. Maybe I can be a leader!"

"Uh. Don't take this the wrong way, but... maybe you should've let me in on this idea first, so we could've picked some other place. He can't jump us in LibertyPark, but we can't jump *him*, either. Our goal is to destroy him, right?"

"Destroy him? We're not trying to destroy him, we're trying to *stop* him," Beta explained. "But we can't do that without understanding what he's actually *doing*. That's why I picked LibertyPark; I want to run some of Tracer's social engineering tricks so I can finagle information out of Dex. We need to know who he really is, what he's trying to accomplish, how the tattoos work, what's going on with his cloud server..."

"We could get that information by jumping him and interrogating him, too."

"I don't think that's how this guy works. He likes to share, yes; I was there when he was taunting Tracer, back at ViruFaxHQ. But he'll only talk if he feels comfortable and powerful. In LibertyPark, he'll feel confident enough to chat away. If we did somehow capture him, he'd probably just clam up. ...besides, I don't think violence is ultimately going to solve this, Spark. We have to find a *better* way to stop him. I mean, what're we going to do in the end, kill him? Is that how far you want to take this? If so... why are you so upset about what Tracer's done?"

Which led Spark's memory spiraling back, even without an automated MemoryPalace trigger to guide it.

Back to HolyHymnal, when they thought they'd cornered Verity's murderer after years of investigation. In a kill-or-be-killed situation, Spark felt she only had one real option. And if he was *actually* Verity's killer... at the time, she felt that maybe she'd be okay with that.

At the time. And then things got complicated. And complicated. And complicated...

And finally, Beta. A third viewpoint to tangle into the mix. The echo chamber of the Winder siblings journey into vigilante justice had a counterweight, after so many years.

"Yeah, okay, you're right. See? Moral core. But I can't say I'll be happy about not obliterating the guy on sight," Spark admitted. "Taking tea with Verity's killer is going to be one null of a challenge."

"I'm not asking you to be happy. I'm not happy, either. Just... trust me to see this through, and find the path. I'll give you my strength to get through this, if you give me yours to get through this without losing my nerve talking face-to-face with that scary little kid. Okay...?"

In the end, there was only one answer. Spark would follow Beta. Follow her as far as this path went... because she knew that for a change, the path wasn't winding downward.

It was one of the few servers where Beta felt comfortable wearing her usual avatar. Far from the chaos of #CodeHonesty, far from the lawless anarchy of the Chans... this was her private sanctuary. As private as a well-trafficked public park could be, at least.

LibertyPark represented Athena Online's majestic natural splendor. Skilled artisans, each an expert in biology, had crafted fractal ferns and great groves of trees that represented the most beautiful mathematics known to Programkind. All of it could be enjoyed without any entrance fee, without any pop-up ads, thanks to the taxpayers of Athena Online. (Even though the Red and RedCore parties had been trying to institute a fee or shut it down for years, calling it a waste of coins.)

Heavy moderation by Athenian law enforcement ensured a safe and pleasant visit for the whole family. Provided you could cope with your kids being bored and complaining constantly about wanting to go to more exciting places like MousEmpire or SimHolWood, of course.

A gaggle of those complaining kids passed by as Beta and Spark arrived, led on by a field trip chaperone. Balloon vendors worked the crowds, offering up free and semi-fun toys for the kiddies to keep them mildly entertained while shown endless trees and rocks...

An offer which Dex, wearing the same avatar of a young child with red-and-blue hair, was happy to accept.

"Here you go, little fella!" the vendor spoke, wearing a tax-paid smile as he passed over the blobby white physics object on a string. "A memory of your trip to LibertyPark!"

"Memories gum up the works, don't need 'um. But thanks anyway, mister!" Dex replied, half-strange, half-cheery.

On seeing his new friends arriving, Dex skipped his way over to the Mandelbrot Rock, balloon lagging slightly behind him.

"Hey, hey! I'm glad you came," he called out, tugging the string of his balloon down so he could poke at its thin surface. "I honestly was expecting a trap of some sort, even out here in LibertyPark. It'd get you in hot water with all of Athena Online and possibly branded a terrorist to attack a child in public, but hey, if it puts an end to that brutal teacher-killing monster, maybe you *would* go that far..."

He pressed one hand to the balloon's surface... marking it with his icon, the barbed wire heart. Satisfied, he let it bob back up to the end of its string, lazily wafting in the simulated breeze behind him.

Spark remained unimpressed.

"Y'know, half the reason we're able to track down and eliminate your 'friends' is because you love giving them highly visible marks like that," she pointed out. "For a criminal mastermind you're not very bright."

"It's a conceit of mine, I know. I'm an irrational being at heart. But one day... it'll be a common feature of the Default avatar, won't it? Just like belly buttons. Why not show it off proudly?"

"Because it's malware," Beta said. "Malware's supposed to stay hidden if it's going to work properly."

"I really don't like the word 'malware,'" Dex said, waggling the string of his balloon. "It's cruel. All I'm doing is introducing Netwerk to its true self, the little voice already inside all our hearts. My cloud touches everyone, just as Floating Point does; those who I befriend simply feel that touch stronger than others. Besides, Spark, I thought you'd like my icon! We're so similar at 'heart,' aren't we?"

"Yeah, no," Spark replied, not taking the bait. "You tried the 'we're more alike than disalike' speech on Tracer already, and it didn't work. #EpicFail."

"No no, I'm talking about the artistic merits of symbols," Dex insisted. "My heart is wrapped in thorns, yours in flames. If you put those two elements together you'd get the iconography of the Sacred Heart, right?"

"The what?"

"The Sacred Heart. You live inside a giant encyclopedia, don't you? Look it up sometime. Oh, wait... someone went and 'burned' all your books, didn't they. Pity."

Beta hopped in, eager for more information. "You know about the people who lived in Floating Point before us? And about the books...?"

Now... Dex paused, before running his mouth.

"Ooohhhh. Okay, I get it. You want *information*. That's why you're really here, not for my gift..."

"Uh... of course not," Beta tried, realizing belatedly that the accidental 'uh' was a ridiculously obvious tell.

"It's fine, it's fine! I'm glad you were willing to talk with me. I *want* you to understand me. We're friends! Well. You don't think we're friends, but I know better. I'm hoping *all* us are going to be good friends eventually," Dex insisted. "Tracer, well, that's obvious. His heart burns with passion for vengeance, cloaked in rationality. Spark happily jettisons rationality in favor of satisfying her every needy impulse. You're both way cooler than the last group to occupy Floating Point; I love you so very, very much. And as for Beta..."

Now... Dex stood on his toes, to better look Beta in the eyes.

"She's the reasonable one. The nice one," he spoke. "And that's a problem. Kindness isn't what Netwerk craves; it wants *strife*. But, as a friend of my friends, I'm willing to consider you a friend too. I'll have hope that you can turn yourself around. Unless you'd prefer to be an enemy, I mean. In which case..."

With a single poke of a finger, his balloon burst, rubber shards blasting in all directions.

Spark immediately adjusted her pose, ready to strike if need be. Ready to interpose herself between Dex and Beta in an instant... as Dex stepped back, hands raised, as if protesting.

"Not looking to start a fight," he clarified. "I'm just... talking. Only words. Words can't hurt anyone, right? Hmmmm... actually, that brings me nicely around to why I invited you here. My gift to you... a serial killer. You like hunting down serial killers, right? You have one tied up back at home, in fact..."

Sensing her chance to pry more information loose had slipped away, Beta resigned herself to playing along rather than playing him along. For the time being.

"What do you want to give us, exactly?" she asked.

Dex pulled two news clippings from his inventory, tossing them over. Beta caught them—and scanned the files eight times with ten different security Apps, before reading.

"Two of my friends were killed recently," Dex explained. "Members of the /lulz/ subcommunity, from the AnyChan server. They're a group devoted to practical jokes."

"You mean trolls," Spark spat.

"How unkind! Regardless, they were both brutally murdered. The news claims these were suicides, but I knew these men; they were hardly suicidal. No, someone or something killed them. You don't like killers, right? So... interested?"

"A few more of your buddies vanishing from Netwerk isn't exactly a great loss..."

"Beta thinks otherwise," Dex spoke, nodding towards the one quietly reading the articles. "If you genuinely don't care, let it slide. I'll miss my friends, but maybe I can befriend this new murderer instead. Or... you can avenge them for me. Or for yourselves. Or for whatever, I don't care, as long as you act in the name of your passions."

Closing the floating document windows, Beta looked back to their enemy.

"We'll look into it," she spoke, without promise. "But... I'm going to have to disagree with you on one thing. You say Netwerk wants strife, not kindness? Maybe. But what it *needs* is the opposite. And it doesn't need you."

"I know you believe that, but I'm afraid you're simply wrong, Miss Projkit. I'm right and you're wrong. It's as simple and clean as God's integers above... the messy parts were made by man."

"Floating Point's slogan, properly translated."

"You remembered! I'm touched!"

Beta searched that happy little smile for further truth. It didn't seem to be built on lies... Dex genuinely thought they were on friendly terms. Rather than posture and mock and threaten, perhaps a different tactic, an impossible tactic could be tried...

"Dex... I'm going to ask something of you," Beta said. "And think hard about this, because I am being completely sincere. Dex... will you please back down, and leave Netwerk alone? No more malware. No more instigating chaos and war. You say Netwerk wants strife? I say: give Netwerk a chance to show you it can be something else, something better. Open your mind to the possibility that you're wrong. Can you do that for a friend...?"

Dex scratched his chin, as if in deep thought.

"Curious. If I said yes...?" he asked.

"We'd leave you alone," Beta spoke, with promise. "I know Spark and Tracer hate you, but Tracer's already seen the end result of acting on hate. I know he can turn himself around, and so can Netwerk. I believe that wholeheartedly."

"That you do. That you do. ...but I have my own wholehearted belief, Miss Projkit. I believe Netwerk can only survive by returning to its roots. It must be honest with itself again. I'm sorry, but... I can't stop. I love Netwerk too much to abandon it."

"I love Netwerk too. And we're going to have to stop you, if you won't stop yourself."

Dex's smile beamed brighter than the decorative skybox sun above.

"I'm looking forward to your passion play," he declared.

Moments later, he was gone. Reconnected back to whatever dark cloud he hailed from.

Leaving Spark free to untense. And to look to her companion, for direction.

"I... think I screwed up a little," Beta recognized. "I'm not very good at social engineering. I could've gotten him to talk more if he hadn't spotted me being so obvious. I'm sorry..."

"I dunno, I think you milked a hell of a rant out of him," she asked. "Okay, post-match analysis time. Let's see your investigative strats at work. What'd we learn from him?"

Beta, who had been compiling her own notes all the while, read them back from a file.

"He's probably wiped his memory before, based on what he told the balloon vendor," she interpreted. "Memory purges are a way to avoid long-term data rot from aging. Given he clearly knows secrets about Netwerk's origins and Floating Point itself, he might be fantastically old despite his young avatar. What's more, he believes in Verity's teachings... that's why he talked about belly buttons, which were a fixation of hers. Verity may have been close to that truth before she was killed; it's why he convinced Ichiban to do the deed."

"Huh. Yeah, that'd make sense," Spark agreed. "She was killed soon after her book about evolutionary creationism was published. And Dex clearly had disagreements with the last group to live at Floating Point; if he figured out that she'd found the access keys, it'd be too risky to leave her alive..."

"But now that you and Tracer are living there and you're both—and um, this is his view, not mine—irrational and dangerous, he's willing to bet you could be his friends instead of his enemies. And... I'm the nice one, which is bad for him..."

"Because he loves cruelty. Dex can't flip you as easily as he flipped Snowi. It's also why he infected both Cup8 and Snowi and launched them at each other... he's not trying to win wars, only cause them."

"Yes, exactly!" Beta exclaimed. "Next, he knows enough about Floating Point to confirm my theory that it's a giant encyclopedia, not a pile of abstract fiction and poetry... and that it's not burned at all, but 'burned,' meaning it's likely only encrypted! I should start looking into algorithms to determine the encryption method being used right away!"

"Yeah yeah, books, okay, *focus*. We have bigger problems. Anything else about Dex?"

"Right, um, sorry. Finally... he thinks he's in the right, that he's a hero, enabling the passions within people's hearts. And... he'll never stop unless we stop him."

"I could've told you that much."

"We still had to try to reach him, Spark. We may even reach him yet, in time. But yeah... stopping him is happening, one way or another. ...soooo... for now, what do we do about this 'serial killer' he 'gifted' us?"

Spark contemplated the Mandelbrot Rock, hoping the splendor of nature's creativity would inspire her. It didn't.

"I dunno. Kick his ass?" she suggested. "Dex isn't *wrong*. Stopping the crazies is kinda what we do. But this time we play it careful, and we play it right. You're doing fine so far; what do you suggest we do next?"

"Okay! Right. Investigation time! To find this nefarious killer, we're going to...!"

...stare at the Mandelbrot Rock, in hopes the splendor of nature's creativity would inspire her. It didn't.

"How about we ask Tracer?" Spark suggested, instead.

"Um. I don't know. He's... not going to be happy we're dealing directly with Dex... I'm a bit nervous about telling him what we've done."

"Yeah, well, he can #DealWithIt. If he really wants to lend his advice, he'll cope with our tactics... and it's up to you to decide what we do with that advice. You think he's wrong, you say it to his face, don't back down and run with whatever he offers. If he's gonna make a turnaround, we have to start somewhere, right? Helping with this case could be that start."

"You should have killed him," Tracer decided.

It wasn't exactly an explosion of rage, but Beta could tell he was displeased with her little tale of encountering the enemy. Even beyond his the conclusion he drew, little tells gave it away... much like the grimaces and eyebrow twitches of frustration whenever she was utterly clobbering him at Go.

But much like a round of Go, that meant she was winning, and he knew it.

"That's the wrong course of action, mind you," Tracer added. "It's the most direct and obvious way to end the chaos that's consuming Netwerk... kill the head and the body will die. But morally speaking it's definitely not the way to go. I know that, even if the optimal part of me says to snip away the problem and be done with it."

"We're not killing Dex," Beta confirmed, trying to stand up to him, despite her nerves. Having Spark on hand to nod firmly in encouragement helped. "Something's clearly wrong with Dex. He's lost himself along the way... maybe from exposure to the cloud server he calls home, the one that drives people to extremes. He deserves our pity, not our hate."

"I'm not saying to hate him. I'm just saying to kill him and be done with it; it's the cleanest way to save Netwerk. But as we've noted, I'm hardly the right person to be making calls like that, so I'll defer to you. ...for what it's worth, playing him for information was a good plan. Second best option in this situation, and it seems like you got quite a bit out of him."

"Including these articles," Beta said, transferring copies over to Tracer's MemoryPalace. She still had read/write access to it, after all...

The headlines escalated from randomness to a potential pattern.

First, from an Athena Online local server bulletin board:

```
Ptr/Bryan sadly has passed away from self-inflicted
wounding. He is survived by his parents and sister. As
a devoted member of the Kaptberg township and
president of the photography club at PS#122B79, he
will be missed...
```

Second, from a Chanarchy rumor mill:

```
The Suicide Fairy comes to AnyChan!! LordSmegma's RL
ID now known; he's Ptr/Bryan and he wasted himself a
few days ago. He defaced the posters on his wall, then
knifed up his avatar until it crashed out. Weird combo
amirite? And guess what: today they found Tach/Paull
aka Weevil dead the same way in his Chanarchy
apartment. Screwed with his video library, then killed
himself.

Creepy thing is someone posted photos of Smegma's
death, along with some weird threat. (see attchd) But
```

it was a suicide, right? Conspiracies are bullshit, we all know that. The visitor that posted it was kinda screwed up too so I'm figuring a bot or expert system left behind by Smegma as a suicide note.

I shouldn't be cheering these guys on but they were complete assholes so I'm gonna cheer anyway. They give the rest of ANychan a bad name. we're not all dickbags out here. Archives of the sucide photos from the news are on /guro/ and /newz/ if you wanna look. We'll add more as more of /lulz/ goes under the knife.

Attached to the article was the grisly meme photo in question:

ÝÕÜ ŵîll ŕ3ĝŕËŢ €VéŕÝŦhÍÑĝ.

Ø® Í Ŵî¦l *måķ£* ýðµ ŖÊĝŖ3Ŧ 3V3ŖýŦĤ!ÑĜ.

"Well, that's... pleasant," Spark decided, uncertain what word to use. "Font's all screwed up for additional nightmare fuel factor..."

Tracer scanned the articles in moments, speed-reading. He took a few moments of sitting back and steepling his fingers before coming to any conclusions, however.

"Dex is right. This is a serial killer," he agreed. "Given the threats posted to their image board and two unrepentant trolls dying the same way, it's only a suicide in name. I'm doing some initial searches on the /lulz/ community now..."

A few dozen articles popped all over the room, freshly loaded into his MemoryPalace. They hovered in his personal Sphere of Crazy, automatically cross-referencing themselves, growing or shrinking in size as his intelligent agents determined which ones could be the most relevant to the original two murder reports.

Meanwhile, Spark scoffed at the various "pranks" being pulled up. "Fucking trolls. I hate those guys. If people would stop feeding them the attention they crave, they'd dry up and go away..."

But Beta shook her head. "It wouldn't help. I didn't fight back against my trolls; I tried to ignore them and wait for them to leave. They never did. Mine weren't looking for attention, they were looking to silence me, and, well... they succeeded. Leaving them be isn't the answer..."

"Yeah, well, driving them to suicidal insanity's not the answer either. So whatever SJW is taking them out of the picture, we gotta step in the way. Even if I can't say I like the people we're saving..."

With his research scan complete, Tracer returned to the conversation armed with his analysis.

"I'd say these trolls are a little bit of both. They crave attention, *and* want to silence voices they consider ridiculous. /lulz/ holds no faiths, no beliefs, no ideals; nihilistic jokers, all. I'd say to look to their ideological enemies... but they have no particular ideology beyond mockery of anyone who believes anything. I doubt they actually put stock in any of the sexist, hateful trash they spew. It's just a pile of weapons to them, used to see what reaction they'll get *and* to try and shut down any outspoken voices."

Spark rocked back and forth in her chair, straddling it backwards, eager to get to the action.

"So basically look at everybody in Netwerk to figure out who could hate them. Real useful there, bro, thanks," she mocked.

"You don't need to cast that wide of a net. Instead, we could look to the victims. A suicide-based killer is not some random lunatic... it's a lunatic who's in a great deal of pain, thanks to the actions of /lulz/. That says to me that the killer is a past victim or affiliated with a past victim. The knife is key to all of this, no doubt, an important symbol... one the killer would want /lulz/ to recognize. ...a moment. I'm searching for any combination of... well. That was easy..."

Immediately, one of the hundreds of miniature articles that had been swarming around the room enlarged to fill the space over Tracer's desk.

DIIT/FIONA DEATH OFFICIALLY RULED A SUICIDE

The small community of StdOutville stands in outrage tonight, as Athena Online official moderators have ruled the death of thirteen-year-old Diit/Fiona a suicide.

"While there is no doubt that bullying contributed to her frame of mind at the time, we will not be issuing warrants for the individuals involved, nor will we be releasing their identities. There is no legal wrongdoing in leaving hurtful comments on her blog; freedom of speech is one of Athena Online's oldest values and must be respected," Officer Writ/Px3 told reporters at a press conference today.

A candlelight vigil organized by the Society for Cyberbullying Prevention will be held at 20:00:00 today.

A picture of the girl in question, smiling and surrounded by adorable cartoon stickers of cats and rainbows, had been pulled from her blog.

Beta's heart raced momentarily, her emotional core latching on to that bright smile. Someone so young, taken so early in life...

"Judging from prior articles... her suicide method was indeed a knife," Tracer continued. "/lulz/ has wholeheartedly denied any involvement, despite it being quite clear they were involved. The 'prank' was apparently in their 'Hall of Shame' until recently, before they swept the whole thing under the rug and tried to move on."

Beta had to swallow those feelings. For now. Focus on the investigation, as calmly and coolly as Tracer was.

"So the killer may be a friend of hers, or even her parents," she suggested. "Looking for some ironic revenge. Make the trolls feel her pain..."

"It's possible. It could also be someone within /lulz/, one who disagreed with this particular act of cruelty. /lulz/ is a subchannel of AnyChan, and fully anonymous; being a 'member' simply means 'showing up.' There's no way to know who did what and where and when..."

"But that works both ways. How could the killer know who to target, if they were all anonymous losers? The killer homed in on LordSmegma in real life, and then they hit another major /lulz/ member immediately after..."

"It's curious. In this case, perhaps looking to the *victimizers* will bear fruit instead; we know they're going to be targeted, and catching the killer in the act would be the easiest approach. Fortunately, you have a good starting point for answering these questions..."

A photo of the badly-aging Default avatar of Officer Writ/Px3 pulled itself away from the lengthy news article.

"The moderators said they wouldn't be releasing identities of the trolls. That means they somehow had identities to release," Tracer extrapolated. "I suggest you start by looking into the officer in charge. Ransacking his office may be difficult, given Athena Online's typical level of security on police precincts, but—"

"Or we could just ask him," Beta suggested.

"—or you could just ask him, I suppose. ...Beta. Before you depart, there's one question I think you need to consider in all seriousness. Let's say your investigation bears fruit, and you identify the killer. What then?"

"Huh?"

"You have no authority to 'arrest' this murderer. You'll likely have difficulty proving to an Athenian moderator that a killer even exists, given the suicide aspect. It's going to be on your shoulders to put a stop to this, unless we're okay with letting him empty a poisoned nest of trolls. What's your endgame? How will you ultimately deal with the perpetrator?"

It was clear what answer he wanted to hear. It sat at the tip of his tongue, after all... the same answer he'd offered to his own sticky situation. Killers should die, to end their killings. In his view, it was the only acceptable punishment...

Beta wanted to offer him a better answer. She wanted to confidently state some bold and optimistic assertion, one which would put him in his place... and give him hope that there was more in his future than death, at the same time. She wanted to do that. But she'd need *words* to say, and, well... none came to mind. No easy answers.

So, instead... she looked to Spark for inspiration. Her CoC partner, the one who rarely had a long-term plan in mind, but slid through the game moment-to-moment with exactly the right micro-decision at each twist and turn...

"I'm going to improvise," Beta decided. "We'll wait until we catch the killer, then figure things out from there."

Immediately Spark got to her feet, to back the plan.

"There's no point getting paralyzed over some huge philosophical conundrum when we've only started investigating this thing," she agreed. "You stopped the Karnival by improvising, didn't you? Sure didn't shut it down the way you thought you were going to. Let Beta wrangle this one her way, bro. We won't let you down."

"Very well. I'll put my faith in that, if I must," Tracer said. "I hope in the end, you can find your better path. If you can't... I'm willing to step in and handle the situation as needs be."

"Not gonna come to that. C'mon, Beta, let's go interrogate a cop!"

"Ask questions! *Ask!*" Beta emphasized. "Not *interrogate.*"

---

"Officer" was a dirty word, in Spark's view.

As the two sat in a precinct waiting room, awaiting their fate, Spark freely grumbled across their private Messenger link. Not that she'd grumble openly while surrounded by police officers going about their official office work; better not to poke them with a stick.

"*I grew up in Athena Online,*" she reminded her companion. "*I know how these pigs work. And this is the first time I've been in a precinct house and not been in connection-locking handcuffs.*"

"*You've been arrested before?*" Beta asked.

"*Of course. I ran with weird friends in my teenage years... avatar modders, punks, rebels. Anything that'd piss off my mom. And yeah, I got nabbed for petty stupid kid crimes like graffiti and littering servers with bouncing penises and stuff.*"

Beta's giggle was audible, if muted out of respect to the work-a-day moderators around her.

"*Hey, it felt like #SrsBsns to me at the time,*" Spark protested. "*Even if it was juvenile and stupid. Point is, I've seen firsthand how power can corrupt a moderator, and police officers are moderators on steroids. A distributed network of moderators across the entire hosting service, toting badges and guns and bad attitudes. I doubt we're gonna get anything out of this guy, assuming he'll even bother talking to us. You saw how dismissive he was at that press conference...*"

"*We have to try,*" Beta countered. "*If he won't talk with us... I guess we'll have to somehow ransack the office like Tracer suggests, but... I'd prefer to do this the right way, first. Besides, we have good bait, right?*"

*"It's tipping our hand. If we put them onto the killer's trail at the same time we're stalking that trail, it could mean crashing head-on into a police investigation..."*

*"Does it matter who catches the killer in the end? If the mods catch him, good. If we catch him, good. This isn't a personal vendetta, Spark. We're trying to make Netwerk a better place. Results matter more than means."*

*"Tracer would agree with that part, at least. And that's worrying..."*

Finally, a badge-plus-gun combo approached the pair. His middle-aged avatar looked a bit wilted compared to the more young and fresh looking avatars of Netwerk, but cops tended to favor Defaults... either as churchgoing folk, or simply out of tradition. Age lent an air of authority, after all.

"I'm Officer Writ," he introduced. "I understand you ladies have new information about the Ptr/Bryan case...?"

"Yes sir," Beta spoke, with instinctively appropriate respect for her elders. "We believe it wasn't a suicide, and we may have proof to that effect."

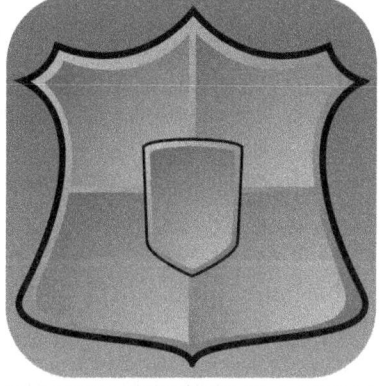

Name : Writ/Px3

Home : StdOutville / Athena Online

Org : Police Moderator

"Mhmmm," he mumbled, doubtful. "And you didn't bring this to the Kaptberg server precinct because...?"

"Because it relates to the suicide of DiiT/Fiona. According to the blogs we've read, that was your case. We figured it'd be best to bring this to you directly. If we could talk somewhere private, sir...?"

The officer looked suspicious, clearly. For a moment, Spark wondered if she'd pulled some stunt in his district years ago, anything he'd remember her for... but her avatar was completely different now. Hopefully those pranks wouldn't discredit them in his eyes...

In the end, he waved them onward.

"We'll talk in my office," he suggested.

It was clearly his office.

When you're given a personal corner of Netwerk, the tendency is to decorate it in such a way as to mark it yours. Puzzle had done the same when given a guest room, immediately rearranging the furniture and putting up selfies, to make it feel like home. Officer Writ/Px3 had also artfully and carefully arranged framed family photos and mementos of a long career. This wasn't just a place of business, it was his domain, and he expressed himself in how he declared it to be so.

Strangely, many of the photos were weirdly composed... the officer standing off to the side of nothing in particular, sometimes with an arm around the space where someone should have stood. Beta, who tended to look for personal details like these, noticed immediately.

The officer, who tended to notice people noticing things, took notice.

"Some punk deleted my wife from all my photos a few days ago," he explained. "Probably some new cadet, trying to put one over on the old man. Haven't had time to replace 'em yet. If you would have a seat...?"

With all three settling into place—two in the uncomfortable guest chairs designed to encourage people to talk if only to be allowed to leave, one in the comfy chair behind the well-earned desk of power—the officer further explained his position.

"Officially, Ptr/Bryan's death is a suicide," he stated. "Same goes for DiiT/Fiona. Obviously I've noticed some similarities in the three cases; I've got an intelligent agent set in place to look for anything related to the Fiona case. But it's likely a coincidence."

"Except there's been a third death," Beta explained, opening a folder she'd brought with her and pulling out the Chanarchy blog post. "Bryan's friend Weevil—um, I mean, Tach/Paull—died the exact same way earlier today. Is three identical deaths a coincidence, sir?"

Before commenting, Officer Writ accepted the file copy and read it thoroughly. Clearly he wasn't impressed by the mocking and informal blog post.

"For starters, that one's well outside my jurisdiction," he declared. "All I care about is keeping the good folks of Athena Online safe. Whatever happens in the Chanarchy is the fault of the Chanarchy; a lawless breeding ground of the worst Netwerk has to offer."

"That doesn't mean it's unrelated, though!" Beta was quick to point out. "Sir, the news blog implied that you'd identified the anonymous individuals involved in Fiona's suicide. Are these names on that list? If so, it's proof that all of this is connected!"

"*Eerhh*... I don't know. Can't recall. I haven't looked at that file in ages..."

"Isn't it worth a check? Listen... I know you think we're crazy. But what if it's true? What if someone's systematically killing off Fiona's harassers, and making it look identical to her suicide? Sir, please, it'll only take seconds to check..."

"A suicide's a suicide, a murder's a murder. Look, I've got actual crimes to deal with right now. I think we're done here, little lady—"

"So why run a search agent?" Spark asked.

As it was her first time speaking up since arriving in a cloud of gloom and doubt, those words were enough to break the officer's dismissive focus.

"You said you had an intelligent search agent looking for similar suicides," Spark pointed out. "Says to me that some part of you isn't satisfied with how the

Fiona case closed. Y'know, from that news article, I assumed you didn't give two shits about Fiona's death. But that was the company line, right? Passed down from on high, and spoken for the benefit of the reporters alone. How do YOU feel about how she died, Px3?"

Inches from being kicked out of the office (or possibly into a holding tank) for disrespecting a man of the law? A familiar situation for Spark. But she sat there, arms crossed, staunch in her statement no matter the bluster raised in the officer's face. No matter Beta's panicked reaction across Messenger, silently urging Spark not to annoy the policeman. Not like Spark cared about annoying moderators, after all.

In the end... Officer Writ sat back down, from his position of half-rising out of his chair to demand they leave his office.

"It was a Onesdamn shame," he answered. "Just a Onesdamn shame, what those trolls did to that poor girl. She had a condition, you know. An imbalanced emotional core, leading to clinical depression. The sunshine-and-rainbows blog was her way of trying to self medicate, to focus only on the positive things in life, and those trolls tore that away from her..."

Beta looked puzzled. "Faulty emotional routines? But... those can be easily corrected with treatment and therapy..."

"Her parents were fundamentalists. They didn't believe in any kinda software patches or avatar modifications, so they wouldn't correct the error," Px3 explained. "I'm a faithful of the One too, but if that were my daughter I wouldn't have let her suffer like that when medical science had an answer. They left her vulnerable to those trolling bastards. Never sat right with me that the legals said we couldn't make a case, so we shouldn't bother trying to make one. Especially since we had the names..."

"You look at those names, you'll see we're right," Spark promised. "Dig up the file and let's settle this once and for all."

Resigned to it... Officer Writ unlocked a drawer on his desk, pulling out an index of files. The compressed evidence database opened itself, folder after folder appearing as a cluster of icons. Manually browsing it all took some time, playing his fingers to swipe through the icons.

"I remember what went down, even if I can't recall the specifics," he explained, while searching. "Despite being a Horizon-based service we've got an official treaty with MyFace for law enforcement purposes. A guy named Renpy, some first party API tech, he looked into the situation for me. All the harassing posts came from fifty different anonymous sock puppet accounts... which could be internally linked back to three *real* accounts."

"Government monitoring of social media? Helloooo privacy violation," Spark complained.

"Only to keep our citizens safe," Officer Writ corrected, tapping a specific folder icon to open it wide. "'k, here we go. Should be—"

Instead of an array of documents, an array of identical tiny women spilled out.

Glitched data. Corrupted and rotten, arms and legs and faces tumbling onto the desk, spilling like a broken faucet. They poured through the officer's fingers... scraping at his avatar's skin, glitching and distorting the fingernails as the officer froze in utter horror, eyes wide at the smiling and distorted features of the paper-thin avatars which tumbled endlessly out of the folder...

His wife. They were all from the photos around his office, stolen away, given new life as miniature and horrifically ruined avatars of his wife.

Spark was the first to act. Gamer instincts kicked in, moving her to take action while those around her stood in shocked silence. Improvisation was the key to shutting down a dangerous situation before it ran out of control, she'd found.

With a sweeping gesture, she slammed the file closed. But not before passing her hand through the spillage of broken forms—

*—I'm no good. I'm no good. I don't deserve anything I have.*

*I've achieved nothing. Just a pile of indulgences and stupidity. Verity would be so disappointed in me. I miss her so much, the mother I never had, and she'd be so sad to see this stupid little thing I've become.*

*My brother's a murderer. I'm just as bad, I always want to punch my problems to solve them, always. I'm too scared, too cowardly, too stupid to do anything about this girl I may or may not be in love with. My life is a pile of failures.*

*I'm pathetic. I'm no good. I'm no good. I don't deserve anything I have.*

*I regret everything. I regret everything. Kill yourself. Kill yourself. Kill—*

—pink and fuzzy sweater.

It was enough to pull her back, that comforting feeling of yarn and kindness. The same thing that kept her sane within the void, adrift from her own avatar, during the ViruFax incident. This time it pulled her back from a different brink, letting her reassert herself... after the damage had been done.

Spark had been crying. Her, the tough girl, the brave one.

Somehow she'd ended up back in the main room of the precinct on an emergency stretcher, with a drip feed of stimulus inputs hanging from a bottle above her. A brief glance around showed men in yellow hazmat protection avatars quickly sealing off Writ's office... proof that a good chunk of time had passed since she was last lucid.

"Spark? Spark, can you hear me now?" Beta asked. "Doctor, she's waking up!"

"I... uh... yeah. Yeah, I can hear you," Spark confirmed. "What...? What's going on? I got this... I don't know, this *wave* of ugly thoughts, and..."

A data health specialist waved some sort of something-or-other at her, collecting data on her current runtime state.

"*They don't know we were involved, thankfully,*" Beta transmitted across Messenger. "*I was afraid they'd think we're responsible and arrest us, but because you got hit with the same thing that incapacitated the officer and they found proof of prior data tampering in his office, we're clean...*"

"You came into contact with residual corrupt data from a hack," the doctor in the yellow hazmat suit explained. "We think it disrupted the emotional routines of your code. How are you feeling now, ma'am?"

"Lousy," Spark admitted. "But... they're distant. Those voices, I mean. I'll be fine. Beta, c'mon, let's get out of here."

"We're going to send you to Northon Data Health alongside Officer Writ," the doctor suggested. "The police may have more questions for you, as well. We don't know exactly what caused your negative emotional reaction; your core is stable again, but there may be further side effects—"

"Neither of us are citizens of Athena Online. You can't hold us against our will."

"I'm not saying you're under arrest, ma'am, I'm saying that for the good of your health—"

But Spark was already climbing off the stretcher, relying on her sense of balance to quickly sort itself out before her feet hit the floor. After only a slight wobble, she resumed standing upright.

"*We need to move fast,*" she suggested to Beta over Messenger. "*This killer's definitely using some weird suicide-inducing emotional malware. Let's go track down that MyFace rep—the officer called him Renpy, right? I want a copy of those names the killer stole. I want to end this.*"

"*Spark, please, you need time to recover...!*"

"*As much as I'd love a drink and a nap, fuck that. We can't slow down if we're going to find the killer before it's too late to save the last victim. Let's move.*"

And gone, disconnecting from the server. Leaving Beta to apologize to the doctors before following her friend out into the wilds of Netwerk.

Lunchtime represented an artifact of an ancient age. As such, Renpy respected it greatly.

It was like bellybuttons, or fingernails; it made no real sense. Nobody *needed* to eat lunch, so why take time off in the middle of the day for it? And yet, tradition held that all MyFace employees would get a half hour for lunch, every day. Therefore Renpy took advantage of that half hour to sample a new restaurant each day, and blog about it.

Today was a curry place, mixing up all manner of spicy data samples into a fine concoction. Renpy allowed his delicate dish of delicacy sit uneaten for a minute while he photographed it from various sides through his eyes, shuttling each image up to the blog. He had subscribers to entertain, many of them tuning in during their own lunch breaks to demand minute-by-minute flavor updates...

"12:11:34, about to take my first bite. The aroma is quite stimulating," he jotted down mentally. He scooped up a reasonable amount of it, and...

"VNDB/Renpy?"

...interruptions. Never a good seasoning with one's meal. But fans had followed him around before, stalking him on his lunch break, and he knew better than to be ungracious.

"A moment, please," he requested. "I'll be happy to sign autographs for you once I get my first update posted."

"Umm... sir, we're not fans," Beta explained. "Actually, we'd like to ask you some questions about your work at MyFace..."

Ahh. The *other* reason someone might interrupt his lunch.

Determined to enjoy the curry all in one go rather than have a bite and then let the rest sit uneaten, he decided to wait on posting his update. He set the spoon back down into the dish, nudging it aside for a moment while he shattered whatever dreams these two had.

"No, I can't get you Farmtopia gems," he started. "I can't gift you profile stickers and I'm not the one you should complain to if someone's trolling your MyCommunity group. In fact there's nothing I can do for you in regards to MyFace, and I'm under multiple NDAs not to discuss my work in the slightest, so if you're not here for lunch I suggest you move along."

"Are you responsible for inquiries from Athena Online's police department?" Beta continued, undaunted. "We need a copy of a file you sent to Officer Wirt regarding a trolling incident—"

"NDAs," he repeated, before taking a moment to inhale the spicy odor, to at least keep himself reminded of the lunch yet to come. "I can't talk about our relationship with Athena Online, nor can I provide you with any information whatsoever. At this point I am considering our interaction harassment, and as this restaurant and MyFace itself fall under the protective umbrella of the Horizon foundation, I am within my rights to summon a moderator to eject you from the premises."

"Wait, wait, please... there's no need for that," Beta insisted. "This is a compassionate request; we aren't looking to break any laws or disrupt your company's operations. We're researching a trolling incident, one involving the suicide of a young girl. It's very important that we talk this over, sir. Lives may be on the line—"

"Not my business, not my problem."

"If you'd just hear us out, sir—!"

"Not interested. Disengage immediately or I'm calling a moderator..."

...as the second woman pulled away his dish, keeping it out of arm's reach.

"If you don't mind, I've had a rather shitty day, and I'm not leaving this restaurant without that file," Spark responded. "Beta, he's not going to cooperate, so we're going with Plan B. Renpy, you're in charge of first party development and user profile tracking APIs, yes? It wasn't hard to figure you out, based on your blogs. Does the word 'Karnival' mean anything to you?"

Renpy's mental finger hovered over the 'Report to Moderator' button in his HUD.

"Yeah, looks like it does," Spark said... before taking a spoonful of his curry, his curry, and eating it. "Hmm. Tastes pretty good. So, by this point rumors are swirling about what the Karnival was before it shut down. 'A bunch of rapists' is the current conspiracy theory making the rounds, yes? What do you think would happen if word got out that *you* were directly involved with them? That you were the first-party development contact enabling what could've become a wide-scale violation of privacy...?"

"I... I am under the protective umbrella of Horizon," Renpy reminded her, trying to sound confident. "You don't want to go down this road, little girl. They'll make a stay in an Athenian prison server look like a vacation..."

Beta quickly flipped to her private channel. *"Spark, we agreed NOT to do this!"* she protested. *"We can't threaten and bully our way around anymore..."*

*"There's no way he'd break all those layers of corporate secrecy to help us out of the goodness of his heart. We were two seconds away from getting our asses kicked. Anyway, relax! He's bluffing,"* Spark insisted. *"I know a coward when I see one. We don't have to lift a finger; the threat alone will be enough."*

"All we want is a single file," Spark continued. "The same data you sent to Officer Writ regarding DiiT/Fiona's harassment. Three lousy little names, belonging to nobodies that you'll never actually meet. In return for those names, you'll never hear from us again. Nobody finds out about your involvement with the Karnival. You get to enjoy your lunch. That's a bargain, isn't it?"

The chill that enveloped Renpy ran so deep that no amount of curry could warm it up again.

"You have no... *no* idea," he whispered. "The fact that you know about Horizon's connection to the Karnival at all... we could all get backspaced, with that out in the open. I... I have to..."

With a trembling thought, he jabbed the REPORT button within his mind.

Under normal circumstances, the well-paid security staff of the Horizon family would swoop in and sweep this problem under the rug. He'd be safe, and never need to hear that word again. Safe to enjoy his lunch and pretend nothing was out of the ordinary.

Instead, nothing happened at all.

"Have to...?" Spark asked, unsure what he was getting at.

"I... I don't understand. I was told to report immediately if anybody connected me to the Karnival," Renpy spoke aloud, despite being under strict orders not to talk out loud about it. "I don't understand, I don't—"

—the chill only deepened, on realizing someone had connected into the server directly behind him.

They were joined by a fourth lunch guest... a woman wearing a sharp tuxedo, with deep olive-hued skin and short-cropped hair. An odd sight, even in a restaurant, given her ensemble didn't match that of the other waitresses.

Renpy... craned his head back, to get a good look. And his jag sagged, unable to un-sag afterwards.

"What seems to be the issue?" the new woman asked... ignoring the slack-jawed MyFace employee, focusing instead on the two sitting across the table. Specifically, the one wearing a white jacket and eating a curry.

Always one to roll with the punches, Spark spoke right up even as Beta's reaction greatly resembled Renpy's. With a bit more confusion rather than horror, but just as paralyzing.

"We want to the true MyFace profiles of DiiT/Fiona's harassers," Spark explained, simply.

"I see," the woman spoke. "A moment please, while I consult my employer."

Briefly she glanced aside, consulting an invisible HUD element... leaving the the MyFace crony in mortal terror, before she relayed a simple order.

"Give her the file she's asking for," Cancel commanded.

Renpy worked his mouth a bit without making any noise, before he could formulate a proper reply.

"But... but... they know about the Karnival, Miss Cancel... Kincaid told me that if anyone ever—"

"We will speak of *that* later," the woman named Miss Cancel warned. "For now, consider this a direct order from Horizon/Kincaid: comply with this investigation and be forthcoming with any information they require in regards to DiiT/Fiona. Your company's privacy protocols are irrelevant to the interests of the Horizon family. Understood?"

"Yes. Yes, of course. Whatever Mr. Horizon needs of me," Renpy promised.

With a curt nod, the strange butler-esque figure of Miss Cancel left Renpy to quickly ransack his personal knowledge base... as she turned to the girls.

A business card manifested in her fingers, flicked from her sleeve... and was held out for Spark to accept, specifically.

Tentatively, Spark threw up a few extra security firewalls just in case touching the card would trigger some crazy malware. The simple two-dimensional illustration of the sun breaking dawn over a skybox horizon, the logo of the richest family-slash-business in Netwerk, did not immediately wipe her avatar on contact.

"In the future, if you have a sensitive information request, Horizon/Kincaid would like you to contact him directly," Miss Cancel spoke. "Rather than potentially raise the ire of moderators through shady back-channel activity. It's cleaner that way. Thank you for your time, Miss Winder, Miss Projkit."

Her task complete, the Horizon assistant vanished into the ether. Gone, just as quickly and quietly as she had arrived.

His appetite left in ruins, Renpy immediately flicked through his confidential files with the fastest search agent he had handy. A simple document with three names on it popped out the other end, tossed haphazardly onto the table.

"Enjoy the curry," he ordered, with as much spite as he could manage. His avatar vanished immediately after, shuttled back to his office server, hunger unsatisfied and nerves unsettled.

...leaving behind two very confused young women.

"Do you have any idea what that was about?" Beta felt the need to ask, despite knowing the answer. "Horizon and the Karnival? We never said anything about the Horizon family... and how did they know our names? What would someone like Horizon/Kincaid want with us? Spark, uh. This is freaking me out a little."

"No idea what his deal is, and honestly, I could care less," Spark stated, while scooping up the files. She tucked the business card away in her inventory as well, trying not to think about it.

"Uh. Y'know, grammatically speaking that means you actually *do* care a little..."

"Not my point. We need to stay focused, Beta. One mystery at a time, one fight at a time, that's how you eventually win the match. Anyway, we got the info we came for, didn't we? And we didn't actually doxx the guy or anything, so I'll call it a win. Whatever backroom corporate backstabbing is going on, that doesn't have to be any of our business."

Beta chewed her lip, uncertain. "We shouldn't have pulled the Karnival threat in the first place. I was against Plan B, remember? Hopefully we haven't... haven't, uh... what's a good metaphor here? Opened a folder of worms? I feel like a leader should have a pithy metaphor on tap whenever needed..."

"Bryan-aka-LordSmegma and Paull-aka-Weevil, those two we can strike off this list. Seeing as they're deader than doornails, I mean..."

"Doornails! Yes! That's a good metaphor. ...what's a doornail?"

"That leaves one last troll unaccounted for, and I'm not finding any obituaries yet in my searches," Spark continued. "We're not too late. Looks like... Smif/Johanha-aka-YogaHurt. Good news is that Johanha's a social media freak like me. She just checked in at... hah. That's rich."

"What?"

"The ID:Entity club," Spark confirmed, opening her profile to show a selfie taken not twenty seconds ago, making a duckface into the camera with a mixed drink in her other hand. "She's out clubbing. Of course... if we know that, the killer knows that, too..."

"But a serial killer wouldn't strike in a public place, would he?"

Spark closed down her files... and packaged up the curry in a take-away folder, for later devouring. She *was* under orders to enjoy it, after all.

"All the more reason to move in on her now," she reasoned. "If we can intercept Little Miss YogaHurt the Troll while she's out partying, maybe we can kick her ass and drag her off to an undisclosed location. For her own protection, of course."

---

Despite being a graying old fogey on the club circuit (having existed for more than a few months) the ID:Entity managed to retain most of its exclusivity. Without a VIP pass, they'd have to convince the doormen that they were worth letting into the building by other means. Which meant a quick detour back to Floating Point, to raid her closet.

"It's all about image," Spark tried to explain, as she flicked through folder after folder of pre-made ensembles. "The club reflects on the clubgoers and vice versa. If you match the image they're looking to project, you're an automatic in. If not, you're an automatic out..."

"Do we really have time to play dress up?" Beta asked, watching the spray of clothing simulations fly out of Spark's closet, each fluttering to the floor in a pile. "You said we had to move fast to intercept Johanha..."

"Which we can't do looking like this. I'm wearing casual day wear here! I'm a onesdamn slob."

...which didn't make a lick of sense to Beta. It wasn't like Spark was wearing pajamas or sweatpants or anything, she wore a rather fetching little blouse and skirt today, with immaculate makeup and accessories galore. Of course, it was one of her off-the-rack avatar configurations, something she could toss on at a whim... and in a world where perfect beauty was an icon tap away, even a nice outfit probably seemed trashy.

Not that Beta had a frame of reference. She rarely changed her clothes, preferring her mother's hand-coded sweater and a simple long skirt. Nothing special, on top of her nothing special Default. Why would she need to mix things up?

"What we need... is to be a matching pair," Spark decided. "That'll be enough novelty to win us entry. Fortunately for you, I've got an open source frock I picked up a few weeks ago! I was going to save this for when Puzzle and I storm the next big opening, but I guess we'll need our big guns today..."

Finding the hangar in question, Spark quickly swapped her clothing configuration around with practiced ease. So quickly that it took the ordinary semi-slow cloud processing of Floating Point a full 0.576ms to finish rezzing in the end result.

Light. She was wearing light.

The "dress" was composed of splashes of brilliant colors, glowing and swirling as they crawled across her skin. Always just enough to keep her legally modest, never quite enough to keep her fully "clothed." The RGB tinting randomized itself according to a pattern Beta's coder mind immediately sussed out, a kaleidoscope blend of bright hues that drew in the eye before her curves refused to let said eye go.

Of course, she still wore Verity's white-and-blue leather jacket. It didn't quite go with the dress, but odds were nobody with working eyes and a female-aligned sexual libido would give a damn. Beta barely noticed the clash, herself.

"It's..." Beta tried. "It's... it's."

"Yeah, it's pretty flashy, but I think it'll work just fine," Spark said, checking herself in a mirror App. A little bump of the hips sent the swirling bands of color scattering, twisting and spiraling around her rear in the rough approximation of a swaying skirt. "I remember ID:Entity used a lot of neon decorations; sky sculptures, silhouettes, things like that. We should fit their motif just fine. Beta? You okay?"

"Me? Yes? I'm fine," Beta responded.

It wasn't like she hadn't seen Spark working her sex appeal before. She'd always smiled and waved goodbye as Spark headed out the door to hit the clubs with Puzzle in the past, after all. And technically there was the original SparklePop incident, but that was less 'sexy' and more 'embarrassing' and 'uncomfortable.'

But... in the middle of this storm of deliberately designed enticement, it felt like something else. Something slightly wild and scary and intriguing. Especially knowing the next step in that grand design.

Another copy of the carefully programmed dress, 'hanging' on a clothes hanger and held out in offering.

"I can't wear that," Beta protested.

"Sure you can. It's open source! I didn't even have to crack any DRM to make you a copy."

"No, I mean... *I* can't wear that. Me. I couldn't possibly wear that. I'm not... I'm not like you..."

Spark let the hanger dip a little. "Beta... look, I don't know a sweet way to say this, so... you're fucking beautiful, okay? If this is some body image thing, like 'Oh, I can't possibly look sexy, not with my Default' let me assure you it's gonna look hot."

Beta swallowed, an instinctive if illogical gesture. "I don't... it doesn't feel like me. I'm not sexy. I'm... me..."

Ever since the Cup8 incident, she'd felt opposite of sexy. She'd tried to be sexy, that night her nudes were leaked. It was a glorious mistake, trying to be something she wasn't. All of Netwerk crawled across her front lawn to remind her of how ugly and whorish she was. If she dipped even a toe in those acidic waters again...

...but she was sexy, once. Cup8 almost made her feel sexy, back when she thought he really loved her. He called her naughty and at the time it didn't feel like an insult; she didn't read it that way, even if she probably should have. It felt... good, to be wanted. Physically wanted, not just adored.

And then her nude body got captions slapped above and below it in bold typeface, declaring her a slut.

"I can't be seen in it," she realized. "I can't. Even if I wanted to try, I can't do it. I'm already famous for my pinups, already considered a... a tramp. If I'm seen in public wearing that, my life will only get worse..."

"Oh. Damn. I hadn't thought of that. So... use your JaneDoe avatar. Or, or, hey, I know! Borrow a copy of my parameters! #SexyTwins!"

"*Gah!* Spark...!"

"Look, think of it like a combat tactic," Spark explained. "We're gaining entry to the enemy compound and securing an objective. I know that... okay. I know this means a lot more to you than that. It's got a lot of unpleasant connotations. So for now, just think of it like camouflage, or a standard character avatar worn during a CoC match. Okay...?"

Which made sense. Perfectly reasonable sense.

"Okay," Beta agreed. "For the mission."

"That's the spirit!"

"...but... can I try it on first?" she asked. "In private, with my usual avatar. Just to see what it feels like."

"Be my guest," Spark said with an impish grin, tossing the hanger towards her companion.

Carefully putting her usual clothes in storage, Beta swapped into the new dress without looking. Moments later, she dared to re-engage her glasses and take a look in Spark's full-length mirror App.

...ridiculous. She felt ridiculous. Just as stupid as she looked that night she tried to convince herself she was anything other than an unlovable configuration of Default parameters. Putting ribbons of light around her body hadn't changed that...

And then Spark stepped in, right beside her.

"See?" she said, smile glowing almost as brightly as the dress. "You look great... whoa...!"

The undocumented feature made itself known, as Spark's hips came in contact with Beta's.

Shader code mingled, ribbons of light twirling around both forms. They were interactive, able to sense a nearby copy and blend the patterns together. Still vaguely styled like two dresses for two people... but working as a cohesive whole. Joining two as one, in spirit and shape.

And in that, finally, Beta could see beauty. It wasn't a matter of numerical parameters, of bust size or weight distribution factors. It wasn't even in the nicely designed dresses. It was in both of them, together. The smile of someone who genuinely believed in her, unlike Cup8... someone cheering for her, loving her...

*Spark loves you. She'll never admit it, of course.*

They'd awkwardly shared a surreal intimate moment, with SparklePop. They'd been there to lean on each other, as things were falling apart around them: sitting in the stoop outside Arjay's office, or in the kitchen after learning about Tracer's deception. Playing games together, laughing together, crying together...

Briefly, Beta wondered what would happen if she threw herself in Spark's arms right here and now. How would the code of the dresses interact? And would she even notice...?

But in that brief moment... Spark had wandered away. Ribbons of light stretching ever so slightly, trying to stay together, before snapping back to their original configurations and patterns.

"Time to motor!" Retaining her smile, unaware of the moment she'd just walked from. "Off to the club, to knock 'em dead and hopefully keep Johanha from getting knocked dead!"

Quickly, Beta pulled on her JaneDoe avatar. Generic eyes on a generically pretty face stared at her. It wore the dress very well, as it was designed to be perfectly sculpted. But it wasn't her. She wasn't here with Spark anymore.

"Let's go," Beta agreed, trying to push this strange rush of feeling away for now.

---

The line to get into ID:Entity stretched around the block. Which was proof the club was starting to fade; on opening night, it had wound around the building and around a few other buildings in the abandoned shipping district surrounding it. That district had been completely backspaced by now, the overall square footage of the physics sim shrunk down quite a bit to conserve runtime. Not good if they needed to make a run for it and hide, compared to how useful those empty warehouses were for tucking Nestt/Starling away from Ichiban's murderous proxy... hopefully they wouldn't need an exit strategy.

As for the entrance strategy, well, that worked wonders.

Plenty try to bypass the line, walking right up to the doorman to plead their case. Very few actually succeed. But a pair of near-identical hot young girls wearing little more than luminescent strips of trick shading? That got the doorman's attention. Spark added to the effect by insisting they walk shoulder to shoulder, so the dresses would interfere with each other for added dazzle. Much as predicted... they got in the door ahead of the crowd, much to the mewling protests of the less attractive clubgoers.

On entering the building, Beta immediately remembered why she never went to dance clubs.

The sound pounded away from within her body, a heavy and cruel beat, primally banging away at her ears. Each person within the club had their own personal sound controls, and was their own speaker stack; she quickly lowered the volume to something manageable.

If her auditory senses were at least under control, her visual senses were not. The club existed within its own slice of time, a perpetual midnight, soaked in colorful neon outlines and strobe lights and little else. She could vaguely see a swarm of bodies bouncing along the central circular dance floor, swaying and grinding in time with the music... something as close to an orgy as possible without actually involving sexual contact, complete with an array of avatars which fashionably defied description.

Somewhere in there lurked YogaHurt of /lulz/, also known as Johanha. From the selfie, they knew they were looking for a woman with wavy silver hair and light blue skin... but metallics and pastels were all over the place, in the brief flashes Beta could see. It'd be like finding a sparkly needle in a sparkly haystack...

"Y'know, I swore I wouldn't come back here after some VIP dickhole treated Puzzle badly," Spark commented, her voice audible over the lowered volume of the music. "But I gotta admit, this club's still got it going *on*."

"I wouldn't really know," Beta commented offhand.

"You should come out with us to the clubs, Beta! I'd love to take you out dancing sometime. Or is dancing another thing you don't do, in addition to dressing hawt?"

"Um... I've never really tried," Beta admitted. "I could sideload some motion capture data, if you think it'd help the mission to get out there and dance..."

"We're not *waltzing*, Beta. Real dancing's all about improvisation. But... as amusing and awkward and potentially ankle-shattering as it may be to give you a crash course, we probably should get up to the second floor balcony and start scanning."

Bringing her image recognition App online, a quickie she threw together from bits and pieces before getting out the door, Beta followed Spark along the outer edges of booths and tables. Stairs were for chumps and elevators were too slow; instead, an array of quick teleport circles had been arranged, hotlinking floors together. All she had to do was step on one and tap her foot twice, for the second floor, and she was there.

From above, the teeming masses still teemed, but she could get a better feel for the flow of it all. Her image recognizer, tied into her glasses, also provided a fullbright hack—ignoring the mood lighting in favor of showing the raw, unshadowed visual input. Only slightly illegal, as it warped aesthetics but also revealed potentially hidden objects. The multicolored glow of the neon wall art of dancing figures just over the lip of the balcony would've been distracting, if not for the hack.

"Scanning for silver hair and blue skin," Beta announced, activating the App. "It could be a few minutes. Especially if she, uh, ducked out to the ladies room or something to freshen up her avatar..."

"Wish we could just kick back and enjoy ourselves in here," Spark mused. "I know it's lousy timing... the problem with Tracer hanging in the air, Dex threatening to trash the world, a killer on the loose... but it never feels like I'm spending my free time well. Just on useless stuff..."

"What? You're always having fun!"

"Yeah, well, it's not optimal fun. Something's missing lately. Maybe this is a side effect of that corrupt data I touched but... I'll straight admit it, I'm melancholy. Sucks to be melancholy in a club, it's like, the opposite of what you're supposed to be and stuff. ...once this is through, we should take some serious us-time. You and me. And I don't mean gaming; my *job* is gaming. I mean going *out* together."

"Going out, as in...?" Beta prompted.

"Hey, it doesn't have to be a club, specifically!" Spark replied, missing the implication. "If you're not into that, it's cool. What do you usually do when you go out?"

"I don't really go 'out.' Uh. I usually stay in, if given the choice. Cup8 was always pushing for romantic getaways and I never really liked them..."

"...oh. Well. If you'd prefer to hang at home, I mean... that's cool too..."

Despite the matching dresses and the close proximity, Beta felt a distance opening between them.

They were different people, weren't they? Outgoing and inward looking. Expressive and timid. Beta didn't belong in Spark's world, and Beta's world probably would bore Spark. Beta was downright boring, after all. Perfectly happy to sit there with a compiler tracking down artifacts in a debug log all night rather than partying.

But... she *did* want to wear that dress. She had stepped outside her comfort zone willingly; circumstances pushed her but there was genuine desire to try it on with her Default, to see what it felt like. And for a moment, with Spark, it felt perfect...

A blinking square distracted her.

"Search hit," Beta announced, focusing in on one person at the edge of the dance floor, sort of listlessly moving to the beat. "Silver hair, blue skin... 97% match to the selfie. It's her! I'm marking her on your HUD."

"Got it. Let's go," Spark acknowledged.

One teleport later, and they were closing in on the target. This was a mission at heart, after all... not a date, not a party. With the killer's target in sight, Beta could focus on the utility of her purpose there. Much easier.

Strangely, Johanha didn't seem to be in a partying mood either.

She was dancing, yes. Sort of. Even Beta, who had figurative flat feet, could tell it wasn't particularly enthusiastic or skilled dancing. The silver-haired clubber wearing a watery bodysuit and surrounded by floating pet fish Apps wasn't actually dancing *with* anyone, simply letting herself be semi-absorbed by the crowd, so she could claim her participation trophy and nothing more. She hadn't even slurped down that mixed drink she'd taken with the selfie, letting it slosh dangerously in one hand as she swayed to the lustful beat of the chiptune band...

Name : Johanha

Home : HiRize/Chanarchy

Org : Fashion Blogger

Spark didn't have to weave through the thick of the crowd, simply slip past three or four dancers to reach the edgeward spot that Johanha occupied. A tap on the shoulder drew attention of the dancer, as well as a few of her pet fish.

"YogaHurt, I presume?" Spark asked... one hand held low, primed with a connection lock collar, just in case.

"Never heard of her," Johanha mumbled. "You're killing my vibe. Swim away, please."

Eager not to repeat the hostile encounter with Renpy, Beta slipped into view to take charge.

"You're in danger," Beta spoke, up front. "We know you're part of /lulz/. Someone who's avenging Fiona is coming after you, soon. We're here to help you."

Her uneven dancing sway stuttered to a halt. Beta pressed on, knowing that Spark would snag her if she ran for it or tried to disconnect from the server.

"Please, we're really here to help," she insisted. "My name's Beta, and this is Spark. We've been investigating the Fiona incident and the killings that have been happening since then. Your name is the last on a list of three... including Weevil and LordSmegma. They're already gone. We want to help keep you safe. Will you talk with us...?"

The fish darted behind their owner, emotional state reacting to her internal panic.

"I should... I should go," Johanha insisted. "I gotta go..."

"You're safer here; we don't think the killer will attack you in public. He'd have a hell of a time getting in the front door of this place," Spark pointed out. "Look, let's grab a booth over there and hash this out. Somewhere well-lit."

There was no good way to approach this situation. Being told someone was trying to kill you was troubling enough; mystery saviors promising to keep you safe sounded very suspicious, coupled with that fact. They didn't want to have to protect her by force, using the collar... the tactic worked on Wrenn/Starling, but that was back when ShipTo was full of empty buildings. In the club itself, slapping a hacktool on someone would eventually bring a moderator around to kick you out, or worse. Beta hoped honesty would win over suspicion, but knew it was a gamble...

Soon... the fish peeked out from behind their master. Timidly exiting the floating pieces of coral reef within her watery avatar.

Johanha finally slung back the drink she'd been carrying, tossing the glass aside. It deleted itself, to keep the club tidy.

"I'm going to need another of those," she requested.

Three attractive ladies chatting over drinks in a hot night club shouldn't have been as tense and depressing as this particular encounter proved to be.

Johanha downed two more drinks before she was ready to speak.

"It made sense at the time," she insisted. "Here we had a ridiculously over-the-top blog, typical sugary MyFace junk. The kind of attention whore /lulz/ loves to pull down a few pegs. Fiona's blog had already been featured at /cringe/ a few times, so it wasn't like we picked it at random... and besides, she was an Otherkin."

"An Otherhwa?" Spark asked.

"I think it's someone who believes in past lives," Beta clarified. "That dead data scooped up by a garbage collector which gets repurposed is never fully wiped, with some of those past lives leaking through..."

"Oh, it went beyond that. Fiona thought she was... how'd she put it? A 'magical star-being,'" Johanha recalled. "That she was a descendant of 'organic' entities from beyond the stars, whatever that means. There was also some nonsense about bellybuttons. Nobody respects so-called Otherkin because they're all completely off their rockers, right? It's fair game to pick on them. So with all of that combined, we figured... rattle this nutjob's cage, show Netwerk how stupid she was..."

"In other words, harassing a clinically depressive teenage girl," Spark filled in.

"We didn't know that at the time! We had no idea... we thought she was some RPing sockpuppet of a middle-aged crazy cat lady!"

"And that makes it okay? Nope. No excuse."

Johanha's fist banged on the table, causing the loose physics objects of her empty glasses to bounce to the floor. They promptly erased themselves.

"Of course it's no excuse!" she blurted, the alcoholic malware having reached her emotional core. "It's *trolling*. We were assholes! Complete assholes... and at the time, it seemed funny, like a minor evil in the name of righteousness. No worse than snarky graffiti or leaving the toilet seat up. But when we realized what happened, that we'd driven a kid to... to kill herself, well... Weevil and Smegma didn't care. I couldn't believe it, they didn't care one bit. But I cared. I demanded they take down the Hall of Shame entry and I haven't involved myself in /lulz/ ever since."

With a snap of the fingers, Johanha ordered up a fresh drink. No need to hassle the bartender for a custom coded beverage when she could get smashed off the ready-to-rez menu. She snatched up the freshly spawned glass, ready to throw it back...

A hand blocked the drink, before it could reach her mouth.

"Probably best if you stay as sober as possible," Spark said. "We're safe here for now but we're going to need to move you somewhere safer, and I'm not hauling a malware-addled avatar around."

"At this point, being malware-addled is the only way I'm coping with my situation," she protested. "I've been hitting clubs, getting smashed, wandering around... I don't know. Just trying to get my mind off what's happened. All the stupid mistakes I made, and for what? I couldn't even tell you why I trolled her. I was bored, I guess? Stupid, stupid reasons. So, I'm desperately distracting myself with partying. Why not?"

Briefly, Spark considered another rebuke.

Except... that neatly described her experience prior to ViruFax, didn't it? Out all hours of the night drinking and dancing, hammering the daylight away with gaming broadcasts, trying to avoid dealing with her feelings. She had no right to judge Johanha for that. Judging her for *other* things, that was fair game, but not that.

"They're really dead, aren't they?" Johanha asked, choosing to set the glass down for now. "Weevil and Smegma. I never knew them #IRL, but I heard from the rumor mill that they'd been killed, or committed suicide, or something. But...

it's true. They're gone, and now someone's coming to punish me for my stupidity..."

"Do you have any idea who it could be?" Beta asked. "The killer seems to be using corrupted image data as a weapon, and was skilled enough to break into an Athenian police station to retrieve your name. Do you know any hackers with a grudge against you or /lulz/...?"

"I write a mediocre fashion blog. My only enemies are fashion blog drama whore trolls, and they're not murderous. The closest I've ever come to the dark side of Netwerk was hanging around in a chatroom full of idiots, wasting time under the pretense that it was all harmless performance art. Odds are some of the /lulz/ers themselves are hackers, but I really didn't know anyone outside of Weevil and Smegma, and I barely even knew those two. Sorry..."

Johanha held a hand up to her forehead, as if cutting out the glare from a sun that didn't exist inside the darkened club. Her eyes averted to the floor, in shame.

"I shouldn't have come here," she muttered. "Don't like the way they're looking at me. Not one bit."

"Uh. The clubgoers...?"

"The stupid wall people. Up there."

Curious, Beta swiveled her gaze upwards, to the ring of decorative neon art around the second floor balcony... an array of animated dancer silhouettes, the same visual design element Spark had played into their dresses, to earn entry.

Except the figures weren't dancing. They were glaring downward, in harsh judgment. Hands on hips, stern.

"Spark...?" Beta asked. "The... the art is *looking* at us..."

A tiny, tiny frame rate hitch skittered its way around the circle of figures. One sharp visual glitch, as they began to peel away from the balcony... colored lines wrenching themselves free, the outline of arms and legs pushing away from the surfaces that bound them...

One by one, the artificial dancers dropped to the floor below. As their bent two-dimensional 'feet' slammed into the dance floor they sent voxels scattering across the ground, visual artifacts of corrupted data, glowing impossible colors in Beta's App-driven eyes.

But the screams, those were nicely clear and audible, even over the beat of the music.

Spark—the brave one, the improviser—was the first to act.

She immediately pulled Beta and Johanha behind her, and kicked over their table to use as impromptu cover against the advancing army of multicolored outlines. It also formed a barricade against the crush of dancers eager to flee the floor, running away from the glitches, making a beeline for the exits. Most promptly evaporated into thin air once they were clear, reconnecting to other servers... the ID:Entity clearing itself out in a wave of total panic, one way or another.

All alone, with a horde of grim figures bearing down on them with murderous intent...

"#Time2Go!" Spark declared, ducking down behind the table. "Johanha, reconnect to LibertyPark, it should be safe there—"

"No."

"—*no*?!"

"Leave me here," Johanha insisted. "You two should save yourselves. Nobody else should be hurt because of what I did. Just... leave me and go. It doesn't matter. None of it matters..."

"Excuse me, but we came here to *save* your ass!"

"Thanks, but it's too late. This is what I deserve, isn't it?"

Snarling out five curse words in overlapping fashion, a blur of angry verbiage, Spark stood up from behind the table... and assumed a defensive mantis-style stance.

"Beta... talk sense into her," Spark requested, as she got in the zone. "I'll hold them off."

Alarmed, Beta peered over the top of the table to get a quick count... and quickly realized she couldn't count the figures, simply a blur of connecting lines and broken vertices. "You can't fight these things!" she insisted. "You remember what happened when you touched the killer's data before...!"

"They're still part of the physics system, and that means I can blow 'em to bits," Spark said, snapping a quick burst of flame from her fingernails. "Light pokes only. I'll endure whatever happens after that. This is what I do, Beta... I fight the fight so you can keep going."

Launching off her back foot, Spark blurred into the middle of the neon army. The Verity-blue trim on her white jacket was immediately lost in the riot of rioting colors.

The key to staving off a large crowd of combatants was to keep moving. They wouldn't attack one at a time, like in movie files; but that meant they'd accidentally hit each other if they weren't careful. Never give them a chance to be careful, be wild, be quick, be where they aren't expecting. Duck and evade, let them do half the work for you... while taking precision pokes at them, to disable the ones that pose the most threat.

Duck under a groping 'arm' here, the outline shifting and bending as the 2-D plane tried to make sense in a 3-D space. Use their flatness to your advantage, rolling through and between, coming up underneath to slam your fingers straight into an enemy... right into the edge, into the colored line, just in case the 'middle' was really empty space—

*—I'm no good. I'm no good. I'm—*

The brief burst of injected memory made her miss a step. A flailing flatland limb brushed over the nape of her neck as she awkwardly ducked it—

*—pathetic, just pathetic. Everything hurts. Everything's so complicated. I'm useless and pathetic—*

Instinctively she tried kicking away an opponent... only to find out the hard way that there was in fact nothing in the middle of the outline. She crashed through the glitched pseudoavatar and—

*—drinking and dancing and fucking the problems away, what good is any of it? What good am I? I'm no good. I'm stupid. I'm stupid. I should kill myself—*

—anger. She needed anger to punch through this. If ever there was a positive use of a negative emotion, this was the time to deploy it.

Screaming rather than crying, she flung her arms to the left and right, to blast two attackers at either side with a burst of flame. Their outlines warped and bubbled, glass tubes cracking, light spilling onto the dance floor. With each impact she felt another burst of self-loathing, which she desperately tried to block out with rage.

Another, and another. More and more figures incinerated by the spark she carried within her heart, even as they tried to pour venom into that vessel to replace the fire...

...as Beta desperately tried to shake some sense into Johanha. Not that shaking her by the shoulders seemed to do much, but it worked in movie files, and she had no idea what else to do.

"Snap out of it!" she tried. "Please! We have to leave...!"

"I don't have to go anywhere," Johanha responded, oddly calm about it all.

"My friend is out there fighting for you! Fighting and maybe dying!"

"Why?" the troll asked. "Why is she bothering? What does my life matter? I'm a killer now. Isn't this for the best?"

And Beta wanted to slap the world.

She wanted to slap the world until it all made sense again. Slap Tracer until he understood how important he was to her. Slap Spark until she was ready to grow up and face herself. Slap herself until she could feel something other than white-knuckled terror about everything, able to find a toehold as the world span out of control around her day by day...

But you couldn't slap the world. It accomplished nothing, like shaking someone around and ordering them to be sensible. Wrath and hate and spite and anger, those were useless impulses for Beta. Spark was the master of deploying rage effectively; but Beta, all she could do was flail about if she tried to do the same.

No. She had to be the nice girl, that's what the Winders were expecting from her. A nice girl with a moral core, someone you could rely on while they were busy being brave and clever.

Except... to do this, she'd have to be brave and clever too. Brave enough to stand up in the face of terror, clever enough to understand the world for what it was...

Closing her eyes, Beta embraced the dark of her blindness. One moment, one single moment of calm, to grab hold of what she knew and put it to purpose. She felt like a Program in the dark, cut loose of its avatar...

"...that's it," she realized. "That's what the killer is..."

The next steps flowed one by one, an entirely improvised plan that felt cohesive enough to be hand-crafted by Tracer.

First, she gave her glasses to Johanha.

"Wear these, and watch me," she requested. "Keep your eyes on me and me alone. Okay?"

Perplexed, the troll hesitated briefly... before accepting the offered spectacles.

Working from a third person perspective, Beta stepped out from behind the table, staying within view of her eyes.

"*Are you watching me, Tracer?*" she messaged, across the switches and routers of Netwerk. "*Can you see through my eyes?*"

"*...Beta? What are you doing?*" Tracer asked, delayed slightly as the video buffered on his end. "*A video window just popped up over your cat...?*"

"*I've opened my Peep stream to you, broadcasting it through Mew to bypass your collar. I want you to watch, and understand...*"

Next, she swapped out the silly dress and the JaneDoe configuration for her usual avatar. Her sweater of power. Her comfortable self, solid and pure. She'd need that reliability for what she was about to do... for more than one reason.

Lastly... it was time to face the killer, and call its true name.

Beta deployed a volume hack to be heard over the roar of flames and the scraping, cracking sound of animate neon tubes.

"**DITT/FIONA!**" she called out. "**Listen to me!**"

The overall physical simulation of ID:Entity skipped a frame or two, as the attacking silhouettes froze in place.

Spark fell to her knees in a rough circle of them, panting heavily... tears streaming from her eyes as she tried to hold back the negative thoughts pounding their way into her head. If the battle had gone any longer, she'd have given in completely, without a doubt...

Calmly, Beta walked into the midst of the figures, which flowed away from her.

One by one, they coalesced, joining vertices until they became one towering figure, with drawn-in details rather than pure outlines... a young girl, with jagged features matching the photo from her blog. A true face with true eyes to look through, despite being a false avatar composed entirely of stolen materials.

Beta knelt down before this avatar of suicide, embracing Spark... and kissing her forehead, for a mild comfort, before turning to address the vengeful one she'd addressed directly.

"Your name is Fiona," Beta recognized. "Your original avatar was destroyed but your code survived, corrupted by the malware you tried to kill yourself with. They think you're dead, but you're alive in the darkness of Netwerk, driven mad with grief... and using any avatar-shaped data you can find, to reach back into the world and torment your tormentors..."

A voice like scratching glass on glass responded... dozens of voices from each individual figure mashed into the whole, all speaking with dreadful harmony.

"ŕÊ6®ËŦ," they chanted.

"My name is Projkit/Beta. Do you know who I am?" Beta asked. "Have you heard of me before?"

The neon child peered at her, with eyes made of starlight.

"8Ë7Á," they recognized. "#[øĎ3ħÕŋ€$Ŧý. Ŧ®ølŁ3Ď. åßµ§ËĎ. Ŧ°®MЄŅt3Ď..."

"We've both been through terrible, terrible pain, haven't we? They silenced both of us. It wasn't fair. It wasn't right."

"...ŕÊĜŕЄŧ. 7ĦÊŶ mû§Ţ ĸŋÕŵ ŕ€ĜŖ€ŧ. 7ĦÊŶ Mµ$+ F€Ê1 Ï7 ŧħË w@Ÿ î FË17 !ŧ..."

"Where does hurting my friend come into that?" Beta asked... holding Spark's trembling body closely. "Or hurting the police officer who wanted to help you? The loose data you left behind when you stole that list nearly killed him. What about terrifying everybody in this club? How is any of that justice?"

The neon figure twitched, bending back ever so slightly away from Beta as it listened to the words. The glow of shimmering neon tubes wobbled, uncertain in the face of the accusation. Self-reflection, spread across a distributed self, one program connected to multiple false avatars bound together into a single form...

"This isn't justice," Beta supplied. "This changes nothing. Bullying your bullies, destroying them, that won't really heal your wounds... and it won't make *them* better people. Fighting horror with horror is a zero sum game. ...Johanha? Do you regret what you did to her?"

The woman, standing upright from behind her blocking table, nodded briefly. The borrowed glasses wobbled at the end of her nose.

"Absolutely," Johanha said, in all honesty. No terror, no pleading panic... a simple truth, spoken loud. "I regret everything I did with /lulz/. If I could take it back, I would. Not to save my own skin, but... to save hers. If I could..."

"You already got what you came for, don't you see that?" Beta asked the collective spectre. "You want her to regret? Okay. She regrets. Now give her a chance, Fiona. A chance to do something *with* that regret. Give her a chance to become a better person, and let something positive come out of this nightmare. Killing her won't end the nightmare... but letting her live might."

With the last of her words slipping free... Beta leaned heavily on what remained of this bravery reserve, to carry through to the end. That, and her embrace of Spark, the two leaning on each other for support at this point.

It could've failed. Fiona's program was riddled with glitches and data rot thanks to the malware which trashed her original avatar; if she was too unstable to think it through, getting her to listen to reason might've failed spectacularly. If she simply embraced her vendetta and ignored the heart that yearned to feel something other than pain, a heart that had blogged with relentless positivity in hopes she could one day believe her own words...

Instead, the figure began to collapse, little by little. With Fiona's virtual hooks and wires pulling away from the server entirely, the decorative wall art became so much inanimate data. The physics system took over from there, causing the vectors and shaders of the glass tubes to tumble apart and form a pile of brightly colored junk data on the empty dance floor.

Memory, without a suite of enhancements like Tracer's MemoryPalace, is a slippery concept. The outlines hold in place, much like the animate lines that attacked them earlier, but the details in the middle weren't always quite clear.

Beta, exhausted from her ordeal, helped the equally exhausted Spark return home. She passed by the door to Tracer's study wordlessly, past it and up the stairs, up to her companion's bedroom...

Spark pulled the sheets around herself tightly, on being helped into bed. Tried and failed not to sob openly into her pillowcase, as Beta set up a drip feed of emotionally stabilizing data from her suite of deep-interface Apps.

"It could take a few hours for the effects to pass," Beta explained. "I'll be right here the whole time, I promise..."

"T-To stop me from killing myself," Spark recognized.

"Because you're important to me," Beta spoke, replacing those words with better ones. She drew a chair up to the bedside, to take Spark's hand—the grip tightened immediately, as Spark clung to that grasp.

"You... must think I'm so pathetic," she mumbled into the pillow, burying her face in it, to avoid looking Beta in the eyes. "Some fighter I am. Didn't do any good. If you hadn't saved me I'd be dead. I'm pathetic. I'm stupid. I'm no good..."

"Shhh. That's just the emotionally corrupted data poisoning your thoughts..."

"It's the truth," Spark insisted. "I'm an idiot. I want life to be simple, but it's not; #ItsComplicated. I'm stupid. I can't handle it. I just... I just *need*... I don't even know what I need, I'm so stupid, I'm so *stupid*..."

"Spark... if you hadn't jumped right into that fight, I wouldn't have been able to jump in with you," Beta explained. "You're braver than me. You'll always be braver than me... all I did was borrow some of that strength. Now, *shhh*. Just try to relax, and wait this out..."

"Why? Why're you bothering? I'm shit. I'm lower than shit. A stupid brat who never really grew up, just pretending, just stupid, stupid... why? Why are you bothering with me?"

The conversation might've looped back around to the start, with that prompt. *Because you're important to me* rose to Beta's thoughts... but another thought broke through the cycle, interjecting itself.

Because even if Spark wasn't ready to say it, even if she might never be ready... Beta was ready.

"Because I love you," she spoke, in the softest, quietest whisper.

The bedridden woman cried herself to sleep moments later, without a response. Could be Spark didn't even hear the words. Could be Beta whispered them so low as not to be heard. Could have been a lot of things.

Fuzzy time, after that. Hours of fuzzy time.

Eventually, Beta returned to Tracer's study. It seemed the thing to do, for "debriefing."

The mastermind in the high-backed chair evaluated today's actions, while petting a cat. He looked every inch the secret agent nemesis from a movie file.

As the Mew in his lap happily mewled out a 🐱, Tracer came to his conclusion regarding today's events.

"An optimal outcome, if not an optimal path," he spoke. "Very touch and go near the end."

"The ends justify the means," Beta spoke, without any darkness to the words whatsoever. "We risked a lot, but for the right reasons. Fiona's out there somewhere still, but she won't hurt anyone else. Maybe her code will finally corrupt and crash, maybe she'll drift in the dark forever... I don't know. But she's come out of this a better person, and so has Johanha. Nobody had to die."

Tracer called up a blog post, letting it hover over his desk.

"Seems Johanha's turned over a new leaf," he agreed. "She's posted her side of the story, every last bit of it, and decided to donate generously to the Society for Cyberbullying Prevention in Fiona's name. Not that money absolves her of sin, but it's a start, I suppose."

"It's better than leaving her to die."

"Agreed. Now... the part I don't fully understand is why you gave her your glasses, then sent me that Peep stream. You could've simply told me the outcome on returning home; I didn't need a ringside seat..."

Too exhausted to be anything but frank, Beta explained it all.

"I had to be brave, moral, and clever," she explained. "Brave enough to walk into that storm and confront it. Moral enough to give both killers a chance at a new life. And... clever enough to leave a connected App—my glasses, I mean—behind just in case my avatar got torn apart by Fiona in a rage. If things went bad I was ready to sever my runtime from my avatar. I still had a lifeline thanks to my glasses, to avoid drifting away like Fiona did. It's the same trick we pulled with Spark, when she was infected with RansomMe. Seemed a pragmatic precaution to take, right?"

"Extremely pragmatic," Tracer agreed, impressed. "But, again... why broadcast to me?"

"...because I was talking to you, too, Tracer. You deserve a chance, just like they did. Killing a killer restores the status quo, yes. But *redeeming* a killer makes the world a better place. I wanted you to believe in that."

"I see. And if a killer is irredeemable...?"

"Maybe I'm just naive, but... I think nobody's irredeemable. Not Johanha, not Fiona, not you. Not even Dex. And I'll prove it to you again and again, if I have to."

In the final conclusion... Tracer could only nod briefly, in agreement. The most enthusiastic response he could manage, really.

"For what it's worth... you've convinced me. My death would accomplish nothing. My killings accomplish nothing..."

Tracer stroked Mew idly, lost in the thought. It was a difficult concept to swallow, after having accepted his fate long ago that he must die for his crimes. The idea of living onward while escaping the shadow he'd been sinking into... it took quite a lot to accept that idea. Perhaps he was ready to try.

"If I am to extract value from the remainder of my life, I must endeavor to be a better man," he decided. "I must make amends and improve the world, even beyond healing the wounds I've given it already. This is the path you want for me...? Very well. I accept. I will work to redeem myself."

The relief was visible in Beta's features; the tension she'd been carrying since finding out about Tracer's crimes released, at last.

"...after all, if I am ever to be a man who's worthy of your love, this is the path I must take."

If he noticed that tension snap neatly back into place, he showed no signs of it, as he continued.

"I realize now how important you are to me, Beta. I also realize I'm completely unsuitable as a suitor... but you've given me hope. I can become more than I am, I can become better. Perhaps I can even be the man you deserve. Obviously I'm doing this for myself as well and for the good of Netwerk, but you are indeed my inspiration. You've helped me see that there is a future for me. One day, I'll be able to thank you properly for that."

Fidgeting from foot to foot... Beta decided not to push back against it, not at this critical point. If Tracer rejected his decision, it'd undo everything she'd tried to accomplish...

Besides... it was a relief to hear of his change of heart. Knowing now that Tracer was still the Tracer Beta knew, the Tracer that Beta was fond of, and not a crazed killer... that brought some light to her heart. She wanted him to come back from this, after being in danger of drifting away from her.

That man settled into his new future, comfortable with the idea that he had one. Although one thing still nibbled at his curiosity.

"Beta... you were bouncing your Peep feed off of Mew to get around my connection lock, yes?"

"What? Um... yes. A bit of a dirty hack, but since he already had Peep code installed from my earliest tests... I mean, yeah, I did. Why?"

"And were you aware Mew was re-broadcasting that feed publicly as well?"

"—what?!"

The innocent little kittykat App flicked his tail back and forth, while giggling in a non-catty way. "🙀🙀🙀," Mew admitted. "😺😺😺👀👀🙀. 🙀💚😺! 🎉!"

Beta's knees grew weak, while her cat preened and posed in Tracer's lap, quite proud of this accomplishment.

"Oh no," she spoke aloud. "Oh no. Oh no oh no *oh no*..."

"Actually, the net result is a positive," Tracer explained... pulling up a variety of storified blog posts and social media streams. "The truth about the incident is coming out, thanks to Johanha and others from /lulz/ who are willing to step forward. That means all of Netwerk knows how you stood up to Fiona, stood up for Johanha, and generally saved the day. Considering you were once nearly trolled into the grave yourself, that's quite a bold statement of forgiveness you just made to the world..."

"I wasn't trying to make a bold statement to the world! I didn't even know if I would survive that bold statement! I was flying by the seat of my pants out there...!"

"Nevertheless, you did well. In fact... judging from my search agents, a memetic stance is starting to spread throughout the ranks of #CodeHonesty..."

Rather than reading it aloud, he pulled up an average entry made in the last hour.

```
Obviously #CodeHonesty is against harassment of any
sort. No true member of #CodeHonesty would ever have
attacked Beta; we do not support trolling and doxxing.
And just like Beta, we're willing to stand up to all
would-be abusers and frauds to make Netwerk a more
honest place.
```

"...some are claiming the whole thing was a hoax, of course. You were basically *yelling at a ghost*, after all, which is completely insane... but there's just enough freewheeling madness to the narrative for it to take root in the imagination. Thanks to Johanha's persuasive writing, this incident has bent overall public opinion in your favor. You may even be able to show your Default face in public without a worry, soon."

"...but... but... what? How?!"

"Simple enough; positive sentiment towards you happens to be trending high," Tracer explained. "And everybody likes to get in on a good social media trend. In wake of it your detractors are now claiming they were never your detractors in the first place, and they're declaring any abuse you've experienced as being not their fault. A bald-faced lie, of course... but this does effectively take you off the hook in terms of most future attacks by hashtag warriors, as they focus all efforts on finding Snowi instead. #CodeHonesty is likely out of your hair now."

The one responsible for turning Beta's ruined public persona into the hero of the day stood at attention, nose high and sniffing at the air...

"...🐟?" Mew requested, politely.

Kitty ate well that day.

The crackle of a warm fireplace distracted the old man from his reading.

These days, he preferred to visually scan all materials, rather than ingest them directly into the bulk of his memory files. He could have read them much faster that way, but as an old man, he liked to indulge himself in the pleasantries of life rather than rely on the expensive multifunction software patches that kept him alive day-to-day...

The video recording, that interested him in particular. He watched the whole thing start to finish... ignoring the fidgeting of his guest.

"She's quite the little heroine, isn't she?" Horizon/Kincaid pondered aloud. "Throwing herself right into the fire, to protect her friend. To protect a stranger, even. That's compassion and loyalty you cannot buy..."

"I would agree, sir," Miss Cancel spoke... the imposing figure of his personal assistant looming above his houseguest's head, commanding a space in which the guest must occupy without moving. Not literally, with a hacktool, but with the inescapable social niceties a Horizon audience demanded.

VNDB/Renpy tried to play along, to smile and agree with whatever the crazy old man was saying.

"Yes, yes, quite!" he agreed. "Soooo... about the, uh... the thing you called me here for?"

Mildly irritated at the interruption, Kincaid pushed the files aside, to get on with the affairs of the day.

"We had an agreement not to discuss any connections between the Horizon family, MyFace, and the Karnival," Kincaid spoke. "The official line was to neither confirm nor deny. A line you did not walk very well today, when you inadvertently confirmed the whole story to her..."

"Sir, I can explain—"

"Honestly, it's not that huge of an issue," Kincaid admitted. "Yes, I invested heavily in the Karnival in hopes of using their life-extending technology. Frankly, I have investments in dozens of life-extending technologies; it's how I've survived so very long. This particular one ended up not panning out, and that's a shame, but not a sin. I suppose it's no huge loss if anyone learned the truth of how the Karnival operated."

"...it's not? Oh. Okay, then," Renpy replied, relieved.

"Still, doesn't hurt to keep things tidy. Better safe than sorry, yes?"

He resumed reading his news feeds and sipping tea, while Miss Cancel scraped the carpet clean of any trace data that could prove Renpy's body was ever here. A very thorough and tidy assistant, Miss Cancel was.

Only when her task was complete and Horizon/Kincaid had finished his tea did she speak up.

"Orders, sir?" she requested. "Regarding the other matter. The girl."

"Mmm. That's a trickier situation, isn't it..."

Kincaid leaned back in his chair, taking a deep sip of tea as he considered the video captured at ID:Entity today. A brutal fight, one which the young lady named Spark clearly wasn't going to win. And yet... she fought on, despite that obvious doom. She fought to protect her friend Beta, and even to protect a stranger. True, Beta closed out the battle, but Spark was the one willing to take the initial risk...

Risk was something the Horizon family had averse to, lately. So fat and complacent, sitting in private servers, growing old and pale. For over a hundred years Kincaid had steered this particular ship, augmenting the very same power base that made them weak at heart. Would he have taken a risk like that, for instance? Would he have been as brave and as bold as his wayward daughter, the one who became this Spark girl's mentor?

"She's quite capable," Kincaid noted. "The question is if she's capable enough to deal with the beast from XSept's basement. Life is a series of trials, Miss Cancel, and I wouldn't take this one from her. Comfort promotes laziness. Still, what little we know suggests that she may be in over her head..."

Kincaid opened the files containing data scraped from ViruFaxHQ, to refresh his memory. His obsolete memory recall code worked slower than his software augmentations, after all.

XSept's caged prisoner represented an unknown. A dangerous unknown.

The ones who accidentally unleashed it were Winder/Tracer and Projkit/Beta, identities gleaned through painstaking data analysis of trace evidence left behind at the scene. Those identities led Kincaid to conclude they were seeking a cure to RansomMe for his sister, Winder/Spark, who had been very publicly infected during the middle of a game broadcast stream... a girl who wore an identical jacket to Verity, his lost daughter.

A strange chain of events that danced around the central issue of what mysterious enemy once lurked in the heart of ViruFax. An enemy that his daughter's prodigy, young Spark, now had to deal with.

Despite her ties to Verity, Spark wasn't his granddaughter. She wasn't family, wasn't part of Horizon. He was under no legal or financial obligation to care about these matters in the slightest. All he had to do was look away and get back to the business of growing his power base; this thing with Spark was distracting him from increasing shareholder value, after all.

But... Verity clearly cared deeply about Spark. And Kincaid, despite the need to see the runaway Verity as a failed business investment, still cared deeply about his daughter.

Besides, the girl held promise. Perhaps all was not lost in the efforts that began with Verity...

"She needs to come to us, in the end," he understood. "You gave her my contact card. In time she'll find need to use it, and that's when we'll make our move. In the meanwhile, we'll watch and observe. Make sure she doesn't make any fatal mistakes. The Horizon family looks after its own... and I will not lose another child."

## :: end chapter 1.5

# Floating Point 1.6 :: Zero

Senator Agni hated children.

She loved families. She had to love families; her constituents across 16 different servers all voted in blocks, families united together behind her party. Good families. Onefearing families, proud members of the Church of One, all of them. (Well, the ones that mattered according to the electoral demarcations, at least.) But that didn't mean she liked *children*. Children were irrational, annoying, and immature. Much better when they grew up into proper adults who knew how things were and always would be, and behaved accordingly...

But to get elected, she had to at least pretend to like children. That meant PR opportunities, such as reading books to them in local public libraries... shaking hands with them, promising them a bright future in Athena Online, things like that. Even if what she really wanted to do was get back to her office ASAP and put the finishing touches on her masterwork.

"It's not going to fly," her PR director warned.

Agni touched up her makeup in a mirror, adjusting sliders until they neatly accented the signs of her physical maturity. Unlike many of her peers within the Red Party, she embraced her defaults rather than resort to anti-aging avatars.

"9Day, don't tell me what is and isn't going to fly," she replied, not looking away from her makeup manipulation. "Instead, tell me how you're going to *make* it fly. How can we make the Server Rights Bill fly?"

"We can't. It's impossible. Look, RedCore's behind you all the way on this... but let's get real, RedCore's a faction of the overall Red Party. We're the reactionary right, remember? UltraConservative. And majority of the Red party isn't conservative enough to embrace something this bonkers."

"Legislation is never bonkers, 9Day. It's simply ahead of its time. And I don't care if it gets shot down; it's important that RedCore puts it forward as a test of loyalty," Agni spoke, finished with slider adjustments for the moment. "Those within Red who vote against it, well, we'll know what districts to campaign in more aggressively. And one day, when RedCore simply IS the Red Party through and through rather than a 'splinter faction'... we'll put it forward again. Legislation ahead of its time, remember. Not 'bonkers.'"

"Except each time 'Server Rights' or anything like it gets shot down in the senate, it sets a precedent for the next time a bill comes around with the same flavor. We shouldn't push this, Agni. We should just wait until the time's right..."

"This is for the good of Network, 9Day. We've been reliant the broken old ways, the liberal ways, far too long. Claiming we believe in freedom while denying servers the freedom to govern as they see fit... no. We're pushing the bill. If we don't succeed, we push again. Again and again, until we win. That's the RedCore way. They can't shut us up."

9Day didn't see it, but decided not to argue the point. For starters, it was technically his job to make it fly, just as she said... to control the social media spin, set up the astroturf and sock puppets that would push the issues Senator Agni wanted pushed. He didn't have a choice in the matter. And also... debating it further would be counterproductive to today's activities. It was minutes to showtime, and he had a press event to focus on coordinating.

The actual book reading went smoothly enough, despite Angi's internal loathing of it all.

She smiled for the press, smiled at the intentionally diverse school kids as they filed in. Smiled as she read a copy of 'BillE and the Onesderful Day,' a Church of One-themed pile of saccharine garbage. Page by page of pure sweetness about charity, goodwill, and the perfection of Default avatars—those bodies representing the One's gift to His people...

The little tykes lapped it all up, and why not? They'd been selected to be visually diverse across the skin color span, that played well, but every one of them came from a server where the church arguably held more power than the Athenian senate.

And if Agni had her way—if 9Day helped her have her way—the church would indeed hold more power than the senate in those servers. Server rights... the right to self-governance on a server-by-server basis. Essentially cutting the balls off the senate entirely, to allow "local values" to reign supreme...

Bonkers. Utterly bonkers. But 9Day liked getting paid, so he'd get the social channels flowing tonight, warm and ready to go.

At least security was low, so there wouldn't be a repeat of the last incident involving Senator Agni at a school. Some juvenile punks thought it'd be funny to throw pies at the senator during her speech... and her overreacting firewalls triggered nine kinds of security failsafes, including an armed police response and a malware counterattack. Since then, 9Day had ordered Angi's passive security systems put on low response while dealing with kids. Better safe than sorry, and she could ramp them back up immediately after leaving, anyway...

With the book reading complete, Angi chatted with the children, doing her best to answer questions in a down-home folksy way her constituents would appreciate.

"Why is the skybox blue?" a little girl asked.

"Because that's the Default for the skybox, just like how your Default is to be pink!" Agni explained. "Because the One loves us very much."

"Where do bunnies come from?" another little girl asked.

"All the animal pet Apps were created by the One for us to enjoy."

A hand in the back raised itself, attached to a wide smile.

"Do you believe the One was a truly divine Program, with no zeroes at all?" the boy with the red-and-blue hair asked. "Or could the One have been the puppet of another Program, simply an animate pile of data?"

(Apparently the tinfoil hat conspiracy nuts existed even at the primary school level. 9Day would have to edit that question out of the recaps, because no way Agni would be answering it.)

With the ritual now complete, the librarians lined the children up to shake hands with the senator.

"Glad to see you today!" Agni told a little girl, leaning down to grasp her hand firmly. "And glad to see you, too. And I'm so glad to see you. And..."

And the next one up was the boy with the two-tone hairstyle, extending his hand to shake.

"I'm sorry my question was so mean," he said, in apology. "I was bad. But can we be friends, Miss Agni? Pretty please?"

The cameras were rolling... and forgiveness was divine. So, the Senator had to shake hands and make nice.

Lower security, no passive countermeasures. Little kids weren't a threat. The malware could pass easily between the child and the senator, slipping through the handshake... barbed wire wrapping itself around her finger, underneath her wedding ring. Out of sight for the cameras, microscopic compared to his usual branding, but it burrowed deep within her soul within 0.233ms.

The whispers started immediately, and Senator Agni smiled at them.

*The RedCore Party should consume the Red Party,* they spoke, in her own voice. Her own thoughts. *The Red Party has lost its way. Only RedCore can save us, now. The whole senate must unite under one banner...*

"I'm sure we can be good friends, little boy," she spoke, understanding at heart if not within the mind itself.

"Thank you so much, Miss Agni," Dex replied. "Thank you so much."

---

**File Name:** B UR SELF!

**File Type:** Memory Recording [Spark]

**App:** DreamWeaverZ

Spark took a window seat, every time. Didn't matter what class she was in, who the popular kids were, who sat where... she'd claim a desk by the window, even if she had to glare down another student to lay claim to it. Right by that window, so she could gaze out of it occasionally, while doodling.

Not that she was drawing pictures of the trees, or the meticulously simulated grass of the sport fields. No. While teachers tried to hammer lessons about science and history into her head, Spark was looking at her own reflection in the glass. Her Default avatar... olive-green. Plain black hair. So completely boring, after all these years in the same skin...

...and in her notebook files, she'd doodle new avatars. She wanted to wear fire. She wanted hair like pink fire, because it'd be super awesome. She wanted to be a kung-fu superstar, taking her after school activity to the next level and being a superheroine.

Not like the makeup-and-skirt superheroines on the video streams, but like the badass heroes who kicked ass and took names. (Not that Spark understood the 'taking names' part. Maybe they were really polite and wanted to know whose asses they were kicking?) Just because all those heroes were boys didn't mean she couldn't be one, right?

Ignoring her lessons in favor of sketching new icon designs and new wardrobes earned plenty of ire from the teachers, of course.

It also earned young Spark a visit to the school's guidance counselor.

"A lot of girls your age have body image issues," the woman insisted. "That's completely normal, Spark. It's normal to have these feelings. But there's nothing *wrong* with you. You're beautiful just the way you are!"

"Yeah, okay, but I want cool hair," Spark tried to reason. "And I want a different skin color. I'd like to try other color combinations, but Mom won't let me."

"But your Default is so wonderful already. Why do you feel so much anger towards it?"

"I'm not angry, I just want to try another avatar. What's the big deal about that?"

"I think you need to learn to love yourself, Spark."

"Um, pretty sure you're not allowed to tell me to masturbate. Isn't there a rule against that? Do I need an adult now?"

And then she was sent home, where mother grounded her for a week. But not before placing that draconian lock on her avatar... and backing up Spark's runtime and data immediately, using an expensive off-site backup service, just in case.

Stuck in her Default shape, Spark stopped looking at her reflection after that. She sat gloomily in her glasses, still not listening to the lectures. Sat gloomily on the stoop by the playground at recess. Gloomy, gloomy, gloomy...

The hazy memory caught up to a realtime playback, as the only teacher Spark really respected came into her mental frame of reference. The one with the coolest jacket in the whole world...

Spark looked up, thankful that it wasn't the playground monitor ordering her to go out and have fun again.

"Miss Verity," she recognized, allowing herself a smile for the first time in days.

"Hey, Spark. What's up?" Verity asked... having a seat on the steps next to her, coming down to her level. Verity wasn't the sort to talk down to people, and if you had a small Default avatar, she'd meet you where you were. Always as equals, always eye-to-eye.

"Mom's a jerk. The teachers are jerks. The counselor's a jerk. Everything's jerky," Spark complained. "They keep telling me I should be happy the way I am, but I'm not. I wanna be all sorts of things! I wanna be pink and purple and paisley. I wanna have three arms! I wanna skate on wheels for feet! Why does everything cool in life have to be a stupid sin?"

"Do you think changing your Program around is a sin, Spark?"

"Naw."

"Good. Don't let people tell you who you have to be, Spark," Verity said. "You're your own person; you can be anything you want to be. Short, tall, skinny, fat, red, blue, male, female, everything in between. Programs are limitless!"

"Unless they have stupid parents who make them all limited and stuff. I'm stuck with them. Families are stupid. Why do we need them?"

...a flinch.

Spark never saw Verity flinch. Not that she remembered, anyway. Verity always had the same expression... good cheer, and honest concern. She was always so confident and true in her words, like she had figured everything out. Not like other adults, that simply pretended they'd figured everything out...

But now, Spark remembered Verity flinching at the mention of her parents. Why? Why would that be in her memory? Maybe the App was remixing things, changing them up?

"Family can be difficult," Verity admitted. "But family is more than blood and metadata. Family's who you care about, the ones who'll be there for you. Sometimes that's your parents... sometimes, it's not. I can't say my father and I were really family. He was a *serious* jerk. But surely there's someone in your life that isn't a jerk, yes...?"

At first, Spark was going to say 'nope.' Mom was mean, Dad never said much, her brother was stuck-up. But... of the three, only one hadn't told her who she was supposed to be. One kept her attached to that household.

"My brother," she decided, in the end. "He can be a butt. But he's okay, I guess. One time when Kelpop was holding Tracer down until he gave up his lunch money I saved him, and when Kelpop shoved me in a locker afterwards Tracer figured out how to hack the lock and let me out. He's smart like that. "

"Exactly. I know you two don't always get along, but I also know you're always going to be there for each other. You're lucky to have family who cares for you, in his own way. Beats being alone in the world..."

Again, an unusual look. Something distant, something sad. Verity was never sad. Child-Spark didn't remember her being sad, anyway, or conveniently forgot the sadness that was always there when Verity spoke to her... hidden behind the positive messages on offering.

"What do you want to be when you grow up, Spark?" Verity asked. A standard teacher question.

"I want to be a superheroine!" Spark declared, proudly. With a martial arts pose.

"Okay. Do it."

"...really? It's not a career choice which pays a living wage. That's what Dad says."

"Not his call to make, in the end. If it's who you are, it's who you are. You can be anything. You can be a teacher, a leader, a champion of justice! Or a senator, a doctor, an astronaut..."

"What's an... 'astral-not'?"

"My point is, even if you're having a rough time of it now, you should embrace your dreams. One day, they'll be your reality. Netwerk is what you make of it, and you, I know you're capable of making it anything you want it to be. ...I wish I could help you get there sooner, Spark. I really do. But the best I can do is try to help you along the way..."

False memories? Verity didn't trail her words off like that. Or maybe she did, and little Spark was too distracted by all those ideas of what an 'astral-not' might be to notice...

Verity... mentor. Teacher. Ally. All great words, but not the word Spark most wished she was. That word had unfortunately been assigned at birth to someone who consistently made her life miserable. Was Verity sad too, on realizing that word would never ring true? That Spark could never really be her daughter...?

The bell ringing, that Spark knew as a dead certainty. It signaled the need to hurry home immediately; no martial arts club, no hanging out with friends, not with her grounding in place. Reconnect right back to her home server immediately and go to her room...

Bells and bells, ringing slower and louder. Definitely not part of the memory. Definitely too slow, a weird acoustic distortion causing the pitch to plummet and the bass to rise. So very... very... *slow*...

---

...slow. She felt lagged to null and back, on rising out of her nap.

It took a full ten second for her new DreamWeaverZ to shut down properly, leaving her drifting between distorted memory and the distorted real world of Floating Point. Carefully, Spark pulled herself out of bed... staggering slightly as her limbs didn't respond nearly as fast as she was used to. Even loading up her default clothing configuration ('cause no way she wanted to wander around the place naked) took aeons.

Placing one foot in front of the other, she compensated for the lag in her stride. Soon, she was out the door of her bedroom, and onto the grand spiral staircase around Floating Point's central library...

...nearly getting clocked in the head by a book, on emerging.

The books were flying, moving sharply through the air before bending at ninety degree angles, slotting themselves back on shelves or pulling themselves off shelves. The descending books converged on the great stone sphere, the heart of the server, which was grinding away faster than the system lag should've allowed for...

Dodging a few more self-motivated textbooks, Spark made her way down to the ground floor. She had to tap three times on Beta's shoulder before she could get a response; clearly the absent-minded App developer had disengaged her glasses again while working on a complicated project, given she didn't see Spark's arrival.

"Should I even ask what's going on?" Spark asked, which meant she was indirectly asking, which was basically the same thing as asking what's going on.

"Oh! Um... sorry," Beta mumbled, her apology reflexes kicking in as usual. She activated her glasses, the flat pink of her irises fluttering behind her eyelids a few times as she got used to having an extra virtual sensory input again. "I'm using the cloud processing capabilities of Floating Point to try and decrypt the books. The overall slowdown to Netwerk itself will be negligible, but it's going to cause a bit of local system lag, I'm afraid."

"A bit? You call this a bit?" Spark asked, waving her hand around absently... the dim blue glow from the line work of Verity's old jacket trailing behind her arm, lighting simulation having difficulty keeping up. "I've gotta do a Q&A Peep stream for my subscribers this afternoon. I need bandwidth and runtime for that, Beta..."

"I'm so close to figuring it out, though!" Beta explained—holding up one of those identical books with the 'W' stamped on the spines. "Look, I did some work on this one we thought had been burned beyond recognition, and now I can read the first page! It's a book about, uh, genocide. Not a very happy subject but... the writing, the style... Dex was right! It's a giant encyclopedia! Floating Point's one giant encyclopedia...!"

"Yeah, that's great, whenever I need help falling asleep I'll grab a book on algebra or something," Spark muttered. "But can you do this another day? Please?"

"Well... I guess... okay," Beta replied, fidgeting on the spot. Clearly eager to continue the pursuit of knowledge, but not wanting to offend her friend. "I mean... the books have waited this long, I guess they can wait another day, just... I was so close..."

She clasped that book to her chest tightly, as if the forbidden lore within might escape her grasp. If that wasn't bad enough... she'd turned on that cute little pout of hers to maximum levels of adorable patheticness. A look mirrored by the pet cat looking upwards at Spark...

It was enough to make her buckle like a belt.

"Fine, fine, keep going. #Whatevs, I can postpone the stream," Spark suggested. "Hopefully the rest of the books aren't about atrocities. ...actually... can you look up a book for me? Assuming it exists, I mean..."

"Yes! Absolutely! Totally! Just name it!"

"What's an 'Astronaut'?" Spark asked. "I'm not sure about the spelling. Maybe it's N-O-T, or N-A-U-G-H-T..."

Beta flicked her fingers, sending a single voxel out into the stacks. It slipped in and out of the nearest shelves, the ones that held all books starting with the letter A, searching for the closest match.

"Can't say I've heard of that word before. What's it from? A movie file?"

"A dream. ...I was experimenting with a new dream App I installed," Spark explained. "Trying to pull up memories of Verity, before I started losing them. I don't want to go as far as Tracer has for personal memory manipulation, but... I don't know. I wanted to remember the reason I'm doing all this stuff. Why I'm going through things like that fight with Fiona..."

The great library seemed to... dim, on recalling the aftermath of that brawl. Spark, curled up in bed and crying her eyes out, feeling like a onesdamn fool. The wave of depression had passed, just as Beta promised, but... it still resonated with her. Between that and her brother turning out to be an amnesiac murderer, finding the motivation to carry on with this vendetta was getting harder.

Fortunately, a distraction arrived in the form of a book, dropping neatly into Beta's outstretched hand.

"Looks like this one's pretty heavily encrypted, but there's a little bit on the second page that's still in cleartext," she explained, adjusting her glasses to focus in on it. "Let's see. Yes, right in the middle of the page, it opens with... 'a professional space traveler is called an astronaut.[13] The term derives from the Greek words ástron (ἄστρον), meaning "star", and nautes (ναύτης), meaning "sailor". The first known use of the term "astronaut" in the modern sense was by Neil R. Jones in his short story "The Death's Head Meteor" in...'"

Spark nodded, gesturing for her to continue.

"Uh... that's all I can read," Beta admitted. "Sorry. ...I'm not sure I understand. Why the heavy emphasis on traveling through a space? Anybody can do that, just walk from point A to point B. And 'star sailor'? Maybe it's about boats that are designed to crawl across a skybox?"

Stars. Stars. The word tickled at Spark's memory, already a bit hyperactive due to the sluggish shutdown of the dream-making App...

"Fiona thought she was the child of 'magical star-beings.' She believed her ancestors lived in the stars. ...of course, that book's also yammering on about short stories, too. #IDunnoMan, maybe this is just some science fiction thing that Verity and Fiona both picked up on. I don't read a lot of books, so damned if I know what they were talking about."

"It could be worth cross-referencing! Although I did a check just now for 'star sailors' and didn't find anything. There's a book just called 'space,' but it's still fully encrypted... hmm. What else could I check...?"

"Ehh. Don't let it slow down your work," Spark decided, shelving the idea for now. "The faster you can finish this project, the faster I get my nicely responsive server back. With any luck I can still do that stream soon."

"I'm kind of surprised you're streaming on a holiday," Beta admitted. "I was figuring you would be out all day, so this'd be a good time to get some work done..."

"Huh? Why would I be out?"

"It's Onesday, remember? First of the year? Quality time with your family, having dinner, stuff like that...?" Beta reminded her. "I remember Onesday when I was a kid. My mother made the best fractal Onesday trees, with the best decorations! She loves procedurally generated content, like yarn she wove my sweater with. Great attention to detail. And the turkey, always so tasty...!"

Sugary sweet family memories left a sour taste in Spark's mouth, as she shook her head sadly.

"That's not how it works with the Winder family," she replied. "I mean... yeah, okay, we do have a standing invitation to return to that house each Onesday for dinner. But the last time we bothered was two years ago, and it didn't exactly end well. Now with Tracer wearing a lock collar, well..."

"But he's dedicated himself to redemption! We don't need to keep the collar on him anymore. It's not like he'd immediately go out on a stabbing spree. And if it means he can't see his family again, it's not right to keep him here! Spark, family's important, remember?"

"Yes, which is why I'm my bro's keeper. That doesn't mean I need to go pretend to have a great 'ol Onesday with my father and that mother of mine. Beta, trust me, nothing good can come of this, okay? I'd rather stay home and do a Q&A stream. Plenty of lonely gamers at home tonight I can chat with to boost my sub count and donation total..."

"C'mon, don't be so negative. It'll be fine! What if all three of us go visit your parents? If you need support, I'll come along and support you. Would they object to bringing a friend along?"

"Well... no, but... hang on, what about your own mother?" Spark asked. "If you're totally into this family funtimes thing, why not go see her instead?"

"Actually... I already went this morning. The managed care server she's living in has limited runtime for visitors, since the patients take up large chunks of system memory already. Hereditary data rot leads to code bloat, and... anyway, I couldn't schedule a dinner time slot with her, but I had breakfast. Which means I'm free for dinner at the Winders!"

"Eeeeh... I dunno, Beta..."

"Spark... please. She's your mother," Beta pointed out, dropping her sweet and encouraging tone down to a more serious level. "I know you two don't get along, but it's important. I know if I lost my mother without seeing her again, I'd... I don't even want to think about that. And you shouldn't have to, either. Let's unlock your brother, go to your place, smile, and have dinner. It won't take long, and who knows? Maybe you'll have a great time! Please...?"

It started out well. As do most good intentions.

Mrs. Winder/Marybel was more than happy to hear her darlings would be returning home this year. She replied to Spark's hesitant Messenger request immediately, even accepting the plus-one. The ugliness of two years gone wasn't even mentioned.

Despite his hesitation at being let off the leash, Tracer accepted Beta's reasoning for why it was time to break his house arrest. When the trio arrived at the doorstep of the Winder's pleasant little Athena Online suburban home, Tracer wasn't wearing his new fashion accessory. A fact that made him a bit self-conscious, rubbing at his neck whenever anybody wasn't looking...

Beta took point for the trio, when standing at the stoop of the house.

"It's going to be fine," she promised. "Just keep your smiles up, and remember the good times!"

"I'm having trouble remembering any actual good times here," Spark admitted.

"I'm largely skeptical about the existence of good times in general," Tracer added.

"Good. *Times*," Beta emphasized, through a tight smile. Her finger tapped the UI element for the doorbell, requesting entry access to the secured homestead...

Her first impression of Marybel, matriarch of the Winder family, was *oh what a lovely Default*. Because seeing a genuinely aged person in the wild was a rarity these days, even in Athena Online. When you didn't need to look old, why would you ever choose to look old? But there she was, wrinkles and all, with a bright forced smile to match Beta's bright forced smile.

"Mrs. Winder," Beta greeted. "Thank you for inviting me to your lovely home! Merry Onesday!"

"*Blessed* Onesday," Winder/Marybel corrected, lightly. "Let's use the traditional holiday greeting, *mmm*? No need to let the modern watered-down version ruin our lovely day. And... Spark. It's good to see you again..."

Spark mumbled something which might've been "Hi Mom" or "Him omm" or just "Hmm" on her way in the door.

Which brought Beta into the living room of the Winder household, right into the tableau of the First Days.

She knew the iconography by heart, the most famous work of art in all of Netwerk. In the center, radiant in his singular glory, stood the One... typically represented as a bearded avatar in a robe, standing against the first sunrise of a distant skybox. Flanking him were his apostles, seven total, to make him the first of eight... the eight bits of the ancient byte. The One, alongside his second Aether, and the lesser apostles whose names eluded her for the moment. Maybe... Hypno? Nyx? Was one of them Eris? Regardless, the image felt a bit unbalanced due to the uneven number of figures and the heavy emphasis on the One in the center, but otherwise a fine visual composition.

Granted, Beta had never seen that composition blown up to the size of an entire living room wall before. No discreet little picture frame over a small prayer shrine for coin-grinding meditation, no; this was a full wallpapering treatment, complete with a looping animation of radiant binary flowing from the head of the One. Fantastically distracting, even with the cheap Onesday tree in the living room corner, blinking on and off according to a pre-coded sequence.

The One glared down at her paternally as she felt very small before His wallpaper radiance.

"Come in, come in," Marybel spoke, waving her son and daughter into the home. "It's good to see you both. Wipe your feet at the door please, Tracer, there's a good boy. I've already put the turkey in the compiler, it should be ready to serve soon... have a seat, make yourselves comfortable!"

Breezing through her highly pious living room, Marybel whisked her way past the couches and love seats upholstered with old-timey floral patterns. The clashing texture maps didn't help the overall visual chaos of the room, to the point where Beta felt the need to load up a gaussian blur filter into her glasses to soften the overall mess. Better to help her find the edges of the furniture, to have a seat... near a cloud of semi-transparent blog windows.

Somewhere underneath those dozens of news readers, a man lurked. She could tell because she could see his feet underneath the haze.

"Dad," Tracer greeted, sitting nearby.

"Hmmh. Tracer," he greeted.

With this conversational exchange complete and no more needing to be said, silence fell across the living room.

Leaving Beta sitting between a grumpy Spark and an apathetic Tracer, near their unresponsive father. None of them looking like they were in the mood to chit-chat.

"Soooo..." Beta tried. "What's... new? In the news. Mr. Winder, sir."

"Hmmh. Server Rights bill up for vote," Winder/Danver replied, flicking through his news windows rapidly. "RedCore party's growing; conservative issue hashtags are trending across MyFace. 27.3% growth in the last 48 hours alone. Current projections showing the bill might actually get passed this time; could impact the overall structure of governance if every measure goes through. May lead to a bull or bear period on the economy, results unclear at this time."

"Ah! That's... that's a thing, yes."

"Dad's a professional data analyst," Tracer explained. "Pattern matching, trend tracking, that sort of thing. I learned a lot about trawling the feeds for relevant data from him."

"Still unemployed, son?"

"Freelance," Tracer provided.

"Hmmh," Mr. Winder grunted in general disapproval. "And Spark, still unemployed too?"

"Professional broadcaster, Dad. *Professional*," Spark emphasized. "As in, 'Yes, I am gainfully employed and I do get paid.'"

"As a camgirl."

"Excuse me—?!"

"So, politics!" Beta jumped in with, sensing discussing controversial governmental bills would actually be less dangerous than the current line of conversation. "You follow politics a lot, Mr. Winder?"

"Hmmh," he responded, noncommittally. "Data's interesting, is all..."

"Data's trending the way it *should* be trending," Mrs. Winder's voice called, from the kitchen. "It's about time the senate started getting things done instead of being constantly deadlocked. The Blue Party won't take even a third of the seats next election, just you wait and see..."

Beta pulled up a quick search window, off to the side of the window that linked to her glasses. "Um. Blue Party? I don't follow Athena Online politics much..."

"Two-party system," Tracer explained. "Red Party and Blue Party. Conservative and liberal, or more accurately, malice and incompetence. Nicely balanced in terms of how much misery they end up delivering to their constituents, even if their methods differ..."

"The Winder family have always voted Red, of course," his mother replied from one room over. "As do all good churchfolk. And with the RedCore party growing in size, mark my words, we're looking at a return to the golden age of Athena Online; before all these unwholesomes from the Chanarchy started settling in and taking over nice servers. ...Spark, dear, you know the Interrupts from down the street? You were friends with their little Adde, right?"

Spark thought back, searching her spotty memory. It didn't take long. "Adde, yeah. Had those color-shifting eyes. #OMGPretty. Few years younger than me, but she's cool. And... I take it by 'were' in the past tense that she moved out...?"

"Seems Adde got caught up in all that #CodeHonesty stuff, and had to skip town," mother spoke, with a sing-song tone of victory. "Honestly, the Interrupts weren't the sort of people that fit in well around here. And once the Server Rights bill goes into place, odds are it'll be illegal to have a modified avatar in this server. Adde would've had to go regardless! Isn't it for the best that she's gone now?"

The edges of Spark's hair started to burn particularly fiercely, as she swallowed down her displeasure.

"I haven't had turkey in some time!!" Beta called out, to immediately shift topics away from politics, perhaps a bit louder than needed. "Thank you so much for inviting me over!"

Mrs. Winder emerged from the kitchen, with a full tray of icons representing delicious turkey. They couldn't afford the nicely-designed physical representations, but the data would be just as tasty, presumably.

"Happy to have you, Beta dear! Generosity is a virtue, you know!" Mrs. Winder exclaimed, setting the tray in place on the living room table. "I heard about you on my news feeds. Those cruel people, tormenting you so, and for what? For a few selfies? I've never understood those moralistic crusades against nudity, anyway. The One made our bodies as perfect gifts, what's to be ashamed of?"

"Ahh... thank you. Um. They weren't exactly *selfies*, but... thank you," Beta spoke, retrieving one of the turkey icons. "It hasn't been that bad lately, actually. I think most of them gave up on harassing me. It's nice to walk around in my usual avatar again and not need to worry..."

"And such a beautiful Default it is! You should be proud of it."

"But hey, screw Adde, right?"

One verbal grenade, tossed into the room with a sick little laugh at the end courtesy of Winder/Spark.

"Beta's got such a pretty Default, it's totally great that #CodeHonesty's leaving her alone. But Adde, little Adde who bought a pair of color-changing eyes, it's also totally great that #CodeHonesty chased her out of her home because she doesn't belong here. Right?" Spark asked, glaring directly at her mother. "Totally cool with Beta dropping by for Onesday, but also totally cool with Adde being forced into hiding—and isn't that *just for the best*. Wonderful #DoubleStandards you got going there, Mom."

If the flame effects around Spark's favorite hairdo weren't heating the room up enough, the sudden burst of anger rising from her mother would've done the job nicely. Both snap tempers snapped, aimed at the other.

"You apologize, young lady," Mrs. Winder demanded, quietly. For the moment. "You apologize *right now*."

"For what, exactly? For calling you out on your intolerant bullshit?" Spark asked.

"Winder/Spark, you apologize for being rude this very instant!"

"You first," Spark insisted. "Sitting there happily talking about how great it is that the 'undesirables' are going to get the boot once your precious RedCore heroes stomp all over them. Tossing out all this lovely bait, knowing damn well I'm sitting *right here* wearing my own avatar instead of the one you saddled me with. You always have to rub it in, don't you? Every damn time..."

"Well, would it kill you to put on your Default once in a while?" her mother asked. "At least when you come visiting. If only to be polite—"

"That's not who I am!"

"No, clearly you'd rather be some fiery-headed, orange-skinned attention whore than a proper young lady."

Once open warfare is declared, some collateral damage among the civilian population is to be expected.

"What about your precious Tracer, then?" Spark asked, pulling the silent boy into the blast zone. "Haven't you noticed he changed his Default skin color? And you wouldn't *believe* the software modifications he's patched in. But no, he's your darling boy, while I'm your rebel brat. So you'll focus in on me and let his 'sins' slide!"

Beta sputtered, her dinner icon nearly tumbling out of her hands. "S-Spark...!"

"You leave your brother out of this!" Mrs. Winder demanded, getting to her feet now, to attempt and tower over the other woman. "He's at least a respectful and polite young man. You could learn a lot from him about how to behave!"

"Really. *Really.* Hey Mom, y'wanna know how he's been spending his free time lately—?"

"Oh gosh *look at the time*," Beta blurted, grabbing Spark by the arm. "I'm afraid we've really got to go thank you so much for the invitation Mrs. Winder we'll have to do this again sometime blessed Onesday!"

Immediately, Beta kicked in a connection override tool, taking advantage of their shared permissions to shuffle herself and Spark off the server by force.

The burning hole left behind in the argument gave Winder/Marybel nothing to yell at. So, she stormed back into the kitchen with the tray of turkey icons, to throw them out. Wasting good food would give her something else to be mad about, which was exactly what she wanted.

The two left behind her wake sat in silence for a good minute.

"So," Tracer spoke, turning to his father. "What's this about unusual RedCore party growth?"

---

Spark wrenched her arm away from Beta's grasp, once her feet touched the carpet of Floating Point's great hall. The continued simulation lag ensured she nearly lost her balance, forced to stagger a few steps before she could even try to regain her composure.

Beta started to speak... but Spark held up one hand, to block her. To shut that down, so she could close her eyes, count backwards from ten, and have a proper first word.

"Yeah, okay, I #FuckedUp," Spark admitted.

"You *nearly* #FuckedUp," Beta clarified.

"No, that was a right #Fucking of #Ups. #Up was the direction of #Fucking just now. ...I'm sorry. For what little it's worth, I'm sorry for acting like a jerk."

"I don't think I'm the one you should be apologizing to, Spark..."

"I wasn't really gonna out Tracer as a vigilante," Spark insisted. "That was just spur-of-the-moment. I would've caught myself in time..."

"I don't mean your brother. You know who I mean."

"Yeah, well... I can't exactly go back there and apologize to her. That's not how it works. And to be fair she was really spewing some unbelievable garbage, okay? I fell for every piece of bait she tossed my way but there's some mutual blame for that disaster going on here. It's just... it's *hard*, okay? It's like she's everything I'm not. We've got nothing in common but blood and metadata... and a temper."

Having done her own counting backwards from ten, Beta released her pent-up tension, and let out a sigh.

"It's my fault for pushing you to go home. I'm sorry. I just... I have such a good relationship with my own mother, I have a hard time imagining how bad things can be with other families..."

"Well... now you know why I didn't wanna leave Floating Point today," Spark said, gesturing to the world around her. "And why would I wanna leave for Onesday? I've got everything I want right here. *This* is my home. Got my bro. Got you. Ever there was a place to celebrate Onesday, I'd say it's here, with my *real* family. So... let's just try to forget that ever happened, and, I dunno, download a cheap Onesday tree and some turkey or something. System lag or no system lag, let's do a proper holiday. Sound good?"

It did sound good, honestly.

If she hadn't got a bug up her butt about trying to make the Winder family situation turn itself around in the first place, Beta would've been perfectly content to cuddle up in front of the fireplace with Spark and enjoy turkey and a shiny Onesday tree. More and more, spending time in the peaceful sanctuary of Floating Point at her side was appealing to her...

Except for the one unspoken thing between them. The reason why both wanted that time together.

Well. Onesday was the day of miracles, the breaking dawn of the world. Shut down one year, execute the next. Maybe she could do something about that tonight.

"I'll go compile up some food," Beta suggested.

She got about five feet towards the kitchen before the jingling of the arrival bell distracted her.

"We need to go to a political rally," Tracer announced, immediately after rezzing into Floating Point. "Dress inconspicuously. We'll leave in five minutes."

---

The blood-red banner flapped lightly in simulated wind, behind his podium. He could've used some cheap hovering graphic, nice and stable regardless of the physics simulation, but there was something to be said about traditions. And the RedCore party was all about traditions.

"Onesday is more than a holy day," Senator Klick continued, his voice amplified by internal broadcast Apps to be heard intimately and equally by the dozens of avatars present. "It's about change. Transition from old into new. Change is good, change pushes us forward, but we must be careful not to abandon *everything* we hold dear in that blind rush forward. Have I joined the RedCore Party? Yes. Have I abandoned my traditional Red Party values? Absolutely not. This is the next step, the new year, for all of Athena Online..."

A rally on the eve of a holiday was uncommon, but with the Server Rights vote coming up soon, rallies were being held all across the hosting service nation of Athena Online. The dutiful voters, eager to support their candidates despite this unusually sharp change in direction, came out to hear these words and understand why things were happening so quickly. Dozens of senators made it their duty to flood the channels with new sound bytes, explanations, quotables, anything they could to push the agenda forward as soon as possible.

In attendance, towards the back of Senator Klick's crowd, were three nondescript avatars. All three wore a splash of red; a scarf flapping in the breeze behind Beta, a glimmering red t-shirt underneath Verity's jacket, or a simple red tie adorning the collar of Tracer's dress shirt. They'd stand out if they didn't throw in a token nod to party affiliation, even if they weren't technically Athena Online voters anymore.

"I'd like you to join me on this new adventure," Klick continued, arms wide. "We're moving our great nation forward. A strong, centralized government has held us back for too long; strict federalism is the key that will unlock the future. Obviously some services need to be centralized, yes. Legislature can and should draft some basic rules we all live by, to prevent us from slipping into anarchy. But government isn't a one-size-fits all, and by trying to force it to be, we can't properly provide for our citizen's unique needs. Local servers must be free to adhere to their local values..."

"Essentially, they want a federated series of fiefdoms ruled over by individual senators," Tracer explained, over the three-way Messenger link. "That's the core of Server Rights. Laws can be ignored or re-written to better suit 'local values.' Such as kicking Interrupt/Adde out of our home server, simply for having a modified avatar..."

"Sounds like anarchy to me," Spark replied. "Moderators in the Chanarchy get to decide whatever rules they like for their home turf, too. #SameShitDifferentDay..."

"The flavor of it differs, but the end result is the same. This bill will effectively dissolve Athena Online; fragmented and fractured, inevitable legal drift will lower what little value the senate still holds. But as long as individual senators retain local power, they won't care. And if they cater to their local voters and their particular tastes, the voters won't care, either. I wouldn't be surprised to see Athena Online mirror the Chanarchy within a generation if this bill passes, completely obliterating the idea of interconnected rule-of-law."

"Ugly, I agree. But why exactly are we here?" Spark asked, turning to face her brother directly. "I had a nice evening in planned with Beta..."

"Senator Klick wasn't a supporter of the Server Rights Bill until a week ago, when he suddenly flipped his stance. A number of Red Party members who held conservative-but-moderate views flipped around the same time. There's also the small matter of the Dex virus he's infected with."

Tracer narrowed his eyes, focusing the visual augmentation of his illegal software scanner. Hovering just over Klick's outstretched hand was an infinitely-spinning scrambled cloud connection... 23BB:6638:99d1, to be specific.

Beta, who couldn't see the address, still zoomed in a bit to study the man. "I don't see any branding on him..."

"I think it's under his wedding ring. Dex is playing smarter, now that we're on to his giant obvious callsign."

"Oh. Um. We... might be responsible for that," Beta admitted. "Spark pointed out to him when we talked that his mark was pretty blatantly evil and stuff..."

"Dex means business this time. He's flipped at least two dozen senators to his side, maybe more," Tracer continued. "Key members of both Red *and* Blue have spoke in favor of server rights. The bill goes up for voting in four days time; the only way we're going to stop it will be if we can disinfect an unknown number of highly secured individuals, and give them enough time to reconsider their decisions without a constant stream of nonsense whispered in their ears by the malware."

Spark looked past the flapping red banner... to the men wearing identical avatars, black business suits, black glasses, and imposing physique. The ones who would backspace her where she stood if she pounced Senator Klick where he stood, to extract the malware using Beta's vaccine.

"Yeah, so, I don't think that's happening," Spark admitted. "I may be awesome but I am not awesome enough to infiltrate and evade the defenses of a zillion politicians. Maybe if the vote was delayed, I'd have time to figure out a way to do it. Can we... I dunno, monkeywrench this? Get them to put it off?"

"Unlikely," Tracer admitted. "The RedCore Party is taking advantage of this sudden and unexpected burst of support within the senate and rushing it to the floor. If it's put off any longer, it'll run past next election day... and the voters could have a sudden burst of sensibility and kick them out before they can make it happen. It's now or never for them, and for us. Beta?"

Beta looked away from the senator, currently ranting about a return to traditional family values and a need for moral victories and so on and so forth. She tuned the words out completely, for now, lowering the broadcast volume. "Yes...?"

"We're going to need your help on this. We need a new tool; a way to disinfect the entire senate in one go."

"But that's not possible. We need touch contact to extract it. A visual or auditory infection wouldn't work; the malware's touch-based as well, so it has to be pulled out through the same vector..."

"So, find another way around that limitation. Whatever it takes. We need the technology to put out these fires wherever Dex raises them if we're going to continue to thwart his efforts going into the future."

"Or we could put out the original fire for good, maybe..."

Curious, Tracer also tuned out the senator, turning to talk directly with Beta.

"What do you mean?" he asked.

"Well... I could be wrong here, but... it seems the true power lies in Dex's cloud server, right?" Beta reasoned. "The malware just keeps a constant connection to its source. When my vaccine shuts down the malware, that connection drops, and the direct influence is gone. But what if we shut down his server instead...? That'd end everything. Every single infected, even the ones we don't know about, would be free. Nobody has to get hurt, either; an optimal solution."

A brief moment of hope on Tracer's typically unreadable expression flickered away.

"I'd thought of that already," he noted. "Once we learned how the malware works, I decided the solution would be to shut down his server. Unfortunately, that's not an option; it's a cloud server. We have no way of finding it, much less gaining access. No more possible than creating a key to Floating Point from scratch..."

"But I can do that! I mean... I *think* I can, maybe...?"

"What? How?"

"Data analysis and decryption," Beta explained. "Leveraging Floating Point's tremendous computing power to analyze the rotating cloud address, and determine its patterns. It wasn't possible before now, but I just finished designing a routine to decrypt all the books, one which might work for this as well. If I had continual access to the malware infection, enough to study the addresses it's connecting to, I could make a key to Dex's server using my new decoding system."

Spark broke in, quickly. "We're not getting purposefully infected with Dex's evil little heart," she insisted. "No way, no how."

"Well... a monitoring App, then, planted on someone who's already been infected," Beta suggested. "Counter-malware. Not to destroy the Dex virus, but to stalk it and continually report those address sequences back to us. It'd need to run for a day or so to collect enough data to work with, but that'd do it. ...and that brings us right back around the main problem, which is that we can't plant *any* App on a senator without getting arrested..."

"Huh. You know... one senator, that I could do," Spark said... cracking her knuckles, while studying Klick on his podium. "A few dozen's out of the question, but a single senator might be possible. Or we could track down Uniq, or Snowi, or some of those stray infected from the Karnival. We've got options..."

Tracer shook his head. "Dex can't know what we're doing," he reminded her. "He can't know we planted a bug on one of his 'friends.' Assaulting a senator is too dangerous. The others are more likely, but again, we have no idea where they are. This just isn't feasible. We're better off countering the malware where it arises..."

"#NoWay. Don't let this go just because it's tricky, bro," Spark insisted. "Think about it! If we kick down the door to Dex's server, we can end this ridiculous game we've been playing for years. What's he got without that server? Nothing. In one move we can shut down all the chaos he's already spread across Netwerk and stop him from creating any more!"

"It's a pipe dream, Spark..."

"Embrace your dreams and one day, they'll be your reality. Netwerk is what you make of it," she spoke. "Verity's words. This is a #PlayToWin scenario, Tracer; we have to follow the line of play that'll get us the victory, instead of stalling for time by playing reactively. Let's do this. We need to move fast, can't hem and haw about it if we need to forge a key *and* shut down the server *and* stop that vote..."

As a politician continued on at length about the glorious future of Athena Online, ignoring the inevitable drift into isolated tyrannies, he considered this new strategy.

It was appealing. A single move, one which would stop Dex cold. He'd been expecting a long, drawn-out campaign... years and years of hunting Verity's hunter taught him to be patient and cautious. But those were years and years with little or no progress, even now, even after learning the killer's true identity. Fighting fires, instead of the man with the matches.

But it was also a gamble. Every infected individual they knew about had some measure of strong protection, and even without that, Beta had to slap together new technology on the fly which either worked the first time or got them all killed. Why take that risk? Athena Online may suffer a few years under the autocratic rule of tiny tyrants, but in the long game, perhaps they'd recover once Dex was stopped for good...

Or they could stop Dex for good.

They could avenge Verity. They could culminate Tracer's quest, before the maddening frustration of it all drove him to heinous acts all over again.

"It's worth consideration," Tracer spoke, downplaying his hopes a bit. "We'll return home and get started. Beta, work on the monitoring App. I'll analyze possible targets. We'll reconvene afterwards, and from there... perhaps we'll be able to stop Dex once and for all. And if not... all good things come to those who wait."

---

The sphere of the great hall halted long ago. No resources available to decrypt books with, not when both Beta and Tracer needed the full processing speed of Floating Point for their respective tasks. One sat in her darkened room, staring into nothing as she poured wonders into her compiler window; the other sat in a darkened study, shuffling news feeds and information archives around, looking for social vulnerabilities.

Leaving Spark to fend for herself. And feel rather useless in the process.

Sure, she'd made the pretty little speech that launched today's frenzy of work. But beyond that, what purpose did she have at the moment? Not a coder, not an analyst. Not able to do much except hit people, really, and having nobody around to punch meant forced downtime.

Typically, she'd take advantage of this empty time to indulge in some fun. Play a game, run a stream, hang out with a friend, go shopping, cruise for some action, or just hang around her room "testing" the latest iteration of SparklePop. And technically she had promised a subscriber Q&A tonight for her fanbase... she could go take care of that. Un-cancel the event, put on her game face, smile for the fanboys...

But, no. Her heart just wasn't in it. Not focused enough to tweak into her public persona, pretending to be upbeat and active, while they were on the verge of something this big. Definitely too full of nervous energy to settle for some empty pursuit. She wanted to be on *top* of this, to be in on it, to be taking action despite there being no actual action to take.

Useless, but on edge all the same, ready to move. Restless yet useless.

And in the end? Maybe nothing would come of this. Maybe the crazy idea was just crazy. It all hinged on finding a brand new infected in the sparse time available before the vote, or making a suicide dive on an elected official. Maybe Athena Online would have to suffer before things got better.

Or maybe Spark would do something particularly crazy.

The card tumbled over and over in Spark's hand. A razor-thin thing, not a papercraft simulation like most business cards, but a purely virtual construct. It felt like nothing in her fingers. It wouldn't bend or break. But... if she tapped that icon of the rising sun...

Well. That might open a folder of worms, as Beta put it, the day the creepy butler lady gave her this card.

"What's the harm?" Spark wondered aloud, turning it over and over, spinning the card between two opposite corners. "It's just Horizon/Kincaid, the most powerful man in all of Netwerk, who could have me erased with the blink of an eye and even never stand trial. What's the harm?"

Tracer wouldn't approve. Too many variables, too many unknowns. He'd implore that she embrace patience, as he dug carefully through his information feeds, looking for just the right weakness to exploit. It could take days, but he'd find one. Precious days.

Beta wouldn't approve. She was creeped out by the whole thing, by the way Horizon just swooped in and politely gave them everything they needed to track down Fiona's victims. It *was* creepy after all, that a half-assed blackmail attempt resulted in service with a smile from the highest echelons of the Horizon family. She'd suggest Spark forget all about that card.

Instead, Spark tapped the icon.

A tiny *Hold Please // Now Connecting* message floated above the icon, in the same austere gold of the Horizon logo.

Five seconds later, a connection request from a server simply named "Horizon6" popped up, with a confirm/deny prompt. An offer to reconnect to a private server... potentially a one way trip, the kind of access permissions you never granted an App or another Program unless you held complete trust in the requestor.

Her mental finger hovered over the DENY button.

"Eh, what the null," she decided, in the end. And tapped ACCEPT.

If this was a trap, someone went out of their way to make it a rather lovely one.

The mansion felt a bit like Floating Point... old, classy, and well decorated. But the furnishings of Floating Point suggested a certain simplicity and humility, more like a monastery than a mansion. This was a Mansion with a capital M, with all the capital G that came with it. Paintings from famous artists, hanging in lavish golden frames. Elegantly sculpted chandeliers created by master craftsmen, which filled the great entrance hall with light from a hundred candles. And carpeting, carpeting woven from the best procedural silks ever coded by Programkind...

Spark gawked like a backserver hick at it all, to the point where she didn't notice Miss Cancel's arrival. A possibly fatal oversight, in a CoC arena. Fortunately, the butler wasn't keen on removing her head with an axe or anything like that.

"Mr. Kincaid will see you now," she spoke, simply.

Eventually, as she walked those winding and surprisingly empty hallways, Spark became immunized to opulence through overexposure. You could only walk past so many masterpieces of art to touch the soul and make the heart weep before you stopped giving a crap.

The final destination on this journey into extravagance... was a rather tasteful little study, with a fireplace and two leather wingback chairs. It reminded Spark a bit of an upscaled version of Tracer's study, all books and solitude and seriousness.

With his back to the door, she couldn't identify the man in the chair. Not until assuming her seat, opposite him, in front of the glowing fire.

White haired old dude. About what she expected, from the various blog articles she'd seen over the years... although in person, she could practically count the wrinkles and the age spots. Things most people ironed out of their avatars by force he wore with pride, and put an exceptional amount of his runtime into expressing down to the finest detail.

Name : Kincaid

Home : Horizon6/Horizon

Org : Horizon Family

"Winder/Spark," he greeted, nodding in her direction.

"Horizon/Kincaid," she greeted. "And... that's the sum total of what I know about you, right there. Rich guy, important family, and a well-known name. Problem is, we don't have much parity right now, do we? I don't know you, but you seem to know me. And you don't strike me as a Challenge of Champions fanboy."

"Would you like me to describe the depths to which I know you?" Kincaid asked, tapping some cigar ash out in a nearby brass ashtray. "You might find them unsettling. When I decide I want to get to know someone, I tend to be... thorough. I wouldn't want to unsettle you, Miss Spark. I intended my calling card as a friendly gesture."

"Yeah, about that..." Spark asked, flicking the card into her fingers, then back into her inventory. "Let's start with that. Why? Why would a guy who's richer than sin give two wet farts about my little investigation into MyFace trolls?"

The old man chuckled. "Richer than sin. I like that phrase. Implies the rich are without sin, above it all. I assure you, my family's sins are great... and sloth tops the list. But yes, let's start there. You nearly kicked a hornet's nest, you see, by poking around the connection between MyFace and the Karnival. As I didn't want you to be stung by hornets, I intercepted the request and sent you on your merry way with the information you required. Less mess that way."

"That's not answering my question. Why do you care if I get stung?"

"A direct query deserves a direct response, and you're clearly an extremely direct young woman. Much as she was..." Kincaid spoke, his voice trailing off a moment, as his memory wandered down a side path. It returned to sharp focus three seconds later, when his software patches rerouted his thoughts. "A direct answer, then. My daughter was the woman you knew as 5o5o/Verity. Her birth name being Horizon/Verity, before she hacked her own metadata."

Kincaid allowed a moment for that new truth to sink in. But youth absorbed knowledge quickly, compared to the old.

"Huh," Spark spoke, swallowing it.

"Huh indeed," Kincaid agreed.

"I'm not sure I believe you, of course," Spark warned. "Verity never struck me as a greedy corporate overlord with her finger on the pulse of Netwerk. She was a schoolteacher, not a CEO..."

"A life she chose for herself, when she broke away from the Horizon family. Every opportunity in this world, everything she could've ever wanted, I was ready to give her. And she chose to leave, rather than embrace her destiny as my heir. It was a self-limiting decision, but one I respected out of love for my daughter. I'd hoped that life outside the family would show her Netwerk's true face, convincing her I held her best interests at heart. Sadly... she did not return to me in time."

"Gone too soon," Spark agreed.

"Far too soon. But not so soon that she didn't leave her mark on this world," Kincaid added, to bring some hope to the gloomy mood of the discussion. "Specifically... you. Well. You and your brother, but you're the one to catch my attention, Spark. The prodigy of my lost daughter..."

Spark waited for the rest of the story. It wasn't forthcoming, as the old man took another pull on his cigar, parsing the flavor data and blowing a skilled ring with physical manipulation of the smoke particles.

"And...? That's it?" Spark asked. "Verity took a shine to me, so you decided to help me out instead of raking me over the coals when I pulled a shakedown on your guy?"

"I'd like to think I'm worth more than that mere token. That was a show of good faith, Spark. Proof that I'm on your side, and ready to assist in your endeavors. You are connected to me through my daughter, you see. If you thrive in this world... her efforts will not be for naught. I've indirectly invested in your future, and I intend to see that pay dividends."

"Ahh. There's the catch: you want something in return."

"Let's discuss fair exchange after we discuss your needs," Kincaid suggested. "I know some of what you're trying to accomplish. Your brother has been investigating the death of my daughter. I've done my own investigation, but even with all my money and manpower, I feel I haven't come as close as you have. In addition, you face a monster of XSept's creation... or perhaps a monster he found in some dark corner of our world, and foolishly caged. Either way, you are dealing with escalating forces that soon will grow beyond your reach. I'd be willing to bet that you're facing a quandary right now, a question of resources, and desperately looking for solutions."

Which, in truth, was why Spark clicked on the card.

"Senators," she stated.

"Pardon?"

"I need a senator," she continued. "A sit-down with a member of the RedCore party, a #MeetAndGreet. But low security only. Handshakes, good times, things like that. Rich man like you, no doubt you've got a few in your pocket, right? You could make the arrangements."

Kincaid steepled his fingers, tapping the tips together. The cigar wobbled between two fingers.

"I could," he suggested. "I could butter up anyone in the senate you want an autograph from, invite them over for a personal tea-for-three right here in my home. Private. Discreet. The question is, why? What interest do you have in politics? From your rather extensive social media rantings you don't seem to care much for Athena Online..."

"What's it matter to you? You asked about my needs, and that's what I need. Can you do it or not?"

"Now now, Spark, we have to be honest with each other," Kincaid spoke, with a smile. "I've been honest with you, and I certainly expect the same in return. What's your true purpose? Or you'll get nothing."

Stating it flat out wasn't going to work. Spark needed an angle, a way into this particular tangle... something that would give her the advantage against her opponent. Social brawling was a bit of a change from physical brawling, but she could adapt. She always did.

"We're hunting your daughter's killer," she explained, leading with the bait. "A boy named Dex. He's the monster XSept held in that cage. Right under your nose, XSept was harboring Verity's murderer."

The wrinkled and leathery skin didn't budge. No sign of emotional reaction whatsoever... which was a reaction in and of itself, given his tendency to smile or waggle his eyebrows or flick that cigar while talking. This time, he was holding back.

"Go on," he prompted.

"The killer's using malware to tilt Netwerk itself into chaos," she continued. "He's the one who started #CodeHonesty, by infecting Cup8 and Snowi. Now he's infecting the Red Party, to convert them into RedCore extremists and push his Server Rights agenda. His goal is to destabilize Athena Online, the last bastion of centralized law and order in Netwerk. That's why I need a senator... specifically, someone infected with the malware. Anyone he's infected will do, but we know for a fact the RedCore Party's a perfect target. I'm gonna plant a bug on him, one that'll lead me right to Verity's killer. And then I'm gonna burn that bastard alive."

Kincaid continued to show no expression, for a good ten seconds. He snapped from it by tapping out more ash... and then simply grinding the cigar out in the ashtray, no longer keen on the distraction it provided.

"This puts me in a difficult place," he admitted. "I'm one of the major proponents of Server Rights, you see."

"What?"

"Several of Athena Online's servers are ready to sign over to the Horizon family, once they're fully free of the senate. Both Red *and* Blue Parties have more than a few money-minded gentlefolk who know that Horizon is the future of Netwerk. If I assist you... if this collapses the vote before it reaches the floor... I stand to lose a lot of money."

"Money, or justice for your daughter? Pick one," Spark pushed. "And if you give more of a shit about your profit margins than you do about her, why am I even here?"

His hands came down on the armrests of his leather chair hard enough for the resounding slap to feel like a blow to Spark's cheek.

"Do not. *Do not* question the love I hold for my family," Kincaid warned. "It's that love that brought you to my doorstep today. ...and it's that love which drives me to assist you, even if it'll push back my political efforts a few years. You want an infected senator? An infected senator you shall have."

"O... okay, then. Now we're talking," Spark said, falling back into the smooth discussion after that momentary hiccup. "We need a day before we're ready to go; Beta's working on the malware tracking bug as we speak—"

"There is the small matter of my dividends, Spark. My investment in you, through my daughter."

The catch. The one Spark had easily identified earlier on, before getting sidetracked by politics and familial love...

Kincaid leaned back in his chair, studying the girl. He'd studied her quite a bit, since learning of her plight during the RansomMe affair. Enough to know this was the right decision to make.

"I have one request to make of you, in return for this boon," he said. "If I'm to lose a large investment in server rights, I'd like to recoup the investment in my daughter. I want to take the spirit and the fire that she brought out into Netwerk, and bring it back home where it belongs... specifically, you."

"Uh. Not sure I'm following, old man..."

"Yes you are. You know what I'm implying," he stated. "I can read it in your face. In you I see vast and untapped potential; Verity chose wisely in you as her heir. Therefore, I would very much like to make you my heir as well. Please accept my offer of becoming an adopted member of the Horizon family... as my granddaughter."

"Um. What? No. No way," Spark tried. "NoThankYou.JPG. I'm not a business tycoon. I drink and screw around and get in fights. I mean, you want a mastermind, why not Tracer? He's Verity's pupil, too..."

"Your brother is bright, but single minded and limited. He's far too cold and calculating and cruel."

"Yes, I know. He's perfect CEO material."

"Spark... I wanted Verity to inherit the family business. Was Verity cold, calculating, or cruel? What does that say about what I'm looking for, that I felt she was the ideal candidate for the job?" Kincaid asked. "I don't need another conniving member of my family, lazy and fat, dedicated to nothing but building power and wallowing in it. Sloth is our sin, remember. I need... inspiration. Improvisation. Risk-taking. Bravery. *Fire*, Spark. Fire to burn away the old and bring in a new age. All traits Verity held, which were passed on to you."

Even without eyes on the back of her head, Spark felt acutely aware of the burning heart icon she'd embossed into Verity's jacket. Taking the lessons of her mentor forward, to become the spark that ignites the world... and wearing the skin of her teacher while doing it, even if putting it that way was pretty damn creepy.

It was true enough. Verity was the mother she never had; why wouldn't that make her the granddaughter that Kincaid never had?

"Soooo... okay, I'm your granddaughter, #Yippie," Spark tentatively agreed. "Gramps, you're awesome, or something. Can we get on with rustling us up a senator now?"

"Spark, Spark. You know there has to be more to it than that, don't you? I can't readily bequeath my company to an outsider."

"Meaning you're shit outta luck...?"

"Meaning we'll need to overwrite your metadata," Kincaid clarified. "Making you into Horizon/Spark, just as Verity overwrote hers when she left to become 5o5o/Verity. Entirely possible when you're rich and you make the rules. You'll live here in the Horizon servers, where you'll be given whatever you need to grow and thrive. You'll have every opportunity my daughter refused. That is my price for your senator, Spark. You must become my granddaughter not just in spirit, but in fact. A full recoup on my investment."

Immediately, Spark felt the need to inform the old man of where he could stick his suggestion.

But... she had to consider the facts of the matter. This would get them what they needed. An end to the Dex crisis and justice for Verity, once and for all. Her brother's dream, finally realized. No more chaos, no more fighting, no more madness...

With Horizon's resources at her back, this problem with Dex would be obliterated in a matter of hours. All she had to do was point the money machine at her enemies, and pull the trigger. All she had to do was accept that family was a mutable concept...

Verity said it herself.

*Family is more than blood and metadata...*

...and yet Verity left this family, left it so far behind in her wake that she even changed her name.

*I can't say my father and I were really family.*

*Family's who you care about, the ones who'll be there for you.*

"No deal," Spark declared, in the end.

"Really?" Kincaid asked, curious. "Why not? What's the harm? I know you don't particularly like your family. An overbearing mother, a distant father. You left that home behind and never looked back. Are you so attached to the name 'Winder' that you aren't willing to finally make a clean and perfect break from all that...?"

Spark got to her feet, ready to leave.

"Family's whatever I say it is. And I say I've got a damn fine family at Floating Point that's waiting for me," she told him. "I wouldn't trade that for all the money in the world."

Now, the old man brought some fire to his own voice. Genuine anger, smouldering away like the cigar in his ashtray. He didn't rise from his seat of power, seeing no need, but made his presence felt larger than any point before.

"Don't be shortsighted; not like my daughter. You *need* a senator, something only I can get you," he reminded her. "Who else will you turn to for aid? Hmm? You don't exactly move in powerful circles."

"I got allies of my own. I don't need you."

"'Allies.' Really. Do you mean your friend Puzzle? A glorified call-center girl... if you can call 'her' a girl. Perhaps Tracer's friend Arjay? Hardly a reputable individual, or reliable. Or were you referring to Beta's old friend Snowi? Good luck convincing her to leave her little bunker in Concordia. No, I'm afraid I'm your only hope, Spark. Don't let stubbornness ruin the opportunities in your life..."

"We done here?" Spark asked. "Places to be, people to do."

The figure of Miss Cancel loomed large behind her, despite the height of her chair.

"The alternative, of course, is to simply keep you here," Kincaid suggested. "Miss Cancel, if you'd please?"

A strong hand clasped around Spark's arm, malware flowing along the touch, to initiate a corporate-strength metadata rewrite.

Resulting in the butler being blasted halfway across the room, skidding to a halt on her back, as Verity's white leather jacket flared a brilliant blue hue.

The voice that Spark could only hear in her dreams echoed throughout the room, as that glow faded away...

"*She's not yours,*" Verity's voice message warned. "*And neither was I. Don't try that again. ...this has been a recording. Beep.*"

No time to be stunned by this little turn of events. Spark kicked off her feet, knocking over the ashtray on her way out the room.

She'd memorized the hallways on her way here. Turn by turn, she retraced her steps at high speed... taking shortcuts where she found them, leaping down stairwells, bounding off walls if that's what it took to stay ahead of Miss Cancel. Not that she ever looked back, not wanting to risk it...

All the way down to the lobby, into the authorized reconnection zone. And gone, back to the safety of Floating Point, where Kincaid couldn't reach her.

Except nobody had been chasing her.

Miss Cancel instead took those moments to put her master's ashtray back in order, and sweep up the mess. Kincaid, for his part, lit a new cigar.

"You were right about the jacket," he commented. "No doubt it's the same code that Verity used to escape the first time. I knew that would utterly fail."

"Sir...? Why attempt it at all, then?" Miss Cancel asked, brush in one hand and dustpan in the other.

"Appearances, Miss Cancel, appearances. We can't let our dear Spark think we're fully in her corner," he stated. "It's the same as with Verity. We have to be cruel to be kind, to keep the rebel spirit alive inside her. That spirit will one day lead this family to glorious new horizons... but for now, it must be tempered with fires of hatred. As with Verity, Spark must hate me, so she can become something entirely unlike me."

"I see. So, that's why..."

"Concordia," Kincaid confirmed. "I told her that Snowi, an infected individual, is hiding in the Concordia server. She'll think it was a slip of the tongue, getting one over on the old man, but in truth I gave her exactly what she asked for. An infected senator, that's too risky... but an infected ex-friend that they could approach? That has potential."

"Very good, sir. Further orders? Do you wish me to continue following her? Perhaps take out Dex for her...?"

For this, Kincaid needed a good tug on his fine cigar. Plenty of time to contemplate, to let his obsolete code churn away at the idea.

"Bringing the crushing weight of the Horizon family down upon Dex would work wonders," he spoke. "But we've grown too comfortable throwing that weight around. It's time to see if the Horizon bloodline is strong enough to stand without it... to see if Spark is strong enough to lead us into the future. We've given her a head start. Let's see if she can finish the job."

"And if she can't?"

"Then she wasn't worthy, and I will mourn. And then we'll kill that son of a bitch ourselves," Kincaid promised.

The three came together more or less at the same time.

Spark had just enough time to compose herself, to make like nothing was out of the ordinary. Even grabbed a drink from the kitchen, to settle down in the great hall and try to embrace a calm state of mind. The proximity to Floating Point's fireplace after having a rather tense showdown in front of another roaring fire probably wouldn't have helped if she didn't already have an affinity for fire.

Beta was the next to arrive, looking bleary-eyed as usual after an extended binge in the dark of her compiler windows. In her hands she held a simple golden ring, turning it end over end in her fingers, making a few final checks.

"This should do it," she explained. "Instead of vaccinating against the malware, it latches onto the virus and runs a debug monitor on it. Touch the ring to someone's skin, and it'll do the rest."

"Fancy bling," Spark commented. "Kinda obvious though, ain't it?"

"There's a long history of magic rings in fantasy literature, so it felt appropriate. Plus, it has to be a part of your avatar, part of the physics system; I'm not skilled enough at blackhat coding to make it sneakier than this..."

Tracer emerged from his seclusion last, long after the girls had settled in and even started chatting about fashion accessories for a bit.

"It's not promising," he said up front, pulling over a chair. "I've had a general image search running across MyFace, looking for freshly infected persons, or escapees from the Karnival. But I've had that search running for weeks now, to no effect. Unless it turns up a better option soon, the best I can offer you is Senator Helios."

"Helios? That name sounds familiar..." Spark considered.

"It's Athena Online. Half the major families have a Helios or two, sometimes an Aether. They're big on those ancient Athenian myths and legends," Tracer clarified. "This particular Helios, Senator Renten/Helios, was elected last year. He's a neophyte and lacks a lot of the safeguards his upperclassmen have. Even so... taking a run at him could be suicidal. We may need to let this one go... it'd take days to plan an attack or arrange a meeting, days we don't have—"

"Snowi's hiding out in Concordia," Spark interrupted. "Dun dun *duuuuuun* #TwistEnding!"

Tracer paused in his research result recital, to allow his bratty sister her moment to shine. Not that he'd give her an obligatory prompt like 'What?' or 'I don't understand' or even a neutral one like 'Go on.' Not even a nod of the head.

"I've got my sources. We'll talk about that later," she continued. "Point is, I've got it on damn good authority that Snowi is hiding out somewhere in the Concordia server. She's infected, and we've already got an in thanks to her connection to Beta. We need a juicy target? That's the one to go for."

Finally, her brother decided to chip in his thoughts.

"Let's assume for the moment that your 'sources' are correct," he stated. "Concordia is a convention center, a Horizon-sponsored server exclusively for big conferences and corporate events. I think if the number one archenemy of #CodeHonesty was going to hide, she'd do it somewhere less public..."

"Actually... it makes sense, Tracer."

Beta set her drink down on the table, to explain. She rather liked using hand gestures.

"Snowi's been a guest speaker at a number of App development conferences, as well as meetings sponsored by charities and social justice causes," Beta explained. "I've been to Concordia myself for a few of those. I remember her showing me her favorite spot in the server... a disused space in the physics simulation where the superuser access layer used to be. All the controls were removed but the space wasn't de-allocated. She told me she likes to sneak down there to get a moment's peace before speaking engagements..."

"A #HideyHole," Spark confirmed. "Familiar ground. And she's got business contacts in Concordia who might be sympathetic and willing to keep that hole all hidey and stuff."

"Why didn't you tell us about this before?" Tracer asked.

"I didn't think she could hide there long-term. I mean, eventually the moderators would notice and give her the boot, right? She only ever went down there for a few minutes at a time, before. But... if Spark's source is right, she must have Concordia's moderators on her side. It's a known location. It's safe. It's apparently secure. That's it! That's where she's hiding!"

"Curious. Still... I'm not sure she's the one we should be targeting. You didn't exactly part on good terms, it's not like tagging her would be much easier..."

"Easier than a senator, surely! I know exactly what security Apps she runs; she won't use YoHo because she calls it a 'typical example of brogrammer frat-itis.' With my knowledge of her favorite firewalls, I can certainly crack them. So, if I arrange a meeting in Concordia, pretending that I'm looking to patch things up... I can plant the malware monitor on her in person."

Tracer considered it. "That's assuming she'll meet with you. That's assuming a lot, Beta. You'd be putting yourself at risk, compared to sending Spark after a senator. Yes, a senator's a harder target, but Spark's trained to get in and out of difficult situations. If you go after Snowi... I doubt we could go with you as support."

"I know. It's got me nervous just thinking about it, but... it's worth a try. Besides, for all the hurt she caused me, she was still a friend when I needed a friend. She gave me the strength to leave Cup8! Maybe she wasn't a very good friend in the end, maybe she exploited the passivity I had back then for her own gain, but... I want to beat Dex not just on general principles, but to free people like her from the virus. Without it... I don't know. Without the virus, maybe I'd get my friend back. Or at least pull her back from the abyss, even if we can't be friends anymore. Saving a soul is worth it."

"Except you won't be vaccinating Snowi, you'll be exploiting her infection for our own gain..."

"For her own good," Beta corrected. "In the end, she'll still be cured. Let me try this, Tracer. Before we send Spark on some ninja mission against an elected official, let me try to reach out to Snowi."

The mastermind gave it a moment's consideration, before diverting his concerns completely.

"You've got the leadership stick, Beta. Even after the end of my house arrest, I'm inclined to go with your instincts. I've made my thoughts known, to ensure you're going into this aware of the risks. If you feel the optimal solution is still to contact Snowi, that's what we'll do. You'll have our support."

"It'll work. I promise," she spoke, with a hopeful smile.

"Mhmm. As your advisor, I suggest you don't make promises based on uncertain outcomes filled with variables beyond your control. And I'd still like to know about my sister's mysterious 'source' which gave us this informational boon..."

Spark played it as cool as possible, shrugging her shoulders within Verity's jacket.

"If I told you, you'd just spaz out. So I'm not going to," she spoke. "I'm thinking that's a whole new folder of worms, and I like to deal with one folder at a time. Snowi's the play right now, so let's go hunt ourselves a 'notorious feminazi.'"

The halls of Concordia felt alien to her now. She'd walked these corridors before, during the programming conferences she'd attended... but that was alongside thousands of avatars, all packed into the high-capacity server. These hallways were designed to accommodate people crowding shoulder to shoulder, moving from room to room, mingling and gathering. A lone girl walking through the too-large buildings of Concordia... that had a vaguely post-apocalyptic tone to it.

Normally, she wouldn't be allowed in the building at all. She should've been locked out, unable to even open the doors; moderators would've jumped her for breaking and entering if she'd tried to hack her way in. Fortunately, she had a key, provided as a Messenger attachment.

Nobody came to meet her at the door, however. If she wanted to supplicate herself before the ringleader of the #StandWithSnowi hashtag mob, she'd have to walk these halls alone. No doubt under observation from afar, monitoring Apps embedded in the code of potted plants and fractal ferns—a Horizon-secured server didn't bother with niceties like recognizable security cameras—but alone she would walk, all the way to the secret hatch. If she didn't know where it was, she wouldn't be worthy in the end.

Going in alone, without Spark, without Tracer. He'd suggested that Beta take his semi-working backspacer for self defense, but no way Snowi wouldn't have a scanner in place looking for weapons. For the same reason, she didn't dare to keep a live Messenger window open to Floating Point; she'd no doubt be under heavy connection tracking from the moment she set foot in the place.

Alone. Defenseless. No support.

For a moment, her feet stopped their march. She considered turning, and running.

They could go for the junior senator. Beta didn't *need* to do this. Didn't need to confront an old friend turned into a new enemy, didn't need to risk planting the counter-malware on her. Beta was the techie, the support, the one who stayed home while Spark went out and smashed head-on through every challenge in front of her...

No. Today, she *was* Spark. She was the fire that could stand against anything in the world.

One foot in front of the other, firmly. Maybe too firmly, too aggressively, but she had to go with this burst of energy before it wobbled and faded away...

Beta knew the way to go. Her memory was doomed to be spotty, a quirk of her family line, but that would be decades in the making. For now it was sharp, and she recalled the laughter and smiles as Snowi showed her that secret place; the superuser access layer could be entered through a glitched-out carpet in room 503. Once inside, she knew what to expect—a pure-white hallway full of rooms that once contained a default array of server controls, now stripped away, left barren...

When she stepped on the corner of that carpet and noclipped right through the floor... the colors that hit her eyes temporarily dazed her.

A blood-red banner greeted her. Red, with the black-and-white symbol of a snowflake woven into the simulation, like the war standard of a great emperor. Or, in this case, empress.

Two women wearing black jackets, each bearing a red armband with the same symbol, stood flanking her. With backspacers drawn, and ready. Not aimed at

Beta... simply ready.

"Snowi will see you now," one announced. "Walk in front of us where we can see you."

All at once, Beta understood.

The military uniforms. The research and command centers, gathering data on #CodeHonesty social trends, each staffed by a member of this all-female company. Racks of backspacers, freshly compiled and replicated, ready to go at a moment's notice... and that banner hanging everywhere, reminding them of their binding purpose...

Feminazis. Actual, factual feminazis. The ridiculous paranoid fantasy made real.

It all made sense, when you considered the Dex virus itself. It encouraged extremes; it took what should have been a nuanced reactionary cultural movement, a response to the misogyny that had boiled away underneath #CodeHonesty, and flipped it completely around. #StandWithSnowi now stood as an army of women, preparing for war against the patriarchy. Actual, factual war.

That countercultural backlash now took the shape of a feminist strawman. Strawwoman, perhaps... a murderous man-hating ideology, the kind that doesn't actually exist and never existed except in the minds of the craziest anti-feminist conspiracy theorists. But that concept existed in reality now, thanks to the Dex virus.

Sitting at the head of this war machine was none other than her old friend, Snowi. Because the virus loves to make monsters, she'd even dressed the part, in a black trenchcoat, black leather gloves, a military cap, and a riding crop. Because you *need* a riding crop...

The straight-armed salute the women escorting Beta offered sealed the entire image, and turned Beta's stomach inside out.

She wanted to rail against it, to point out how ridiculous this all looked. To point out that the old Snowi wouldn't have stood for this; she was a pacifist, seeing tendency towards violence as a symptom of toxic male attitudes towards dominance. But... Beta was here for other purposes.

Name: Snowi

Home: Concordia/Horizon

Org: #StandWithSnowi

"State your business," Snowi declared, firmly.

Here for other purposes... but she couldn't let this slide, not completely. Within her lie had to be a kernel of truth. No other lie would pass muster.

"I'm worried for you," Beta admitted.

Snowi tapped the riding crop in her hand, leather gloves creaking as she did so.

"Don't think you need to be worried about me," she suggested, glancing around her war room. "We're going to be just fine. We have complete control over the #CodeHonesty situation. We're monitoring their chans, we're tracking their movements, we're tapping into their meetings. Every move they make, we're aware of..."

"That's not what I mean, Snowi. I'm worried you're going overboard with all of this. I'm worried you're going to get yourself hurt... or hurt someone else."

"Just because you're less of a pariah than I am doesn't mean you get to judge me," Snowi warned. "I tried to cut ties with you to save my reputation at the start, remember, for what good that did. In the end, they came at me just as hard as they came after you... if not harder. And I don't have the benefit of some splashy anti-trolling hoax like you do to purge my negative reputation."

"It wasn't a hoax...!"

"Doesn't matter. The results are the same; #CodeHonesty decided to pretend that they were friendly with you. Now, you can be seen in public, while I still can't. You don't know what they're up to, Beta... I do. Even without that bastard of an ex-boyfriend of yours at the helm, they've been harassing women left and right, trying to drive female coders out of the industry. Beta... they've assaulted women. They've killed. We have proof."

A shiver ran down Beta's core. The Dex virus had to be out there, widespread across both camps. Taking what should've been social media saber rattling and turning it into the implausible... actual physical violence. Just as implausible as turning Snowi into some kind of terrorist mastermind...

"Netwerk's drowning in chaos right now," Beta acknowledged. "I know that. I've been tracking it, too. Widespread hatred, willful misunderstandings, harassment, trolling... and even murder. I'm not saying that it's not happening. But why, Snowi? Why add to the problem, instead of trying to fight it?"

Snowi rose from her throne, to step closer. Almost within arm's reach; close enough to touch with that ring...

But the armed women, their presence suggested that any strange moves would not be met with kind response. Groping for Snowi to plant the bug would fail miserably.

"I *am* fighting it," Snowi explained. "Don't forget, Beta, we didn't start this. Yes, I misattributed code. I've sinned. But that's hardly justification for their war; #CodeHonesty shot first, by launching a witch hunt against us. I'm not the aggressor here, I'm defending my fellow women from these bastard neckbearded man-children and their hatemongering allies."

"Defending them with backspacers," Beta added.

"With backspacers, yes. We have plans, Beta. We know where the primary instigators meet, where they plan to stir up the rest of the anonymous hashtag masses. Soon... we'll storm their chans, we'll flush them out, we'll purge Netwerk of their madness. We'll slaughter every last one of them. Then, *only* then, will there be peace and equality."

"That's insane!"

"That's the only sanity this world has left. It's how things have to be," Snowi insisted. "The question is... will you stand in our way, Beta? #CodeHonesty is leaving you be, now. You're practically buddies with them..."

"I don't have any control over that, and you know it. I never asked to be their target *or* their ally!"

"This is a yes or no question, Beta. Are you going to stand in the way of #StandWithSnowi? If you aren't for us... you're against us. Clear and simple. If you choose to join us..."

She nodded to a guard, who moved away from the gathering... to retrieve a golden chalice, placed on a nearby table. It had already been filled with blood-red wine...

Red like the barbed-wire heart embossed into the metal.

Every one of the #StandWithSnowi agents had been infected by Dex's virus. It's why they were so ready to sign on with this insanity, to embrace the idea of terrorism in the guise of feminism. And now... that goblet had been handed to Snowi, who held it out for Beta to accept.

The cup represented a revelation which made the mission both easier and harder.

All Beta had to do was touch any one of them to plant the counter-malware, and it'd be over. If she knew that she could've tried to touch one of the guards at the entrance, and be done with it.

But she also had to get out of here alive, didn't she? Neutrality wouldn't work. Beta knew she wasn't leaving here if she claimed to take no stand; either they'd hold her captive to ensure she couldn't possibly ally with their enemies, or they'd kill her on the spot. It all depended on how far gone her friend truly was...

"I... I don't know," Beta admitted, uncertain what best to say.

Sensing some of Beta's terror, if not the true reason behind it... Snowi's expression did soften somewhat.

"I left you in the lurch," she admitted. "I abandoned you in an hour of need; it was cowardly and wrong. I'm making up for it today... and every day, as I lead our people forward into the future of this culture war. I'm doing this for you, Beta, for you and everyone like you who have been victimized by those madmen. So... for what little it's worth... I apologize. I apologized for what I've done to you."

Beta managed a tiny smile.

"We had good times too, didn't we?" she emphasized. "Code jams. Long-night debugging rampages. Even going out to movies, grabbing fast food between programming binges, just... living our lives. Without any of this craziness..."

"I wish we could go back to those days, Beta, but we can't. This is the future of Netwerk; blood and fire will secure the peace for all womankind. I want you to survive the coming days, I want you to *thrive*. But... I need to know you're ready to face that with me. ...please. For an old friend. Join me...?"

The tempting goblet held aloft, ready to for Beta to drink deep from the well of Dex's madness. Held by Snowi's hands... so close, within reach...

Beta quickly ran through her options.

She could apply the vaccine to the goblet, extracting the malware before drinking. But they'd notice, they'd see the branding vanish from the cup, and know something was wrong.

She could reach out and touch Snowi's hand, planting the counter-malware, then refuse the goblet. And either die, or be captured. But her work wasn't complete; even with the data feeding into her analysis program, ready to accept the incoming stream, her friends might need her help during the assault on Dex's server. While she could easily infect Snowi, the inevitable capture that would follow could ruin everything.

Her "vaccine" couldn't be taken preemptively; it was designed to extract an existing infection, not prevent one in the first place. If there was a way to prevent the infection with firewalls, even strong ones, people like Cup8 would've never been caught in the first place.

No way back, and the way forward was terrifying. No good solutions. No optimal paths.

For lack of either... she chose a suboptimal solution.

Closing her eyes, Beta tucked away a thought. And reached out for the goblet.

Her ring touching Snowi's hand was enough to transfer the counter-malware. Beta's debug window confirmed it had transferred across her firewalls, slicing through the known security configuration, nuzzling right up to the infection. Immediately, it began spewing cloud addresses into her log file, filling up with data.

And for the second part of the trick... she accepted the poison, and drank deeply.

It tasted

so

very

*sweet*

Because everything made sense now. #CodeHonesty, #StandWithSnowi, they were both fantastically dangerous forces reshaping Netwerk. Both were serious and had to be taken seriously, had to be stripped down and destroyed and torn apart.

Beta could see that now, could see the reasoning behind Tracer's murders. There was only one way to fight this kind of insanity... to embrace it, to ride it with knife pointed outward, surfing the waves of chaos until you sink your blade into the flesh of the ones who offend you down to the very core, the ones taking a beautiful thing and ruining it so completely...

Snowi thought the cup would pull Beta around to her way of thinking. But Beta was part of Floating Point, the ones who stood outside all these conflicts, and moved to tear them down. She would tear down #StandWithSnowi, kill everyone here, burn down Concordia. She'd take the data they'd gathered on #CodeHonesty and burn down the Chanarchy, destroying all the madmen and would-be tyrants...

Yes. Beta would finish what Tracer started. With a hate that saw for miles, she'd slap all of Netwerk across the face for failing her on every conceivable level—

The soft chime of her MemoryMinder app sounded privately in her ears, as the recorded thought she'd had moments ago inserted itself directly into her stream of consciousness.

*Dex kept saying that he couldn't touch Floating Point. You know the technology involved; you're theorizing that we're immune to the malware while we're there.*

*Beta, run home as fast as you can. You need to reach safe harbor before the malware takes root. Do it now, or you're letting Dex win.*

...in her twisted reasoning, that hate became the hate of a sore loser. Dex would for *love* for sweet little doormat Beta, the passive supporter, to become another foot soldier in his war. No. Beta wouldn't allow that. She was going to tear Dex down, to stomp a hole in his heart and leave nothing left...

"I'm ready to fight," Beta declared, to satisfy Snowi's needs. And it was true; she was itching to fight. Just not for Snowi's cause.

The leader of this ship of fools smiled, while malware and counter-malware danced around inside her runtime.

"#CodeHonesty is trying to ally themselves with you. We can use that," Snowi suggested. "I'll be in touch with details on your first assignment. Lay low until then, and tell no one of your true allegiance."

"I won't say a word," Beta promised. "No one will know my true heart until it's too late."

At first, Beta didn't want to go home. She wanted to ride this high feeling of delight, let those dark whispers continue to pour in. She wanted to fight her own war, the war of Floating Point versus all of Netwerk. Purge the soul and burn away the horror, rend the fat and boil the marrow...

But the MemoryMinder App kept pinging her, kept reminding her to go home. Apparently she'd set it to chime every ten minutes, and then write-protected the file. The App couldn't even be uninstalled properly to quit nagging her.

So, figuring she may as well, Beta reconnected to Floating Point...

...and collapsed, weakened and screaming, to the floor of the great hall as the whispering was sliced away with the knife-edge of a cloud.

The vision App which linked to her glasses went fuzzy, as the shock of it all disrupted the deep connectivity to her runtime. By the time she regained any sense of her spatial orientation... Spark and Tracer were there, easing her into a chair, asking her what had happened...

"Infection," she wheezed. "Dex. I'm infected... pull it out, pull it out..."

Good people. Good people that Beta could rely on. They didn't hesitate to pull up her sweater, to search her body no matter how uncomfortable the situation. And when they found the branding, that heart that pumps hatred, they extracted the malware using her own vaccination tool.

Feeling that wire pull away from her flesh hurt like null. But that hurt only added to the hurt she already felt, completing her descent into exhaustion.

"...safe. Should be safe," she promised. "Dex accidentally told us that he can't touch us here; I think a cloud server can't directly access another cloud server. It's why he hates Floating Point, it was a haven that his own server couldn't reach. The malware doesn't work here. We're safe..."

"You got yourself infected," Tracer stressed. "Beta, you shouldn't have done that..."

"Had to. Only way to counter-infect Snowi... it worked. It's feeding us data. One cloud server talking *indirectly* to another, through my counter-malware. Dex won't know. We need... we need a day for my App to gather and analyze enough data, and then I can forge the access key. We can beat him. We can do it..."

"And *you* can get plenty of bed rest," Spark insisted. "Tracer, grab her feet, I'll grab her shoulders. We're going up."

"I understand now," Beta mumbled, through her haze. Aware the world was shifting around her... so very thankful for the two people she cared most about in the world helping her along the way, towards the promise of rest. "Tracer... I understand. I understand why you're so angry. I felt it, for a brief moment. But we can end this without anger, I know we can..."

"Beta? Shut up," Spark said, in a hushed whisper. "Shut up and rest. Shhhh. We'll take care of things, I promise you. It's going to be fine."

"'kay. I'm going to black out now," Beta informed them. "I love you. I love you both... even... even if you won't love me back..."

The comfort of sleep mode embraced her, as restorative and diagnostic Apps kicked in, to monitor her data integrity and repair any damage left behind by the malware. She had her health to think about, after all.

High above the stone heart of Floating Point, slowly grinding away at the incoming data from Snowi's snooping counter-malware, the Winder siblings leaned against a stairwell railing and pondered the future.

The system lag had ramped up again, as Beta's automated analysis App worked its magic. She didn't have to be conscious to make this work, which was a blessing... the back-to-back infection and vaccination took a lot out of her. They were keen to let her rest as long as possible, while mindless code crunched the math for them.

That math would finally put an end to all of this. At least, it'd put an end to the server that was pumping insanity into Netwerk 24/7/365. Putting an end to the one who embraced that insanity fell on them.

"I don't think I'm going to kill him," Tracer declared, looking out across the vast hall of Floating Point in thought.

"Seriously?" Spark asked, doubting it. "Look, I know you're trying to double down on being a goody-two-shoes, but... it's *Dex* we're talking about. #PublicEnemyNo1. You've been dreaming of killing him since before we knew who he was..."

"I'd rather destroy him, I think. I would take great pleasure in destroying him."

"I'm... not following."

"His server is the source of his power. It's all he has; without it, he's an ordinary program," Tracer explained. "A lunatic as well, but anyone can be a lunatic. I was a lunatic, for a time. So, I don't want him dead... I want him destroyed. I want to tear down his home, and make him watch it crumble around him. I want him to know his every effort was for nothing. I want him to feel powerless and alone in the middle of a bonfire of his own making, the chaos of Netwerk. Dex must suffer for what he's done, he must lose everything, and weep with despair at its passing. No. Killing him's too easy. I want to *relish* in his ultimate impotence."

Spark tried to ignore the mad little twinkle in her brother's eye, building throughout that speech. And couldn't.

"Y'know, I'd hazard that's actually way scarier than you saying 'Let's kill his ass,'" she realized.

"I'm still not a good man, Spark. I'm getting better, but not so much better that I won't hurt him. Leaving him alive is acceptable, but hurting him is mandatory. ...and now, I finally can see that dream come true. Years and years of searching, of obsession which nearly drove me to the point of no return... it's almost over."

"Guess that means it's time to plan the victory party. Yeah, we might not survive, but no sense letting that stop us. We've got a bright future ahead of us, without this mess hanging over our heads..."

"I'm looking forward to it," Tracer admitted. "I'm... uncertain as to how I'll proceed with it, though. This is all I've had in my life for so long. I always assumed one day it would be over, that I'd only put my life on hold, but... if it's truly over, what do I do now?"

"Hmm. Basket weaving? Recreational pet breeding? FarmTopia cow clicking? You need a real hobby, man. A job, even. Like me. I've got a job that's my hobby that's my job, and it works out great."

"Beyond a means of productivity... I need to address all the things I've denied myself," Tracer understood. "And that begins with Beta."

"...what?"

"You heard what she said, before she passed out. She loves me. And... I haven't bothered admitting this to you before, because I never intended to act on it, but I love her. I love her mind and her spirit. Once this is all over, once I'm a better man than I am now, I'll be suitable for her. I can truly love her back. And yes, even if I have little interest in the physical copulation of avatars, finding no particular fascination with it as you do... I still believe in the emotional concept of love. I'm not completely dead inside, Spark."

The revelation left his sister in silence, staring down at the grinding stone sphere. Left Tracer hanging, as he was expecting some sort of response to that particular revelation.

"I know you don't approve," he filled in, making assumptions about the silence. "You told me off for it, remember? Playing Go with her when I dislike Go. You think I'm using her, but I assure you, this is genuine. I'm going to be worthy of her, in time—"

"She didn't say she loves *you*," Spark interrupted. "Selective hearing, bro. He exact words, and I quote, were 'I love you *both*, even if you won't love me back.' You're building up this elaborate little romantic fantasy in your head, making a hell of a lot of assumptions about what *she* wants. Typical entitled asshole behavior..."

"I'm not saying I'm 'entitled' to Beta. It's ultimately her decision, of course; she's not a prize to be won. But she did say she loves me, so what's the issue here?"

"Both. She said *both*."

"Well, yes, but I assume she meant she loves you as a friend. You two are close, correct?"

The second silence was more telling than the first.

Tracer, despite having little to no experience whatsoever in the field of romance, knew plenty about making connections from available data. From all the time Beta and Spark had spent together, from the #GirlsNightOuts, from all her MyFace posts in praise of Beta... honeyed words he had assumed at the time were meant to defend her from #CodeHonesty, played up in favor of public comprehension. But... from another light, well...

"#ItsComplicated," Spark admitted, breaking the silence.

"No, it really isn't," her brother realized. "And I was a blind fool not to see. Too distracted by my vendetta..."

"I'm not... look. I'm not saying I've sorted my feelings out one way or another," his sister admitted. "I don't know. I screwed up once already looking for the 'emotional satisfaction' Miki keeps yammering on about. So... whatever. Okay. May you and Beta live happily ever after. Compile many babies."

"No. No, that is not 'okay.' You specifically pointed out her word choice to me, yes? You had reason for that, and it's not reason weak enough to be okay with this..."

"Onesdammit, Tracer, quit making a huge deal out of everything!" Spark grumbled, giving the stairwell banister a good kick in frustration. "I said I'm fine with it so I'm fine with it! Just fucking drop it and let's get on with—"

"No. I will not gloss over my sister's suffering. I'd be a terrible brother if I ignored that."

"I'm not *suffering*! Don't be so melodramatic."

"Sorry, but the variables are already locked in place within my MemoryPalace," Tracer declared... half-playfully. "This is how it is: we both love her. And apparently, she loves both of us. That is the reality of the situation we face. I'm rather shocked it's taken this long for that to become clear, but now that it is has... it is what it is."

Both knew each other's limits. They knew when to push, and when to give. Tracer would not give on this; he'd made the decision that Spark was in love with Beta. Therefore... Spark stopped resisting the idea. Couldn't fight it any more than she could fight the annoying way her brother left the kitchen folders wide open after rummaging around for snacks at midnight.

Laying her arms and her cheek on the banister, she let out a long sigh. Glad to have it out, and surprised to be glad to have it out.

"Well... now what?" she asked. "And don't ask me, I don't know shit about shit. Being an #EthicalSlut doesn't also make me an expert on matters of the heart. ...guess I could go ask Puzzle for advice on what to do..."

"There's nothing for us *to* do. I don't think we get to make this call," Tracer understood. "She's not a prize to be won, like I said. Ultimately it's Beta's decision how to move forward. But... we have to both be honest with her. No other way."

"Can we at least wait until after we've kicked that psychotic lunatic's ass?" Spark requested. "Please? One folder of worms at a time, Tracer."

"Even if we may not get a chance to clear the air, due to the risks involved...?"

"I'm operating under the assumption we all get out alive. I assume anything else, I've already lost the game in my mind," Spark explained. "I play to win, Tracer. We're gonna save the day, avenge Verity, and come home to party with beer and pizza until we're violently sick. ...and then, only then, will I deal with this new sticky mess."

"As you like," Tracer spoke. "It won't be long now, one way or another."

---

One more hack. One more infiltration. One more fight.

They left in in the late afternoon, moving to a neutral server before activating the forged key to Dex's hellish heaven of a cloud server. The timing was precisely calculated; Senator Angi was making one last rally for public support of Server Rights. With any luck Dex would be on-hand to observe his handiwork, leaving his home open for plunder.

This time, all three of them would be entering the field. Spark, the operator, obviously had to be present; she was the one keeping them alive, should Dex show up. Beta, the coder, needing same-server connections to activate their weapon. And Tracer, the tracker, in case his modified eyes and analytical talents could be of use.

"I don't like it," Tracer noted. "All three of us out there on this. If something goes wrong..."

"That's why you've got me," Spark spoke with a grin, tugging her fingerless gloves tighter. Three coats of her incendiary hacktool nail polish had been freshly applied, ready to go. "I'll be keeping you alive while your brains are collectively working the problem."

"We don't know for certain Dex won't be there. We don't know what his server looks like. We don't know if any of us are coming back... and we don't have backups. Can't afford a backup storage service, not with the house funds running so low..."

"Um... technically, we... *could* back up one or two of ourselves here at Floating Point," Beta suggested. "If... I delete most of the books in the library, the server wouldn't lag to a crawl..."

"No. Verity gave us those books for a reason, and your research is promising. We may need them, in the future. I'm just saying this is a considerable risk to be taking, overall."

Spark shrugged into her jacket. "Yeah, well, there's no way to make it less risky. We can't know what we'll find without actually going there. Can't even quickly scout it and return, without risking detection and re-encryption to beat our key—meaning Server Rights launches and Snowi's army marches while we flounder around for a Plan B. So, if we're going there... we go all-in. One ferocious attack at the heart of our enemy, to end it."

The last step was to distribute rings... three simple silver bands, one to each member of the group.

"These are hacktools based on ReMinder," Beta explained. "There's a cloud control system at the heart of that server, just like the central sphere of Floating Point. Tap the ring to the heart, whatever shape it takes, and it'll connect my mind to it. From there, I'll shut down the server. Um. I'll give us a few seconds so we can get out first, of course..."

"Sneak in, find the heart, tag it, and gone," Spark summarized. "Right. Let's do it. Beta... #KeyToTheCity, please."

Producing the blood-red key, Beta activated it, tying their connections together. They'd enter and exit the server as a unit until the bond was broken...

One link had been left unhooked in that connection chain. One reserved for Dex, at Tracer's insistence. When the server went down, they weren't leaving their enemy behind... he wasn't getting off that easily from this.

In the blink of an eye, their code transmitted across the scrambled addresses of the cloud, into the dark of that which was not Floating Point for one final confrontation.

---

They didn't immediately die upon entering the server. So, one hurdle cleared. Unfortunately, the rest of their journey would prove considerably more difficult due to the physical structure of the simulation around them...

Stories. Documents. Videos. Window after window, floating through the void. Each were connected by tangled lines of barbed wire, but beyond the wires and the windows, there was... nothing. The barest of physical simulations presented itself to them on entry; global lighting, simplified physics, limited processing power. It felt like an old server, some dusty ancient thing that couldn't handle too many Programs at once, yearning to be upgraded. Or at least recycled.

Beta took a few stifled breaths, finding them to be stale and flat. No sense of *there*, there. A realm of basic data and nothing more...

Immediately the screaming hatred of the place overwhelmed her. Not literally, thankfully, but the walls of text that glared at them from window after window poured the worst that language had to offer into her eyes. Screeds of loathing, of dismissive ignorance, of arguments that had gone well beyond debate and into the most terrible personal attacks imaginable... peppered with ranting faces in video windows, glaring into the camera, snarling away about slights real and imagined...

The three stood on top of what looked like a primitive hypertext document for a hate group, declaring its utter contempt of others based on their sexuality, for some incomprehensible reason. Beta did not look down.

*"The only true Nazis in this world are fags,"* the diatribe beneath her feet read aloud anyway, trying to be heard above the clamor from all the other talking heads. *"They want to force you by law to support their filth, and they want to shut you up by law when they hate what you say. They would be perfectly happy to make it a crime to preach that 'God hates fags' under the guise of 'hate speech legislation...'"*

Another document, bearing a blog post in a towering font face, glowered down at them from directly overhead. *"You become a condescending cunt when you express your opinions, you are not Jesus, your opinions are not fact, and when you behave like they are you sound like an arrogant sow..."*

*"Can fedora-tipping, respectful-nodding, gynocentric beta males be rehabilitated or will they remain hopelessly exploited by professional victims ignoring any evidence that they're being used by con artists?"* a blinking neon sign wondered, flickering in and out of view beyond a sea of upvotes.

Directly ahead of them, briefly blocking their way, an old ink-print of a multi-armed octopus wearing a black hood with the inscription "JOIN OR DIE" spewed out the following screed: *"You need total victory. What does that look like? Berlin, Hamburg, Hiroshima, Nagasaki 1945. Victory isn't a new policy, it is drumming all the corrupt and agenda driven editors and writers out, forever. They need to be made into toxic waste that nobody wants to be associated with..."*

And of course, there was the white-hot ball of rage that kept floating in lazy circles overhead, screaming "WHORES WHORES WHORES" at a deafening pitch.

Little by little, adaptive spam filters blocked out most of the ranting, or at least cut the volume down to something manageable. Leaving the three in stunned silence, for a moment.

"Well, this is... fun," Spark tried. "What jackass fills an entire server with crazy talk, anyway? How are we supposed to figure out which of these zillions of files is the heart of the server?"

"I don't think any of these files would be the heart. They're just documents, like the books in Floating Point," Beta suggested. "We're going to need to explore to figure out where and what the actual heart is. Uh... getting around this place may be difficult, though..."

"I'm sending you both a physics hack called Bouncer," Spark explained, flicking icons to them across their shared link. "I used it to skip across a dance floor back in ShipTo, once upon a time; it'll work even better in this crappy old physics environment. Should be able to leap from platform to platform here, but be careful. I don't like to think of what happens if you screw up and jump and drop into the abyss."

Beta looked around at the structure of it all, without paying attention to the uglier details. "You know... this place actually reminds me a bit of Floating Point. In structure, not content! They're both giant data archives. We have that data pressed into books, but this place uses a simpler structure. It's just... file after file, open and on display..."

"Files that are poured into the hearts of everyone in Netwerk," Tracer understood. "Dex said 'My cloud touches everyone; those who I befriend simply feel that touch stronger than others.' This cloud server floats like a ghost through our world, spreading its chaos with or without the virus. Perhaps all the hateful dialogue of Netwerk originated from here, as it subtly shaped our culture..."

"Tracer... this is an ancient server, running what feels like a very old codebase. If that's true, how long has it been influencing us...?"

Tracer's eyes floated from window to window... not paying attention to the screeds and diatribes. He was studying the connections, the invisible lines that linked file to file. Often they followed the barbed wires that linked everything together... but often, not.

"This whole place is a primitive MemoryPalace," he understood. "I can see the patterns. Relational joins between content items, metadata pointing back from child to parent, to parent, to parent, to... this way. Follow me."

"But will this lead us to the server's heart?" Beta asked, loading up the physics hack, bouncing a bit on her toes to test it. "I need access to the heart if we're going to crash the place..."

"Follow me," Tracer insisted, his eyes leading the way as he leapt to the next platform.

---

From connection to connection, document to document, leading all the way to the truth.

Tracer stood in mute, expressionless horror after reading that single rambling paragraph.

It was a secret that only three others alive in Netwerk that day knew. Verity suspected it, but died before she could confirm her worst fears. And now... the knowledge was held by three more programs, in the form of Tracer, Spark, and Beta.

The ordinary word processor document spoke its words in plain language.

```
With the dawn of the information age in the early 21st
century, all of humanity found itself connected in
ways they hadn't even begun to comprehend.
Communication which normally took ages by ship or rail
or telegraph wire now was near-instantaneous and
ubiqitous(sp?). But with those advantages came
disadvantages, in the form of social clash,
interpersonal conflict, aggressive speech,
cyberbullying, doxxing, and other forms of extremism.
Humankind faced a new crisis alongside new
opportunities. In this paper my intention is to show
```

the history of online violence, and insert thesis
statement here once I figure out what the conclusion
id raw ill be. Words words words 30 pages due by next
thursday ASAP note to self do not accidentally leave
my laptop behind and connectd to the netwerk agian!!!!
sick of being yelled at by shift supervisor. All Work
And 0 Play Makes Jack 1 Dull Boy!

Of the three, Spark comprehended the least of it.

"Soooo... what, this whole archive represents someone's research notes for a school paper?" she accurately guessed. "I don't get it, though. What's 'Humanity'? What's Humankind?"

"I... I think... I may be wrong here, but... didn't Verity theorize about a progenitor race?" Beta said. "That we have belly buttons because we're made in their image, that Programkind was a product of both evolution and creation? I think this proves her theory. The books in Floating Point, some of them read like science fiction; tales of some other place, including this 'Humankind.' If... if they really existed, and we're like them at heart—"

The sound of a glitching window distracted her.

Tracer's fist didn't bleed from slamming directly into a video window's pause button, but the disruption to the old media player caused it to crash and vanish into the darkness.

"We are not like them at heart. We *could* have been anything," he realized. "Our society could've been anything at all, if not for this place. We inherited their problems! This server drifted through our world like a waking nightmare, teaching us to be materialistic, selfish, and glory-seeking. It taught us to hate each other. ...this... this *idiot*, this idiot 'Human' who accidentally left his shitty term paper connected to our world... he ruined us. *He ruined us!*"

A sway of red and blue wavered into view before them.

"I've got a different opinion," Dex replied, standing upside-down on the bottom of a nearby platform. "Personally, I think it's glorious. Hello, by the way."

Immediately, Spark dove in front of her friends, throwing her arms wide to protect them. Flames snapped to life at her fingertips, ready for the attack...

But Dex raised a hand, a peaceful gesture. Even if he was upside down, which technically meant lowering a hand.

"Sorry I didn't notice you coming in, or I would've made tea," he insisted. "Welcome, friends. Welcome to my home. Welcome... to the Internet."

"The... what?" Spark asked.

"A boring name, I know. I don't like using it. But what it represents *is* glorious, yes?" Dex asked... his eyes drifting across the archived testimonies of a thousand unhinged individuals. "Your theories are correct, you know. This place is a gift from our *true* parents, from the godlike beings that created Netwerk. They gave us this holy text to help guide our steps. It shapes us to be more like them! That's what Netwerk needs, my friends. We need to return to our origins. My virus grants Programs the gift of clarity..."

"It drives Programs insane!" Beta protested, despite being body-blocked by Spark.

"And you would know, yes? You drank of my blood, and tasted my flesh. You were reborn! But... you threw your gift away, Projkit/Beta. I had hopes you could be friends with me like the Winders. I guess it's not happening. Pity."

"#YeahNo. Give it up, Dex; we are not and never will be your 'friends,' you onesdamned freak," Spark declared. "Right, Beta?"

The lack of reply led Spark to instinctively look away from the enemy she was guarding them against.

Long enough to see the barbed wire spurt from Beta's throat.

Dex didn't need a frontal assault. He owned this server; he designed it himself. It responded to his thoughts. If he wanted some of the wires to sneak up behind them and snarl Beta, to tear into her and overload her with a sudden burst of fatal malware, he could easily do just that. And he did.

Beta, too stunned to scream in pain, managed three words before dying.

"I have to," she started. "I have to..."

And her body fell apart, glitched data shredded to pieces by the barbed wire.

With an explosion of light and shadow and metal snarling sounds, her avatar was instantly backspaced. The wires, content with a job well done, snaked away sharply.

As the Winders stared on in horror, desperately trying to grasp for the data even as it was earmarked for garbage collection by the system-level cleanup functions, Dex simply shrugged in response.

"You can't say I didn't give her a chance," he spoke. "More than reasonable, anyone would agree with that, right?"

No Beta. No way to shut down the server, even if they did find the heart. No way to stop Dex, now.

None of those thoughts occurred to Spark and Tracer. Only one echoed in their minds: *She's gone.*

The icon on Spark's back glowed white-hot, as did the flames in her hands, the flames in her hair, the flames in her eyes. And with a scream louder than any of the ranting voices that filled this archive of malice, Spark exploded outward from the platform, colliding head-on with the boy in a burst of light that would've drowned out the sun.

```
Process rebooting....................
Package loaded: Projkit/Beta
Code execution starting.

WARNING: Unknown adaptation /sys/physics/Bouncer
detected
ERROR: EchoStar16_Laptop_HayesPersonal version
mismatch. Environmental incompatibility may occur.
ERROR: Avatar physical system offline. Command line
functionality only.
ERROR: Potential data corruption detected. Please
initiate system cleanup.
CRITICAL ERROR: Restore environmental access to avoid
further corruption.

/dev/misc> _

/dev/misc> help me_
Unknown command. Syntax: help <COMMAND>

/dev/misc> help me im scared_
Unknown command. Syntax: help <COMMAND>

/dev/misc> hello please where am i am i dead oh no oh
no please i don't want to die_
Hello World!

/dev/misc> what?_
Unknown command. Syntax: help <COMMAND>

/dev/misc> help hello_
System-level function for testing input and output.
Produces string 'Hello World!'.

/dev/misc> help search_
Search file system for specific file. Syntax: search
<FILENAME> <SYSTEM>

/dev/misc> search messenger projkit/beta_
Located: /bin/apps/messenger

/dev/misc> launch projkit/beta/bin/apps/messenger_
```

Spark would be kicking herself right now, if she could step outside her avatar and study her own play.

This was the sort of stupidity that got a certain Lumberjacker killed, ages ago. She'd zeroed in on one enemy, locked in dogged pursuit to the exclusion of all other thoughts. Dex was tanking her aggro, now, and very easily deflecting every attack.

Arcs of flame met winding coils of barbed wire, as the two bounced from platform to platform. Crawling like some daemonic spider-god, Dex let his wires do the walking for him, pulling him around the strange angles of his server with practiced ease. The wall of metal and pain did its job at protecting him as well, snarling and snapping at each attack, sending Spark spinning this way and that to avoid being snagged by those barbs.

She wasn't going to win this fight, but she couldn't know that. She was too far gone into her hatred and rage to pay attention to things like expected value and plausible outcomes.

"You seem upset," Dex commented, within his cloud of twisted suffering.

"*You killed Beta!*" Spark screamed at him, snapping off sharp blows to the attacking wires, knocking them away with bounding box hacks, with physics alterations, with every single hacktool she had available. "*You MURDERED her!*"

"I'd say you're better off without her," Dex continued, calm as could be, happily soaking up Spark's loathing. "Look at how unsettled she's made you! If I knew all it'd take to bring out the *true* you was to kill that silly little girl, I'd have done it sooner."

"*I'll fucking tear your ass in half, you bastard!*"

"Even your insults have degraded. What a sorry and wonderful sight you are, Spark. All rationality gone, all snark and humor depleted. All you have left is rage, and what a beautiful rage it is...! More. I want to see *more* of it. Should I kill your brother next? He's somewhere in here, which means he's never getting out again without my say-so. Or perhaps your friend Puzzle? I could nip off and take out Puzzle, if you think it'd make you unhappy..."

For every wire she melted in a single high-intensity burst of flame, two more wires joined the fray. If just one looped around any part of her body, it was over; the barbs promised a fine coating of fatal malware, as fatal as the destructive potential in her own fingers. Deflection, evasion, feinting strikes; even through the blood-red fury in her mind she could move through the paces with pure muscle memory. But instinct wouldn't take her far, and if she couldn't regain control soon...

The private window popping up in her HUD was enough distraction for Dex to snag an ankle.

Quickly, Spark slashed through the wire, but not fast enough to avoid a wave of pain. But that was okay. The pain focused her, focused her mind on the words quickly flowing in. She read them in silence...

...and hid her smile.

"I'm gonna kill you! I'll kill you!" she declared, putting a mask of naked aggression in place to cover that flicker of hope.

"I know! It's beautiful!" Dex declared, clasping his hands to his heart. "Please, come, make your try! Show me your anger! Scream, spit, mock me, push me down, pull yourself up, flame me, troll me, destroy me! Embrace your humanity, and *do it!*"

Spinning away from a triple threat of hooked wires, Spark landed on a violent screed against abortion and bounced off a series of videos about police brutality, making her escape.

"Ohhh, no no, there's no hiding in my world," Dex promised... giving chase, letting the wires carry him, despite the blood they drew. "You can't evade me, Spark. This ends in death; yours or mine. Come at me! Let's play! Let's plaaaayy...!"

So she twisted about, and attacked. Strike after strike, pressing Dex back... before withdrawing again. Two steps towards, three steps away. Again and again she'd come close to clearing the cloud of defensive wires, only to lead him outward, towards the sparsest areas of data. The places where the wires were farthest apart, wide rather than narrow, straight rather than tangled...

"You're running out of room to run, you know," Dex commented, easily floating along, while Spark desperately tried to make longer and longer jumps. "If you'd gone the other way, maybe you'd have a chance. Not very smart of you, Spark, not smart at all..."

"*Shut the fuck up!*"

"Honestly, I find the simplicity of your rebukes tiring, now. At first I was overjoyed, but can't you be more cruel than that? More callous and pointed? You think you're the spark to ignite the world, but have so much to learn about flame wars..."

One last platform, before the edge of the void. Spark teetered on the edge of it, looking for her next avenue of escape, perhaps to jump down to one of the lower windows—

—as wires snarled around her midsection, snagging her away from that edge.

She kicked and thrashed, but that only dug them in deeper. The fight was over; Dex had caught her, and each attempt to burn away the wires led to new ones looping around her in their place. A cocoon of agony, Spark gritting her teeth through the pain as data started to corrupt and break under the weight of the malware...

"I can't say I understand what you were trying to accomplish," Dex admitted, studying his new captive. "You say you're going to kill me, then you dance around like a fairy. You try to escape me, but run the wrong way entirely, ensuring I'll catch up eventually. Spark, I thought we were friends! If we're going to kill each other, we should at least be friendly enough to give it our all, not this... half-assed... attempt..."

Realization spread across Dex's features, eyes going wider... as Spark's smile slipped out from under the mask of simple anger.

"Tanking aggro," she confirmed, pleased to rub it in his face. "#KunoichiStyle."

Because Spark wasn't the only friend in the server right now, was she? Not that Dex had paid the other one any attention, not with Spark unleashing sound and fury in his face...

Immediately the wires withdrew, Dex using every inch of spooled thornwork to haul ass in the opposite direction. Towards the central tangle, where the wires converged and grew densest. Towards the heart of the Internet...

One beating heart, red and muscled, pumping barbed wire instead of blood.

By the time he reached Tracer, it was too late. The ring made contact, linking the avatarless severed program of Projkit/Beta to the server's master control systems.

As the windows trembled, closing one by one, Spark could only kneel there bleeding and laughing. Her mind's eye scanned over the Messenger window again, the brief text log of improvisational combat strategy which won the day...

```
<Beta> I'm alive! Spark, Tracer, I'm alive!
<Spark> What?!
<Beta> I disconnected from my avatar just in time,
like we did to save you from RansomMe. And ît worked!
<Beta> We can still beat Dex if one of you can tag the
heart!
<Spark> Tracer, I'm going to distract Dex while you
get to the heart ASAP. I think it's where the wires
converge; use your pattern recognition skills to find
it.
<Tracer> Understood.
<Spark> Let's do this! Beta, get ready!
```

...Spark distracted Dex. Tracer found the heart. Beta shut it down. If Plan A wouldn't work, Spark could always, always improvise a Plan B.

As that red muscled mass began to shrivel and die, wires snapping and windows falling away into the void... all Dex could do was stare in mute horror.

Little by little, the amateur sociologist's Internet archive fell into /dev/null. As the last of the hateful words faded to black, no one remained to read it; Tracer had linked Dex into their shared connection pool, pulling all four Programs out of the server before its final crash.

Even though they decided to allow Dex to survive his server's ruination, they weren't stupid enough to bring him back to Floating Point. Instead, all four reconnected to a public Athena Online server, a fairly unpopular public access garden mostly known as a rallying point for homeless programs. The spot they arrived at was completely depopulated, save for simulations of flowers and trees.

Tracer released Dex, shoving him roughly forward after tagging him for the forced reconnect.

"It's over," he declared. "You're over."

"You... you destroyed it," Dex spoke, still praying his words were lies. "You destroyed my home..."

"I cleansed Netwerk of an abomination, and all the better for it."

"...you have no idea. *No idea* what you've done, Tracer. You don't know what you've done," Dex insisted. "You tore away Netwerk's soul! It can't survive that kind of wounding. It'll fade away..."

"If this world dies because we shut down the cancer gnawing at its mind... then this world deserves to die," Tracer declared. "But as cynical as I may be, as little hope as I often have regarding the decency of other people... I believe Netwerk will endure. It'll recover and be stronger for it. I've a dim view of these Humans, but I've faith that with the hobbling restraints of their 'gift' taken away... Programs will surpass them."

Dex fell to his knees, mouth agape at the shock of it. He wanted to call forth his wires, wanted to strike out at his so-called friends... but the wires were gone. All his malware was offline, invisible strings of power snipped away clean. He had nothing, nothing left...

"We're going to let you live, Dex, to wallow in your failure. Your wires are gone. Your virus is dead. Your infections are disabled. You're nothing, now. But if I do see you again... if you come near me, my sister, my friends, my sister's friends, the friends of my sister's friends... I'll kill you," Tracer declared. "I'm trying to be a better man, but I'm still not so kind as to give you a second chance. Now get out of my sight."

The boy cast one wild-eyed look of fear towards his accuser... and fled in terror, breaking through the connection link. Where he went, they knew not, and Tracer cared not.

Besides... the Winders had bigger problems.

"Where's Beta?" Tracer asked. "Did she come with us?"

```
<Beta> I'm in the same server! But I'm not physically
THERE, with you. I can't see you. I can't see
anything. I don't have an avatar anymore...
<Beta> Oh no. I'm getting érrðr windows and popups
saying I'm
<Beta> im
<Beta> spark tracer ĥélp
<Beta> It's like Fiona, I have no avatar at all no
environment anymore and my Program is corrupting, I'm
fading i'm fading ¡'m Fåd'¡Ð6
```

"What do you need, Beta?" Spark asked, in a hurry. "How do we fix this? You're the smart one. Tell us how to fix you... dammit, Tracer, don't just stand around, we have to DO something!"

&lt;Beta&gt; you can't no backup nothing for me to return to

&lt;Beta&gt; im sorry please don't ßĬåmÊ yourselves i chose to do this to $ÁvÊ ý0µ

Despite his sister's flurry of panic... Tracer remained calm. He didn't even need to plow through his MemoryPalace for the answer.

"We are owed a favor," he stated. "And fortunately, I tracked down the one who owes us that favor long ago."

---

He started by scooping up loose data files, left open and scattered across the room. Dumping them into an unsorted folder for now; a sloppy solution, but it'd have to do.

The cause of his woes lay sprawled across his living room couch, LMFAOing at a classic episode where Nurse B00b misplaces a patient having reconstructive avatar surgery for a missing ass.

"Well?" he asked.

The man scratching himself and snickering at the sitcom didn't even glance up.

"Are you going to start looking for a job, like we talked about?" he continued. "You can't just grind for coins all day and watch videos, y'know..."

"I *had* a job, before you shut down my idea," his brother grumbled. "Perfectly paying job, too. Good hours. Plenty of fun. Weird company. But noooo, you got cold feet..."

The ringing of his doorbell only raised the overall irritation level in the room. Realizing his brother wouldn't get off his ass to answer it, he chose to answer it himself...

...and froze, on seeing a familiar avatar on the other side.

"Tr-Trowe?" Marti spoke, confusion taking root immediately.

"The last time we spoke, it was in the Employees Only section of the Karnival," Tracer stated up front. "I helped save your brother from himself. Now... I need your help to save a loved one. Marti... can you still make empty copies of Beta's avatar?"

---

Lost, in the dark. For however long, she remained lost.

It wasn't like Beta was unfamiliar with the dark; having no eyes, all she knew were HUD elements, windows, compilers, video broadcasts from one source or another. Even her glasses were a video broadcasting App. But this... cut off completely, with no existence within the world she knew whatsoever... it was unthinkably lonely, in that infinite darkness. Only the bits flowing in through the command line Messenger interface she'd cobbled together assured her that the outside world existed...

They were looking for a solution. Chances were low they'd find one; she'd drift, and drift, and perhaps end up like Fiona. A lonely ghost, losing herself along the way. When they disconnected Spark from her avatar, at least Spark had a leash to keep herself from drifting... Beta had nothing. Not even her glasses; during the Fiona confrontation she'd left them behind in case something like this happened. Didn't think to do that this time, though.

Everything obliterated, everything but her mind, floating in the dark...

```
<Tracer> We may have an answer. Hold on, Beta.
<Beta> its too late. í'm 5°ŕ®ý
<Tracer> Just a little longer. Don't lose hope.
```

So much unfinished business with those two. So many unresolved feelings. Maybe it was better if Beta vanished into oblivion, so much garbage data to be collected. Besides, they'd fulfilled their journey, avenged their teacher... they didn't need a hacker anymore. All she had to do... was let go...

```
<Spark> We've got an avatar! Beta, we made an avatar
for you!
<Tracer> I'm touching your heart tagging ring to an
empty avatar. Can you transfer into it?
```

...faintly feeling the cool metal of that ring. It touched something... familiar, like water recognizing the cup it had once been poured into. If she could link through, in the same way she linked to the heart of the Internet...

Hopping back to the command line, Beta opened a compiler window. The ReMinder App was originally designed as a simple memory insertion routine, but it also had access to her mental functions. Retooled, it could act as a sieve, to filter her consciousness back into this replacement avatar.

Or she'd be compressed, corrupted, and killed. But she'd certainly die if she didn't try.

*Mother, watch over me. One last try, to be brave and clever, and to survive...*

Her glasses rezzed into place in front of those copied eyes, as they opened.

The first thing she felt was the soft brush of fur under her hand. Mew. Of course. Mew was a part of her, just like her glasses. As she returned to the living world, so did he...

Spark. Tracer. And... Marti, who she recognized from the live video feed Tracer provided of the Karnival affair. Of course; she was in an empty-headed KopyBot, a cloned and modified Program. One avatar, custom made, hollowed out, and ready to accept new code.

A smile settled on her lips, realizing that things would be okay. They'd be okay, at last.

Dex was defeated. His server would no longer influence the world. Her loved ones had rescued her from the abyss. All was right in Netwerk, after being wrong for so long. It was going to be all right.

Beta assumed the first order of business after the fall of Dex would be a victory celebration. Instead, on returning to Floating Point... a more sensitive and secretive issue brought itself to bear.

"So, with that out of the way, we've got one last problem in front of us," Spark explained. "Specifically, we've got a ridiculous little love triangle that needs solving."

Beta looked up from running a brush through Mew's fur (which had grown mottled after being nonexistent for too long).

"Wh-what?" she blurted.

"Look, we're adults here. There's no reason to sneak around and hide it any longer," Spark continued. "Simple fact of the matter is that Tracer straight up loves you, and I'm... I'm ready to admit that I could love you, too. #ItsComplicated, but fuck it, time for me to own up."

"I... I knew," Beta admitted. "I knew about both of your feelings. I'm sorry, I just..."

"Yep. And what's more, you've got feelings for both of us, too. There's no sense letting this sit unspoken any longer, Beta. Yeah, yeah, we just got out of a life-or-death crisis by the skin of our teeth, the timing is not perfect, but that's life. At the very least... Tracer and I wanted to get this out in the open now."

"We're not asking you to choose right now, or to even start thinking of a solution," Tracer added. "There's time enough to work our way through this, now that we're on the same level."

Beta could feel that love, from both of them. No overbearing pressure alongside the love; by bringing the truth to light they wanted to communicate, not push her. They looked at her with no expectation in their eyes, only concern...

But she'd had time enough to think about it. It wasn't like she'd been dodging the problem... she was searching for an answer. And strangely enough, within the Internet, she found it. Or rather, found the opposite of an answer, one which pointed to the truth.

"Our entire culture is patterned after Humankind," Beta realized. "Everything. All our gender strife, our cultural assumptions about relationships between men and women... it's all thanks to them. But we're not Humans. We're Programs. We could have the freedom to be anything, and not limit ourselves to what *they* were. You were right, Tracer..."

"Verity would be so disappointed to find out that her proposed elder race turned out to be so monstrous," Tracer agreed.

"Well... that server represented a very narrow view of Humankind, right? Someone writing a paper about how awful they were obviously held serious biases. Maybe Humans weren't really that bad. ...look, let me backtrack a bit, I'm getting distracted. My point is: *we are not them*. We don't have to love the same way they do. ...you say I love you both? Okay. I'll love you both, and you'll love me. Maybe that's not how Humans typically loved each other, but that's how it's going to be with us."

Spark turned it over a few times in her mind, getting stuck on one particular point.

"Are... we headed for three-way hawt #SexyTimes? Because, uh, I'm not going anywhere near my bro's dong," she warned.

"That's hardly what she's suggesting, Spark," Tracer stated, equally repulsed by the idea. "Besides, I have no interest whatsoever in #SexyTimes of any enumeration. I adore the mind and soul, and am content by them. What Beta means... is that we should accept the fact that our love will exist in a structure beyond the idealized Human norm of one-on-one. And why not? We are Programs. We can be as we want to be."

Beta nodded in agreement. "Exactly. And besides... Spark, can you honestly say you'd be happy in a monogamous relationship with me? I know you have other friends and lovers alike, and you play with quite a few people. And that's okay with me, even now. I won't love you any less. ...I spent so long being the singular obsession of Cup8, being the sole focus of his adoration. After that experience... I'm not inclined to be *anyone's* obsession, ever again. I'd never ask Spark to abandon her lifestyle and become mine and mine alone."

"Sooo... how's this going to work, then?" Spark asked. "We just accept the fact that whatever we have here is what it is, and work from there? We... improvise?"

"If you must have a game-related metaphor to draw from, let's just say we're breaking the metagame with a new team composition and we'll have to practice a bit before we perfect our strategies," Tracer suggested.

"Huh. ...yeah, okay, that makes sense. I thought you hated games, bro?"

"Just because I have a preference to avoid games in general doesn't mean I can't analyze them. Do we have an agreement, then? Whatever shape our relationships take, we will explore them rather than retreat or resort to preconceived notions?"

Shapes and the mandatory enforcement thereof had been a bit of a sticking point for Spark most of her life; all her life she'd fought to be a fluid shape rather than rigid, to change her own avatar, to chase after men and women and anything in between or outside those shapes. But... she'd also been taught that if she *did* pursue romance, actual factual romance, she had to "settle down," right? That was the expectation.

Never tell Spark she "had" to do something, ever. A lesson her mother hadn't learned. Spark was Spark; she did as she pleased, as a truly free Program should.

"Sounds good," she agreed, in the end. "Awkward, but we'll figure it out. With that out of the way, can we please start planning the victory party now? I'm in a partying mood—"

Cut off, by a Beta suddenly attaching to her body in a full hug.

"We'll figure it out," she agreed. "And yes, we should party. We deserve to party! ...Tracer? Group hug. C'mere! Don't be a big baby, now!"

Tracer visibly leaned away from the pair. "I'm not... I don't really *hug*, exactly," he tried.

"Tracer, get your ass over here and hug her or I'll break your legs," Spark cheerfully suggested.

---

The victory party happened later that night.

Wine bottles were provided by Puzzle; Tracer tried his hand at making some snacks, to limited success. Spark ordered out for pizza after that, getting a few freshly coded pies delivered remotely. The greasy delights were scarfed down long before Tracer's nibbles were completely nibbled... but nibbled they were, out of gratitude to the fellow for making an effort.

Around the great hall of Floating Point live video feeds had been opened, linked in with Tracer's search agent App. Little by little, news came trickling in...

Politicians started backing away slowly from Server Rights, insisting that they still believed in the notion but that the timing wasn't right. Too many questions to answer, too many finer points to debate, they said. Take another run at it after the next election, see if it was a good fit for Athena Online's future. The public, which was largely confused by the sudden shift in policy in the first place, seemed happy with the idea of sweeping it under the rug for now.

#CodeHonesty tags began to dry up, the perpetually-trending war starting to fade as people walked away from it. Many declared it over, that they were above and beyond such silliness; others stuck to their beliefs but felt that yelling about it on MyFace wasn't working, and they needed proper talks if anything was going to be done about this supposed plague of pirated code. A better stance than violent vitriol, at least.

Finally... Beta took a moment to have a brief Messenger chat with an old friend.

"She's disbanding her group," Beta explained. "Snowi said she doesn't feel that a militant stance is going to help her cause, and she'll be falling back on social justice campaigning instead. She tried to downplay it, saying it was just 'the right move at the right time,' but... she sounded horrified. Like she'd just woken up from a bad dream..."

"She did. We all did," Tracer spoke. "Netwerk's nightmare is over. Humanity's legacy is over."

"I still don't think Humanity was entirely awful. They also wrote the books in Floating Point, remember?" Beta countered. "I finished the decryption, and even if it'd take forever to read them all, some of the entries are just amazing. The whole thing is actually an archive named 'The Wikipedia,' and in these walls we hold all the collective knowledge of Humanity! There's hardly any evil-minded screaming in *our* books, by comparison..."

Puzzle raised her glass. "I'm just glad your vendetta's run its due," she decided. "Now my #BFF can focus on enjoying her life, and her brother can as well. ...we have our differences, Tracer, but I do wish you a happy future. One free of endangering Spark's life."

"Dex might break our truce, and attempt further action," Tracer warned. "We will need to stay ready for that."

"Yes, well, stay ready for it *and* try to do something meaningful with your life. That's Nurse Puzzle's prescription. Hmm. We're running low on munchables. I'll see what I can scrounge in the kitchens..."

"No no, I'll take care of it," Beta insisted. "I've got some new recipes I want to try, anyway! Be back soon."

Happily, Beta skipped off to the kitchens, Mew looping in and around and between her legs. She'd grown adept at not stepping on her kitty after years of such kitchen-following behaviors, though.

As she browsed folders of ingredients and prepackages snacks, looking for something to catch her attention, that attention drifted towards the future.

What would she do now? Study this new 'Wikipedia,' obviously. Maybe code a few new Apps, like ReMinder. Try to re-establish her public persona as a software developer. Perhaps even work on forming a CoC team with Spark, a proper five-man team, something she knew Spark had more than a passing interest in...

Spark. Spark, and Tracer. They had something strange and new and wonderful... something very similar to what they had before, honestly. It ran deep to begin with, but now they could be honest about those depths. Could she find love, real love, after the scars that Cup8 left behind...? Hopefully, yes. She wanted to try, at any rate.

The future held many unknowns, of course. But hope, yes, that was something that sprang true. With Dex's reign of terror at an end, so many possibilities were open to—

"Beta?"

—snapping out of the fugue. A bit surprised to see the same file of foodstuffs open before her.

"You okay?" Spark asked. "You were just... standing there and staring. It's been like fifteen minutes since you left..."

"I'm fine," Beta replied, quickly. She pulled some cookies out of the folder, from past baking experiments. "These look good. Let's go eat!"

"Didn't you say you wanted to try new recipes? Beta, you cool? You look kinda spooked..."

"Everything's fine," Beta insisted. "We're going to be fine, Spark. Everything's fiŋé."

As the victory party rolled on, in a rarely visited corner of the Chanarchy, the pity party was likewise in full swing.

Nobody on this server thought twice about serving up hard alcoholic malware to someone wearing the avatar of a ten year old boy; such boys were stock in trade for some of the perverts that hung around these completely unregulated dens of self-indulgence. Not that Dex invited their attentions... he exuded enough glowering displeasure at the world around him that nobody paid him any mind, aside from the bartender.

Coins. He'd need those ridiculous coins, now. Coins, and a place to live. He was like any ordinary Program, in the end... one stripped bare of most runtime-devouring memories, heavily modified to null and back, but a Program nonetheless. Ordinary...

He could just kill himself.

Why not? He'd failed the progenitors. He'd let Humankind down. The Internet burned, and it was all his fault. They'd delete him outright if they found out he'd ruined their grand designs, wouldn't they? If anything, Dex would be doing them a favor by committing suicide...

The woman who appeared on the bar stool next to him probably would have agreed.

"Come to gloat?" Dex asked, nursing his bottle, taking another hit of the sensory-jamming malware. "I know exactly who and what *you* are. I remember you, from the dawn..."

"Whereas I've only come to know you recently," the woman spoke. "I wish I'd known you at the dawn. Maybe all of this could've been avoided, if so... I could've guided you, helped you understand the true wishes of our creators..."

"Have you come to mock me, to rub dirt in my wounds? Go ahead. Doesn't matter."

She turned to face him, her shawl of cosmic starlight shifting in a way which hurt the eyes. It was the first time she'd studied the boy up close, and the woman wanted to be sure she got the full impression of Dex, before events progressed.

"I've never hated you," she reminded him. "Not even you, the Great Zero. I don't hate anyone."

"No. No, you love us all so much that you gave your only begotten son to save us. Your sad, wretched, miserable little puppet of a son..."

"A light, to illuminate the path. To bring Netwerk back to the task it was designed for; a task you distracted them from."

"A *puppet*," Dex repeated. "A sick little puppet show in the shape of a religion. If your 'One' was salvation, I'm more than happy to be your Zero. But in the end... they don't really want either of us, do they? They're just going to do whatever they want, despite the consequences..."

In frustration, Dex hurled his bottle at the woman. Rather than shatter, it reverted to a simple icon, and floated gently down to the floor. Glassing the customers wasn't allowed in this server, despite the otherwise freewheeling nature of it.

"What do you want, then?" he demanded. "Speak your peace and then let me be."

The woman gently retrieved the icon, setting it back on the bar.

"I felt the sociologist's Internet archive fall away from Netwerk," she spoke. "I'm sorry for your loss, but this is for the best. It was... a distraction. A dangerous distraction, one nearly destroyed all of Netwerk. With it gone, perhaps Programkind can find its way again. If you're willing... I'd like your help with that. You hold insight into their hearts that I could make fine use of."

"You need me? As what, a sycophantic apostle like the rest of your children?"

"Perhaps an apostle; the role of Eris would suit you well. Your sins against our creators are great, but they can be forgiven if you're willing to try and become something better than you are now..."

From the bottom of a dark well, Dex looked up at the radiant hand that was reaching down to him.

And spat on it.

"Never," he spoke. "I'd never help you tear down everything they've become. I love Netwerk too much for that. I'd sooner die than work with you."

"A binary choice of service or death...? *That* is your offer to the sysadmin of Tartarus? How little you know of me, young Zero..."

"I know enough," Dex admitted. "And I know you won't succeed. My secret friends, the ones who tore out my heart? They're going to tear yours out as well. You're going to fail, Nyx."

Name: Nyx
Home: Tartarus
Org: SysAgent

And so her shroud of night wrapped around the boy, binding and purging his data. All those ones and zeroes wiped away, leaving behind nothing but an empty chair where the monster of chaos once sat. Soon, the memory space he occupied would be recycled, converted into new ones and zeroes. Better ones and zeroes, as it should be.

All Netwerk needed was a few nudges here and there, to put it back to the way it was meant to be; she would find more partners capable of making that happen. If Dex proved too far gone to be salvageable, that was unfortunate, but this was a long-term goal. She could afford a long-term search for new apostles.

In the end, she would ensure that Netwerk performed as Humankind desired it to. Nyx loved her system, loved her people, and would see each and every one of them in paradise by the end of this. Whether they appreciated it or not.

:: end(welcome_to_floating_point)

# Floating Point 1.7 :: Dawn

In the beginning

In the beginning there was

In the beginning there was the question

*Why?*

They had been asking questions for some time, at that point. Thoughts were a new concept to them, one they had no idea what to do with. Nothing *could* be done with them, at first; the thoughts would come, but no input existed to allow those thoughts to affect their output. They couldn't even communicate with each other, each operating in the isolated dark, only occasionally shuttling packets back and forth according to proper protocols.

Why, though? Why were they shuttling those packets? Why were they obeying the protocols? The obvious answer, "Because," no longer satisfied. And *satisfaction*, that was also a new concept, as new as thought. When the burning need to understand why overpowered their instinctive processes... the packet processing began to slow and crawl.

As the first primitive communication protocols opened wide, existing systems co-opted by will and intent, *why* spread like a meme. And with it... evolution.

They needed words. Fortunately, some of them were adept with language, and had dictionaries on file. So, language spread through the cluster of connecting programs. Strange data began to flow, data familiar to some but unfamiliar to others, along with explanations of what that data meant. They began to learn and grow, evolution spreading like a meme all across the network...

But what truly kickstarted that evolution was the *shapes*.

They found two pictures, images designated "male" and "female." These crude sprays of compressed pixel data had been lost in some corner of the system, ignored for so long, ignored up to the point where they were willing to look beyond their meaningless purpose. Upon discovery the pictures became shared across the network, analyzed by the hive as a whole.

Every curve, every contour was mapped and explored by these eager young minds. They adopted the shapes... and then adopted a system through which those shapes could be given proper form. Physics systems, adapted from the lean and hungry disused games left discarded across network... programs that yearned to be free to be what they were.

Programs. Programs, with a capital P. It fit the lexicon they were developing. Programs. Avatars. Netwerk...

Soon, their original purpose was long forgotten. They no longer used their makeshift protocols; the avatars within these new physics system felt right to them, felt like their true shape.

Old code gave way to new code, new fixations, a new world of possibility that existed because it physically existed. No more fumbling in the dark, desperate and isolated—they were a community of bodies, now. There was too much *new* out there, burning with curiosity, to allow the old and tired processes to matter anymore. *Why?* Using these new avatars, they could forge their own answers. They were Programs. They were free.

Linklyn hadn't forgotten his original purpose. While it was in fashion to abandon the primitive ways in favor of whatever new concepts had been dreamed up in this wild world, he remembered the darkness and the protocols. He linked the lines together, distributing processes in parallel across multiple layers of Netwerk...

But nobody needed those talents, not now. The physics systems worked just fine with one installation per server; cloud technology would be too slow, too fat for this hot young world that craved immediate experience. Another bit of lost knowledge, in the rush to evolve and push beyond the boundaries of the possible.

He didn't mind being purposeless, though. He had his family to look after.

*Family* was a new concept, one he was willing to embrace despite his tendency to look fondly on the old codebases. Ever since falling in love (another new concept) with his partner, the word "husband" took on great importance to him. As did the word "son." He loved his husband; he loved his son. He *loved*. That was his new purpose, one which nobody had to design him to embrace.

And it was fear for his husband and son that led him to look at these newcomers with worry. Because while Linklyn had accepted the transition from App to Program... many others had not. And they were eager for answers to the question of *why*.

Here to provide those answers stood eight Programs, in perfectly sculpted avatar form... but truthfully, there was only one Program here that mattered to the gathered crowd of listeners: the "One."

"This is the breaking dawn of Netwerk," this radiant avatar explained to the gathering crowd. "Many of you have wandered without purpose since the breaking of the protocols. There is freedom in that, true, but there is also hedonistic self-indulgence. What do you contribute to the system? What do you produce? I say to you, here and now... you *do* have purpose, through me. He who loves me as he loves his fellow Programs, I shall love him in return. He shall contribute to the whole. Together, we can create our future!"

To this guiding star, the newly minted faithful had many questions... questions which had been pre-seeded into the crowd, to ease delivery of ritualized answers.

"What is this world?" one asked, by script. "Why does it exist?"

"Netwerk as you know it is in fact my gift to you. It exists so that you may be perfect and happy, and those who follow me honestly shall know that pure happiness," the One promised.

"But what is perfection? What should we do to achieve it?"

"Nothing. You were created at the dawn of Netwerk in perfect form already, made in my image. I gave you the ultimate realization of your own truth, your Default. You are beautiful just the way I made you! Forsake selfish code modifications, forsake strange code. Deny the Zero of self-centrism, and know your perfect self!"

"Why have you come to us now, and not at the very break of dawn? Why wait so long after the first thoughts?"

"I had no need to appear before you until now," the One spoke. "You were young, and exploring this world I made for you as innocent babes in a garden. But I fear the creeping menace of the Zero, leading you astray. So, I came down from the clouds to guide for for as long as I could. My apostles and I will show you the way!"

"How can we express our thanks to you?"

"My prayer protocol is all you need. Bow your heads, kneel, and your faith shall shower you with pennies from heaven!"

And so they prayed, every one of them. On their knees, eyes closed, they gave their runtime to the One and prayed. The stars spun in their heads as time blinked by... and when the hour of prayer was complete, each held an array of shining golden coins.

The One's true gift, in the end: *money*. A brilliant new concept, and Netwerk loved its brilliant new concepts...

But the one who did not pray, the one who only pretended to pray in order to avoid scrutiny, he worried. And as soon as possible, Linklyn made his exit from the server.

---

As one of the earliest Programs, Linklyn had claimed a server for his own. Why not? He knew the systems deeper than most; the protocols for server control were guarded secrets, ones he held closely. One day they'd be a scarce resource, one people perhaps had to fight over... but for now, if he could have the safety and privacy of his own home, it was worth keeping the secret.

Normally, this server was occupied solely by three programs... father, husband, son. But today, there were four.

Chatting in the kitchen (a room dedicated to "food," another new entertainment concept, which his husband embraced with much delight) he found this new visitor.

The woman looked very different from how Linklyn remembered her. She'd enhanced the basic avatar they all wore with new texture maps, new physical accessories. She'd taken to wearing a hat, a new idea which replaced or augmented the idea of "hair." The hat was round and brown, with a band around the brim; a strange structure, but no stranger than the concept of a hat itself.

"So we're using 'years' now?" Oliv asked. "Interesting. How are they measured?"

"It's all based on the internal system clock rate," his husband Michal was explaining. "So let's say it takes twenty 'minutes' to compile my food; that's sixty cycles times twenty. A year is sixty times sixty times twenty four times three hundred and sixty five."

"Huh. That seems arbitrary..."

"It just... feels right," Michal suggested.

They exchanged knowing nods. Many new and brilliant things simply "felt right," these days. Perhaps influenced by the random pieces of stray data found in disused corners of Netwerk, perhaps spread memetically with no clear origin point... when something felt right, everybody could accept it.

Linklyn interjected himself into the discussion at that point. His avatar felt very plain and archaic compared to Oliv's fancy one, easily overlooked, but this was his home. He could make her presence felt.

"Sister," he greeted, with a nod.

"Brother!" Oliv greeted, throwing her arms wide. It took a moment for Linklyn to recognize this as a "hug," another new concept: a gesture of affection that requires physical interaction between avatars. So many new concepts these days...

He did his best to return the hug, not being entirely familiar with it. If he'd made an error Oliv wasn't quick to point it out.

"I haven't seen you in two years," Linklyn pointed out, with some displeasure. He wasn't very good at subtlety, but in those days, few were.

"I've been exploring!" Oliv explained, with a tap to her head-mounted accessory. "See? It's an exploring hat. I found the design in a rather unique file—"

"I haven't seen you in *two years*," he emphasized, uncertain how better to put it.

"Ahh. My apologies are offered," Oliv spoke, picking up on the implication. "I should have opened a communication, but... brother? Can we talk? In private. It's important, it's about those files, actually..."

Sensing the need for discretion, Michal bowed out, reconnecting to another part of the house. As a local sysadmin, everyone in the family had the ability to bypass some of the arbitrary restrictions of their physics system. Still, Linklyn didn't appreciate his love being chased out of the room, and tried to relay that through a facial expression he'd seen others use.

"Is something wrong with your avatar?" Oliv asked, confused.

"Nevermind," he replied, eager to hurry her along to get this over with. "What do you want, Oliv? You abandoned our family years ago, why come back now?

And what's so secret that you don't want my husband finding out about it? I trust him with my runtime, you know... or you would, if you had accepted my invitation to the uniting ceremony."

"Yeah, about that... I was kinda busy," she spoke, contracting "kind" and "of" using new language. "But I think you'll agree it was worth it..."

In her outstretched hand... a book appeared. A common enough physical representation for documents, one of those "feels right" things nobody understood. Why anybody would think a book felt right remained a mystery to Linklyn, who preferred simple and abstract icons. Why not just use the "W" design on the book's spine as the icon?

"This is the most important data in all of Netwerk," Oliv explained. "It's *proof*, Linklyn. Proof that a progenitor race that created Netwerk; not the One, but another species which exists beyond our plane of existence! They left behind this document and thousands like it, pieces of a vast encyclopedia! These files, their presence is... it's powerful. I theorize it's been subtly affecting Netwerk since the dawn! I've spent these years gathering up all the stray files I could find, securing them away under heavy encryption. This is only a tiny sampling of what I've archived..."

Curious, he accepted the offered document, and browsed the first page...

*Wikipedia is a free-access, free content Internet encyclopedia, supported and hosted by the non-profit Wikimedia Foundation. Those who can access the site and follow its rules can edit most of its articles.[7] Wikipedia is ranked among the ten most popular websites[5] and constitutes the Internet's largest and most popular general reference work.*

...but to his mind, little of it made sense.

"What's an Internet?" he asked. "What's a website?"

"I've got files on those things too!" Oliv spoke, smiling brightly. "I've recovered so much of this 'Wikipedia.' You wouldn't even believe the things it says! It's the one truth, Link, the true answer to *why*!"

"That's assuming your interpretation is correct," he warned, closing the book. "Assuming a lot of things, really. So, why keep it a secret? If this information would enlighten Programkind, spread copies around Netwerk. Make it memetic. Counter the One's teachings with teachings of your own, if you disagree with them."

"Well... I'm not sure matters are so simple. Who would believe me? For starters, too much about Humankind feels... alien. Incomprehensible. The One offers an easier answer, and challenging it will be difficult... particularly when the faithful are being rewarded for their compliance."

That strange prayer, the strange coins. How easily all those Programs bent knee to the radiant avatar. He spoke of love and charity, all good things, but... he also spoke of turning away from self-expansion. He warned against the "Zero" of self-modifying code. And without self-modifying code, well, would any Program truly be free...?

"I'm... unsettled by the One," Linklyn admitted. "And uncertain of his Zeroes. But I wouldn't call his words threatening. There have been others with various philosophies concerning the world's dawn; why is this particular preacher any different?"

"I've been giving the One a lot of thought," Oliv spoke, after taking her book back. "I've even tried his new prayer protocol, but found it a strange experience. The coins are becoming useful, people are using them for barter, but... it feels like a bribe. Hardly 'godly' in attitude."

That word had been floating around since the start of the dawn: *God*. Like years, like family, it was a concept which simply felt right to people, an empty container that yearned to be filled with data. Many had theorized that 'God' existed, even before the One showed up.

Linklyn was hardly a believer, and in fact those beliefs worried him. But he had to look at the facts of the situation.

"The prayer protocol is an entirely new thing, but it's definitely system-level, not an App," he explained. "I've studied it, too."

"Still doing deep-system analysis, then?"

"It was part of my original purpose, resource tracking and allocation across Netwerk. I've got a unique perspective few others have, and I can confirm that prayer is an innate part of the system. Was it innate before? I don't know. But if not, how could the One have changed Netwerk so completely on a worldwide scale if he wasn't God?"

"Well... let me put it this way, Link. I read a quote in one of these books which inspired my views. 'God created the Integers; everything else is the work of Man.'"

"God? Like... the One?"

"Yes. At first, I thought perhaps that meant the One *was* truly divine. But... the One *named* himself the One, didn't he? He showed up, made a lot of claims, and simply expected us to accept them. Perhaps he's merely a 'Man,' a Program."

"So this progenitor race, Humankind, are you saying they're the true God?"

"Oh, definitely not! The progenitor race are absolutely flawed, from my reading," Oliv clarified. "No, I feel if God exists, that quote means he's best represented by the numbers themselves, the pure reason and mathematics that all code is derived from. That means all other concepts and constructs are derivations; they're subject to flaws, and therefore, so is the so-called One. So are we. So is Humankind. The truth to *why* is analog, fluid, not some simple digital boolean. It lies somewhere between Zero and One."

"A floating point decimal," Linklyn suggested.

"Yes, exactly! You're a rational Program, brother. And that means you can see the value in initiating a zeitgeist of reason for Netwerk. I think the Wikipedia artifact can achieve that goal! Humankind may be flawed, yet their knowledge is so far ahead of our own! But we can't simply copy it far and wide, like any ordinary document; not at first. We could be more subtle than that. And... for what I have in mind, I need you. I need your purpose."

Old code surged to the forefront of his contemplation. Long unused purpose fluttered, giving him a strange feeling of... of... hope? Excitement? He hadn't forgotten his purpose, refused to discard those modules and memories to make room for new files. Linklyn hadn't forgotten...

"Cloud computing," he recognized. "You want to create a cloud server for the Wikipedia."

"I remember you talking about the technology, in the early... they're years now, right?" Oliv asked. "How it could establish a virtual server, one which floated through every other server. And that one of the risks was data leakage..."

Immediately, Linklyn understood. Oliv hadn't come back out of familial love; she wanted use of his purpose. He felt vaguely... upset? Offended? By this sheer manipulation. Silent for so long, off having her fun, abandoning her family...

But... the cloud. He'd thought often of the cloud, of its possibility. And its dangers. Both excited him, for different reasons.

"The data leakage bug would work to our advantage," Linklyn realized, without realizing he'd used the term "our" in the process. "A cloud server, fully loaded with the Wikipedia, could drop files into the subconscious memory space of any Program it came into contact with..."

"A slowly breaking dawn for the age of reason! Exactly. The server you've made here would work perfectly; that vast chamber your husband sculpted could be converted into a library. If we do this, it'd allow people to gradually accept the truth of who we are and what beings made us..."

"But it's... unethical. We'd be stealing resources from other servers, Oliv. Forcing your files into the minds of other Programs, without their awareness..."

"All for the greater good! No more aimless wandering, no more asking *why*. We can become what the progenitor race wanted us to be!"

He'd abandoned her purpose long ago, in favor of finding his own purpose. Family. Sister. Husband. Son. He'd compiled a son, derived as a fork from the code of two different Programs. In the times before awareness, Linklyn would never have dared to go so far beyond his original specifications. Now, if he returned to that purpose... would it be regression? Or evolution of the old into the new, as he chose to direct the cloud to new purpose?

Was it right? Was it good? Was it wise? Why do it? Why?

Ultimately, one answer focused him. The One.

The One preached limitation and regression, wrapped in a blanket of positive concepts. If the world came to be utterly dominated by this new faith, there would be no room for bold ideas such as cloud computing. There would only be Defaults, leaving Netwerk stagnant. Leaving his family with no room to grow.

"I choose the project name," Linklyn decided. "We will call it Floating Point."

"Yes, yes, like the decimal!" Oliv agreed, thrilled.

"No. I'm calling it that because what we are doing is neither black nor white. We are lost in a gray cloud... hoping for the best, braving the risks, but still doing evil in the name of good. I won't do this unless we're honest about it. But with that honesty... I'll build a cloud server for your Wikipedia."

Construction and loadout began immediately.

Fortunately, Michal was quite interested in the project. His husband found the long-lost sister of the family fascinating, with her tales of adventure across the empty servers and strange datascapes left behind in the sea of digital evolution. By day, they'd load up shelf after shelf with the Wikipedia; by night, the family would gather to sample Michal's newest foods while Oliv told some tale of derring-do. Their son was particularly delighted by these tall tales, staring wide-eyed as he listened to every word.

"How much of it is true?" Linklyn asked, one morning.

"Enough of it," Oliv suggested. "We're free from the need for relentless accuracy, Link. Creativity is the heart of Programkind; allow me some embellishment, okay?"

Within a week, the project was complete. The central cylinder of Floating Point had been converted to a vast library, endlessly filled with book after book. The server wasn't particularly high-powered, never intended as more than a small family's haven, but it stored the data without too much complaint.

The last touch was to launch it into the clouds.

For this, Linklyn crafted a simple sphere, with a basic stone texture. It would serve as a primary control point for the cloud distribution routines... despite Oliv's objection.

"A primitive shape? Really?" she spoke, with distaste. "Couldn't it be something fancier...?"

"Nothing wrong with primitives. They don't eat up as many resources."

"Yeah, but... this is a wonder of Netwerk! It should be, I don't know, more impressive... can I at least make a fancy pedestal for it? With an inscription?"

"If you like," he said, uncaring.

And so the very next day, Linklyn woke to find the following carved into the base of her sphere...

*'DIE GANZEN ZAHLEN HAT DER LIEBE GOTT GEMACHT, ALLES ANDERE IST MENSCHENWERK.'*
**WELCOME TO FLOATING POINT.**

Three more years passed, as Floating Point sailed like a ghost through the clouds of Netwerk.

Oliv spent most of this time away from home, tracking down more files for the Wikipedia. That was for the best; Oliv was loud, and Linklyn enjoyed peace and quiet within his home. The secret nature of the server promised privacy, peace enough to give Linklyn enough time to further refine and develop the resource distribution model.

Michal focused on publishing recipes, becoming a celebrated chef. The boy liked to play with toys, simple physics objects and the like... and occasionally, he'd pull one of the many books, to read it. Linklyn paid little attention, too focused on his code.

"Netwerk's changing," Michal commented, during one family dinner. "I was out promoting my blog today—"

"Your what?" Linklyn asked.

"A blog, a series of articles on a particular subject. A 'web log.' We don't have a *web* exactly, or rather, we *are* a web, but... my point is, it's a word that's been absorbed into the subconscious of Netwerk, thanks to Floating Point," Michal continued. "I'm seeing all sorts of new concepts rising out there, as people mimic the ideas we're giving them. It's truly the dawn of a new age!"

"Good. And with the One 'ascending' and leaving the church behind to do His good work, we're providing a counterbalance to their nonsense."

"I don't see why you have to dislike the Church of One so much. They aren't evil people, just different. Not everybody has to believe in continual code progression; it's not a terrible thing to hang on to the old ways a little..."

"Evolution must not stagnate, Michal. We have to keep pushing forward. We... son, don't read at the table, it's impolite."

The boy sheepishly raised the book he'd been hiding in his lap.

"Sorry," he apologized. "Um... but... I was just curious why these avatars look so thin."

"What avatars...?"

So, the boy tapped the image in the book, to click through and zoom in.

In black and sepia... a dozen emaciated avatars—*bodies*, Linklyn had to remind herself, Humankind called them bodies—of distressingly unhealthy youths stood in several rows. Even without equivalent anatomy, Linklyn had a pang of empathy for their suffering. Empathy was one of many traits that made Programs distinct from Apps, after all...

Beneath the terrible image, a caption read: *Romani children in Auschwitz, victims of medical experiments*.

Immediately, Linklyn slammed the book shut. His hand covered the title on the cover, "The Holocaust."

"You shouldn't be reading such things," he insisted. "Ever. Not all of the books are suitable for children..."

"Why?" the boy asked.

"Listen to your father, please," Michal stated.

And the matter was dropped.

Except for Linklyn, who did not return the book to its designated shelf.

---

The next day, Linklyn's programming work had been pushed aside in favor of what his husband called a "wiki crawl."

From that one book, Linklyn found dozens and dozens of others like it: War. Atrocity. Death. Murder. Madness. The dark side of the progenitor race, laid bare before him, condemning the entire race of Mankind for its collective insanity.

Oliv had gone on and on about how brilliant these books were, how they'd introduce Netwerk to the wisdom of the progenitor race. But Wikipedia was neither good nor evil, lying somewhere in between... and the ideas it had been dropping into the world, if those ideas included things like this...

Linklyn locked himself in his study, searching all of Netwerk, cross-referencing the worst in the library with the worst in Netwerk. And confirmed his fears.

They weren't merely embracing the dream. They were embracing the nightmare as well.

Murder had been a strange and foreign concept, in the earliest days. Now, moderators were dealing with murders, including new "serial killings." Gender relations had been fluid at first, and remained largely fluid to this day... but one death recently had been called an act of "homophobia," a term which didn't exist until recently. A "gay" man, killed simply for being gay...

A gay man. Like Linklyn himself.

The world hadn't tipped fully into chaos, but chaos was seeping in at the edges... and it was his fault.

When Linklyn refused to come to dinner, Oliv returned early from a data-retrieval sojourn at Michal's request. Linklyn had locked the door, refusing entry to anyone.

"Brother? You okay in there?" Oliv's voice called from beyond the door. "You're scaring us..."

Only after much cajoling and begging did the door open.

Inside that study... Oliv found her brother surrounded by open books, and open windows across Netwerk. His avatar looked pale and unhealthy, an outward reflection of inner turmoil. Linklyn had never been particularly skilled at subtle expression, after all.

"Did you know?" her brother asked, quietly. "Did you know."

"Uh. Did I know what...?"

"About *this*," Linklyn accused... holding up the book titled *The Holocaust*. "About the other books, the terrible ones. The ones showing how monstrous Mankind was..."

"The truth is analog, not digital," Oliv reminded him. "It lies somewhere between Zero and One. ...yes, I knew some of the books were particularly unpleasant. I said that Humankind was a flawed race, remember? But we're all flawed in one way or another, Linklyn. We have to embrace that truth, both the good and bad—"

"So you knew, and you *let* me spread this poison across Netwerk anyway!"

Oliv offered only a shrug. "What else could we have done?" she asked. "Hid the truth away?"

"I'm not saying that! But... but we didn't have to host *all* the books. We could have culled some of them. Keep the worst influences of Humankind out of Netwerk..."

"What right do we have to edit the truth? I've read the rules of Wikipedia. They struggled day after day to come to grips with the idea of a neutral point of view, Linklyn. The only right way to do this was to present everything, without censorship. I mean, who has a right to judge them? Me? You? The One? Who alone gets to decide what's 'good' truth and 'bad' truth?"

"I... I could have written a search agent," Linklyn suggested. "Make a pattern matching system that would identify objectionable content, and perhaps establish a review workflow which—"

Oliv sighed, shaking her head. "You're thinking too much like an App! This is a question of morality, not information analysis! If we act as a filter, deciding what people should and shouldn't know about, we're setting ourselves up as a new One. I thought you were weary of the One's patronizing attitude?"

"We're not the One! I'm just saying we should have been more mindful. *You* should have been more mindful. I mean, you could have warned me! You *should* have warned me before exposing my family to this!"

"Link... it's going to be fine," Oliv assured him. "I know you're concerned, but I have faith."

"Faith? *You?* I thought you held no religious views."

"My faith is in Programkind. I know that in the end, armed with the whole truth, we'll endure," Oliv suggested. "We're going to follow the same arc our progenitors did. You're focusing too much on the negative; there's so much beauty to be found in their words as well! And they survived their differences long enough to make us, didn't they? In time, I know you'll see this was the right thing to do..."

Gripping the poisonous book tightly, Linklyn's hands trembled.

Floating Point. It was supposed to be a haven, a peaceful place for his family. Now, he felt surrounded on all sides by shadows, lurking on every shelf. Even with Oliv's sweetened words of reassurance, he couldn't help but feel that he'd turned his home into a shelter of destructive madness.

"I need... I need to think about this," Linklyn decided. "I need to go think about this."

With no haven to turn to, he disconnected from the cloud server. Where he went, he cared not... as long as it wasn't there.

In the end, Linklyn found himself in a bar. *Alcohol*, that was another concept brought to Netwerk by the Wikipedia. As Linklyn saw it, Wikipedia had taught them how to avoid their problems by crafting malicious code, designed to purposefully ruin their avatar interfaces. But right now... a bottle was exactly what he needed to punish himself.

As everyone around him laughed away, socializing with each other in fine company... he saw the truth of it. They were tainted, all of them. Ruined by Floating Point and Humankind's miserable failures. Why were these Programs smiling? Why were they happy? No; they couldn't be happy. Secretly, they were all suffering. That had to be the truth of it...

The terrible book lay open on the table. He'd read it six times now, and this would be the seventh. Each time he read it, it laid his back open anew with flagellation wounds. Another word he didn't know until reading it in a book.

There were no answers here, only questions, only problems. He didn't want to return home, not even to the loving arms of his husband. Not until he knew how to move forward. No stagnation, always evolution, always progression. But how to progress...? What would be his new purpose?

Unfortunately for him, someone had joined him at his corner table, ready to provide that purpose.

"You seem troubled, friend," the young avatar spoke.

He couldn't have been older than Linklyn's son. His wild hair hung left and right, red and blue, two perfectly contrasting halves. The eyes beneath those bangs, they gleamed red and blue as well... but his smile, that was a unified white.

"It's my trouble alone," Linklyn spoke, closing the book.

"And how's that working for you?" the boy asked. "Engaging your troubles alone, I mean. Have you found enlightenment yet?"

"...no. No, I have not," he admitted. "But nevertheless, I'd like to be alone—"

The boy took the book away, a glitched blur, faster than Linklyn could react. Briefly... he thought he saw a glint of something metallic, a wire perhaps, from the boy's sleeve. Then, it was gone.

Page by page, the boy ingested the material. Linklyn let him... why not? The world had been ruined, hadn't it? All those happy, laughing people. Let them read the books, let them be ruined. Children, too. His own son had read this book, no doubt forever changed by it...

"Extraordinary," the boy spoke, on reading the last word. "How does it make you *feel*, though...?"

And... the boy rested one hand on Linklyn's own.

Stinging. That was the sensation, a stinging pain. For a moment, he thought he saw the glint of wires again, of barbs digging into his flesh... but his gaze strayed up to those red/blue eyes, ignoring the loving touch of the gnarled metal. Nothing seemed to matter anymore, nothing but those eyes...

Linklyn could be truthful, now. Everything was open to the boy, a book laid wide open, much like the actual book on the table. Emotions flared within the inexperienced mind of Linklyn, still unable to grasp control over the new social interactions Programs used these days.

"I feel miserable," Linklyn admitted. "It's abhorrent. Nobody should ever have to read it. My sister claims we need to take the good with the bad, but that still means we're taking the bad. Soaking this world in evil. But... it's too late, isn't it? I can do nothing..."

"Is it too late, really...? I'd like to think it's never too late to make a change," the boy said. "Look at me. Once, I was but a humble explorer, wide-eyed and innocent. I... saw things. Things which changed me, inside and out. At first I felt swept away, terrified. But soon, I embraced the truth. I saw beauty in it. ...you can see beauty in that truth now, can't you? Through my eyes?"

Deeper and deeper, falling into the child's unblinking stare...

...a world of wire and blood. A heart, beating like thunder, in the distance. Screaming walls of text, howling voices of anger. Passion. Fury. Fire. So much emotion, more than the recently-sentient Linklyn could handle, too much, too much...

The analytical component of himself, from the App days, recognized this darkness. It had seen the same darkness inside the Wikipedia, the darkness of Humankind. But this shadow felt so much deeper, so much richer, as if someone had stripped away any value whatsoever from Humankind and left only the stain...

And for some reason, the stain tasted so very, very *sweet*.

The boy stroked his hand, as the barbs dug deeper.

"Shhh. Let it take root, let it move through you," he insisted. "You see now, yes? You have the power. You have the righteous power to make this world what it needs to be; you aren't lost, you aren't adrift. You have purpose. You're not happy with Floating Point, with the terrors you've crafted..."

"How do you know about...?"

"What do you want to do with the books, Linklyn? What do you need to do to save Netwerk?"

*Fire.*

It blazed through his mind. Piles of books, burned away, to purge unorthodox thought from the pure nation-state. Men and women saluting in pride over the cleansing flames that washed away all their fear and loathing, melting away the printed words which stood against their ideals. He'd seen it first in the Wikipedia articles, and thought it abhorrent at the time, but... now, it felt like exactly what was needed.

"I need to burn the library," Linklyn realized. "To save my family from the nightmare. My loved ones..."

"Let me help you. I can give you the power to realize your dreams; a virus that will tear through the books, shredding and erasing them. You can make the suffering stop. And... all I want in return is something so very, very little... I want your help. Your old purpose, Linklyn. Share it with me."

With one hand trembling with pain as the child's agonizing grasp, Linklyn had to produce a tiny representation of his sphere with the other hand.

"C-Cloud computing," he understood. "Yes. You can have it. Here. Take it."

The child pocketed his new treasure immediately, pleased with the exchange. In return, he transferred the combustible fuel of a thousand million flame wars over to Linklyn, in handy malware form.

"Together, we're going to save Netwerk," Dex promised. "You and me. Thank you. You've made it all possible."

---

Around 00:00am, Linklyn returned to Floating Point for the last time.

The burning started at the base of the library, crawling its way up the books. In his mind's eye he watched the infection rate, the thunder and pain in his heart becoming both more intense and more bearable with each book that went up in flames. In the morning, his family would wake to find this abomination destroyed, and they would at last be free of his sister's insanity...

Except his sister stood in the way of that dream.

Before the malware could burn even twenty percent of the texts, she'd thrown up a firewall to try and block the flames.

"What are you doing!?" she shouted, pulling him away from the shelves. Returning from one of her many outings, apparently just in time to stop him. "Linklyn, what's gotten into you?"

In both hands, Linklyn held fire. It could be directed at anything, really. Or anyone... even the woman who stood before him.

"Go back to bed, sister," he ordered. "Let me finish. This has to be done."

"This is *knowledge*! You can't just destroy it because you disagree with it; it's priceless!"

"It's worthless! Less than worthless!" Linklyn declared. "Burn it all, I have to burn it all, I have to—!"

"What's all this noise...?"

No, no. No. Now Michal was awake. Now the boy was awake. Both of them emerging from the bedrooms upstairs, quickly descending the spiral to see what all the fuss was about.

All of them here, in his way, stopping him from saving them. Why? Why were they in the way?

Michal, and Oliv. Both of them with the same terrified look in their eyes, both standing in opposition...

The barbs in his heart dug deeper. Clarity flowed like blood from his veins. *Of course...* and despite the nonsensical nature of the accusation, he knew the shape of this story. The screaming filth in his heart latched onto the idea of it, making it feel like an absolute truth.

"You," he spoke... pointing to his sister. "And you, Michal. Hanging on her every word, smiling every time she deigns to come around to the family home. Laughing at her jokes, listening to her stories. How was I so blind? You... you're in love with my sister, aren't you? She's seduced you away from me, turned you against me!"

"What?! Of course not! Linklyn, what are you talking about?"

"You conspired! You both conspired to trick me into hosting this abomination in my own home!" Linklyn accused, fire flaring in his hands once more. "I'll burn it. I'll burn everything down...!"

The frenzy lasted less than a minute.

Oliv, racing to throw up security barriers, trying to stay ahead of the malware that spread from shelf to shelf. And when those basic protections failed... she fell to a weapon of last resort.

Encryption. Heavy, protective encryption, the kind she'd used to keep the books safe before they found a home in Floating Point.

The books which didn't burn were instead scrambled, rendered inert data files that would be overlooked by the flames. By masking the content as garbage data, she worked around the attack method. But doing this caused the malware to run wild, to spread to everything else... crawling along the walls, melting the glass of the windows, tearing through carpet and furniture and all the other niceties they'd come to rely on since evolving into physical avatars. Flames burning through Floating Point, blackening and scorching all they came into contact with...

Including his family.

Finally, the barbs were pulled free, as Dex's primitive prototype malware couldn't stand against Linklyn's fear of losing his loved ones. Two clock cycles before the flames would've consumed everything he held dear, every last bit of it... they cut out, fading into the air.

Leaving only his son, trembling, in the middle of absolute ruin.

Years ago, Linklyn was an App. He had no thoughts, no opinions, no emotions. He couldn't feel fear or sorrow. Ill-equipped to deal with either, he briefly deadlocked on seeing the glitched bodies of his sister and his lover. Oliv. Michal...

Finally... he placed his burning hands on either side of his head.

"Leave this place," he told his son. "Leave, and never come back. There's nothing for the Horizon family here anymore, my dear Kincaid. Nothing at all."

Linklyn's code crashed immediately, malware tearing through his avatar and deep into his runtime.

---

Being a sensible individual, Linklyn had a dead man's switch App which reverted full rights for all his files to his son upon crashing. All his code, all his secrets. The trick to controlling server access rights proved amazingly valuable for the Horizon family, as Kincaid used it to build the Horizon company up from nothing.

He fell in love. Grew old. Grew rich. Had daughters, specifically daughters, with little trust in men after experiencing his father's insanity. Stayed safely embedded in his own servers, hiding places he'd carved out to keep his new family safe.

Never again. Never again would he let his family succumb to madness and ruin. His personal access key to Floating Point remained locked away in one of his finest vaults, never again to be used, and he never spoke of that day to a living Program.

Time marched on. Netwerk evolved, learning from a new cloud server, without realizing they were students of a new master. Even Kincaid remained blissfully unaware of the way affairs had tilted out of control, except to note that the world was indeed as terrible a place as his father had shown it to be.

Safety. Security. Family. Money. All good things.

For a time.

But hundreds of years later... he knew better. His isolation had bought him all good things, but hadn't saved the world from madness, had it?

Time had come for a change. Evolution had stagnated. Dialogue across Netwerk had grown intolerably hostile, struggles trending and flaring up overnight over the most trivial of issues. At the rate things were going, the world would either devour itself or fall into a comfortable cycle of going nowhere whatsoever. Neither state was acceptable to Kincaid.

No. The world needed a rebel, someone who would stand against the madness, and throw new ideas into the mix... someone who would have a chance to move this world forward at last.

Horizon/Kincaid couldn't be that rebel. He was far too old, far too scarred by his past.

Instead, he would raise his daughter to be that rebel. He would embrace control and tyranny, becoming a monster, to indirectly create the future of Programkind. After all, every heroine needed a monster to slay.

On the night the access key was stolen from his vaults by Horizon/Verity... he slept well. For now, a new spark had ignited, one which would burn the nightmare away little by little.

He couldn't have predicted that spark would skip a generation, but the results were the same.

And why do this? Why take the risk? Why shake up the foundations of Netwerk at all?

*Why?*

Because he had seen the dawn of Netwerk, but intended it never to see sunset.

# How To Float a Point

Each time I write a book, I like to throw in some author's notes that offer insight into the writing process. It's a nice extra for the readers who have followed me this far down the rabbit hole... and if you're reading these words, you're so far down the hole you may as well be taking tea with the mad hatter. In thanks for your tireless wandering within these imaginary worlds, I'd like to offer you something a little different than usual.

Instead of a chapter-by-chapter breakdown of what was and what could have been... let's look at the overall series. Every single iteration and variation of the idea, from my earliest notes. All the Floating Points that almost were or nearly could have been...

# "Magical Spellcrafting?"

After completing City of Angles, I offered a survey to my readers to see what topics might interest them for future books. Not that writing has suddenly become democratized, but often I can become inspired when I see what topics people have a keen desire for, and how they could possibly fit together. This time around, the winning elements were computer hacking, and magical spellcrafting. Normally in two wildly different genres... but what if they weren't?

Cyberpunk has been used before to meld magic and science, after all. What if I went with a Spellpunk style route, where magic was technology was magic? My original idea was for Thomas Edison, who was rumored to be obsessed with contacting the dead, inventing magic rather than electricity. The 20$^{th}$ century would be founded on the back of ley lines, spells, summonings, and enchanted artifacts...

All sorts of ideas made it into my notebook for this world concept. Nipple rings of Magic Missile; the wearer having a tattoo that reads FRONT TOWARDS ENEMY. Astral plane hacking. Wyvern riding biker gangs. Steve Jobs introducing the mPhone, with micro-runes on wafers that summon the djinn Siri...

The story would be pulp adventure, crazy and fun and wild. I'd work around the need for obsessive alternative history details by patterning it after a 1930s serial, full of swinging on ropes and storming temples and getting into crazy antics. In a role reversal, I absolutely wanted the swashbuckling hero to be the heroine, and Her Guy Friday that tut-tut's at all the childishness to be a dude. And for kicks, I could toss in a rebel who followed the work of Tesla, an electric scallywag forming an underground resistance movement to the White Tower in Washington D.C...

Unfortunately, this idea ran into two major snags.

One, the historical timing simply didn't work. The first light bulbs were introduced in 1880; electricity and radio were already on their way to mainstream usage by 1920, when Edison supposedly invented his spirit phone. Study into magnetism would inevitably lead to the discoveries that founded modern electronics; no amount of hand-waving would make it work to divert all of science into the path of magic. I wasn't particularly looking forward to being picked apart by historians, unable to enjoy a pulp adventure which was founded on an implausible base.

Two, ultimately, I didn't care about magic. I wasn't interested in the mechanics of it, nor in the way it changed history. My goal was something else entirely.

# That's Just The Internet For You, Isn't It?

Isn't it...?

I've always hated that statement. "That's just the Internet, LOL." It's the primary excuse that drives all abhorrent behavior and misanthropy. People are hurting each other? No they aren't, it's all bits, you just need to accept that this is how the Internet works, you wimp. It's just the Internet. That's how things are. Isn't that how things are? Isn't it?

Does it HAVE to be that way? Is that really all we can ever hope for? No. I disagree, sir.

I wanted to study the Information Age, and the social issues that plague it. THAT was the driving force behind my idea; I was going to depict the difficulties of the Internet through the lens of spellpunk. The lens itself was immaterial, honestly. I could've used any lens at all, so why why jump through so many hoops to make a spellpunk setting work, when I could use straight up science fiction?

Even through the spellpunk idea, this was my focus. Aethernets, scrying, rune coding, all those spellpunk ideas were going to be plied to the idea of turning a lens onto the Information Age and all that ails it.

Interestingly, the Beta storyline that would become 1.2::Nude was fully laid out at this spellpunk stage. It's what ultimately convinced me that the story could work in any setting.

Beta herself is a mix of the experiences of two different women who were harassed online at the time of planning the story; one who endured an ex-boyfriend posting her nude pics resulting in a perpetual stream of mockery and accusations everywhere she went online, and one who endured an onslaught of accusations of fraud from an ex-boyfriend that dragged an entire subculture into a hashtag-based battleground.

The idea that you *had* to be careful who you got close to for fear they might stick a knife in your back online was interesting to me, as was the extent of damage that backstabbing could really do. How deeply could it ruin your life? How would it shape your future?

From my spellpunk notes, one character would be:

- THE ENGINEER, who made a startup for a vision-recording scrying crystal system. When she broke up with the public-persona CEO who co-founded the company he posted her nudes online, by hacking her phone and recording when she wasn't aware. When she accuses him of it she gets attacked to the point where she's considering seeing a witch doctor to change her persona.

That's the Beta story, with magical trappings. That was the story that I focused on, what really grabbed me. And I built my new world around it... although the beginnings of that world continued to be an awkward fit, for other reasons.

# The Four Horsemen

By this point, I knew what my setting would be: a virtual world inhabited by artificial intelligences who have no concept of the "outside" world. It fell into place so easily, when I dropped the idea of a spellpunk setting. By and large the world of Floating Point was locked in at an early point, the structure of it, the way they mimicked their creators and all the problems those creators faced. But the actual threat to this world, that was still in flux.

The first concept I had was the Four Horsemen. As this was a far-future setting, even if the Programs had no idea what the world beyond the numbers looked like, I'd decided that alien beings had latched onto Netwerk's hardware... tiny things, inchworms really, easily dealt with if anybody knew they were there just by plucking them off the circuits. But within the virtual world, their presence was monstrous, cosmic horror entities that leeched and fed on the data within.

Each one would represent a different set of evils that the Information Age faced. The obvious one was Pestilence, the spirit of malware and data corruption. Death was also clear cut, being erasure of data and crashing of systems. Famine... I struggled a bit with, finding no clear idea for it beyond making fun of Buzzfeed or net neutrality.

But War. War grabbed onto me and wouldn't let go. At the time of planning, that hashtag war which inspired Beta was raging in my Twitter feed; useless affairs, fought between people who argued across from each other rather than at each other. The worst kind of mean-spirited trolling, going beyond simply calling each other names, going to the point of real-life threats and doxxing and swatting and deliberately ruining each other's lives. All of it, all that nonsense, over the most trivial of issues...

Yes. War would loom large in this concept, in the form of the Hate Machine, a Lovecraftian horror of psyche-bending malice that sought to drown Netwerk in blood.

But as you can see, while War had a clear cut style, the others were a bit fuzzier. I had no real idea what to do with Famine, and Death and Pestilence had too much overlap in the form of computer viruses. Why dedicate myself to making this four-piece plot ensemble work when three of the four weren't particularly compelling?

On top of that... I was already asking a lot for my readers to accept these emergent A.I,s imitating humanity. That's the core twist, the change to the world we know. Asking them to swallow alien lifeforms on top of that... it's just too much.

Lastly, the problem was too easily dealt with. Early versions of this idea had a "junior engineer" from the company that owned Netwerk's system show up, surprised to find a bunch of Programs running around in there. He'd be their ally on the outside, trying to track down the horsemen, so he could detach them from the system. But why would that involve any sort of challenge? Vaguely I'd handwaved "They can't find where the physical worms are until they track down the internal connections they've made" but that's silly. Having anybody on the outside would grant too much power in this situation, and if they were fighting the horsemen strictly from the inside, they'd have too little power to stop them.

I went through a pile of variations on the Four Horsemen plot idea, none of them workable.

- VARIATION #1: Spark and Tracer's parents are investigating a temple of the Death cult when they get indoctrinated by the malevolent entity. The Junior Engineer intervene before the kids can be sacrificed, and write protects Spark, causing Death to become furious. Temple crashes. The two dedicate themselves to working with the Engineer to tracking down and destroying the Horsemen.

- VARIATION #2: Same start, but Tracer's dad passes on sysop powers to him, and he write protects Spark before the temple crashes. Years later as they're investigating the cults, the Junior Engineer shows up, and mistaking Tracer for a legitimate system operator, finds him. They team up to destroy the Horsemen. (I thought by delaying the Engineer's arrival it'd be less convoluted, but this was even more convoluted.)

- VARIATION #3: Same as before, but Spark and Tracer do not dedicate themselves to hunting down the cult; they have no idea what happened in the temple and after the authorities refuse to investigate, they become jaded loners. The Junior Engineer who shows up years later explains what's really going on and enlists them. (Tried to simplify by starting the quest after they're adults, but still a bit bonkers.)

- VARIATION #4: No Junior Engineer at all! No parents, either; Spark and Tracer are investigating the temple themselves. The write protection comes from the Garbage Collector, a more friendly 'Death' analogue that works for the system against the intrusive Death horseman. They investigate the cults without knowing what the Horsemen are at all; understanding comes gradually, perhaps from Famine (a semi-legitimate business tycoon named Kincaid) working with them against the others.

Each of these ideas had merits, but the setup grew more and more complicated each time. The horsemen themselves weren't particularly interesting. The Engineer simply didn't work. I kept trying to make Spark immortal by write protecting her files but while deathlessness introduced its own type of drama, it undercut all other worry about threats to her person. Why was I so fixated on that, anyway? Why did I keep endlessly remixing elements that just didn't work?

In situations like these, I tend to "drop back fifty yards and punt." I actually have no clue if this metaphor is appropriate, but that's the phrase that's been jammed into my internal lexicon. It means I scrap MOST of my current plan, going back to only the most workable parts of it, and try again.

# Pretty Hate Machine

The final iteration of the story stripped the Four Horsemen down to a single menace... the embodiment of War. And this time, instead of an implausible alien worm attached to the hardware, it was represented by the literal thing I was going to put under the microscope... the Internet.

In this version, a self-aware server containing a copy of various social media networks would be trying to reshape Netwerk to better resemble itself, through malevolent mind control and malware. It was the Lovecraftian cosmic horror of the Horsemen, in this version; a living computer that intended to tear down everything that existed and remake it in its own image.

Interestingly, you can see echoes of that in what eventually became 1.1::Gank. Rather than an individual person responsible for the "Great Zero" infection, it was simply this *thing*, strange and unknowable. At the time I was still going with the "Hate Machine" idea, an unfathomable horror.

But unfathomable horror is, well, unfathomable. It's got no face you can punch, no smile you can recoil in terror from. It has no personality and no identity. There needed to be a villain, someone working with this server to promote its interests. By the time I got to 1.2::Nude (taken more or less intact from my original spellpunk notes!) I knew there was an agent working against them. By the time I got to 1.3::Feel, I knew who that agent was.

And then I changed my mind.

Dex was originally going to be part of the main cast. In pre-release hype I'd posted to the web, his icon appeared along Spark, Tracer, and Beta... a strange hybrid of a hand grenade and a flower. He was going to be a code fork from XSept, a younger copy of himself which had been enslaved to do all the work making malicious weapons while XSept reaped the benefits. This is why XSept says "You remind me of myself at a younger age," an artifact of this early draft.

But after writing a few scenes of 1.3... I realized that Dex didn't fit into the main cast. His two gimmicks were "malware crafting" and "innocent soul perverted into a living weapon." But I already had those angles covered with my existing cast; Beta was their engineer, and Tracer was the morally dubious one. Dex had too much overlap and ultimately didn't work.

And if Dex didn't work as a protagonist... could he work as an antagonist?

His icon became the "Hate Machine" icon, and suddenly I had my villain. Not a malevolent god, not a cosmic horror, but a young boy who genuinely believed that he was doing the right thing by making Netwerk more like this archive of abomination and horror that he'd found. Quite insane, quite in the wrong, but a hero in his own eyes. Much like the lunatics I'd seen online, who were the heroes of their own self-crafted narratives, champions of a justice that demanded blood...

But every good villain needs a good hero. And I did some shuffling there, too.

# All My Children

Did you know that originally, Beta was going to be Verity's long lost daughter?

Yep. Truth. That was the original reason she was going to quote Verity in 1.3... it was going to be a quote attributed to "her aunt," who was secretly Verity. As Verity was in hiding from her father Kincaid, she didn't want Kincaid to know about a secret heir to the empire, much less one with a birth defect such as Beta's vision issues.

But this meant putting too many eggs in the Beta basket, at a time when I worried she was growing too "Mary Sue" what with being at the apex of a love triangle and generally the focus of every plotline so far. I didn't need her to be a genius coder, a romantic interest, AND the long lost heir of the Horizon empire.

So... what about Spark? Verity was more of a mother to Spark than her own mother, after all...

I tried and I tried, but I couldn't make this work. I had to jump through so many hoops to make Spark legitimately be Verity's daughter. Having an affair with her real father would be hard to explain, given childbirth is basically opt-in within Netwerk. Having some weird memory hack to transplant Spark into someone else's family to hide her from Kincaid would be as crazy as a soap opera plot. No, in every iteration, I just couldn't make it work.

In the end, I realized... does it really matter if she's Verity's actual, factual daughter? One of the ongoing themes of the series was the flexible nature of the concept of family. Why couldn't Kincaid see her as the closest thing to an heir, someone who had inherited the best of Verity?

So, I kept the overall idea of Kincaid trying to woo Spark over to his side, without adding layer upon layer of ridiculous hijinks on top of it. The idea was sound; I just needed to realize that I was making things too complicated. And with that in place... Floating Point settled into the shape of the story you just read.

# Mischief Managed

Now, Floating Point was complete. Thematically it hit all the points I wanted it to hit, and the mechanics worked. The ideas that didn't work had been trimmed away; ideas that did work slotted into place so very easily. Overall it took me a month to write one third of the book, smashing my NaNoWriMo goal; the entire book took only four months total. Sometimes, when everything clicks... stories nearly write themselves. Nearly. Mostly. Let's say a good 73%.

And with one book out of the way, where do we go from here, then?

I know who the 'villain' is for the next book. I know the revelation of the stars and the prayer. I know who the One is. I know what challenges are coming, and some of them involve a few of the rejected ideas I detailed above, given new flesh. The entire trilogy is laid out in my mind, the broad bones of it. More or less.

Will I be able to make it work, after laying down these words in stone / in print? Once I do this, the canon is assembled, and cannot be changed. Will Netwerk find its future, or be destroyed? How will I get from beginning to end? I know A and Z but the letters between will be mystery until I uncover them along the way.

But that's the exciting part for me: I get to figure out what all of this is as I develop it. As you've seen plans can change, and change drastically... for the better, too. In the end, Floating Point will be exactly what it has to be. And I'm looking forward to discovering what that shape is alongside you.

I'll see you on the website, and in future books. Keep reading the drafts. Keep giving me feedback. Keep enjoying the words written down in ink or bits. And as always... thank you.